IG]

Fighting the Vacra was no easy chore. The insectoids were double-jointed in an unfamiliar fashion, making it difficult for Maker to apply his martial training. Nevertheless, he was initially holding his own until he slipped in something — probably blood or gore. His feet flew out from under him and he banged his head hard on the floor.

For a moment, Maker saw stars. At the same time, klaxons started going off in his brain as he sensed more than observed movement next to him. He shook his head to clear his vision, and then his eyes widened in shock as he saw a Vacra kneeling next to him, stabbing down with a knife.

Acting more on instinct than conscious thought, Maker reached out with both hands and caught the wrist of the limb holding the descending blade, halting its momentum. (Thankfully it wasn't the vibro-blade, but the weapon didn't need any special properties to finish him off; any old stabbing implement would do the trick.) The Vacra then leaned over, putting its weight on the knife, which slowly began to drop toward Maker's chest.

Someone shouted nearby but Maker ignored it, putting all his energy and concentration into stopping the descending blade. However, he found himself slightly distracted when a shadow unexpectedly fell over him. Still fighting for his life, he risked an upward glance and felt unbridled fury at what he saw.

Skullcap.

More to the point, the Vacra leader was still holding the battle-axe, which he had pulled back like a lumberjack attempting to fell a tree in one swoop. And then he swung the axe towards Maker.

IGNOTUS

Kid Sensation Series
Sensation: A Superhero Novel
Mutation (A Kid Sensation Novel)
Infiltration (A Kid Sensation Novel)
Revelation (A Kid Sensation Novel)
Coronation (A Kid Sensation Novel)
Replication (A Kid Sensation Novel)
Incarnation (A Kid Sensation Novel)

Kid Sensation Companion Series
Amped
Mouse's Tale (An Alpha League Supers Novel)

The Warden Series
Warden (Book 1: Wendigo Fever)
Warden (Book 2: Lure of the Lamia)
Warden (Book 3: Attack of the Aswang)

The Fringe Worlds
Terminus (Fringe Worlds #1)
Efferus (Fringe Worlds #2)
Ignotus (Fringe Worlds #3)

Boxed Sets
The Kid Sensation Series (Books 1–3)
The Warden Series (Books 1–3)
Worlds of Wonder

Short Stories
Extraction: A Kid Sensation Story

IGNOTUS

IGNOTUS
Fringe Worlds #3

By

Kevin Hardman

IGNOTUS

> If you purchased this book without a cover, you should be aware that this book is stolen property. It was reported as "unsold and destroyed" to the publisher, and neither the author nor the publisher has received any payment for this "stripped book."

This book is a work of fiction contrived by the author, and is not meant to reflect any actual or specific person, place, action, incident or event. Any resemblance to incidents, events, actions, locales or persons, living or dead, factual or fictional, is entirely coincidental.

Copyright © 2020 by Kevin Hardman.

Cover Design by Isikol

Edited by Faith Williams, The Atwater Group

This book is published by I&H Recherche Publishing.

All rights reserved, including the right to reproduce this book or portions thereof in any form whatsoever. For information, address I&H Recherche Publishing, P.O. Box 2727, Cypress, TX 77410.

ISBN: 978-1-937666-50-7

Printed in the U.S.A.

IGNOTUS

ACKNOWLEDGMENTS

I would like to thank the following for their help with this book: GOD, who has blessed me in more ways than I can count; and my family, for showing exceptional patience, love, and understanding when it comes to my writing.

IGNOTUS

Thank you for purchasing this book! If, after reading, you find that you enjoyed it, please feel free to leave a review on the site from which it was purchased.

Also, if you would like to be notified when I release new books, please subscribe to my mailing list via the following link: http://eepurl.com/C5a45

Finally, for those who may be interested in following me, I have included my website and social media info:

Website: http://www.kevinhardmanauthor.com/

BookBub: https://www.bookbub.com/authors/kevin-hardman?follow=true

Amazon Author Page: https://www.amazon.com/Kevin-Hardman/e/B00CLTY3YM

Facebook: www.facebook.com/kevin.hardman.967

Twitter: https://twitter.com/kevindhardman

Goodreads: https://www.goodreads.com/author/show/7075077.Kevin_Hardman

And if you like my work, please consider supporting me on Patreon: https://www.patreon.com/kevinhardman

IGNOTUS

Ignotus -

    1. unknown;

    2. strange;

    3. weird;

    4. alien.

IGNOTUS

Chapter 1

To Bain Browing, it felt like an interrogation.

At present, he sat at a broad, circular conference table capable of seating (and currently accommodating) a score of people. Hefty and ornate, it had been hand-carved from a single block of wood taken from some rare, arboreal colossus on a distant world. It was the type of table meant for the discussion of weighty matters, issues of import. Moreover, Browing recognized that the table's round design — with no clear "head" — was meant to further such discussions by giving the impression that those who occupied seats around it were equals.

Browing was operating under no such illusions at the moment. Glancing around at those seated at the table with him, he plainly understood that he was not an equal here. He had some very powerful connections, but there was no doubt that he was currently out of his depth.

First of all, the sheer amount of military brass was almost startling, and — judging by the stars on their uniforms — they were far from rank and file. Nothing but top-level generals, field marshals, fleet admirals, and more. It seemed to Browing that there were more stars in the room than in the night sky.

Not to be outdone, the civilian sector was also well-represented. Those present included high-ranking civil servants, powerhouse political appointees, and incredibly influential elected officials.

All in all, Browing estimated — conservatively — that at least a quarter of humanity's government (including military might) was controlled by the people sitting with him.

IGNOTUS

No, he was not an equal here — not by any stretch of the imagination. Therefore, the fact that he was here at all could only mean one thing: they wanted something from him. More to the point, there was only one commodity he might possess that the people in this room couldn't procure elsewhere, and that was information.

"Thanks for making time to meet with us this morning," said a fleet admiral seated near Browning, plainly dismissing with the courtesy of formal introductions. "We realize it was short notice."

"No problem," Browning assured the man, whose nametag said Lafayette. "Although I'm not sure why I'm here."

"We have a few questions about what you observed on the *Black Pearl*," stated a statuesque brunette whom Browning recognized as an interstellar senator.

Browning frowned. "I'm not sure I understand. I — along with everyone else involved — have already been fully debriefed regarding the events on the *Pearl*."

As he spoke, Browning reflected on the crisis that had occurred a few weeks back — when he and a group of Marines he was working with found themselves on the front lines, facing an invading alien armada. Miraculously, with only one ship (and a little help from a bizarre entity known as Efferus), they managed to defeat the invading aliens — an insectoid race known as the Vacra.

A field marshal named Steiner cleared his throat, snapping Browning out of his reverie. "Ahem. For our current purposes, we're less concerned about the invasion and more focused on the personnel on the *Pearl* who responded to it."

IGNOTUS

"Personnel?" Browing repeated quizzically. "You mean Lieutenant Maker's squad?"

"Exactly," stressed Steiner. "We'd like to get your opinion of the lieutenant and his group."

Browing frowned. Lieutenant Maker was the commander of the contingent of Marines who had been involved in defeating the Vacra. In fact, despite facing daunting odds, Maker had actually managed to thwart the Vacra *twice* in the recent past. That said, it wasn't surprising that senior officers might have questions about him, as the man's methods were often unorthodox, to say the least, but there were better channels for obtaining that type of information.

"That still leaves me confused," Browing admitted. "Ariel Chantrey is one of the best behavioral scientists we have, and she's done a complete psych profile on Maker and everyone under his command. Assuming you have her report, she's probably the most appropriate person to direct any questions to regard—"

"We have Dr. Chantrey's files," interjected one of the civilians — a handsome blonde woman named Goya whom Browing recognized as a political appointee, like himself, but far above his pay grade. "However, there's concern that her reports might be tainted by" — she took a moment to determine the proper word, then settled on — "bias."

Ahhh, Browing thought. *So that's it.*

"Dr. Chantrey is in a personal relationship with Lieutenant Maker, is she not?" asked Lafayette.

Browing almost laughed. "If you're suggesting that Dr. Chantrey would allow her professional judgment to be swayed by personal sentiment, I can assure you that you're wrong. *Dead* wrong. Anything she's written will be

IGNOTUS

based on her expert opinion and nothing more. In addition, Maker himself would object if he thought she was doing anything along those lines."

"What about the rest of Maker's team?" asked a Star Forces general named Grasso.

A look of bewilderment crossed Browning's face. "Excuse me?"

"Would those serving under the lieutenant also be adverse to receiving favorable treatment?" Grasso clarified.

Browning reflected for a moment, then stated, "There's an old military saying: the leader sets the tone."

"So you're saying his people wouldn't expect special consideration, either," Steiner concluded. "Does that include Master Sergeant Adames?"

"Adames is Maker's right-hand man," Browning replied. "They tend to think alike, so I'd say 'Yes.'"

Steiner gave him a hard-nosed stare. "So does that mean Maker is a scoundrel as well? I mean, that's how you described Adames in one of your reports, where you highlight the fact that he's twice been demoted from *chief* master sergeant."

Browning frowned. Adames hailed from a family of smugglers, and as a result had individual skills and personal contacts that caused Maker to label him as an "acquisitions specialist." In short, there was little that the man couldn't procure (although occasionally he did so by questionable means). That aside — and despite the demotions — he was a first-rate NCO (non-commissioned officer), an experienced veteran, and a reliable sounding board.

"You're probably referring to my initial evaluation," Browning noted. "If so, then I have to admit

IGNOTUS

that my early assessment of Adames was probably overly harsh and gave more weight to the man's background than was warranted."

Steiner responded to this information with an unimpressed grunt, but otherwise didn't comment.

"Well, at least he's mentally stable," chimed in the senator while looking at her p-comp. The way her eyes scanned from left to right, she was obviously reading something on the palm-sized computer. "The same can't be said of this mind reader — Isis Diviana."

"Sergeant Diviana doesn't read minds," Browing corrected. "She senses thoughts."

The senator raised an eyebrow in curiosity. "The difference being…?"

"I believe Diviana likens it to being inside somewhere but hearing someone speaking *out*side," Browing replied. "You can hear them, but can't make out what they're saying."

"So, in your opinion, she's fully recovered from this breakdown she suffered?" the senator continued.

Browing fought to keep his face impassive. Prior to joining Maker's team, Diviana had been an intel agent and then part of a special ops group. She had been mentally connected to other members of her unit when they had been killed on a mission. As a result, she had felt each of their deaths intimately. In his opinion, it was more than most people would have been able to bear, and the senator's attitude seemed to trivialize what Diviana had gone through. However, he felt it prudent to keep those thoughts to himself.

"As far as I can tell, Sergeant Diviana has fully recovered," Browing stated truthfully. "She's as

IGNOTUS

competent as she was when she worked in the Intel and Special Ops divisions — if not more so."

"Moving on," said Goya. "What about this Edison Wayne? Is he done trying to kill his fellow soldiers?"

"That was an accident," Browing shot back almost defensively.

"An accident?" Goya echoed, plainly skeptical. "He built a booby trap that sent another member of his squad to the infirmary in critical condition."

"It was actually an anti-theft device intended to discourage some ongoing larceny," Browing corrected. "In short, the 'victim' — who fully recovered from the incident — was a criminal, and any harm he suffered he brought upon himself."

"Still, this Wayne sounds like a menace," Goya declared.

Browing shook his head in disagreement. "On the contrary, he's an asset — a technological whiz and an engineering genius. Give him a bit of metal and some wires and he can build almost anything. From the standpoint of sheer ingenuity, he's without peer."

"So the fellow has some redeeming value," Lafayette concluded, then glanced at his p-comp. "What about these other two: Cano Snick — who sounds like an oafish brawler — and this blind woman, Luna Loyola?"

"Actually, Snick is a quiet man given to introspection and meditation," Browing stated. "As you all know, we live in a time when humanity is greatly fractured in terms of mores and manners. Snick grew up in a society where martial skill is not only prized, but determines your station in life. That being the case, he was trained in martial arts almost from the moment he drew breath. As a result, he's probably one of the best hand-to-hand combatants you'll ever meet."

"As to Loyola," he continued, "she's technically blind, as you said — lost her eyes in an accident. However, she's able to see through the use of synthetic oculi and advanced optics technology."

"So she's got no eyes," Lafayette proclaimed. "And she operates as a sniper?"

"With or without eyes, there's no one more accurate with a gun," Browing commented. "You'd be hard-pressed to find her equal — male or female — in any branch of the service."

There was silence for a few seconds as Browing's words seemed to sink in, and he took the opportunity to once again scrutinize those seated with him. Not everyone was asking questions, but he didn't take that to mean that the others were disinterested or indifferent. In truth, it was quite the opposite; they all seemed captivated by the discussion taking place, although he'd done nothing more than state information they all had at their fingertips.

"Moving on," Steiner said, interrupting Browing's thoughts, "I'd like to talk about the Augman in Maker's group."

"He goes by the name Fierce," Browing offered. "He's the team doctor."

"It's odd enough having an Augmented Man in the military, but reports have surfaced that he actually participated in combat," Steiner stated, almost gushing. "I don't have to tell you what that's worth if it's true. It could change the entire complexion of humanity's armed forces."

IGNOTUS

Browing nodded in understanding. Augmen were genetically engineered super-soldiers, created to be the finest fighting force mankind had ever produced. With strength, speed, and stamina well beyond that of ordinary human beings, they should have been the backbone of mankind's military. However, instead of being feared combatants, some design flaw had resulted in Augmen being pacifists. They were doves rather than hawks, rejecting war and violence in all forms.

A soft cough from someone near him brought Browing back to himself.

"Reports of Fierce fighting are exaggerated," he attested.

"So you're saying he's as worthless as any other Augman in combat," Steiner concluded.

Browing contemplated his response for a moment, then said, "There's a perception that Augmen are useless in war because of their nonviolent nature, but that's completely untrue. Their presence during a skirmish can be incredibly beneficial, even if all they're doing is carrying wounded men off the battlefield."

"If you can get an Augman to do even that much, it's practically an evolutionary leap forward," Steiner opined.

"Speaking of steps forward," the senator said, "what do you think should happen to Maker's alien pet?"

Everyone at the table suddenly seemed to perk up even more. If they were captivated before, they were completely engrossed now.

So this is it, Browing thought. *The* real *information they're after*.

IGNOTUS

"Erlen's not a pet," Browing swiftly replied, surprising himself since he had generally referred to Maker's exotic alien companion by that term in the past.

"What is it, then?" the senator asked.

"It's Niotan," Browing answered. "From a planet called Niota, according to Maker."

"So it says in your report," Lafayette chimed in. "But leaving aside what you consider to be fact for a moment, what's your honest opinion of this creature?"

Browing frowned in concentration. He needed to choose his words here very carefully.

"I'd say he's singularly unique," Browing offered. "And quite possibly a higher lifeform."

There was stunned silence for a moment as his words sank in.

"A higher lifeform?" Steiner blurted out incredulously. "This thing goes around licking the ground!"

"It's a living chemical factory," Browing explained. "It can synthesize and reproduce almost anything it tastes, so licking things is in its nature." He didn't add that Erlen also had papillae on his footpads, which meant that the Niotan could also taste things just by touching them.

They can read my report — instead of some underling's summary — if they want the nitty-gritty details, he thought.

"So what kind of value would you put on something like that?" Goya inquired, interrupting Browing's thoughts.

"With respect to Erlen, I would posit that he's *in*valuable," Browing declared.

"In that case," uttered Grasso, "is Maker the best person to be taking care of him?"

IGNOTUS

Browing shrugged. "He's done a pretty good job so far."

"No doubt," Grasso agreed, nodding. "But you've just described Maker's unit as being exceptionally talented. You also designated this alien Erlen as an incomparable asset. Bearing those facts in mind — and in light of his penchant for, shall we say, unwonted tactics — are they best utilized in the hands and under the authority of someone like Maker?"

"Hmmm," Browing mumbled, appearing to think on the question. "Regarding his team, in my opinion they're all pieces from different puzzles. Even though they aren't supposed to, they somehow fit together perfectly under Maker" — he interlaced his fingers for effect — "with the whole turning out to be greater than the sum of its parts."

"Are you saying that they would be ineffective under someone else's command?" queried Steiner.

"Not at all," Browing insisted, "but you have to understand that these were people whom the military was ready to throw away, misfits who didn't fit in anywhere. Maker didn't just give them a second chance — he gave them purpose, believed in them. More to the point, his faith in *them* is reciprocated tenfold by their faith in *him*. The result is that they put forth a hundred-and-ten percent on every assignment."

"And you don't think they'd do that for another commander?" Goya asked.

"Actually, I think they would," Browing countered. "But for Maker, they'll always do more. For him, they give something extra — something that can't be defined or quantified. Frankly speaking, I think they'd rather die than fail him, and that level of devotion not only increases the value of what they bring to the team but also gives Maker a considerable edge."

"As to Erlen," Browing continued, "even if I agreed that he should be under someone else's care — which I don't — I'm not sure how you could effectuate that. Maker will never give him up willingly, which means you'll have to go *through* Maker to get him, and that's going to cost you an army. He will litter the landscape with bodies before letting you lay a finger on the Niotan. And even if you get past Maker, there's Erlen himself to deal with. Just so you'll know what to expect in that regard, he's got claws that will slice through flesh and bone like they're made of water. He can cough up an acidic compound that will eat through steel. He can breathe out poisonous fumes that will kill you in seconds. And all of that is just the tip of the iceberg."

There was a momentary silence while everyone absorbed what Browing had just said.

"We're getting ahead of ourselves here," Grasso stressed after a few seconds. "No one's talking about breaking up effective units or forcibly taking possession of anyone or anything. We're simply getting an assessment of certain individuals."

"Fair enough," Browing noted.

"Now," Grasso went on, "based on what you just said and prior reports, it sounds like Maker may not necessarily be the type to obey orders."

It wasn't posed as a question, but all eyes in the room were on Browing, clearly anticipating a response.

"That's not how I'd put it," Browing said. "Based on what I've observed, I'd say he's a loyal and devoted Marine whose first instinct actually *is* to obey orders. However, he doesn't simply check his brain at the door. I

IGNOTUS

think when it appears that a situation has changed, he feels confident with improvising rather than blindly following orders that may get him or his people killed."

"Sounds like you admire him," noted the senator, "which would be a notable about-face from your early reports, when you said his nicknames of 'Madman' Maker and 'Maniac' Maker were well-deserved, albeit understatements of the truth. Are you two friends now?"

"Ha!" Browing barked humorously. "I'd say there's mutual respect between us and we generally speak in cordial tones to each other, but calling us friends would be a bit of a stretch. That said, if I were in trouble and could cherry-pick one person I could call for aid, it would be Lieutenant Arrogant Maker."

IGNOTUS

Chapter 2

The ambush happened pretty much in the exact spot where Maker expected it: a secluded area of the park that he had recently incorporated into his morning jog.

There were three of them — two men and a woman. Maker had first noticed them about a week earlier at the gym where he typically went to work out after his morning run. Dressed in matching T-shirts bearing the logo of some special ops unit, the trio had been loud and boisterous at the time. Maker had ignored them (mostly in hopes that they would show him the same courtesy), but it wasn't long before the sidelong glances had begun, accompanied by fervent whispering. Once again, Maker's reputation had preceded him.

Even so, Maker had been hopeful that the three — like most others — would simply come to tolerate his presence, assiduously ignoring him to the furthest extent possible. No such luck. That first day, they had left the gym when he did, keeping a respectful distance but blatantly tailing him as he jogged back to his room at the Visiting Officer's Quarters.

Since then, they had trailed him every day — clearly focused on getting a handle on his routine: how far he ran, the route he used, how long it took, etcetera. In addition, over the past two days, they had stepped up their game, assuming strategic positions along the path he took.

Of course, they hadn't been overt about it. They had stayed out of view for the most part, a testament to the fact that they were well-trained and good at their jobs. Maker, however, was better, and had picked up on enough telltale signs for the trio to give themselves away:

IGNOTUS

an errant cough, inadvertently stepping on a twig, and so on. It was enough to give him a heads-up regarding what was going on.

But even if he hadn't noted the conspicuous signs of their presence, he'd still have known something was amiss. His instincts were honed to the point that he could generally tell when there were eyes on him, when a threat or menace was in close proximity.

In short, not only was Maker well aware of the fact that he was being surveilled, his gut also told him that his watchers would soon take action. And in this instance, his intuition was spot-on.

On this particular morning, he had just finished his workout at the gym and was jogging back to the VOQ when the trio made their move. They appeared on the path about a hundred feet ahead of him, stepping into view from behind a ten-foot hedge, at a place where the jogging trail turned at a moderately sharp angle. It was the spot at which Maker himself would have attempted to waylay someone, if such had been his desire. (He probably would have waited, however, until his target was closer, but the three ahead of him were either impatient or overconfident.)

Having expected this maneuver, Maker didn't break stride or do anything to indicate that he was aware of the trio's intentions. In fact, he casually drifted over to the right — off the path — plainly giving way to the special ops soldiers in a last-ditch effort to avoid confrontation. (Quite often, simple deference was all that was needed to avoid conflict, and if it was an option here, Maker would take it. He didn't have pride or ego with respect to these matters.)

IGNOTUS

However, rather than take the olive branch being offered, the trio spread out, plainly intent on blocking Maker's path. Smiling with malicious glee, the woman walked in the center of the jogging trail while her two companions — one a dark-haired fellow and the other bald — strode parallel courses on either side.

Oh well, Maker thought. *I tried…*

He slowed to a halt and then went down on his left knee, noting that the approaching trio were about thirty feet away. Massaging his right calf as if he'd gotten a sudden cramp, he took a moment to surreptitiously size up the threesome.

In terms of appearance, the two men were about what one would expect from special ops members: tall and muscular, with an air of confidence about them that manifested itself in a sort of swagger as they walked. They were elite soldiers and they knew it; still, Maker was confident that he could handle them. The woman, however, was an entirely different story.

She was only about five feet tall, but was built like a block of granite. Squat and square-shaped, her body appeared to be formed of nothing but corded muscle and sinew that stretched the tank top and shorts she wore to their limits. (Even her hair — tied into what appeared to be a French braid that fell down her back — looked fibrous and brawny.)

Maker recognized the body type; it was indicative of a native of a high-G world. Coming from a planet with greater-than-normal gravity, the woman would be stronger and faster than the average person. (Not as strong or fast as an Augman, but she'd have an edge over most in terms of strength and speed.) That made her infinitely more dangerous than either of her male

IGNOTUS

companions — especially on a standard-G world like Baskin, where Maker was currently stationed.

The trio was about ten feet away when Maker went into action. Rising suddenly, he swiftly flicked his right shoe (which he had stealthily taken off while bending down) in the direction of the woman. The thrown was intentionally low — in the area of the woman's shins — and she responded as he expected, instinctively leaping to avoid the projectile. In her case, however, her jump took her about twelve feet straight into the air.

Her companions, momentarily distracted by the woman's vaulting of the thrown footwear, watched her in awe for a second. Maker, on the other hand — although he noted the woman's impressive vertical with his peripheral vision — was in motion almost before the shoe even left his hand. Flinging himself at the man who had been on the woman's left (the dark-haired guy), he hit the fellow with a cut block, striking him dead-on at the knees.

In terms of a fair fight, it wasn't exactly according to Hoyle (but then again, neither was three-on-one). The man was just turning back in his direction when Maker made contact. With his feet planted, the impact immediately and powerfully forced the soldier's knees back into a locked position — and then, under the strenuous pressure of Maker's forward momentum, something in the man's leg (or *legs*) snapped.

Maker and his target went down in a tangle of limbs, with the man wailing in agony. Under ordinary circumstances, one might expect a foe to still be putting up a fight — punching, clawing, grabbing — even on the ground. Going with his momentum, however, Maker

IGNOTUS

managed to roll free of his adversary without issue. As experience had taught him, there was nothing like a broken bone to take the fight out of an opponent. As evidence of this, the man he'd tackled didn't even make a feeble attempt at combat after being taken to the ground, choosing instead to simply stay where he'd landed, moaning in pain.

That said, Maker didn't have time to pat himself on the back with respect to taking out one antagonist; there were two more to deal with, so he wasn't out of the woods yet. Not by a long shot.

Coming up on the balls of his feet, he found himself with his back to the remaining oppugners. Rather than attempt to turn around, he immediately flung himself to the side — and none too soon, as something like a human missile went streaking through the space where he'd been a moment earlier. He knew without being told what it was: the woman, who had (upon coming back to the ground) promptly dove at him, perhaps preparing to visit the same treatment upon Maker that he had bestowed upon her companion.

His maneuver had probably kept him from getting T-boned (or worse) by the woman. More importantly, it had bought him a little time, as the force of her jump was likely to propel his assailant much farther than was practical under the circumstances. Still, Maker didn't kid himself. He had earned a few extra seconds, at best.

At this juncture, Maker was still low to the ground, having rolled and come up on his fingertips and the balls of his feet after evading the woman. It wasn't as bad as being on his hands and knees, but put him at a distinct disadvantage as he noted the third attacker — the

IGNOTUS

bald man — bearing down on him fast. In fact, the fellow was almost on top of him.

Maker rose swiftly and immediately threw a roundhouse kick at the man's side with his right leg. When properly executed, it was a blow that could be devastatingly effective, doing everything from winding an opponent to breaking ribs. But in this instance, Maker had attempted the kick without having properly set his feet. Thus, his form was far from perfect. In addition, he had practically telegraphed the strike, giving his adversary advance notice of what was coming. Finally, he was up against what was most likely a well-trained combatant who would be experienced in dealing with an attack of this nature.

As a result of all these factors, the kick — although it connected — did little damage. More to the point, the bald man ended up catching Maker's leg, snaring it in the crook of his left elbow and using the same joint to pin it against the side of his body. Simultaneously, he brought his right hand over to help hold the leg in place.

Ordinarily, this was just about the worst thing that could happen following a roundhouse kick, as the bald man now had a variety of options he could employ against Maker: sweeping the latter's free leg, forcing him backward (or forward), and more. All of this flashed through the bald man's mind in an instant, and he was on the verge of smiling when he got a look at Maker's face. The grin that had been on the cusp of forming on his lips froze in place. Something in Maker's eyes told the fellow the truth: that he hadn't gained an advantage or the element of surprise by grabbing Maker's leg. Instead, he'd done exactly what Maker had *wanted* him to do.

IGNOTUS

Without warning, Maker used his free leg to propel himself toward his attacker. With his hands preoccupied holding Maker's leg, the fellow had left huge swaths of his body open to attack, and Maker used the opportunity to ram his forehead straight into the man's nose. Plainly stunned, his assailant wobbled for a moment and then collapsed, pulling Maker down on top of him. As they went to the ground, Maker followed up his headbutt with a hammerfist to the bridge of the man's nose, connecting just as the fellow's head hit terra firma. Sparing a quick glance toward his opponent as he scrambled away, Maker noted that the man seemed to be unconscious, his nose reminiscent of a squashed tomato.

As with the dark-haired fellow earlier, Maker didn't have time to gloat. Swiftly coming to his feet, he suddenly picked up on a sound that was both familiar and unmistakable: the distinct patter of footsteps striking the ground in quick succession. Someone was running towards him. Spinning in the direction of the sound, Maker found himself facing the last member of the trio.

The woman closed on him fast, but seemed to check her speed as she drew near. Twice now she'd been spurred into taking action that could be construed as imprudent — namely, leaving her feet. Doing so had allowed Maker an opportunity to engage her companions individually and had cost them the advantage of numbers. She appeared wary of making any more missteps.

On his part, Maker knew that he was seriously outclassed. This particular opponent was stronger and faster than him, and had far greater endurance. More to the point — judging from the look on her face — if she got her hands on him, she'd break him in half.

IGNOTUS

Bearing that in mind, Maker worked on keeping a healthy distance between himself and the woman. Stated plainly, he retreated from her advance, constantly keeping his feet shuffling backwards. Needless to say, it didn't take his opponent long to catch on to his game.

"Come on, cutie," she said in a surprisingly feminine voice. "Don't play hard-to-get."

A moment later, she lunged at Maker, barely missing as he scooted hastily aside to evade her grasp. She was even quicker than he had suspected, with cat-like reflexes. The only advantage he had was that — given the woman's height — her legs were short and she didn't have a great deal of reach, despite the fact that her arms seemed slightly elongated.

"Please, handsome, just one little kiss," she mocked, puckering her lips teasingly. "I promise I'll make it worth your while."

Maker ignored her quips, refusing to engage with his adversary either physically (which would have been foolish) or verbally (which would also have been folly). Exchanging words with her would simply have winded him, and his opponent had a lot more stamina than he did.

In addition, he didn't need the distraction that conversation would evoke; he had enough to do just keeping an eye on his adversary while also sparing the occasional glance behind him to make sure he didn't inadvertently trip over anything while keeping a safe distance between them. Not helping matters was the fact that he still only had one shoe on, which had the effect of throwing his equilibrium off to a small extent.

Despite appearances, however, Maker wasn't just randomly retreating; he had a plan of sorts, which he

IGNOTUS

stayed mindful of as they moved through an area of the park populated by towering trees with broad, rectangular trunks.

It was around that juncture that the inevitable happened: as Maker continued to fall back, his unshod foot, covered only by a sock, came down on something hard and unforgiving — presumably a stone or something similar. Pain shot up through his foot, and Maker drew in a sharp breath through clenched teeth as his leg buckled slightly. He recovered almost immediately, gingerly moving away from the offending object, but the episode gave his opponent the opening she had been looking for.

Noting that Maker was now favoring one foot, the woman dashed forward, arm cocked back. Hampered by his injury, Maker instinctively realized that he'd lost the ability to be evasive. That being the case, he steeled himself, and a moment later the woman rammed a meaty fist into his midsection.

Air exploded forcefully and painfully from his lungs as the wind was literally knocked out of him, and Maker's body essentially folded around his attacker's clenched hand. In fact, her fist was the only thing holding him up, as he otherwise would have collapsed to the ground.

Leaning towards his ear, she whispered, "Guess I kind of took your breath away, huh? I tend to have that effect on men."

Then, giggling at her own joke, she made a flicking motion with her hand — like someone trying to shoo away an annoying insect — and the next thing Maker knew he was flying through the air backwards.

IGNOTUS

He coasted for a few feet before hitting the ground hard, then pitched and rolled for a couple of yards before fetching up against a tree. He lay there for a moment, simply trying to get his bearings, then started to rise as he saw the woman heading towards him. He had just come to his feet when she placed a vise-like grip on his neck with one hand, hoisted him from the ground, and then slammed him against the tree that had stopped his helter-skelter tumbling a few moments earlier.

"You know," she mused as she held him aloft, "I have to say I'm a little disappointed. I expected more of a challenge from the famous 'Madman Maker.' Considering the way you took out Frost and Marco" — she nodded in the direction of her two companions — "I just knew I'd have a real fight on my hands. Instead, though, it feels like you should have called for reinforcements."

As before, Maker didn't allow himself to be baited by her words. Instead, he busied himself with trying to pry the woman's hand from around his neck. She wasn't squeezing, hadn't tried to choke him out (at least not *yet*), but — leaving little leeway for him to draw in air — it was far from what he'd describe as comfortable.

He might as well have saved himself the trouble. The woman's flesh felt as though it was chiseled out of stone, and trying to pry her fingers away was an effort in futility. He'd have had better luck trying to pick up a cinderblock with a pair of paper tongs.

At the same time that he was trying to free himself from his opponent's grasp, Maker was also kicking wildly. However, rather than aim at the woman holding him, he instead slammed the heels of his feet repeatedly against the tree where he was pinned. He suspected that the image was reminiscent of a petulant and unruly child, kicking and screaming in a tantrum while being held by a long-suffering parent. Unfortunately, it looked as though his antics were having no effect (other than causing additional pain to shoot through his injured foot), and then it happened.

Movement out of the corner of his eye drew Maker's attention. Turning his head to the side (or rather, as much as he could with his throat gripped), he saw an oversized insect crawling out of a hole in the tree trunk just a few inches away. It was about six inches long, with a navy-blue body and white wings, along with a pair of mandibles that twitched almost spasmodically.

Maker recognized it immediately: a razor-wasp — an insect native to Baskin, but which was exceptional in a number of ways.

The razor-wasp beat its wings for a second, as if testing them, and then took to the air. A soft droning reverberated as it flew a lazy path that brought it near Maker's face. It hovered there for a moment as if scrutinizing him.

On his part, Maker stayed as still as possible, having ceased both his kicking and his efforts to pry the woman's hand from his throat. After a few seconds, the insect seemed satisfied. It then spun around and began drifting towards the woman, apparently intent on giving her a similar perusal. Regrettably, it never got the opportunity.

From Maker's perspective, it was almost as if the razor-wasp had vanished. Of course, it hadn't simply disappeared, but it *was* gone — batted viciously aside by the woman with her free hand. (Her other hand, of course, still graced Maker's neck.) The action had happened so fast that Maker had barely noted it visually,

IGNOTUS

although he couldn't miss hearing the painful chirp that escaped from the insect as it was struck. It now lay on the ground a dozen feet away, crumpled and dying, letting out a curious warbling sound.

"What the hell was that?" the woman asked, staring at the insect. The question was more rhetorical than literal. Nevertheless, Maker answered.

"Reinforcements," he hissed, a grin starting to form on his face.

The woman simply stared at him for a moment, probably astounded to finally hear him speak and simultaneously confused by his answer. But before she could respond, the air began to fill with sound — the same droning the razor-wasp had made while in flight, but much greater in volume and pervasiveness.

The woman's head quickly swiveled from side to side, and her eyes widened as she suddenly took note of something Maker had already observed: all of the trees in this area had holes in their trunks similar to the one near Maker's head. More importantly, swarms of razor-wasps were now filing out of said holes and taking to the air.

One of the insects seemed to light momentarily on the arm being used to pin Maker to the tree. The woman jerked it back reflexively, unceremoniously dropping Maker in the process. Because of his adversary's stature, he'd only been held a few inches off the ground so he managed to stay on his feet. He then watched as the woman slowly backed away, holding the arm that the razor-wasp had touched, which now seemed to be red and swollen where the insect had made contact.

She looked around wildly, all thoughts of Maker forgotten as she realized she was in the midst of a swarm of angry insects — more specifically, angry insects with

IGNOTUS

razor-sharp stingers. As if proof of this was needed, the woman suddenly yelped and slapped a hand at the back of her neck.

At that point, the air was thick with razor-wasps. It was as if the trees were industrial smokestacks, but ones that belched out hordes of insects instead of clouds of gas and exhaust fumes.

Maker's erstwhile adversary yipped sonorously, arching her back in pain. She then reached with her left hand towards her lumbar region while reaching over her shoulder with her right, giving the impression that she was trying to grab something on her spine. At the same time, she quickly spun around in a half-circle, and Maker noted that there was indeed something on her back: a host of razor-wasps. (And from what he could discern, they appeared to be stinging her repeatedly.)

As Maker watched in fascination, more of the insects converged on the woman. Within seconds, they were a writhing mass, swarming all over her to such an extent that no part of her body could be seen.

Panicking now and obviously in pain, the woman took off, running on a course that was tangential to the spot where she'd dropped Maker. Frankly speaking, Maker was curious how — as blanketed as she was by razor-wasps — she could see anything. A few seconds later, he had his answer as his former opponent ran pell-mell into a tree, plainly indicating that she had been running blind.

Although she had hit the tree hard enough to shake its branches, the woman stayed on her feet — at least initially. She staggered around for a few moments, clearly stunned, and then — swaying like a drunkard —

she collapsed to her knees before pitching forward face-first onto the ground.

    Maker continued watching her prone body for a few seconds as if in a trance, only coming back to himself after a sharp pain lanced through his wrist. Looking at it, he noted that he had been stung by one of the insects. It was a stark reminder that, while the razor-wasps seemed focused on his former attacker, he himself was not completely out of danger. With that in mind, he lay flat on the ground, tucking his face into the crook of one elbow to protect it.

IGNOTUS

Chapter 3

Maker lay hunkered down for what felt like an hour, but was probably no more than five minutes. During that time, he received two more vicious stings to his back, but otherwise suffered no harm.

Eventually, the droning of the insects diminished, receding so quickly, in fact, that it took Maker slightly by surprise. Taking a chance, he raised his head — just in time to see what appeared to be the last of the razor-wasps retreating back into one of the tree-holes. Assuming that any danger was now past, he slowly rose to his feet.

Glancing around, Maker couldn't help noticing how peaceful and serene the park looked, with shafts of sunlight shining down through the treetops and branches swaying gently in the breeze. It felt somewhat surreal considering that, just minutes earlier, the air had been filled with throngs of angry, hostile insects. Counting himself fortunate to have escaped their wrath essentially unscathed, he decided to see how his female attacker had fared. Walking in the direction where he had last seen her, he soon got his answer.

The woman still lay on the ground, and her condition was such that Maker would actually have been shocked if she'd been capable of movement. Every square inch of her body appeared markedly puffed up — incredibly swollen and inflamed — as if she had acquired a rampaging case of massive boils that had infected her from head to foot. Even her scalp hadn't been spared and now bulged ominously, giving her head a misshapen and malformed appearance, as if her brain had outgrown her skull. Moreover, many of the lumps on her body gave the

IGNOTUS

impression of being infected by either weeping pus or oozing blood.

Frankly speaking, she was an unsightly mess, and if it hadn't been for the fact that the form before him seemed to regularly expand and contract — a sure indication of breathing — Maker would have been hard-pressed to say whether she was even alive (although he harbored no doubt that she was unconscious). The razor-wasps had obviously had a field day with her, stinging her repeatedly with complete and utter abandon.

Surveying the area, Maker saw a few of the insects lying dead on the ground. Obviously some would have been crushed when the woman ran into the tree. Others surely met their demise when she collapsed to the ground (and possibly rolled over).

Needless to say, Maker owed the razor-wasps a debt of gratitude. They had come to his rescue like the proverbial cavalry, although in truth it was something he'd been banking on.

Basically, there was a reason why this area of the park was deserted, and Maker's female opponent had found out (the hard way) what it was: the razor-wasps. Not that the insects were territorial — far from it, in fact; they seemed to take a live-and-let-live approach with respect to other lifeforms. However, they were extremely protective of their own, viewing an attack on one as an attack on all. As a matter of fact, they were known to fly miles in order to exact revenge — for lack of a better term — on anyone or anything that assaulted one of their number. This would be the case even if the assailed razor-wasp was nowhere near any of its fellows. (Entomologists had postulated that this ability to unerringly identify and track down attackers was due to some sort of hive mind

IGNOTUS

or collective intelligence, which might even be psychic to some degree.)

Considering that human beings had an almost instinctive tendency to swat insects that got too close, putting people and razor-wasps in near proximity to each other was a bad idea. Thus, the local advisory — a written pamphlet for those new not only to Baskin but also this specific geographic region of the planet — had suggested avoiding the area of the park where the insects nested (which was how Maker typically found himself the only jogger on the nearby trails).

Obviously, Maker's female assailant had known none of the facts about razor-wasps, or she never would have made herself a target by striking that first one. She had clearly failed to read the advisory, an oversight that had ultimately cost her dearly. (On his part, Maker always thoroughly reviewed the advisory of any planet he was visiting. It was a habit he had picked up during his first mission as a Marine, after another member of his squad lost three fingers to a carnivorous plant on a strange planet.)

Still, Maker's slapdash plan, which had been premised on using the razor-wasps to level the playing field (or maybe even gain some type of advantage), had required more than a bit of luck. For starters, it was the beginning of hibernation season for the insects; he hadn't been sure they were still active or — if they weren't — whether they could be roused. In addition, he hadn't been certain that the woman would play along; there had always been the chance that she'd realize that Maker's retreat from her was more purposeful and deliberate than seemed warranted. Thankfully, she hadn't been

IGNOTUS

particularly astute and had allowed herself to be led down the primrose path.

Standing over her now, Maker almost felt sorry for the woman. The stingers of razor-wasps were about an inch long, sharp as scalpels (hence their moniker), and full of potent venom. That said, attacks from the insects were seldom fatal; it was if they knew exactly how much punishment a victim could take and would break off an attack before it became lethal. That, however, was small consolation to someone on the receiving end of one of their assaults, as Maker could attest: he had been stung only three times, but as a result he could positively affirm the potency and effect of both stinger and poison. He couldn't imagine what it would be like to be repeatedly stung by them all over his body.

Satisfied that the woman was incapacitated for the nonce, Maker turned and walked away, heading for the area where he'd left his two male attackers. When he reached them, he noticed that both men seemed to be unconscious. The first — the one Maker had tackled — had white bone sticking out of one leg in a grotesque manner. Surprisingly, however, the injury hadn't bled as much as Maker would have suspected. (Presumably some kind of auto-meds had kicked in, stopping the bleeding and perhaps inducing unconsciousness to keep the man from going into shock.)

As to the other fellow, it was no surprise that he was still out of it. Having taken two blows to the noggin at roughly the same time — Maker's fist-to-the-nose while striking his head on the ground — the guy would be lucky to escape without a concussion.

Satisfied that neither man was in any condition to attempt further shenanigans, Maker turned his attention to the real reason he'd returned to this area: his thrown shoe. It only took a few moments to locate it, as his missing footwear was in the same general vicinity of the two unconscious men. Maker was in the process of slipping it back on when the sound of footsteps, approaching from the rear, reached his ears.

Suddenly alarmed, he quickly spun around, assuming a fighting stance as he did so. A moment later, he relaxed, letting out a deep breath when he saw who had been coming up behind him: Bain Browing.

Browing spent a few seconds taking in the scene around them, letting his eyes linger momentarily on the two prone figures on the ground. Then, turning to Maker, he said, "I see you've been making friends again."

IGNOTUS

Chapter 4

Maker never got to finish his run. Instead, he found himself in Browing's hovercraft a short time later, heading toward the latter's apartment. He stared out the passenger-side window as they zipped along, sitting quietly while Browing completed a call to a local medical unit, informing them of three unconscious individuals in the park they had just left. After completing the call, Browing cast a sideways glance at Maker.

"So you were just going to leave them there?" he asked.

"Well, when you say it like that, it makes me feel ashamed," Maker retorted sarcastically. "After all, had they beaten me to a pulp, I'm sure calling for a medic was the first thing on their agenda."

Browing gave his passenger a judgmental look but didn't say anything.

"How'd you find me, anyway?" Maker continued.

"Ha!" Browing guffawed. "You're a creature of habit in a lot of ways, such as morning exercise. Every day you leave at roughly the same time, take the same route, jog at the same pace…"

Maker frowned as Browing trailed off. "So, what? You've been watching me?"

Browing snorted derisively. "Hardly. I just asked Ariel where to find you."

Maker kept his face impassive, but mentally he scowled. This was the risk inherent in developing a romance with someone like Ariel Chantrey. As a behavioral scientist, her job was observing and dissecting attitudes, actions, and conduct, which segued nicely into her specialty: discerning and predicting human behavior.

IGNOTUS

More to the point, it wasn't something she could simply turn off, not even for someone who she was involved with, like Maker. (In fact, Maker had been — and actually still was — her specific work assignment.)

As to their personal relationship, it was still fairly new — only a few weeks old. To be honest, Maker wasn't sure how to define it (and hadn't yet decided if he was truly comfortable with it), but found himself with few complaints. His primary objections were two in number: first and foremost was the fact that any attempt to predict his behavior always gave Maker the impression that he was being handled. He generally had no problem with being given or carrying out orders — even those he disagreed with — but he detested the thought of being manipulated.

The other issue was the likelihood that their relationship was damaging to Chantrey's career. Their involvement meant that any report she made on Maker was liable to be viewed with a jaundiced eye. That said, this was a topic that Maker actually fretted over more than Chantrey herself, as he didn't like the possibility that he was tainting her in some way. Chantrey, on the other hand, seemed to view it as a non-issue.

Reflecting on his relationship with Chantrey, Maker considered how — just a few months earlier — both she and Browing had ranked near the top of his "Do not trust" list. (Truth be told, Maker had felt at one juncture that he'd probably have to kill Browing.) Glancing at the man now as they drove, Maker had to acknowledge that they had all come a long way since then. (As further proof of this, he had recently given Chantrey the passcode to his quarters, despite his misgivings about their relationship.)

IGNOTUS

"So," Maker droned, "since you're making me deviate from that fixed routine you just mentioned, do you want to tell me what this is about?"

"Sure," Browing responded with a nod. "But I'd prefer only having to tell it once, so it would be great if you could wait until we get to my place — Ariel and Adames are meeting us there."

"Fine by me," Maker replied, then went back to staring out the window.

IGNOTUS

Chapter 5

They arrived at Browing's place roughly fifteen minutes later. Unsurprising to Maker, it turned out to be the penthouse suite of a high-rise hotel. It was just another overt sign that Browing hailed from a family with money and connections.

As had been indicated, Adames and Chantrey were already inside when they arrived. Seated and chatting in the living room, they both rose when Maker and Browing came in.

"Hey," Browing stated in greeting to Chantrey and Adames. "Any trouble getting in?"

Chantrey shook her head. "No, the temporary passcode you provided worked fine."

"Excellent," Browing declared with a nod as he took up a spot next to Adames, who had been sitting on the living room couch. (On his part, Maker joined Chantrey, who had been occupying a loveseat across from the master sergeant.)

"I hope you don't mind, but I took the liberty of helping myself," Adames said, raising a tumbler full of burgundy-colored liquid that Maker hadn't noticed before. With glass in hand and dressed in civilian attire, he looked more like he was unwinding at the end of the day as opposed to preparing to get his morning started.

"Not at all," Browing assured him as they all sat down, "although — as your host — I would have let you sample my private stock rather than that swill the hotel keeps on hand and brazenly markets as liquor."

"Thanks," Adames said with a laugh, "but this is actually just juice from your fridge."

IGNOTUS

"Well, let me know if you want something stronger," Browing intoned.

"Maybe after the boss leaves," Adames quipped, nodding towards Maker. "He's a jerk about folks imbibing before the workday begins."

Maker chuckled and was about to make a witty retort when movement in the corner of the room caught his eye. Turning in that direction, he saw a familiar shape rise lithely from the floor and stretch as if from a nap: Erlen.

Looking like the sleek, hybrid offspring of a salamander and a spider monkey (in addition to a few other species), the Niotan was about the size of a large canine. He yawned, and then began padding across the room in a beeline towards Maker.

"Sorry," Chantrey muttered apologetically. "I didn't know how long we'd be and didn't like the idea of Erlen being cooped up for an indefinite period of time, so I brought him along."

"No problem," Maker assured her, "although he's generally able to entertain himself if left on his own."

At that point, Erlen had reached Maker, taking up a position next to where the latter was sitting. The Niotan seemed to give him a once-over, then made an odd rumbling sound.

"I'm fine," Maker insisted, in response to an unasked question.

"Fine?" Chantrey echoed, raising an eyebrow. "Did something happen?"

"Just the usual," Browing chimed in. "Maker had to show some folks why he was voted 'Most Congenial.'"

"Another fight?" Chantrey murmured in surprise. For the first time, she seemed to notice that Maker had an

IGNOTUS

odd assortment of bumps and bruises. "Was it about the *Orpheus Moon* again?"

Maker shrugged. "They didn't really say, although that's a fair guess."

As he spoke, Maker reflected back on the incident in question. The *Orpheus Moon* was the ship he'd been on when mankind first encountered the Vacra. Unfortunately, first contact, in that particular instance, had not gone well. The Vacra had previously raided a sub rosa ship — a Gaian vessel full of secret (and in many cases banned) weapons and tech. The insectoid aliens had shown little compunction about using said weapons, and as a result Maker ultimately found himself the lone survivor of the *Orpheus Moon* (not counting Erlen).

Ironically, had he died like everyone else on board, Maker probably would have been hailed as a hero, along with his fallen comrades. Instead, surviving had made him not just infamous but also a scapegoat, with people generally blaming him for what had happened to the *Orpheus Moon*. (Ultimately, he had been drummed out of the Marines over the incident, although he was eventually reinstated with the specific mandate to hunt down the Vacra.) More to the point, the military was a lot smaller in a number of ways than the general public realized, and Maker typically couldn't throw a rock without hitting someone with a connection to the *Orpheus Moon*: a friend, a relative, or the like. Thus it was that, wherever he went, stares and whispers usually followed, and it wasn't uncommon for individuals — like the trio of special ops soldiers — to occasionally feel the need to punish the notorious "Madman" Maker.

The feel of something wet near his hand brought Maker back to himself. Looking down, he saw that Erlen

IGNOTUS

had licked his wrist where the razor-wasp had stung him. The area was swollen and irritated (as were the stings to his back), but not debilitating in any way. In all honesty, Maker had essentially ignored the nicks and scratches he had received during the morning's escapades, as they were small hurts that — in his opinion — didn't require a great deal of attention.

With that in mind, and not wanting to make a mountain out of a molehill, Maker shooed Erlen away, watching as the Niotan padded softly back to the corner he had occupied earlier. It was then that Maker realized that Adames had been saying something to him.

"Excuse me?" Maker muttered, turning to his NCO.

"I said that your altercation this morning may not have been about the *Orpheus Moon*," Adames repeated. "It may have been about the Hundred-and-Twelfth."

Maker's brow wrinkled in confusion. The Hundred-and-Twelfth Fleet had been part of the Star Forces, under the command of a bumbling general named Roche. Unfortunately, thanks to Roche's incompetence and ineptitude (not to mention delusions of grandeur), the Hundred-and-Twelfth had been completely wiped out by the Vacra during their most recent skirmish. (Ironically — and as proof that there was no justice in the universe — Roche himself actually survived, as his flagship had been well to the rear of the action.)

Maker and his squad, aboard their own ship (the *Black Pearl*), had wound up with front-row seats to the entire episode. In fact, they themselves had only survived thanks to the efforts of the enigmatic alien entity they had dubbed Efferus.

IGNOTUS

"I don't understand," Maker finally said. "How does what happened to the Hundred-and-Twelfth result in people coming after me?"

"The same reason people come after you about the *Orpheus Moon*," Adames answered. "You survived, while the rest of the fleet was annihilated."

"Except that's not true — the fleet wasn't completely destroyed," Maker pointed out. "Roche made it through unscathed. His flagship wasn't even touched."

"So riddle me this," Adames said. "Which of these is more titillating: an idiotic no-name general who survives a skirmish because his flagship is so far to the rear that he's never in danger, or the notorious Maniac Maker being on the front lines but somehow managing to cheat death once again — this time by being the sole survivor of the Hundred-and-Twelfth Fleet?"

"But the *Pearl* wasn't even part of the Hundred-and-Twelfth," Maker protested.

"Doesn't matter," Browing noted. "You were there."

"Well, it wasn't just *me*," Maker insisted. "We were *all* there."

This statement was met with a stony silence on the part of Maker's companions. A moment later, the truth hit him.

"Wait a minute," he blurted out. "Have you *all* been getting targeted in some way because of what happened to the Hundred-and-Twelfth?"

"'Targeted' is a strong word," Chantrey noted. "But…" She let the rest go unsaid.

Maker shook his head in disbelief. "This is a bit beyond the pale."

IGNOTUS

Browing raised an eyebrow. "Did you seriously not know this was happening?"

"How would I know?" Maker demanded. "People have been gunning for me over the *Orpheus Moon* for so long that I've incorporated it into my daily routine: shower, shave, fend off attack, go get breakfast…"

"Like the three this morning," he went on. "These psychos don't always convey their motivations. If a guy tries to knife me in the back in the locker room at the gym, he generally doesn't shout 'This is for the Hundred-and-Twelfth' first. He just pulls out a blade and goes for my spine."

"Wow," Adames droned. "Sucks to be you."

Maker simply stared at him for a moment, and then everyone burst into laughter. More importantly, tension Maker hadn't even been aware of seemingly dissolved.

"Well, at least there's a silver lining to this entire affair with the Hundred-and-Twelfth," Chantrey intoned after regaining her composure a few seconds later. "Skullcap is dead."

At the mention of the name, Maker sobered immediately. Skullcap was one of the Vacran leaders and the closest thing Maker had to a mortal enemy. Or rather, he *had* been. The insectoid commander had apparently been killed when the invading Vacra armada he was leading was "transitioned" — moved to a remote, unknown region of the cosmos by the mysterious entity Efferus. Once there, Efferus's race had destroyed the entire Vacran fleet by essentially snuffing it out of existence.

Of course, "Skullcap" was just a nickname. The insectoid's given name was actually Ni'xa Zru Vuqja.

IGNOTUS

However, Maker had labeled him "Skullcap" due to the fact that the Vacran's body armor had the skull of some alien animal grafted to the helmet. It had given Skullcap an imposing presence, which was fitting since he had been a formidable adversary. (And adding to his striking appearance was the fact that a ring of skulls, embedded in the breastplate of his armor, encircled his neck.)

The sound of Chantrey's voice unexpectedly cut across Maker's thoughts, snapping him out of his reverie.

"What's on your mind?" she asked. "You look so serious all of a sudden."

"I was just thinking about Skullcap," he admitted. "It's still hard to imagine him dead."

"Well, he *is*," Browing declared confidently. "We all watched his invading fleet get vaporized."

Maker nodded in acknowledgment. When Efferus had transitioned the Vacran ships, he had also taken the *Black Pearl*, which was manned by Maker's unit. Thus, they'd had ringside seats with respect to watching the insectoids get obliterated.

"I know what we saw," Maker said, "but it just doesn't *feel* like he's dead. I can't shake the sense that he's still out there."

"Come on, Gant," Adames interjected. "You're talking like the two of you are twins with some kind of psychic connection. I don't often agree with Browing, but this time I think he's got it right. Skullcap's dead."

Maker's brow creased as he contemplated his friend's words, but he didn't say anything. Instead, he glanced at Erlen. The Niotan's uniqueness was known to the Vacra, and capturing him had been job one for them. Thus, even if Skullcap were truly gone, Maker didn't

IGNOTUS

imagine that the Vacra would give up their quest to capture his alien companion.

"Look," Adames went on, "I know you expected Skullcap's demise to herald the advent of a new era. The sun would shine brighter, the singing of birds would be sweeter, and so on. But the fact that the universe hasn't acknowledged his death in some memorable fashion just means that, ultimately, he was nothing special — no different than bad guys that we put down before in skirmishes on a hundred different worlds."

Maker didn't immediately respond, choosing instead to sit quietly while he contemplated the NCO's words. As usual, Adames made a lot of sense. The problem was that his instincts — his gut — were telling him something different.

After a few seconds of introspection, Maker sighed. "Maybe you're right. Maybe Skullcap *is* dead, which would mean it's time to move on to the next challenge. Speaking of which" — he looked in Browing's direction — "I believe you said you had something important to discuss."

IGNOTUS

Chapter 6

It didn't take Browing long to bring the others up to speed on the meeting he'd had. They sat silently, but listened intently, as he relayed the conversation he'd been privy to earlier.

"So what — they plan on breaking up the band?" Adames asked when Browing was done. "Shipping everybody in the squad off to different units?"

Browing shrugged. "I don't think that was their main area of concern, but it certainly seems to be something they're considering."

"Well, they can take their consideration and shove it," the NCO uttered fiercely. "No one's interested in a transfer."

"Maybe it's for the best," Maker interjected unexpectedly. "I mean, let's be honest. I've been toxic for years — ever since the *Orpheus Moon*. But now I'm radioactive, thanks to this thing with the Hundred-and-Twelfth. People have a tendency to paint with a broad brush — especially in the military — and anyone near me is going to get smeared. It's going to cause them issues both personally and professionally. My people don't deserve that, so maybe it's in their best interest to serve with another commander."

There was silence for a moment after Maker finished his impromptu speech. Needless to say, it wasn't anything he'd planned or rehearsed, but the thought that his people were now experiencing the kind of persecution he'd endured for years was galling to him. However, before he could dwell too long on the issue, his thoughts were interrupted by his NCO.

IGNOTUS

"Well, if we're being honest, let's put all the cards on the table," Adames stated. "Every member of our team was broken when you got them, Gant. The military had pretty much written them off as damaged goods. But you believed in them — found that busted thing in each one of them and fixed it."

"I didn't really fix anything," Maker countered, shaking his head, "because they actually weren't broken. They just needed a second chance."

"However you style it, those people were able to get back on their feet again because of you," Adames offered. "You've forged them into what's probably the finest squad in uniform, and — despite the situation with the Hundred-and-Twelfth — there's a host of soldiers out there who'd love to trade places with them."

"I find that hard to believe," Maker scoffed.

"Don't take my word for it," the NCO insisted. "I've got an inbox full of transfer requests, all asking to join our unit."

"What?" Maker muttered, unable to hide his surprise.

"They started coming in a few days ago," Adames said. "I was hoping for a chance to sort through them before bringing it to your attention, but just haven't had a chance."

"Hmmm," Maker mused. "Kind of a coinky-dink that you start getting transfer requests around the same time Browing is quizzed about moving people from our unit."

All eyes shifted to Browing, who stated, "As I said, it just seemed to be something being considered — not anything set in stone."

IGNOTUS

"Plus, that was just the undercard," Maker noted, recalling what Browning had said earlier. "Let me guess: the main event was Erlen."

At the mention of his name, Erlen suddenly sat up, at the same time emitting a low, rumbling growl.

"Yes," Browning acknowledged. "Your Niotan buddy seemed to be the subject they were most interested in."

Suddenly tense, Maker asked, "So, are they weighing the notion of handing him over to the Vacra?"

As he spoke, Maker felt anger flaring in him like a supernova. In the recent past, the powers that be had made secret compacts with the Vacra to hand over Erlen in exchange for the tech the insectoids had taken from the sub rosa ship. Ultimately, those efforts had been thwarted, but Maker still saw red every time he thought about it.

Browning shook his head in response to Maker's question. "Unlikely. They understand that Erlen's unique characteristics essentially make him a weapon, and an incredibly powerful one at that. Handing him over to an alien species — even for sub rosa tech — would be like trading a tactical nuke for a handful of magic beans."

"Well, thank heaven for small favors," Maker intoned mockingly.

Mentally, he let out a sigh of relief. It meant a lot to him to know for certain that Erlen was no longer on the auction block. Of course, Browning could be lying; the man had misled him before. However, the two of them had seemingly reached an understanding that, at the very least, involved open and honest communication. Thus, Maker felt that Browning was telling the truth. Still, there was obviously more to the story here.

IGNOTUS

"Anyway," Maker continued, "if the top brass no longer plan to use Erlen for bartering and they also have an idea of what he can do, that seems to imply their next course of action."

Adames frowned. "Which is what?"

"Taking custody of Erlen," Chantrey said, essentially verbalizing what Maker had been thinking.

"Hold on," Browing interjected. "I'll admit the subject was touched on, but nobody embraced the idea or even suggested a plan of action in that regard. That part was almost a sidebar conversation."

"That's what you've been saying about everything," Maker interjected. "Breaking up our team, taking possession of Erlen… They're all on the periphery of what was discussed, but you've yet to mention what the main topic was."

"That's just it," Browing shot back in exasperation. "They asked a lot of questions, but it wasn't explicitly clear what their main focus was. I know it relates to Erlen, but beyond that I couldn't glean much. It's like they danced around the real issue but never turned the spotlight on it directly."

"Come on, man," Maker said dubiously. "You're as connected a guy as I've ever seen. Are you saying you can't find out what those folks were after?"

Browing shook his head. "I don't think you understand the level of clout that was in that room. Sure, I've got connections, and I could probably reach out and get joint meetings with two, maybe three of the people I met with today. But a score of them, all together in one place, at one time? No way. I mean, they were all there in *person* — no aides, no assistants, no underlings. That

IGNOTUS

means that whatever was being said was something they each had to hear and assess *personally*."

"So whatever's going on, it's big," Adames surmised.

"That's a certainty," Browing agreed. "But beyond that, I just don't have any info to impart."

"Great," Maker muttered. "Like most bureaucrats, you're useless when your own interests aren't at stake."

Ignoring the barb, Browing said, "Look, all I know is that — based on the questions asked and the level of interest shown — this issue the bigwigs are focused on involves you and your Niotan friend."

Casting a quick glance at Erlen, Maker asked, "And you're sure they won't try anything, like forcefully taking possession of him?"

Browing shook his head. "No, the conversation honestly seemed to lean away from that type of action. They did, however, express concern over whether you were the best person to care for an asset like Erlen. Given your proclivity for dragging him into battle with you — as well as your affinity for adopting unconventional strategies and tactics — they seemed to feel that it might be in Erlen's best interest to be in an environment that was more…*stable*, shall we say."

"You mean it would be better for him to be with some*one* more stable," Maker corrected. "Well, you can tell them that I'm no less stable than when they reinstated me in the military."

"I did," Browing insisted. "Oddly enough, it failed to reassure anybody."

IGNOTUS

Chapter 7

Their impromptu meeting broke up shortly thereafter, with Browing promising to dig for more information, while Adames returned to his quarters to get into uniform and start reviewing the transfer requests. It was simply assumed that Chantrey, who had driven her own vehicle to the meeting, would give Maker and Erlen a ride back to the VOQ.

Conversation during the drive was dominated primarily by small talk, most of which consisted of Maker and Chantrey generally discussing dinner plans. It wasn't anything that had ever been officially declared, but they typically spent every evening together — a state of affairs that had come to include supper. Like Chantrey taking his hand while she drove (and which she did on this occasion), it was something that had come to give meaning to their relationship without defining it.

Once at the VOQ, Chantrey accompanied Maker and Erlen to their room, ostensibly to tend to the former's injuries (despite Maker insisting he was fine). Upon entering, Erlen immediately leaped upon a nearby sofa, while Chantrey dragged Maker to the bathroom.

"Take off your shirt," she practically commanded after they were inside.

While Maker complied without question (revealing sculpted pecs and well-developed abs), Chantrey opened a cabinet under the bathroom sink and pulled out a first-aid kit. Although he didn't comment on it, Maker found it somewhat telling that she knew where to find the kit without asking. However, he didn't have time to put any more thought into the subject as Chantrey turned to him, holding an antiseptic swab.

IGNOTUS

"Hmmm," she droned, looking him over. "You don't seem as bruised and battered as you did at first blush."

"What can I say?" Maker responded with a shrug. "I heal quickly."

Chantrey gave him a skeptical look but didn't comment. Nevertheless, he knew what she was thinking: that in licking him back at Browing's place, Erlen had applied some type of healing agent to Maker. It was one of numerous abilities the Niotan possessed, and one which Chantrey was well aware of.

"Well, my skin is still a little irritated from some razor-wasp stings," Maker announced suggestively.

"Fine," Chantrey said with a sigh. "Show me where."

Smiling, Maker held up his wrist, which was slightly discolored where he'd been stung.

Chantrey dabbed it with the swab almost dismissively. "What else you got, soldier?" she demanded.

"They got my back as well," Maker stated, turning around.

"What, these two little pinpricks?" Chantrey muttered dubiously, eyeing a couple of diminutive protrusions that might be generously described as bumps. Sighing almost disgustedly (which caused Maker to chuckle), she began swabbing one of the tiny lumps.

There was silence for a few seconds as Chantrey tended to the injured area, then she blurted out, "So, are you going to ask me?"

Maker frowned. "Ask you what?"

"The question that's been burning a hole in your brain since we left Browing's place," Chantrey replied.

IGNOTUS

"What I think the bigwigs were after with their questions about your squad and Erlen."

Maker turned around to face her. "The only question I had for you was about dinner, which we discussed on the way here."

"No, that was idle chatter that you engaged me in so that we wouldn't have to discuss what was *really* on your mind. It's called avoidance."

"I wasn't avoiding anything," Maker shot back, although in truth he couldn't recall who had actually started the conversation in the car. "Regardless, if you had an opinion on the subject, you should have spoken up back at Browing's place. Now that I think about it, you barely said a word when we were there."

"That's because I was listening and *formulating* an opinion."

"And I take it that you have one now?"

"Of course," Chantrey replied. "Would you like to know what it is?"

Maker simply stared at her, not saying anything.

She met his gaze without flinching, looking him directly in the eye.

After a few seconds, Maker let out a long sigh. "You know I can't do that. It wouldn't be appropriate."

Chantrey giggled, then gave him a sly look. "Considering all the things we've done to each other lately, I'd say propriety is rather low on the totem pole."

"You know what I mean," he admonished. "I'm your assignment. You draft reports about me that the higher-ups use to give me orders. It wouldn't be proper for me to basically start asking you for reports on *them*."

IGNOTUS

"Well, let me ask *you* a question," Chantrey said. "If we weren't in a relationship, would you ask my thoughts on the subject?"

Maker barely hesitated before declaring, "Yes, probably."

"Then what's the difference?"

"The difference is that your judgment can be construed as being warped by the fact that we're together. It makes your work appear tainted — makes *you* appear tainted. It could ruin your career."

Chantrey put her arms around his neck. "As I've said before, why don't you let *me* worry about my career."

Maker shook his head in disbelief. "I don't understand how you can be so nonchalant about this. No career means no job. No job means no income. No income means…"

He trailed off as an odd thought suddenly occurred to him. He then looked Chantrey up and down, as if seeing her for the very first time.

Understanding immediately what this new scrutiny meant, Chantrey withdrew her hands from his neck and simply looked down.

"Geez, I'm blind," Maker muttered, almost to himself. "I can't believe I didn't see it before."

Looking down at her hands, Chantrey simply said, "I knew you'd figure it out sooner or later, although I was hoping it would be much further down the road."

"You're like Browing," Maker stated as if she hadn't spoken. "A trust-fund baby."

Her head snapped up unexpectedly and there was a fierce look in her eye. "I don't like that term."

"But it's true," he stressed. "That's why you're not concerned about money or your career. You're rich."

IGNOTUS

"Yes, I am," Chantrey admitted, crossing her arms defiantly. "I come from a wealthy family and I *do* have a trust fund — several, in fact. But that's not why I'm not worried about my employment or income. I'm not worried because I'm the best at what I do, and no amount of money could buy the knowledge and skill set that I have. So if they want to replace me, they can, but they'll be getting an also-ran."

"Great — you're irreplaceable," Maker conceded almost sardonically. "What about *me*?"

Chantrey looked at him in befuddlement. "I'm not sure what you're asking."

"Am *I* replaceable?" he clarified. "Am I just a boy toy that you'll play with until something new and shiny catches your eye?"

She gave him a steely look. "That's insulting, Gant. You're saying my feelings are true-blue as long as I'm a pauper, but somehow being rich means my emotions are insincere."

"No… That's not…" He let out a deep sigh and took a moment to collect his thoughts. "I'm sorry, okay. That's not what I was trying to say."

Chantrey reached out a hand, gently caressing his face while looking into his eyes. "Do you really think that's all you are to me?" she asked. "A boy toy?"

"No," he admitted, shaking his head, "but it's not like we've defined this thing."

"That's because you walk around on tenterhooks about it all the time — constantly worrying about what people will say and how it will be perceived."

"It's more a concern about how it will affect *you*," Maker corrected. "But I see now I've been worrying for nothing."

IGNOTUS

"That's what I've been trying to tell you," she insisted, then leaned forward to give him a quick peck on the lips. "I don't need special handling."

"So I should just act as I did when our relationship was purely professional," Maker surmised. "Treat you as I did before we became an item."

"Well, maybe not when the lights go out," she muttered coyly with a wink. "But otherwise, yes."

"Well, in that case, I've got a question for you," he said. "What's your impression of that meeting Browing had?"

IGNOTUS

Chapter 8

The way Chantrey broke it down, there were essentially three takeaways from Browing's discussion with the top brass.

"First," she began, leaning back against the bathroom counter, "I think they want to replicate what you did with your unit."

Maker frowned. "I'm not sure what you mean."

"Well, it's just like Adames said: you took a bunch of soldiers the military no longer had a use for, and molded them into not just a functional fighting force, but a formidable one."

"And as *I* keep saying, I didn't do anything special," Maker insisted. "All I did was give them a second chance — present them with an opportunity to excel."

"If we're being honest, it's more than just that, because plenty of folks get second chances — or even a third — and still manage to botch things at every turn. I'd say the view from the top is that you've hit upon some kind of process or procedure that lends itself towards success in terms of getting troubled soldiers to straighten up and fly right. Now they want to take the Maker magic formula, add soldiers, rinse, and repeat on a widespread basis."

"Except there *is* no magic formula," Maker insisted. "And even if there were, how do they even know lightning would strike twice?"

"They don't," Chantrey conceded. "Not yet, anyway. But it sounds like they're willing to prove up the theory, and it's not like they have a shortage of test subjects. The military is full of screwed-up soldiers."

IGNOTUS

"As well as soldiers who are complete screw-ups," Maker added, "and you can't always tell one from the other. At least now, though, the allusion to breaking up our squad makes sense — especially in light of the transfer requests."

"You might want to make sure those are actually transfer *requests* and not *orders*," Chantrey suggested. "Someone may be trying to shove a bunch of castoffs on you."

A distasteful look settled on Maker's face. "They can't do that. Part of the deal for me agreeing to reinstatement in the Marines was that I get to pick my own crew."

"That was for a specific mission — hunting down the Vacra," Chantrey argued. "In case you forgot, Skullcap's dead and the Vacra fleet is destroyed. Ergo, mission's over."

"Correction: we destroyed an invading armada of Vacra ships," Maker declared. "I doubt we took out every vessel that they have, just like their obliteration of the Hundred-and-Twelfth didn't wipe out all of *our* spacecraft. As for hunting them down, we still haven't located their homeworld. Finally, we were also tasked with retrieving the sub rosa tech the Vacra stole, and we're nowhere near completing that part of our mission."

"Well, it's been weeks since we faced off against the Vacra invasion force. Don't you think you'd have gotten new orders by now if you were expected to pick up where you left off?"

Maker simply stared at her, unsure of how to respond. It was true that his unit was currently confined to Baskin, but he attributed that to the fact that they had been extensively debriefed — on multiple occasions and

IGNOTUS

an ongoing basis — following the destruction of the Vacra invaders. Compared to what he endured after the *Orpheus Moon* (which had included about six months of debriefing), the weeks they'd spent on Baskin had been a breeze. But to Chantrey's point — outside of having to make themselves regularly available to discuss what had happened — they had no specific duties. Fortunately, Adames was an adept NCO and kept their team from being idle with a fair amount of training exercises, war games, and the like.

"Anyway," Chantrey droned, interrupting his thoughts, "moving on to the second nugget I gleaned from what Browing told us."

"Yes?" Maker intoned, his interest obviously piqued.

"I think they were assessing Browing himself."

Maker's brow wrinkled in confusion. "You'll have to explain that."

"Well, I'm sure you'll recall that — family wealth aside — Browing is a bureaucrat. He's not on the lowest rung of the ladder by any means, but there are still individuals that he reports to — people he takes orders from."

"How could I forget?" Maker blurted out. "Those orders once required that he essentially betray us."

"And you almost killed us by detonating a banned weapon," Chantrey chided, "so some would call that even. But I digress. Now, you're probably aware that, much like me, Browing has occasionally had to file reports on you."

"It's not a surprise," Maker stated, "if that's what you're asking."

IGNOTUS

"Great. Now, I can tell you without having seen it that his initial assessment probably described you as a basket case who pulled together a bunch of sideshow freaks and started calling them a military unit. Since then, however, I think he's come to the realization that you're a capable and competent officer, and on your part, you recognize that he brings a lot to the table."

"I'll admit that I'm no longer actively looking for a reason to shoot him," Maker acknowledged.

"Fair enough," Chantrey said, trying not to smile. "But my point is that his reports on you and your team have probably mellowed of late. In fact, I assume that the most recent ones are probably complimentary to some extent. That being the case, the powers that be want to assess where his loyalties lie."

"So they ask him a bunch of questions they already know the answer to," Maker concluded. "And depending on how he responds, they know if his loyalty is still to them and the task they assigned him, or if he's become aligned with me and my crew."

"Something like that."

"Okay," Maker muttered, mentally digesting what he'd just heard. "I have to confess that it's surprising to think of Browing as being at odds with the puppet masters over him, but I'll give more thought to it later. In the meantime, what's the third thing you picked up from what Browing told us?"

"Exactly what he said when we were at his place," Chantrey answered. "That something big and complex is in the works."

Maker nodded, although this wasn't really news to him.

"Anything else?" he asked almost casually.

IGNOTUS

"Only that — whatever this thing is — it's going to happen very soon."

Her last statement turned out to be more prophetic than either of them would have guessed, as seconds later, both of their p-comps began to beep and flash, indicating an incoming emergency message.

IGNOTUS

Chapter 9

Chantrey left immediately after glancing at the message on her p-comp. Maker didn't ask, but assumed that the missive she'd received was similar to the communication he'd gotten, which was to report to a certain location in an hour.

With time ticking, Maker took a quick shower and then hurriedly got dressed.

****

Not knowing the exact nature of the summons, Maker decided to leave Erlen in their room and go alone. Upon his team's arrival on Baskin, he had been granted the use of a military vehicle, which was what he used to get to the rendezvous point. Truth be told, however, he didn't really do any hands-on driving on this occasion; he simply input the location (which consisted solely of latitudinal and longitudinal coordinates) into the car's navigation system, and the vehicle did the rest.

The drive took about half an hour. Baskin was essentially a military planet — a base for humanity's various armed services. Thus, Maker didn't find it unusual that, despite finding himself in a region that was primarily rural, he still had to pass through multiple checkpoints before reaching his final destination.

Ultimately, the car pulled into the parking lot of a nondescript one-story building that, from the outside, appeared to be about two thousand square feet in size. Maker exited the vehicle and headed towards the building entrance, noting that it was guarded by an armed soldier on either side. The two guards saluted smartly as Maker

IGNOTUS

drew near, while the door — which appeared to be fashioned of steel — opened by sliding sideways into a recessed compartment.

Maker returned the salute and then stepped inside; the door closed behind him with a slight hiss. Glancing around, he found himself in a nigh-featureless white room that was completely and utterly devoid of even the most basic *accouterment*: no windows, no furniture, no decorations… The only thing of note was a set of elevator doors set in the far wall; like the building entrance, it was manned by two guards who were standing at attention.

With nowhere else to go, Maker approached the elevator, at which point one of the guards turned to a scanner set in the wall. The guard placed his right palm on the scanner and muttered something Maker didn't catch — presumably a code-phrase. The elevator doors opened almost immediately, and Maker, understanding what was expected of him, walked in.

As the doors closed, Maker noted a control panel set in a wall of the elevator. However, instead of having multiple buttons for various floors, there was only a single button available for selection.

Only one direction for this elevator, Maker thought as he pushed the button. *And one destination.*

As the elevator was housed in a one-story building, Maker wasn't surprised that it started moving down. What was unexpected, however, was the depth to which it descended. Starting when the elevator went into motion, he mentally ticked off forty-seven seconds before it came to a halt. That meant he was well below ground — a fact confirmed when the elevators opened and he

IGNOTUS

stepped out to find himself on a subterranean railway platform.

As in the building up on the surface, there were guards on the platform — seemingly half a dozen: two by the elevator doors, two near the edge of the platform, and two near a side door set in one of the walls. Frankly, the number of soldiers present struck Maker as overkill. There was nothing down here but a single railway line, on which, at the moment, sat a lone train car with heavily-tinted windows. But he, of course, did not run this particular outfit, so it wasn't his place to say how many guards constituted a glut.

Not needing directions, Maker headed for the train car, the doors of which were open. Once inside, he immediately noticed that he wasn't alone. Sitting on one side of the railcar was Browing.

After giving a cursory "Hello," Maker took a seat across from him. A moment later, the doors closed and the train started moving.

IGNOTUS

Chapter 10

The journey took about five minutes, with the train car traveling at what felt like high speed the entire time. With the windows tinted on the interior as well, Maker couldn't see anything outside (not that there was much to see in an underground tunnel), but he got the impression that they passed several other railway platforms.

Neither he nor Browing spoke while in transit. Maker took this as indication that his companion, like himself, suspected that the railcar was bugged. Besides, other than rehash what they had already discussed earlier, they wouldn't be able to do anything more than guess at what was going on. More to the point, the need for speculation was minimal, because they would clearly find out soon enough.

Eventually, the train came to a halt. When the doors opened, the two passengers stepped out to find themselves on a railway platform similar to the one from which they'd departed. The only difference was that this particular platform seemed to be functioning at full capacity, with a steady stream of railcars pulling up and allowing passengers to disembark. As a result, the place had far more people milling about, including civilians as well as soldiers. In fact, the platform appeared to connect to what looked like a sizeable underground facility — a bunker or fortification of some sort.

"Lieutenant Maker?" asked a feminine voice, interrupting his thoughts. "Mr. Browing?"

Maker turned to find a Marine sergeant standing just a few feet away. He had been so busy assessing their surroundings that he hadn't even noticed her approach.

IGNOTUS

"That's us," Browning said to the sergeant.

She gave a curt nod and said, "Follow me please." She then turned and began walking away, without waiting to see if they would follow.

****

The sergeant led them into the bunker Maker had noticed earlier. Once inside, he noted that it was even more expansive than he'd initially assumed, with wide hallways leading off in various directions.

Following the sergeant down a corridor, Maker asked, "What is this place?"

"That's classified, sir," she responded without breaking stride.

"Its name or its purpose?" Maker inquired.

"Both," the sergeant replied flatly.

Browning gave her a skeptical look. "You can't even tell us what this place is *called*?"

"No," she stated rigidly.

"Surely we're cleared to know *that* much," Browning insisted. "After all, we're *here*."

"Except you don't know where 'here' is," the sergeant admonished. "All you know is that you're in a subterranean facility, but you can't tell anyone where it's located or how to get here. You arrived in a train car, but you don't know the direction it went or the distance it traveled, not to mention how far underground you are."

"Speaking of the train car," Maker said, "any reason why it's running on rails instead of using anti-gravs?"

"I'm afraid that's classified as well," the sergeant declared in a bored monotone.

IGNOTUS

Maker merely nodded, but didn't say anything. He had been assigned to numerous classified facilities in his time, and was therefore able to glean a fair amount of info from the sergeant's responses. However, he kept his thoughts to himself.

Eventually, their guide led them to — and through — a door that opened up into a room that was eerily similar to the building Maker had entered earlier: devoid of furniture and almost anything else other than armed soldiers. This time, however, it was just a door in a side wall being guarded rather than an elevator.

One of the soldiers stepped forward and muttered something inaudible to the sergeant, who nodded and then turned to face her two charges. "My apologies, but we're going to have to check you for weapons."

"Haven't you done that already?" Browing practically demanded. "I mean, none of you people have asked me who I was or demanded I show any sort of identification, and I assume Maker had the exact same experience. That means you've probably been scanning us since the moment we stepped out of our vehicles and satisfied yourself as to who we were via facial recognition, biometrics, and so on. I find it hard to believe none of that encompassed a weapons scan."

"The methodology we use to verify bona fides is confidential," the sergeant explained. "But if it makes you feel any better, the weapons check only applies to the el-tee."

She then waved over a big, burly soldier who was at least a head taller than anyone else in the room. The fellow took a position in front of Maker and simply stared at him for a moment with an *are-we-going-to-have-a-problem?* expression on his face.

IGNOTUS

Maker glanced at Browing and shrugged. He wasn't armed, and therefore didn't see the need to make things difficult. Ergo, he lifted his arms and held them out to the side at shoulder level, inviting the soldier to do his job.

Thankfully, the soldier performed the pat-down quickly — although perhaps a bit more thoroughly than absolutely necessary. (Maker couldn't tell if the guy was simply meticulous, or if he just enjoyed his work.) When done, the fellow simply nodded at the sergeant, apparently indicating that Maker was clean.

"You good?" Browing asked Maker.

"Oh, yeah," Maker replied, "although I think I might be in love now." As he spoke, he winked at the soldier who had searched him; caught off-guard, the fellow suddenly looked like someone who had accidentally stepped on a landmine.

"Okay, you're clear," remarked the sergeant, plainly ignoring the raillery between her guests. As she spoke, the side-wall door slid open.

Browing and Maker did as expected and stepped through the door into the next room. Calling it a room, however, was incredibly generous. It was more of a closet, if anything, that could accommodate perhaps six full-grown men (assuming they weren't adverse to being packed in, jowl-to-jowl).

They had barely entered before the door behind them slid shut, followed by a series of mechanical clicks that seemed to indicate that it was locked and bolted in position. Maker was perplexed for a moment, as the other three walls were bare. He and Browing shared a confused glance, but before either of them could comment, the wall opposite the door they had entered began to move.

IGNOTUS

From all appearances, the right corner of said wall appeared to be hinged, allowing the entire wall to swing outward. It put Maker in mind of the door to a vault, and a moment later he realized that was exactly what it was: a vault. Something valuable was on the other side, and Maker suddenly found himself itching to know what it was.

As soon as the opening was wide enough, Maker slid through. He was in another white room, about twenty-by-twenty feet in size. However, his attention was immediately drawn to the fact that the entire wall opposite the vault door was made of glass, revealing another room that was almost a mirror of the one he was in except for one distinct difference: there was a single individual in the other room, standing maybe ten paces away from the glass.

Maker drew in a ragged breath, recognizing the other person immediately.

Skullcap.

IGNOTUS

Chapter 11

Maker instinctively reached for his sidearm, but it wasn't there. He typically didn't wear it outside of battle conditions (and if he *had* worn it, it would have been confiscated during the pat-down), but going for his gun wasn't anything that he had consciously thought about. It was a natural impulse, a reaction, to seeing Skullcap.

The insectoid wasn't in his battle armor or wearing his namesake helmet, but Maker had no trouble recognizing him. Although bipedal, the Vacra had six arms, and Skullcap was distinguishable by the fact that one of his middle arms was stunted and deformed. It was actually a regenerated limb; the original arm had been normal, but Skullcap had lost it during his first skirmish with Maker. His body had attempted to regrow the appendage, but with less-than-stellar results.

"Looks like I owe you an apology," Browing muttered. "He *is* alive."

Maker didn't even hear him. From his perspective, the rest of the universe had fallen away, receded to a distant point. The only thing that existed was him and Skullcap.

Maker dashed to the glass wall separating the two rooms. He pounded on it with a fist, then hit it again. It felt like he was striking steel. The glass was obviously made of some kind of reinforced material — probably meant to withstand anything up to and including a grenade blast.

Skullcap, roughly seven feet tall and dressed in something like a gray tunic, stepped towards the glass.

"Maker," the insectoid said, pronouncing the name as "Make-her," with two separate syllables. "News of your demise was conveyed to me. I told them it could not be so. Death cannot claim you — not while the Senu Lia grants you protection."

Maker ignored him, although it registered somewhere in the back of his mind that the voice had seemingly come from overhead — speakers — rather than in front of him. Instead, Maker scanned the framework of the glass wall before him, looking for an access point, some way to breach it.

Somewhere near him, he picked up on an odd noise — a type of chattering — but his mind filtered it out, mentally waving it away like the buzzing of an insect. His focus stayed on the problem at hand as he continued to look for a way to get into the room with Skullcap.

"There's gotta be…" he murmured to himself, eyes examining the glass partition between the rooms. "How do I…"

The chattering sounded again, louder this time. Closer. Still, Maker's disregard of it persisted. Skullcap was all that mattered.

The chattering increased in volume, almost enough to become an irritant. Maker turned in the direction of the sound, not to see what it was but as part of an effort to survey the room. In his mind, there had to be something on hand he could use to try to break the glass wall — a chair, a table leg, a light fixture… *Some*thing. *Any*thing.

That's when he noticed that the source of the chattering was a person. More specifically, it was a man in uniform sporting the rank of a Space Navy fleet admiral. He was red in the face at the moment, and seemed to be screaming something in Maker's direction. No, not just in his direction, but *at* him, to be precise. At that moment,

IGNOTUS

the singlemindedness that had gripped Maker vanished, and the chattering he'd been hearing suddenly became words he could understand.

"—ay it again!" the admiral bellowed. "Soldier, stand down!"

IGNOTUS

Chapter 12

"What the hell is going on?" Maker practically demanded. "What's Skullcap doing here?"

"Ambassador Vuqja is here as our guest," said the admiral who had yelled at Maker to stand down. His name tag identified him as "Lafayette," and Maker now remembered him as one of the officers who had been present during his debriefings.

"*Ambassador* Vuqja?" Maker repeated, not bothering to hide his surprise.

"Yes," said Lafayette. "He's here as a dignitary and official representative of the Vacra."

Maker frowned, trying to process this.

They were currently in a small chamber in the general vicinity of — but not adjacent to — the room where Maker had seen Skullcap. He had been so taken aback by his archenemy's presence that he hadn't even noticed that there had been other people in the room at the time besides himself and Browing. (In addition to Lafayette, there had been a field marshal named Steiner and a Star Forces general named Grasso present.) After his initial astonishment at seeing his archenemy — and subsequently being ordered to stand down after trying to get at him — Maker had been hustled out of the room in question.

A few minutes later, he'd found himself at his current location, along with Browing and the three general officers. (En route, Browing had managed to convey that these were three of the people he'd met with earlier.) At Lafayette's insistence, they had each taken a seat at a table located in the middle of the room, at which point Maker had launched into his questions, seemingly

IGNOTUS

without regard for the fact that the other officers in the room outranked him by a mile.

Now, upon hearing Skullcap labeled as an ambassador, all Maker could do was shake his head in disbelief and say, "Can someone explain to me how a piece of flotsam like that gets to be an ambassador?"

"Funny that you should describe him as flotsam," Grasso said, "because that's exactly how we found him."

"What?" Browing asked, plainly bewildered.

"After your incident with the Vacra ships," Grasso explained, "we found him floating in a lifepod."

"Incident?" Maker echoed. "You mean the battle where their invasion force was destroyed?"

"The ambassador describes the encounter a little differently," Steiner interjected. "But, yes, that's where he was found."

Maker's brow wrinkled as he struggled to process what he was hearing. "So what — any piece of sentient trash that we pick up can just declare himself a dignitary?"

"Well, we didn't just take his word for it," Lafayette assured him. "We had your reports to go by."

Upon hearing this, Browing let out a groan of agitation and shook his head in solemn frustration.

"What am I missing here?" Maker asked him. "Did you call him an emissary in your report or something?"

"Not exactly," Browing stated. "But I did refer to him as a leader of the Vacra and one of their military commanders."

"Actually, you *all* did," Grasso clarified. "Including you, Lieutenant Maker, when you were debriefed."

Maker shrugged. "So what?"

IGNOTUS

"Think about it," Browing said. "He's the only representative of his species that we've managed to have sustained contact with, he says he's an ambassador, and our own people vouch for him being a leader of his race."

"Basically, we had no reason to doubt his claims," Grasso said. "Not to mention the fact that some of our people have, ahem, had prior contact with him."

Maker balled his fist, remembering how certain individuals had tried to hand Erlen over to the Vacra, but tried to keep the anger of his voice.

"So that's what this boils down to," Maker muttered. "You still want the sub rosa tech the Vacra took."

"Of course we still want it," Steiner admitted. "It's generations of work — not to mention weaponry that is incredibly potent, powerful—"

"And illegal," Maker interjected.

There was an uncomfortable silence following Maker's last statement. He had highlighted a harsh and galling truth: most (if not all) of the tech taken was banned and forbidden by either law, treaty, or common decency. It should never have existed in the first place.

"Look, let's just talk straight," Lafayette said. "We've got to get that tech back. Not only is it dangerous in the wrong hands, but just the fact that it exists could tear apart dozens of treaties that mankind has with other species. So the physical damage these weapons can do is only part of the story. The political fallout can't be measured."

"So you're politicians now?" Maker asked, his disdain evident.

"We're here representing a lot more than just military interests," Lafayette answered, gesturing to include Steiner and Grasso. "There's a score of people who wanted to be part of this conversation, but it was felt that you'd respond better to folks in uniform."

"And these special interests groups, first and foremost, all want to reclaim the missing sub rosa tech," Maker concluded.

Grasso nodded. "Absolutely."

"Well, you've got the people who took it," Browning noted. "At least one of them, anyway. Just make him tell you."

"Again," Lafayette droned, "he's a foreign dignitary. That means he's a guest and will be treated as such."

"Ha!" Maker barked. "He's not a guest. He's a prisoner. This little subterranean site" — he spread his arms in a gesture encompassing the entire facility they were in — "is a holding tank. A place to stick people you may never want to see the light of day again. That's why it's buried a mile underground. That's why there are guards at every door. That's why the train cars are on rails instead of having anti-gravs. All those things are obstacles, make it more difficult to get away should one of your 'guests' ever manage to break out."

"Regardless of appearances," Lafayette countered, "his official status is that of ambassador. As to having him in this 'holding tank,' as you put it, that's for his protection. Apparently we've got people around here who will shoot him on sight."

"That's called displaying good judgment," Maker stated, "and it's not too late to exercise some."

"Hold on," Browning said. "Before we talk about putting someone in front of a firing squad, I'd like to know a little more about how our guest survived that last

IGNOTUS

battle. I would have sworn he died when the Vacra invaded our region of space. In fact, that's what I reported."

"Well, there are two versions of what happened," Grasso began. "There's the official record of what occurred, and then there's the *un*official record."

"Why don't we take the official version first?" Maker suggested. "Might as well get the lies out of the way as soon as possible."

"That's fine," Grasso assured him, ignoring Maker's taunt. "But just to be clear, this is the only narrative that will be cleared for public consumption, and it's the story that Ambassador Vuqja will articulate if asked about it."

"Oh?" Maker droned. "So what exactly is our esteemed visitor's recollection as to what happened?"

"That it wasn't an invasion, for starters," Grasso explained. "Simply put, he came to open a dialogue between mankind and the Vacra — to initiate contact between our two species and see if we could treat with one another in mutually beneficial ways."

"And the armada he brought with him?" Maker asked. "I suppose that was just for show-and-tell?"

"The ambassador states that he was accompanied by an escort befitting his rank and title," Steiner replied. "It wasn't an invasion force, but we, unfortunately, treated it as such."

"So how does he explain the obliteration of the Hundred-and-Twelfth fleet?" Browing chimed in.

"He says there was some weird spatial anomaly," Lafayette answered. "It destroyed both his escort and the Hundred-and-Twelfth. However, much like General

IGNOTUS

Roche's flagship on *our* side, the ambassador's vessel was out of range of whatever force came into play."

"How convenient," Maker uttered sarcastically.

Browing frowned. "So if his ship wasn't destroyed, how does he end up in a lifepod?"

"Despite everything that happened, he still wanted to make contact," Lafayette explained. "However, he didn't know how he would be received after what happened to the Hundred-and-Twelfth, so he ejected in a lifepod while ordering his crew to return home in his ship."

There was silence as Lafayette finished talking, with the other two general officers nodding satisfactorily at his narrative.

"That's a good story," Maker admitted with a nod. "Did Skullcap come up with that on his own or did we coach him?"

Steiner seemed to bristle at this and was on the verge of responding but didn't get a chance.

"I believe the lieutenant's question was rhetorical," Browing stated. "That said, I think we can all agree that it's a plausible cover story, but it does raise the question: what does the crew of Roche's flagship say happened?"

"Frankly speaking, none of them are sure," Lafayette assured him. "They just know that one second the Hundred-and-Twelfth fleet was there in all its glory; the next, it was gone."

"And a moment later, the alien armada had vanished as well," Steiner added. "So there's no one who can really contradict this version of events."

IGNOTUS

"No one except the people who were on the *Black Pearl*," Maker corrected. "Namely, the people in my unit, along with Browning and Dr. Chantrey."

"Well, let's address that," said Lafayette. "First of all, you and your people claim that all the destruction was the result of contact with an anomalous entity that you refer to as Efferus. Call me crazy, but that seems to dovetail nicely into the official story.

"Next, your operation was classified, as are any reports on it and any related debriefings. Plainly speaking, while we appreciate your efforts to complete your mission and your candor in reporting what happened, none of that info is ever going to see the light of day."

"In short," Maker concluded, "there's no formal evidence to dispute your version of events."

Lafayette shrugged. "Don't take it too hard, son. This isn't an unusual course of action, and based on your record, this can't be the first time you've encountered something like this."

"I've been on missions where a cover story was required," Maker admitted. "Recon, skirmishes, and so on, where it was necessary to sweep things under the rug. But we're dealing with the Vacra here — a new breed of enemy. This is different."

"It's no different than a thousand times in the past when we made peace with an enemy," Grasso argued.

"But that's just it," Maker stressed. "The Vacra don't want peace. They never did. They want something else entirely."

Lafayette studied him for a moment. "You're speaking of your, uh, 'friend.'"

IGNOTUS

Maker nodded. "Erlen. They'll do anything to get him."

"Not anymore," Steiner blurted out.

Maker's eyebrows went up in surprise. "Excuse me?"

"They're no longer asking for him," Steiner continued.

Maker frowned. "I take it this is another instance of there being an official and an unofficial story?"

Grasso shook his head. "No, not this time. There's only one rendition of the facts."

"Hmmm," Browing mused. "The Vacra have always stressed a trade: Erlen for the sub rosa tech. If they no longer want him, there must be something else they're asking for."

"There is," Steiner agreed with a nod. "Since he's achieved his aim of making peaceful contact and paved the way for cooperation between our two species, Ambassador Vuqja just has one request: he wants to go home."

There was silence for a moment as Maker waited expectantly, then he realized that no more information was forthcoming.

"Wait," Maker murmured in confusion. "That's it? He just wants to go back to Vacra Prime or wherever he comes from?"

"Yes," Lafayette confirmed. "And he'll hand over the sub rosa tech in exchange if we allow it."

Expecting someone to expound, Maker quickly glanced at each of the general officers in turn. After a moment, it became clear that none of them was going to speak without prompting.

IGNOTUS

"So what's the problem?" he finally asked. "Just get the tech back, then pack him up in a ship on autopilot and send him on his way. Good riddance."

"He's asking for an escort," Lafayette replied. "Someone to shepherd him back to his homeworld. In fact, he says that part is nonnegotiable."

"Okay, so assign a squadron to take him back to whatever dung heap he crawled out of," Maker practically dictated.

"It's not that easy," Lafayette insisted.

"Why not?" Maker asked, looking nonplussed.

"Because part of his demand is that a specific individual be assigned the duty of escort," Lafayette explained. "*You*, to be precise."

IGNOTUS

Chapter 13

Maker stood in stunned silence for a moment, then blurted out, "What?!"

"The ambassador wants you to escort him home," Lafayette repeated.

"And I want to be a hologram star," Maker shot back, "but neither one of those things is likely to happen."

"And if you were ordered to take him back?" Grasso inquired.

"Then I'd say the odds are high that he'll suffer an 'accident' before reaching his destination," Maker said.

"Well, I'm sure you'll do all in your power to keep that from happening," Lafayette retorted without missing a beat. "After all, from what Browing here says, you're a stickler for obeying orders and completing the mission — even if it's an assignment you don't care for."

Maker frowned, not liking where the conversation was going. "Are you ordering me to do this?"

Lafayette shook his head. "No, but I'm curious as to why you're so adverse to it."

"Because it's Skullcap," Maker declared, as if that explained everything. "He's as devious as they come. If he's asking for this, that means it's a trick or a trap."

"And if I could add my two cents," Browing chimed in. "I don't often agree with Maker, but I think he's right. Who's to say that when we take him home, we won't drop out of hyperspace and find ourselves hemmed in by battleships?"

"I think that's unlikely," Grasso asserted. "Regardless of the official story, they just lost an armada

IGNOTUS

— a lot of ships, and even more people. I don't think they're eager to tangle with us again."

"I wouldn't bank on that," Maker said. "I'm sure they have some hive mother or monarch bug that can lay a million eggs a day. They'll be back at full strength before your afternoon tee time."

The three general officers exchanged glances. Plainly disregarding the comment on how they spent their afternoons, it seemed that Maker's assessment posited a theory they hadn't considered.

"While we're mulling over egg-laying queens," Browing suddenly interjected, "I wanted to ask how, exactly, this exchange is supposed to take place. Does the ambassador have to hand over the sub rosa tech before being taken home, or vice versa?"

"He'll take us to the tech first," Steiner said. "Apparently realizing how dangerous it was, the Vacra didn't want it anywhere near their planet, so it's being stored in a distant star system. After it's retrieved and fully accounted for, our new friend gets to go home."

"So this is actually a multi-stage trip," Maker summed up in a frosty tone. "That means the Vacra will have *two* chances to stab us in the back. Skullcap has to be practically giddy that anyone's even considering this."

Lafayette drummed his fingers for a moment, eyeing Maker critically.

"I suppose I should have led with this question," he finally said, "but what exactly is your relationship with the ambassador?"

"Relationship?" Maker echoed, visibly taken aback. "We want to kill each other, so to the extent that implies relations, there you have it."

IGNOTUS

"Well, it's just odd," Lafayette commented. "When we picked him up, he inquired about you. We told him you were dead — that all evidence pointed to the *Black Pearl* being destroyed in that incident with his, uh, Vacran escort."

Maker simply nodded. He already knew that he, along with everyone on the *Pearl*, had been presumed dead when the entity Efferus took them to his part of the cosmos. When Efferus returned them several days later, there had been general shock at the fact that they had survived.

"Anyway," Lafayette continued, "despite proof to the contrary, the ambassador insisted you were alive. He said that the Senu Lia — your alien companion, Erlen — wouldn't let you die. Lo and behold, he was eventually proved right. And on your part, notwithstanding the fact that you had seen the Vacra armada destroyed, you seemed convinced that somehow, some way, the ambassador had survived. More importantly, no one could disabuse you of the notion during the times you were debriefed."

Maker shrugged. "So what's your point?"

Lafayette leaned forward, steepling his fingers. "Just that you and the ambassador, in spite of evidence and information to the contrary, were each convinced that the other was still alive, and you were both right."

"And you think that means something," Maker concluded.

Lafayette shrugged. "If nothing else, it implies that you have an understanding of this individual — and maybe his entire species — that no one else does."

Maker shook his head. "There's nothing deep or profound about my understanding of the Vacra. Just assume that they'll do nothing but lie and be treacherous, and voilà — you're an expert."

"Be that as it may," Lafayette intoned, "it's imperative that we get that tech back, and you're the only person who can do it. Assuming we won't order you to do this, what will it take for you to accept this mission?"

Maker contemplated for a moment, then said, "I'll think about it and get back to you."

IGNOTUS

Chapter 14

At the conclusion of their meeting with the general officers, Browing and Maker quickly departed the underground facility. Upon gaining the surface, the former cryptically stated that he needed to reach out to some people and would be in touch; he then got into his car (which Maker hadn't even noticed when he'd parked his own) and zoomed away. On his part, Maker headed for his current base of operations, which consisted of a moderately-sized warehouse space that had been designated for his squad's use.

When he arrived, he found Adames alone in the warehouse, having sent the rest of their unit out on a training exercise. It gave Maker an opportunity to solicit his NCO's opinion on what had happened, and Adames was brutally honest in that regard.

"What's there to debate?" he asked rhetorically after Maker gave him an overview of what had occurred. "You have to do this, Gant."

Maker didn't immediately respond. At present, they were in a walled-off (and soundproof) area of the warehouse that he generally used as his office. Maker sat at his desk while the NCO occupied a chair across from him.

"Without beating around the bush," Adames went on, "you know what those sub rosa weapons can do. If we have a chance to get them back, we have to take it."

"I agree that *some*one has to take the chance," Maker countered. "I disagree with the notion that it has to be us."

"But who else is really qualified?"

IGNOTUS

"According to the bigwigs, it's just escorting Skullcap home," Maker replied. "Basically babysitting. You don't really need any special qualifications."

"Come on, Gant," Adames implored. "This mission is right up your alley. What's *really* bothering you about this?"

Maker stared at him a moment, then let out a deep sigh. "Look, if it was just me, I probably wouldn't have an issue with taking on this assignment, but I've got our entire team to think of. I can't put them in that kind of danger."

Adames frowned in confusion. "What the hell are you talking about? Everyone in our unit is a Marine, and they understand that danger goes hand-in-glove with what we do. It's part of our daily constitutional. If you start worrying too much about danger to your people, you're going to lose sight of the mission."

"I can lead others into danger," Maker assured him. "It's what we were trained to do, and I have no problem with it. That's the job. But I can't just waltz my people into what I *know* is a trap, and that's what this thing feels like."

"And if it *is* a trap, who's better equipped to handle it: our unit with you at the helm? Or some green lieutenant fresh out of the Academy who doesn't know which end of a rifle to shoot from, leading a bunch of chuckleheads who don't know what the Vacra are capable of?"

"But you heard Browing this morning. Our people aren't the dregs the military previously thought they were. They have options now. They don't have to keep risking life and limb by charging into minefields behind me."

IGNOTUS

"As I just said, they're Marines — they're going to be risking their lives charging in behind *some*body. Better you than some clown who doesn't care if they come home in a box."

"What I care about may not matter if I parade us into an ambush," Maker stated. "That said, I see your point."

"So what are you going to do?" Adames asked.

"Well, I've been given a choice as to whether to take on this mission," Maker replied. "In light of all the facts, it's only fair that I give my people the same option."

IGNOTUS

Chapter 15

"I'm in," declared Edison Wayne, the youngest and least-experienced member of Maker's unit.

At present, the entire team was seated around a small conference table in the middle of the warehouse. After Maker had opted to let his subordinates choose whether to join the proposed mission, Adames had called an early end to the training exercise and ordered the other five members of their squad to report in. Once they were present, Maker had quickly brought them up to speed on the situation. However, he had barely finished speaking before Wayne announced his readiness to volunteer.

Sergeant Diviana, a striking woman with an exotic appearance, turned to Wayne. "We all realize you're still wet behind the ears, but did you miss the part stating that this entire mission is probably a trap?"

"No, I heard it loud and clear," Wayne assured her. "But if the el-tee is taking this on, he's got my unwavering support."

"Mine as well," said Cano Snick. He was generally a reserved man whose shorter-than-average stature masked the fact that he was a deadly martial artist.

"Us, too," Sergeant Loyola chimed in, speaking on behalf of herself and the man seated next to her. As usual, Loyola wore tinted goggles that fit snuggly over her eyes (or rather, the place where her eyes would have been, if she'd had any).

The fellow next to her, whom she'd spoken for, was Fierce Augman — an Augmented Man who stood over seven feet tall and whose body appeared to be comprised of solid muscle from head to foot. For a moment, he looked as though he had a comment to add,

IGNOTUS

but then he merely nodded in agreement with Loyola's statement.

"I guess that leaves me as the lone holdout," Diviana said, noting that everyone was staring at her.

"No pressure," Wayne muttered jokingly.

Diviana ignored him, stating, "Needless to say, I'm in."

"Great," Wayne practically gushed. "I knew you wouldn't want to miss out on the action."

"No," Diviana said, shaking her head. "I'm just trying to avoid attending six funerals after you people get yourselves killed."

IGNOTUS

Chapter 16

Following Diviana's acquiescence to joining the mission, Maker brought the meeting to a close and dismissed everyone. There was a lot to do, but thankfully everyone knew their job and could be counted on to make the necessary preparations for departure with minimal supervision.

On his part, Maker retreated to his office in order to reach out to Lafayette. (He had a secure comm link there that could be used for confidential transmissions.) As he entered and closed the door, he reflected on what he knew of the admiral.

For starters, Lafayette wasn't a Marine, so he wasn't officially in Maker's chain of command. That said, he had been present at Maker's debriefings and had presented credentials which had made it clear that he had *carte blanche* to exercise authority over Maker's team if he so chose. In short, he actually *could* have ordered Maker to escort Skullcap home, but the fact that he hadn't (and didn't seem inclined to do so) gave the impression that he was a decent fellow.

That fact aside, however, it was pretty clear that Lafayette (and whatever shadowy group he represented) was single-mindedly focused on reclaiming the tech that the Vacra had taken. It was the nigh-desperation in that regard that made Maker wary; higher-ups had previously made secret deals with the Vacra for the tech, and he couldn't be sure that the same thing wasn't happening now. Basically, he didn't know if he could trust Lafayette.

In the end, he mentally shrugged, deciding that there was just no way to know for sure how much faith he could put in the admiral. He'd just have to play it by

IGNOTUS

ear and keep his guard up. Mind made up, he got on the comm and sent a message to Lafayette stating that he wanted to meet the following morning and providing a time. (It occurred to him as he was firing off the communiqué that the proposed meeting time might conflict with something on Lafayette's schedule, but Maker didn't care; the admiral could work it out.)

After sending the message, Maker took a moment to lean back in his chair, feeling a bit smug and self-satisfied. His self-approbation was short-lived, however, as a moment later someone rapped resonantly on the door.

"Enter," Maker barked.

Almost as soon as he spoke, he saw Diviana step inside. After closing the door behind her, she marched smartly to Maker's desk and saluted.

Maker returned the gesture and then announced, "Be seated." Diviana did as instructed and sat down in a chair across from him.

"At ease," Maker said, then sat back and eyed the sergeant critically. "Okay, out with it."

Diviana raised an eyebrow in curiosity. "Out with what?"

"Oh, come on," he said. "You come to me before every mission with some request or complaint. So what is it this time?"

For a moment, it looked as though Diviana was going to protest, but then she seemed to relent. "I wanted to ask what you were planning to do about Planck."

"Of course," Maker muttered. "I should have known that's what you wanted to discuss."

Solomon Planck had been the lead scientist aboard the sub rosa vessel at the time it was raided by the

IGNOTUS

Vacra. He'd spent the next few years as their prisoner, suffering extreme amounts of abuse (including having a bomb implanted in him). He'd ultimately been rescued by Maker's unit, but he was still recovering — mentally and physically — from his ordeal. Plainly speaking, he was a basket case in some ways, but had proven invaluable during their last run-in with the Vacra.

"We need him," Diviana declared, interrupting Maker's reverie. "Planck knows the Vacra better than anybody."

"Agreed," Maker said with a nod, "and asking him to join our little expedition is on my to-do list."

Diviana gave him a critical look. "That's probably a bad idea."

"What — asking him to join us?"

"No," she replied, shaking her head solemnly. "Having *you* ask him."

"What's that supposed to mean?" Maker demanded.

"Just that you took the lead on asking him to join us last time, and completely mucked it up."

"Well, I wouldn't say *that*," Maker droned sheepishly as he reflected on the incident in question. "He was just hard to convince."

"Whatever," Diviana grumbled. "I was able to fix it *then*, but I thought maybe we'd skip the part where I have to clean up your mess by letting me take first crack at him this time."

Maker spread his hands in a magnanimous gesture. "Be my guest."

"Thanks," Diviana said with a smile.

"Anything else?"

"No, sir," Diviana answered, coming to her feet.

IGNOTUS

"Good," Maker stated approvingly. "Dismissed."

Diviana gave a salute (which Maker returned), then swiftly departed. However, it seemed that the door had barely closed behind her before another knock sounded. Upon being told by Maker to enter, Fierce came into the room. After exchanging courtesies, the Augman sat down in the chair recently vacated by Diviana.

"Well, this is a rare treat, Doctor," Maker declared. "Usually someone's lying prone in the infirmary when you and I have a conversation."

"I wouldn't worry about it," Fierce shot back. "Given how our missions have typically unfolded, I'm sure it will happen soon enough."

"I guess we'll just consider this practice, then," Maker noted, chuckling. "Anyway, what's on your mind?"

Fierce frowned, appearing to struggle for the right words for a moment, and then simply blurted out, "Loyola's pregnant."

Now it was Maker's turn to be at a loss for words, and for a second he simply stared at the Augman, completely dumbfounded.

"Are you kidding?" Maker finally managed to say.

Fierce shook his head. "Unfortunately, no."

"How'd that happen?" Maker almost demanded.

Fierce looked at him in surprise. "I'm sorry, Lieutenant. I just assumed that at this stage of your life, on at least one occasion, you'd have met a woman who–"

"I know *how* it happened, wise guy," Maker interjected. "Physically, that is. My question was from the biological perspective. I thought Augmen and normal humans couldn't procreate without some help from science and medicine."

IGNOTUS

"That's always been the prevailing sentiment, and it's what years of in-depth research and testing would seem to indicate. Bearing that in mind, we probably didn't take as many, uh, precautions as we should have."

"So what happened?" Maker asked.

"Don't know," Fierce admitted with a shrug. "But my best guess is that some outside factor came into play. Something with the ability to affect bodily functions and reproductive systems — perhaps through chemical or biological compounds."

Maker leaned back, lifted a hand to massage his temples and at the same time let out a frustrated sigh.

"Erlen," he said flatly.

"That would be my first guess," Fierce conceded with a nod. "It certainly seems like something that falls within the ambit of his talents."

Maker didn't say anything, but Fierce was right. Just as licking Maker's hand earlier had conveyed some healing element to deal with his injuries, what was being suggested was quite likely within Erlen's capabilities.

"But Erlen wouldn't do that," Maker insisted. "He wouldn't just do something to make you guys compatible unless…"

Maker trailed off, his thoughts going down an unexpected path as something new occurred to him.

"So tell me," he said, leaning forward, "did you and Loyola talk about having kids?"

"We've discussed it," Fierce admitted, "but it was something that we knew wouldn't happen on its own."

"But it's something you wanted?"

Fierce nodded. "Yes — it was more of a 'when' as opposed to an 'if' discussion."

IGNOTUS

"And how does Loyola feel about the baby? I mean, is she happy about it?"

"Are you kidding? She's over the moon about it! She can't wait, and she—"

Fierce stopped speaking practically mid-sentence, and his brow crinkled. Maker smiled internally, knowing that the good doctor was coming to the same conclusion he had reached.

"Wait a minute," Fierce muttered, finally getting his thoughts together. "Are you saying Loyola may have *asked* Erlen to do this?"

Maker raised his hands defensively. "I'm not saying anything. However, you two obviously have a lot to talk about."

"Clearly," Fierce said in agreement. "But the pregnancy is only part of why I wanted to speak with you. I also wanted to discuss Loyola's role on this mission."

"Say no more," Maker insisted. "I'll make sure she's taken off hazardous duty and—"

"No," Fierce objected, shaking his head. "That's exactly what you *shouldn't* do. She doesn't want to be treated any differently, which is why she hasn't told anyone — especially you."

"My hands are a little tied here," Maker insisted. "There are rules about expectant mothers in the theater of battle. She can go on this mission because technically it's nothing more than escort duty, but there are limitations on the tasks she can be assigned."

"I get that, but can you try to find something that makes use of her talents without making it seem like you're deliberately taking her out of harm's way?"

IGNOTUS

"She's a sniper!" Maker blurted out, throwing up his hands in exasperation. "There aren't a lot of subtle ways to take advantage of that skill set."

Fierce didn't reply. Instead, he simply gave Maker an expectant look.

"Fine," Maker muttered in acquiescence a moment later. "I'll find something to keep her occupied. Anything else I can do for you?"

"There is one other thing," Fierce said, now looking incredibly concerned. "This baby — it's going to be unique."

"That's for sure," Maker agreed. "The conception alone makes it one-of-a-kind."

"Yes, and the military has been looking for a way to enhance Augmen for generations now. Anything that looks like a new development in that arena is going to pique their interest."

Maker nodded, understanding what Fierce was getting at. "You're saying that they're going to try to take this baby."

"What I'm saying is that I don't want my child to end up in a bell jar," Fierce stated hotly. "Or being raised as a lab rat."

There was a scowl on the doctor's face as he spoke, probably the closest thing to anger Maker had ever witnessed an Augman display.

"That's never going to happen," Maker said flatly. "I give you my word: I won't let any harm come to this baby."

Fierce didn't say anything but merely nodded solemnly, obviously reassured by Maker's comment.

IGNOTUS

Chapter 17

Fierce left almost immediately after Maker made his promise about Loyola's unborn child, staying only long enough to hear — and agree to — an odd request from his commanding officer. Afterwards, Maker found himself contemplating the commitment he'd made (and how he'd fulfill it). However, no more than a minute passed before a knock once again sounded at his door.

Now what? he wondered, then yelled out, "Enter." The door opened and he saw that, much to his delight, his latest visitor was Chantrey.

"Well, this is unexpected," he said, rising as she headed towards him carrying a couple of brown paper bags. "To what do I owe the pleasure?"

She gave him a quick peck on the lips then sat down in the visitor's chair, placing the bags on his desk.

"I'm afraid I won't be able to make dinner," she stated as Maker sat back down. "I'll be tied up with work, but I thought I'd make it up to you with a late lunch — assuming you haven't eaten yet."

"I haven't had time to even think about lunch," he said, noting that it was early afternoon.

Taking that as her cue, Chantrey began taking items from the bags. Moments later, she had unpacked a couple of sandwiches, fruit cups, cookies, and bottles of a local beverage that tasted like a cross between onions and bananas. (Maker was certain she bought the drinks just to see his reaction.)

"*Bon appétit*," Chantrey said, and then took a bite of her sandwich. Needing no more of an invitation, Maker followed suit.

IGNOTUS

There was initially silence as Maker chewed and swallowed the first bite of his lunch. Then, as was typical for them, conversation ensued as they continued to eat.

"Missed you earlier today," Maker muttered between bites of his sandwich.

"Awww," Chantrey droned. "That's so sweet."

Maker shook his head. "No, not missed as in longed for your presence. Missed you as in you didn't show where you were expected."

"Oh?" Chantrey said, as if surprised.

"You got a message on your p-comp at the same time I did," Maker explained. "I didn't see it, but I assumed yours read the same as mine. However, when I show up at the designated meeting spot, there's me and Browing, but no Dr. Chantrey."

"Oh, is Papa Bear grumpy that I wasn't there?" she teased.

"No, because I assume you were watching," Maker said in a matter-of-fact tone.

Chantrey eyed him for a moment, looking slightly dumbfounded. Although she knew Maker exceptionally well from the dossier the Marine Corps had on him — as well as by virtue of their budding relationship — she still found herself occasionally astounded by how astute and perceptive he really was.

"They had cameras on you from the moment you entered that first elevator," she said after a few seconds. "They wanted to know if you'd accept the mission."

"And what did you say?"

"I told them your psych profile, along with everything I saw today, suggested that you probably would."

IGNOTUS

"Hmmm," Maker mumbled, brow wrinkled in disapproval. "So Lafayette was probably *expecting* to hear from me."

"Yes, but expecting to hear from you and knowing exactly what you'll say are two different things," Chantrey noted.

Maker's brow crinkled. "What's that supposed to mean?"

"Well, if you recall when we first met, I had correctly concluded that you'd accept the initial mission to go after the Vacra, but didn't foresee all the questions you'd ask or the demands you'd make."

"So is that what you'll be working on tonight — determining what demands I'll make?"

She shook her head. "No, because that would be a waste of my time."

He raised an eyebrow. "Are you saying I'm that unpredictable in that regard?"

"Hardly," she clarified with a smile. "Truth is, they're so desperate for the sub rosa tech that they'll give you almost anything you want. Still, I wouldn't get too crazy with the ask."

"I hadn't planned to," Maker averred, although he did have some things in mind. "So if it's not my demands, what are they asking you to do — a work-up on the team?"

"That's part of it," Chantrey acknowledged. "But the main thing they want are assurances that you aren't going to fill Skullcap full of holes or jettison him into space the second you take off."

Maker laughed. "I can give them better odds on the likelihood of building a snowman in Hell."

IGNOTUS

"I'll just let them know the jury's still out on that issue," she said with a smile.

Maker grinned back at her. As usual, Chantrey found a way to lighten the mood, even when the topic was serious. However, despite their previous conversation, discussion of her work — especially in regards to *him* — made him worry.

"So," he said after a few seconds, "do your puppet masters know that you've kind of been an open book in terms of your work for them?"

"What they've learned from past experience is that a certain level of probity is required to solicit your cooperation. That means answering your questions candidly, and they've left it to my discretion to determine how much to disclose. I choose full disclosure."

Maker's eyes narrowed. "You didn't mention any of that when we talked this morning."

"I didn't?" Chantrey said quizzically, her eyebrows going up. "Must have slipped my mind."

Maker rubbed his chin in thought. "So you tell *me* everything you tell your bosses, and tell your *bosses* everything you tell me."

"Sounds convoluted when you put it that way, but yeah."

"So you're basically a double agent," Maker concluded, his tone suddenly serious.

She gave him a confused look. "How can I be a double agent if we're all on the same side?"

"Hmmm," Maker mused, ignoring her question. "I just realized something else: I'm less like a boy toy, and more like a mark."

"And there it is," Chantrey said, throwing up her hands in exasperation. "That's why I didn't tell you about me fully disclosing everything to everybody, because I knew you'd reach that conclusion — that you were being hustled."

"So how do I know whether anything you tell me is true?"

In a move that was uncharacteristic for her, Chantrey let out an audible groan of frustration and spent a moment rubbing the bridge of her nose with her thumb and forefinger.

"I swear, Gant," she grumbled, "sometimes you make me want to scream when you start giving me the third degree like this."

"So scream," he said. "This office was built for confidential communications. The walls are soundproof. Scream your head off if you want. And after you get it all out, please answer my question."

Chantrey sat back, crossing her arms and giving him a steely look.

"Okay, here's the truth," she stated. "Your thinking's outmoded. You're still operating under the belief that the powers that be want to keep you in the dark as much as possible. Well, here's a news flash for you: we are well past the point of them worrying about what bits of knowledge are bumbling around like tumbleweeds in the head of Lieutenant Arrogant Maker."

"What's that supposed to mean?" Maker demanded.

"It means that the people in charge don't care what you know. They don't care who you date. They don't care if you get the recommended daily allowance of vitamins and minerals. All they care about at this point in time is what you're going to do with respect to this mission. More importantly, if my answering your questions truthfully and honestly gets them their desired outcome, they don't care about the rest."

Maker didn't immediately comment, choosing instead to ruminate for a second on what Chantrey had just said. In all honesty, it made sense and his gut instinct told him she was being straightforward.

"Well?" Chantrey said expectantly, cutting across his thoughts.

"All right, all right," Maker conceded. "Your point is well-taken."

"And?" she inquired, lifting an eyebrow.

"And I don't think I'm a mark or getting hustled."

Smiling slightly, Chantrey twirled her hand in a keep-it-coming gesture.

Maker sighed. "And I'm sorry for suggesting that you might have been disingenuous."

"Hmmm," Chantrey droned, crinkling her brow as if contemplating something. "Not the greatest apology I've ever heard, but probably the best I can get out of *you*. Anyway, let's just fast-forward to the part where you make it up to me."

"Fine," Maker said almost sheepishly. "What can I do to make this right?"

"Well, there is something," she cooed with a mischievous glint in her eye. "I seem to recall you making mention of soundproof walls, so that just leaves one question." Smiling coquettishly, she hooked a thumb over her shoulder towards the entrance to Maker's office and asked, "Does that door lock?"

IGNOTUS

Chapter 18

"What are you so chipper about?" Adames asked, eyeing Maker warily.

"Huh?" Maker replied, caught unawares.

"You were whistling," Adames noted.

Maker stared at him for a moment, eyebrows raised. "Was I?"

"Yeah, and you've been grinning like the Cheshire Cat ever since Ariel brought you lunch."

"Oh," Maker muttered. "Guess I've just been thinking about how great it would be to shove Skullcap out an airlock on this mission."

Adames grunted noncommittally in response, as if Maker's answer barely bordered on the edge of being acceptable.

They were currently alone in the open area of the warehouse, taking inventory. Following Chantrey's departure, Maker had come out and told everybody to add a couple of items to their individual chores.

"By midnight tonight," he'd announced, "I'm going to need each of you to provide me with a wish list — whatever supplies, equipment, gear, or materiel you'd ideally like to have. Not what you think we can *get*; whatever you'd like to *have*, no matter how far-fetched. In addition, I want everybody to update their dream sheet."

His statement had been met with silent surprise. However, rather than brook questions, Maker had essentially ordered everyone but Adames out, ostensibly to do research on (and put some thought into) complying with his request.

"You know," he now said to Adames, "my earlier comment applies to you as well."

IGNOTUS

"You mean regarding the dream sheet?" the NCO asked. "My ideal assignment? I'm doing it. In case you didn't notice, I love this job."

"I was talking more about the wish list."

"Pshaw!" the NCO uttered disdainfully. "I appreciate what you're trying to do, Gant, but wrangling stuff that's purportedly impossible to get is half the fun for a guy like me. Having a wish list that gets filled just by asking will suck all the joy out of my work."

Maker chuckled. "I wouldn't worry about it. There's always another unattainable item popping up on the horizon that someone will need you to get."

"In the past, sure. But now? Let's face it: you've got a mindboggling amount of leverage. You could probably ask to be promoted to general and they'd agree."

"Yes, and it would be followed by an equally fast *de*motion as soon as this mission's over," Maker shot back, although the comment did tickle something at the back of his brain. "Basically, this bargaining chip we've been handed has an expiration date."

"But let me guess: you've got some ideas about how to extend its shelf life."

Rather than respond verbally, Maker gave his NCO a sly grin that told him all he needed to know.

IGNOTUS

Chapter 19

Maker stayed up late getting ready for his meeting with Lafayette, but had no trouble rising early the next morning, courtesy of a scheduled wake-up call. After a light breakfast consisting of cereal and milk, he said goodbye to Erlen and headed out. Upon leaving the VOQ, however, he was surprised to see a staff car with tinted windows hovering just outside the exit.

A young sergeant — apparently the driver — stood near the rear door of the car. After seeing Maker, he opened the door and saluted. Understanding what was expected of him, Maker returned the salute and climbed inside. As he could have predicted, Lafayette was in the vehicle, waiting on him.

"I hope you don't mind if we do this in transit," Lafayette said as Maker got comfortable. "You didn't appear to be flexible on the time, so I'm having to squeeze this in between other commitments. Plus, as I'm sure you realize, time is of the essence."

"Not a problem," Maker replied as the young sergeant got in and started driving.

"Great. We'll make sure you have a ride back to your quarters."

"Works for me," Maker stated indifferently, "although I'm curious as to how long you were outside waiting for me."

"Not as long as you might suspect," Lafayette said with a grin. "We have computer modeling and simulations which can extrapolate roughly how long it takes to get from the VOQ to the 'holding tank,' as you put it. Pairing that with the time you proposed for

IGNOTUS

meeting, and we had a pretty rough idea of when you'd be stepping outside."

"Or you just had the hotel tell you what time my wake-up call was for and made an educated guess based on that."

Lafayette gave Maker an appraising stare, almost as if he were seeing the lieutenant for the very first time.

"Anyway," the admiral said after a few seconds, "you asked for this meeting, so I'm at your disposal."

"I'll do the mission," Maker stated without preamble.

"Excellent," Lafayette commented with a smile.

"But I've got some conditions," Maker added.

"Of course you do," Lafayette acknowledged with a nod. "I would, too, if I were in your position. So what is it that you're asking for?"

"A new ship, for starters. Something top-of-the-line and state-of-the-art, with the latest in offensive weapons capability, defense systems, etcetera. All the bells and whistles."

"Not a problem," Lafayette assured him. "In fact, your buddy Browing already got the ball rolling in that department — started reaching out to folks yesterday."

Maker frowned. Browing's actions had not only implied that he'd take the mission (seemingly at a point in time before Maker himself knew), but also hinted at something else that Maker didn't particularly want to dwell on.

"That can't be all," Lafayette declared, interrupting Maker's thoughts.

"It isn't," Maker replied. "I also want medals and commendations."

IGNOTUS

"Oh, really?" Lafayette said sarcastically. "And which specific honors do you find yourself deserving of, Lieutenant?"

"Not me," Maker clarified. "My people. They've gone up against the Vacra twice now, facing incredible odds each time, and managed to come away victorious on both occasions. I've nominated them for a slew of awards because of their valor, gallantry, and distinguished service, but haven't heard anything back yet."

Lafayette nodded approvingly. "We'll take care of it."

"*Before* we leave on this mission," Maker insisted.

"Of course. Now, what's next on your list?"

"Our ambassador friend," Maker said acerbically. "If we're going on a road trip together, I want to know everything about him."

"Like what?" Lafayette asked, frowning. "His pedigree? Whether he went to an Ivy League school? If he's married or has kids?"

"I'm not talking about any of that crap," Maker grumbled. "I'm talking about him *physically*. How much can he lift, how far can he see, how good is his hearing, and so on. I want to know as much as possible about what I'm dealing with in case he gives us trouble."

Lafayette seemed to reflect for a moment. "I'll have to check to see how much of that we have."

"Fair enough," Maker said, although he had no doubt that from the moment Skullcap had been found, the necessary folks had been scanning the insectoid from top to bottom (not to mention doing whatever they could to get a sample of anything he *se*creted or *ex*creted).

"So what's next?" Lafayette inquired.

IGNOTUS

"This," Maker replied, handing the admiral a data chip that he'd been holding in his palm.

Lafayette stared at the chip for a moment, then asked, "Okay, what's on it?"

"For starters, a Christmas list from each member of my team — everything Santa forgot to bring them last year."

"Done," Lafayette said flatly. "What else you got?"

Maker eyed him suspiciously. "Don't you even want to know what they're asking for?"

"Doesn't matter. As long as it's not overtly or blatantly illegal, we can make it happen. So what else can I do you for?"

"There's also some other stuff on there about my people getting hardship duty pay…"

"You got it."

"…hostile fire pay…"

"No problem."

"…imminent danger pay…"

"Stop," Lafayette ordered, holding up a hand, palm outward, for emphasis. "I can't give you hostile fire pay *and* imminent danger pay. There's a slight difference in the definition between the two, but for pay purposes the military considers them the same. In essence, if you're under hostile fire then you're *in* imminent danger. Ergo, you can get one or the other, but not both."

"Oh," Maker muttered in a contemplative tone. "I guess I didn't realize that."

"Or you were testing me," Lafayette suggested. "Seeing if I'd be truthful, or just promise you anything under the sun in order to get you to take this mission."

IGNOTUS

"I'm just a dumb Marine, sir," Maker said, almost defensively. "You give me too much credit."

"Or maybe not enough," the admiral countered.

Ignoring Lafayette's comment on his purported shrewdness, Maker asked, "Are you saying you can't do it?"

"Ha!" Lafayette boomed contemptuously. "Let's be honest: the money's not the problem. I can pay you pretty much anything you ask for, and probably would. The issue is how I get it to you. In this instance, to avoid the appearance of double-dipping, I think I'll pay you officially for the hostile fire and give you the imminent danger compensation as a bonus."

"What does it matter?"

The admiral looked at him askance. "Okay, smart guy, let's say you ask for a million simoleons. I could transfer it into a bank account that only you have access to, or I could walk into the Officer's Mess while you're having dinner and dump it all on the table in front of you while everyone's watching. The difference, I'm sure you'd agree, is that one way is more palatable than the other."

"No argument there," Maker said.

"Likewise, forcing the military pay system to issue two forms of remuneration when it's only designed to distribute one will cause numerous people — including me — to jump through various hoops unnecessarily, as well as draw unwanted attention. It's a lot easier to call the money a bonus and give it to you that way."

"That's okay," Maker declared. "Let's just forget about the imminent danger pay."

Lafayette raised an eyebrow. "You don't want the bonus?"

"Not if it's double-dipping."

IGNOTUS

"So you *were* testing me," Lafayette concluded.

"I'm just not interested in the Marines compensating me for something I'm not entitled to."

"Does that mean you don't want the hardship pay, either?"

Now it was Maker's turn to give the admiral a sideways glance. "Excuse me?"

"Hardship pay is usually reserved for units serving in locations with onerous living conditions. Things like a desert planet with perpetual sandstorms, or a world full of plants that human beings are allergic to. You and your crew are basically taking a leisure cruise."

"Well, I appreciate your assessment, Admiral," Maker intoned. "However, you seem to have overlooked the fact that hardship pay also applies to unhealthy *psychological* conditions. I'd say this mission qualifies."

"The conditions in question have to be documented as extreme or egregious in order to qualify on a psychological basis," Lafayette noted. "Otherwise every soldier would be entitled to it."

"Just in case you forgot, my team will basically be serving as bodyguards to someone who wanted to wipe out the entire human race, starting with us. That's taking quite a mental toll — a fact which you'll find documented by a physician in the files on that data chip."

"A physician?" the admiral repeated skeptically. "I don't suppose this doctor happens to be an Augman attached to your squad."

"I don't think his duty assignment affects his qualifications," Maker noted.

"No, but he could be biased."

"Then let me put it another way: I'm Maniac Maker. The general consensus is that I'm a basket case

IGNOTUS

anyway. On top of that, I lead a crew of circus freaks who obviously have mental issues if they're willing to follow *me*. In short, no one's going to challenge any assessment that says the psychological condition of my people is less than stellar, regardless of who wrote it."

Lafayette just stared at him for a moment, then said, "You don't miss a trick, do you?"

Maker frowned. "I'm not sure what you mean, sir. I was just trying to justify the request for hardship duty pay. Nothing more."

"Nothing more, huh?" the admiral muttered, eyes narrowing. "Then why do I suddenly feel like I've been suckered into playing a game of chess with a grandmaster?"

Maker chuckled. "I don't know, since the guy you're talking to is nothing but a pawn."

"Don't sell yourself short," Lafayette advised. "A pawn has the ability to become the most powerful piece on the board."

"Depends on who's playing," Maker stated, "and I'm not that good."

"So you say," the admiral retorted. "Anyway, as I've already stated, money isn't an issue, so why don't we just cut to the chase and I'll state for the record that we will approve all of the assignment incentive pay requested, *sans* any double-dipping."

Maker nodded. "Sounds reasonable."

"Great. So rather than go through everything else piecemeal — and assuming that we'll comply with essentially all of your requests — why don't you highlight for me those things you think might be problematic, so I can start working on them if I have to?"

IGNOTUS

"Fine by me," Maker declared. "First, there's a statement regarding the makeup of my team. I don't want any mandatory transfers in either direction. None of my people get sent elsewhere involuntarily, and we don't get any losers shoved down our throats."

"That's easy enough," Lafayette asserted. "What's next?"

"I had my people update their dream sheets. When they're ready to leave the team, they get the assignment of their choice."

"Consider it done."

"Finally, I want Adames promoted to chief again."

Maker's statement was followed by silence, as for once Lafayette seemed at a loss for words.

"Are you sure about that?" the admiral asked after a few moments.

"Of course," Maker declared emphatically. "He deserves it. I'd have given him a field promotion when we were battling the Vacra if I'd had the authority."

Lafayette rubbed his chin for a moment, then said, "Look, we can certainly make this happen, but here's the thing: he's made chief master sergeant twice already, followed by demotions both times. I get that he's your second-in-command and you want to do right by him, but maybe this isn't the way."

Maker crossed his arms. "I beg to differ."

The admiral simply looked at him, frowning, then asked, "You ever hear of the Peter Principle?"

"Sure," Maker answered with a nod. "It's an old-school management theory which says that individuals in an organizational hierarchy will rise to their 'level of incompetence.' Basically, it means that people in an

IGNOTUS

organization will continue to get promoted as long as they're competent at their job; at some juncture, however, they reach a level at which they become *in*competent, and after that they don't get promoted anymore."

"Exactly," Lafayette said. "In shorthand, it means that not everybody is cut out for top-level management, and it sounds like Adames isn't. Maybe he's got all the stripes he needs to wear."

Maker almost glared at him. "Are you telling me you won't do it?"

"Not at all," Lafayette clarified, shaking his head. "All I'm saying is that, based on his history, it may not stick."

"We'll cross that bridge when we come to it."

"Okay. Any other promotions we need to push through?"

Maker shook his head. "No. Nobody else has enough time in grade."

"So is that it then?" the admiral inquired. "We've covered the main issues you're concerned with?"

"Well, there's some other stuff on the chip dealing with the practicalities of life — things like medical care, family leave, and so on."

"Okay, none of that should be a problem."

"And I'm going to want it all in writing," Maker added. "And signed by someone with appropriate authority."

"That's a given," the admiral stressed. "Now, if you're all done, we've got some conditions of our own."

"Why am I not surprised?" Maker muttered rhetorically, then looked pointedly at the admiral. "Okay, what?"

IGNOTUS

"First of all, the mission gets underway within three days," Lafayette said.

Maker frowned. "I'd argue that's contingent upon us getting the ship in a timely fashion, as well as everything on the wish lists I gave you."

"You'll have it all tomorrow," the admiral asserted.

"Still, it's going to be a pretty tight schedule."

"Make it work," Lafayette said dismissively. "Next, Browing goes with you."

Maker's brow crinkled in thought, but he simply nodded in response. This was what he had suspected the moment Lafayette had mentioned Browing reaching out to people about a new ship: that the man was coming along for the ride.

"Ostensibly, this is a diplomatic mission," Lafayette continued, "so it's necessary to have an appropriate government liaison in attendance. Browing has the requisite credentials, and — despite your past issues with him — I thought you'd find him preferable to someone new."

"I'm fine with Browing," Maker admitted truthfully. "Any conflict we previously had is water under the bridge."

"Good to hear. And by the way, you yourself will officially be designated a military attaché." Noting that Maker frowned upon hearing this, the admiral went on, saying, "It just means that you're a military member—"

"Who's attached to a diplomatic mission," Maker interjected. "Yeah, I know what an attaché is."

"Sorry," Lafayette murmured. "You just looked confused for a second."

IGNOTUS

"I'm looking confused because you've been selling this as simple escort duty. Now I've got Browing tagging along as a diplomat and me as a military attaché. What's with all the skullduggery?"

"Ambassador Vuqja has bought into our approach to diplomacy," Lafayette explained, "including the application of certain concepts, such as diplomatic immunity."

"I get it," Maker said with a nod. "If this thing blows up for some reason, we're protected. *Allegedly*."

"Assuming you mean blowing up figuratively as opposed to literally, that's the general idea."

Maker snorted in derision and shook his head, muttering, "Unbelievable."

Lafayette looked at him with raised eyebrows. "What's the problem? I thought diplomatic immunity would give you some peace of mind."

"Even if I thought the Vacra would respect and honor the concept, this just opens a new can of worms."

The admiral frowned. "In what sense?"

"Diplomatic immunity is generally a two-way street," Maker explained. "That means Skullcap will be protected while we're on this little jaunt."

Lafayette seemed to ponder this for a moment before stating, "I suppose that's true."

"So Skullcap gets escorted home by his enemies, and even if he does something untoward along the way, we can't touch him," Maker noted, then shook his head in disbelief. "He couldn't have planned this any better."

Lafayette gave Maker a somber stare. "Does this mean you're having second thoughts about the mission?"

Maker seemed to contemplate for a moment, then shook his head. "No. As long as the members of your

IGNOTUS

little Star Chamber agree to everything I've asked for, we have a deal."

"Star Chamber?" Lafayette echoed. "You don't think much of us, do you?"

"Would you prefer it if I called you a 'cabal'? Because that was my first inclination."

The admiral chuckled. "A rose by any other name, Lieutenant."

Maker acknowledged the comment with a slight nod before asking, "So, are we done?"

"Just one other thing," Lafayette said. "Dr. Chantrey goes along as well."

"I assumed as much."

"Great. Now that we've gotten all of that out of the way, I think this is where you get off."

The admiral must have sent some surreptitious signal to their driver, because as he spoke, the staff car slowed and came to a halt. Glancing out the window, Maker noted that they were in a rustic region. He saw nothing but trees and grass nearby.

"Hmmm," Maker droned. "I suppose my ride back is that car that's been pacing us since we left the VOQ." As he spoke, he hooked a thumb over his shoulder toward the vehicle's rear window.

The admiral once again gave him a discerning look, clearly updating his assessment of Maker. Then he smiled and said, "I didn't realize you'd spotted it, but I guess I should have known better. As previously noted, you don't miss a trick."

Rather than respond, Maker simply opened the door and stepped out. However, before closing it, he turned back and looked the admiral in the eye.

IGNOTUS

"Just to be clear," Maker avowed, "if Skullcap makes the slightest misstep, if he so much as looks at me sideways, I'm going to shoot him in the head — diplomatic immunity be damned."

He then shut the door.

IGNOTUS

Chapter 20

The rest of the day essentially flew by. After being driven back to the VOQ, Maker had immediately headed to his unit's warehouse. Once there, he had apprised his squad of recent developments — namely, that they anticipated departing in three days. He had then dismissed everyone for the day, simply telling them to be ready to get to work bright and early the next morning. (He did, however, pull Wayne aside for a moment to give him some specific instructions before letting the young man leave.) A short time later, only he and Adames were left in the warehouse.

"Once again," Maker said to his NCO, "my orders also apply to you."

"I appreciate it," Adames stated, "but I've got too much to do. Still, it was nice of you to give the rest of the team the day off."

"Well, assuming the admiral comes through, the next three days are going to be extremely hectic. Seemed to make more sense to give them some R-and-R now instead of later. Plus, who knows what we're walking into with this mission? There's no guarantee that any of us are coming back."

"You like this admiral?" Adames asked. "You trust him?"

Maker shrugged. "Seems straightforward. Didn't appear to be blowing smoke up my nether regions."

"Well," Adames uttered, chuckling, "that's always a good sign."

Grinning, Maker was on the verge of commenting when his p-comp indicated that he had a message coming in on a secure network.

IGNOTUS

"Speak of the devil," Maker said, then went into his office to review the communiqué, which turned out to be the first draft of a document memorializing the agreement to his demands.

****

Maker spent the remainder of the day revising the document and trading drafts with Lafayette until he ended up with an agreement that essentially encapsulated everything he had asked for, with verbiage that both parties found acceptable. Upon completion, the admiral promised to have it signed and get a copy to him as soon as possible.

Satisfied with the progress he'd made, Maker suddenly realized that it was past quitting time. He honestly didn't know where the day had gone. Working on the drafts hadn't been fun, per se, but he had taken a certain amount of joy in knowing that he was getting his people a fair deal for the risks they'd be taking.

Stepping out of his office, he immediately noted that the warehouse bay doors were open. As he watched, Adames closed the rear of a transport vehicle parked there, then slapped the side of the vehicle twice with his palm. The driver, already in position, stuck a hand out of the window in acknowledgment, and a second later the vehicle was in motion. Adames watched him drive off for a moment, then stepped over to a control panel located on a nearby wall. The NCO pushed a button on the panel, and the bay doors began to close.

"Hey," Maker called out, causing Adames to spin around. "We good?"

IGNOTUS

"Yep," Adames replied with a nod. "All the stuff we're taking with us is on standby, waiting for me to say where it needs to be delivered. Anything that belongs to us but isn't making the trip is slated to go into storage. Almost everything else is headed back to the depot for redistribution."

As the NCO spoke, Maker glanced around approvingly, noting that the warehouse was essentially barren. Almost nothing was left aside from furniture and fixtures. (There were a few personables in his office, but he'd pack those and take them with him.)

"You know," Maker observed, "operational logistics is heavily automated these days. You just enter your request in the computer system and you're done. In other words, you didn't have to personally oversee the actual loading of our stuff."

Adames snorted derisively. "You'd feel differently if you were the person having to sign off on it."

Maker laughed. "That's what NCOs are for."

"*Now* you tell me," Adames remarked, shaking his head in mock melancholy. "Anyway, it's not like I did a lot outside of simply cataloging our *accouterment*. I mean, the transport guys are the ones who actually bagged and tagged everything and loaded it up. However, that reminds me: we didn't get anything from your office because you were in there working."

"Don't worry about it," Maker said. "There are only a few items in there that need to go, and I'll grab them on my way out."

"Works for me," Adames assured him, then seemed to grow contemplative. "Hey, do you remember our old unit commander?"

IGNOTUS

"Captain Boggan?" Maker queried. "Of course. Good guy — and an even better officer."

"Yeah. I recall that whenever we had a dangerous assignment — with odds of somebody not coming back — he'd bring us together the night before we deployed and break out a rare bottle of wine, an exotic delicacy, or something along those lines."

Maker nodded, smiling. "I remember — and it was always something wildly expensive. He said he did it so that, in case we died on the mission, the Corps would have at least allowed us to experience something exquisite and bonne bouche."

"Bonne bouche," Adames repeated, chuckling. "Yeah, that was the phrase he used. Anyway, it occurred to me that we should continue the tradition he started."

As he spoke, he reached into a box on a nearby table that Maker hadn't paid particular attention to before. A moment later, he pulled out what looked like a bottle of wine and two glasses.

"What's this?" Maker asked as Adames handed him the bottle.

"Just a little bubbly I managed to get my hands on."

Examining the label, Maker stated, "Wine's not my forte, but I'm guessing this is a rare vintage. It's certainly old." He handed the bottle back to Adames, who had produced a wine cork from somewhere. "Where'd you get it?"

"I pinched it from Browing's stash," Adames replied, and they both began laughing. A minute or so later, they were partaking of the bottle's contents.

"Mmmm," Maker droned approvingly. "As I said, I don't have the palate to truly appreciate fine wine, but this seems really good. You'll have to steal from Browing more often."

"Actually, he gave it to me," Adames retorted. "Said he thought I'd enjoy it."

"Really?" Maker muttered in surprise before taking another sip.

"Yeah. All things considered, he's really not such a bad guy."

"Well, I'm sure it's obvious by now, but he's grown on me, too," Maker admitted.

They took a few more sips of wine in silence, simply enjoying a brief respite at the end of a hectic day.

The calm before the storm, Maker thought.

"So, this mission," Adames uttered, interrupting Maker's introspection. "You got any particular thoughts on it?"

"Like what?" Maker inquired.

"Well, that first time our unit went up against the Vacra, you secretly reconfigured our entire ship to be a nova bomb."

"And you're worried I might do something like that again," Maker surmised.

"Not exactly. Setting aside the fact that it's a banned weapon and you should have spent the rest of your life in prison for setting it off" — Maker snickered at this — "it was actually the right call and saved everyone's life."

"Stop," Maker gushed, feigning modesty. "You're making me blush."

"My point is this," Adames said, ignoring his commanding officer's comment. "You were the only person who really had an inkling of what we were up against with the Vacra. You were the only one who understood how to deal with them."

"You're forgetting about Planck," Maker chimed in. "He was their prisoner for years and knows them better than I know the back of my hand."

"Sure, he *knows* them, but he doesn't *understand* them. You do. That was the case then, and it's the case now. So with that in mind, here's my question: what do you *really* think we're up against on this mission, and how do we deal with it?"

Maker looked him in the eye and then, shaking his head, admitted, "I don't know."

IGNOTUS

Chapter 21

"Have you been drinking?" Chantrey asked.

"Yes and no," Maker replied.

They were currently in his quarters, with Maker having just walked in to find Chantrey sitting on his living room couch, waiting for him. She had greeted him with a kiss, then frowned, obviously noting the alcohol on his breath.

"It's not really a question with a lot of gray area for a response," she retorted. "Either you've been drinking or you haven't."

"I split a bottle of bubbly with Adames," Maker admitted, setting down a box of personal items he had brought in with him. "But it was wine, so it doesn't count."

Chantrey gave him a skeptical look. "Alcohol is alcohol. It doesn't have to come with a head of foam."

Ignoring her jibe, Maker bent down to rub Erlen's back, who had just padded over to him.

"Sorry about leaving you inside all day," he said as the Niotan made a low rumbling noise. "Couldn't be helped."

Erlen made a noise that was something between a growl and a cough, then moved away. He clearly wasn't bothered to any large extent by having spent the day indoors, and Maker hadn't been particularly worried about him. Truth be told (and as Maker had noted on more than one occasion), the Niotan was fully capable of taking care of himself, including getting food from the kitchen and pantry when he was hungry, as well as keeping himself entertained.

IGNOTUS

"So," Chantrey droned, getting Maker's attention. "Did you get so tipsy that you forgot I was coming over?"

"Is that a rhetorical question?" Maker asked as he flopped down on the couch, subtly alluding to the fact that Chantrey typically came over every night.

"It *shouldn't* be," Chantrey replied, allowing Maker to pull her down onto his lap, and then placing her arms around his neck.

Maker gave her a befuddled look. "What does that mean?"

"It means that you've got the passcode to *my* place, and I'd argue that it's usually presentable. Ergo, we could occasionally spend some time there instead of always staring at *these* four walls, if you weren't so paranoid about people finding out about us."

"Well, I'm turning over a new leaf in that regard, remember?"

"Yeah, right," Chantrey muttered sarcastically.

"You don't believe me?" Maker asked. "We can go right now if you like."

Chantrey looked him solemnly in the eye for a moment, then uttered in a surprised voice, "You're serious, aren't you?"

He smiled. "Of course."

"Well, I'm tempted to take you up on the offer," she said with a smile. "But I'm afraid if I did, you wouldn't get much sleep."

Maker raised an eyebrow in a wanton fashion. "Is that a promise?"

"That's not what I was suggesting," Chantrey insisted, giggling. "What I meant was that I need to pack,

IGNOTUS

same as you. In case you forgot, I'm going with you tomorrow."

Suddenly, a serious expression settled on Maker's face, as if some dark cloud of thought had suddenly entered his brain and altered his temperament.

"Maybe you shouldn't," he declared somberly.

Chantrey gave him a perplexed look. "What, I shouldn't pack?"

"No," he answered, shaking his head. "Maybe you shouldn't go."

Thoroughly confused now, Chantrey slid from Maker's lap and sat down next to him.

"Gant, do you know something?" she asked.

"No," he replied. "Just a feeling."

"About what?"

Maker ruminated for a moment on how to answer, then said, "On the drive back here — after I left Adames — I kept thinking about my conversation with Admiral Lafayette and my list of demands."

"He didn't agree to them?"

"That's just it — he agreed to everything I asked for."

Chantrey frowned. "Then I guess I don't understand. What's the problem?"

"I keep thinking that maybe he readily agreed to everything because he doesn't plan on doing what he said."

"You think he's disingenuous?" she asked in consternation. "I didn't get that impression when I met with him."

"Oh, I think he'll provide the *pre-departure* things I asked for. I'm not so sure about those that are due post-mission."

IGNOTUS

"You believe he's going to break his word," Chantrey concluded.

"Don't know," Maker confessed with a shrug. "But it suddenly occurred to me that he doesn't have to break his word — no matter what he promised us — if nobody comes back alive."

IGNOTUS

Chapter 22

Putting aside thoughts of the mission, Maker only had a brief opportunity to spend some quality time with Chantrey before she left, stating a need to get her packing done. Following her lead, Maker went ahead and got his own belongings together in preparation for departure.

Although he couldn't speak for Chantrey, packing for him rarely took more than half an hour, as — aside from toiletries and a few personal items — his possessions generally consisted of a sparse amount of civilian clothing, his military habiliments, his battle armor and his weapons. Years in the Corps, coupled with numerous eleventh-hour deployments, had taught him the value and necessity of being able to leave at a moment's notice. (That said, he did have a fair number of items, including household goods, that he kept in storage on a nigh-permanent basis, although they were unlikely to be retrieved until he and the military parted ways.)

Not long after he finished packing, Maker made a sandwich for dinner and then turned in, anticipating the need to get an early start and hoping that Lafayette would deliver as promised.

Thankfully, the admiral was as good as his word — at least on the front end. Maker had barely arisen the next morning when a message came through on his p-comp stating that a new ship, assigned to his command, was docked in a private bay at a space station orbiting the planet. Maker immediately reached out to Adames, letting him know their vessel had arrived. He also forwarded the craft's schematics, which had been included in the message. (He knew without asking that his NCO would relay the information to the rest of their team.)

IGNOTUS

Next, Maker roused Erlen and got breakfast for them both (which mainly consisted of a protein bar for each of them). A short time later, they were checking out of the VOQ and within an hour Maker found himself on his new ship, the *Nova Gallant*.

Ordinarily, it would have taken him longer to reach the vessel. Although checkout and driving had taken a bit of time, the real holdup was generally the queue for the shuttlecraft after arriving at the spaceport. There was always a waiting list for the transport, which constantly ferried people to and from the space station, and the current day was no exception. However, when Maker entered his credentials in order to get a spot on the next available shuttle, he was informed that several private craft had been reserved for the exclusive use of his unit. Moreover, he was given priority status, including immediate clearance to leave for the space station.

Maker didn't delude himself. The preferential arrangements had less to do with him personally and more to do with the mission. Simply put, it highlighted the importance and value that Lafayette and his Star Chamber (for lack of a better term) placed on recovery of the sub rosa tech.

Once aboard the *Nova*, Maker noted that he seemed to be the first to arrive. He immediately went to the captain's quarters, which — needless to say — were to be his and Erlen's new home. He unpacked quickly, but found the place far more posh than he was used to. In addition to the furnishings (which were more upscale than he'd expected), the place was more sizeable than he felt was warranted, and included an office and a separate sitting room.

IGNOTUS

"All right," he said to Erlen. "Let's scope this place out."

IGNOTUS

Chapter 23

Walking around the *Nova*, one of the first things Maker realized was that the opulence he'd previously noted wasn't limited to the captain's quarters. Every room that he peeked into struck him as luxurious in one fashion or another — from the cabins (which were more like suites) to the conference room (with its high-back executive chairs) to the galley, which appeared to be designed for a celebrity chef, but was actually automated and could make almost anything requested. Frankly speaking, it all seemed devised to accommodate blue bloods more than rank-and-file soldiers.

That said, Maker had to admit that, from a practical standpoint, the ship appeared as capable as any he'd ever seen. The weaponry and armaments were everything he'd asked for, and then some. In fact, the entire ship seemingly boasted the latest-and-greatest on all fronts.

Maker and Erlen were still roaming the hallways and getting the lay of the land when, much to the former's surprise, a nearby door opened and Browing stepped out.

"Oh, sorry," Browing muttered, stopping short when he saw Maker and Erlen. "I didn't realize anyone else was on board yet."

"We haven't been here long," Maker stated. "When did you arrive?"

"I actually got word when the ship was en route and was already waiting when it docked."

"Hmmm," Maker droned, rubbing his chin in thought. He then nodded towards the door Browing had come out of and asked, "Your cabin?"

IGNOTUS

"Yes," Browing replied, "and for the record, I'll admit that it's one of the larger staterooms on the ship."

Maker didn't say anything, but Browing's statement jibed with his recollection of the *Nova*'s schematics.

"However," Browing continued, "it's not what you're thinking."

"Oh?" Maker uttered. "So what exactly am I thinking?"

"That I commandeered one of the largest cabins out of a sense of entitlement."

"Not necessarily," Maker countered, although in truth it was *precisely* what he'd been thinking.

"If you recall," Browing went on, "we butted heads on our last road trip because you told me that there was no room for some of the cargo I wanted to bring aboard, and if I wanted to take it I needed to store it in my room."

"I remember."

"Well, I just thought I'd stave off any potential conflict by getting a room that could accommodate anything I wanted to bring aboard."

"So claiming one of the larger suites was for practical purposes rather than a sense of privilege."

"Bingo."

Maker simply nodded. It was a plausible explanation, and in truth the items Browing had previously wanted to bring aboard had ended up serving an important purpose.

Bearing that in mind, Maker took a deep breath and said, "Look, maybe I was too harsh before, but you've managed to convince me that your requests for cargo space are reasonable. Going forward, I'll make sure

IGNOTUS

we make room in the hold for anything you want to bring aboard — within reason."

Browing gave him an odd look. "Was that an apology?"

"Don't push it," Maker advised, grinning.

"I won't," Browing confirmed with a chuckle. "Anyway, what do you think of the *Nova*?"

"I'm not sure," Maker admitted. "It's like a battleship and a pleasure yacht had a baby, with the result being something that defies classification. Too decadent to be military, but too practical to be a leisure craft. Frankly speaking, I can't quite make out what it's supposed to be."

Browing laughed. "For a guy who doesn't know which label to apply, you kind of hit the nail on the head."

Maker's brow furrowed. "What do you mean?"

"Basically, the *Nova* is a military craft, as you gleaned, with the most current upgrades on both the offensive and defensive fronts. However, she was never really expected to be in actual battle. She was essentially fashioned as a showpiece."

"What do you mean?"

"Well, I'm sure you're aware of the fact that the military answers to the civilian sector."

"Yes," Maker stated. "It's been that way for ages."

"Well, occasionally some government official with the requisite authority decides that they want to see what their bloated military budget is buying. They want to eyeball the weapons, see the defense systems at work, witness how new tech is being integrated, and so on. The *Nova* was designed as a platform for them to do that."

IGNOTUS

"I get it," Maker commented. "Some bureaucrat from the Armed Services Committee wants to see how the latest gee-whiz, super-duper cannon works, so he comes on board the *Nova*, where the weapon is incorporated into the ship's systems. It's demonstrated for him, and he goes home happy and willing to continue writing blank checks for the military."

"Pretty much on the nose," Browning noted approvingly, "except occasionally these officials stay on board for extended periods. And since they're used to accommodations of a certain standard…"

"…we made every stateroom a VIP suite," Maker stated, finishing after the other man trailed off.

"Now you've got it," Browning said. "And in the interest of full disclosure, I was previously one of the 'bureaucrats' who witnessed the *Nova* showcasing her capabilities."

"I guess that explains how you knew about the ship."

"Well, as soon as I heard what Lafayette and the others wanted, I knew you'd need transportation. Based on my personal experience, I felt the *Nova* was ideal, so I started working on getting her."

"It was a smart move, but did you ever consider that I might not take the mission?"

"Not for a second," Browning replied without hesitation.

IGNOTUS

Chapter 24

Maker was still chatting with Browing when a message came through on his p-comp a few minutes later. Recognizing it as a high-priority missive, he excused himself and hustled back to his cabin, with Erlen right on his heels.

Once there, Maker headed straight to the office, casually saying over his shoulder, "We'll finish the tour later." Clearly unconcerned, Erlen leaped onto a couch in preparation for a nap.

Like the rest of the ship, the office — despite being rated for secure communications — was rather swank. It was home to an elegant executive desk and chair, as well as stately, built-in bookshelves. There was also an art niche in a corner that held a weird metallic sculpture, as well as a wall safe tucked away behind a painting.

Maker only casually noted the ritzy décor. With only one thing on his mind, he flung himself into the chair and then linked his p-comp to a computer monitor that sat on the desktop. A moment later, he was staring at information he'd been waiting on with mouth-watering anticipation: the report on Skullcap's physiology.

****

The report was about thirty pages long and turned out to be equal parts anatomy, physiology, morphology, and biology. Much to Maker's surprise, Skullcap had actually allowed himself to be physically examined, so the narrative was more detailed than he had expected. However, none of the documentation was dated, so it

IGNOTUS

wasn't clear if said examination had occurred prior to Maker's request or in response to it. (Not that it made a huge amount of difference from Maker's point of view.)

Unsurprisingly, whoever drafted the report had made it a point to shun layman's terms as much as possible. That said, Maker didn't have too much trouble deciphering the content. For instance, one of the things that came through loud and clear was that Skullcap didn't have the proportional strength of an insect. Ergo, he wouldn't be lifting fifty times his body weight or anything like that (although — based on their previous run-ins — that was something Maker was already aware of).

In addition, the insectoid didn't have a venomous bite, or anything akin to a stinger. Moreover, he didn't secrete any type of toxins. That said, the compound eyes conferred an advantage in terms of visual acuity, and he could seemingly hear far better than the average person. Finally, he had a respiratory system that allowed him to breathe gases that were inimical to human beings.

On the whole, however, it appeared to Maker that he and his team wouldn't have to go to exorbitant lengths in order to deal with Skullcap if the insectoid got out of hand — something he felt was more likely to happen than not.

IGNOTUS

Chapter 25

By the time Maker finished the report on Skullcap, several hours had passed. Based on the ship's schematics, the *Nova* had an audiovisual and PA system that could be accessed from the bridge and the captain's cabin. After a few minutes of trial and error, Maker was able to view both internal and external images on his desk monitor, and was happy to note that most — if not all — of his people were aboard. (The ship's interior cameras were apparently limited to hallways and common areas such as the rec room, so he couldn't tell who might be on the ship but in their quarters.)

In addition to personnel, Maker was also pleased to see that supplies were also arriving: a camera focused on the cargo bay showed Adames overseeing the unloading of various crates. Suddenly feeling idle, Maker turned off the monitor and left the office.

"Come on," he said to a sleeping Erlen as he headed towards the door. "Let's go welcome the team aboard."

The Niotan came awake instantly and bounded over to Maker's side.

****

They didn't immediately see anyone upon leaving their quarters, but that wasn't particularly surprising. The *Nova* was actually built to accommodate a more sizeable crew, so occasionally hallways and such were going to appear deserted. Fortunately, many of the ship's operations were automated, so a small group could man the vessel without feeling overwhelmed.

IGNOTUS

Maker's initial inclination was to head to the cargo area to see if his NCO needed a hand. However, he hadn't gone farther than the next hallway before he bumped into someone unexpected: Solomon Planck.

Planck was carrying a duffel bag, which gave the impression that he had just come aboard, and walking with purpose — like he knew exactly where he was headed. It had been weeks since Maker had seen him, and — although the man had put on a little more weight — he still appeared gaunt. Thankfully, he didn't look as haggard as he had in the past, but he was clearly still recovering from his time as the Vacra's prisoner.

"Lieutenant," Planck said in greeting. "It's good to see you."

"Likewise," Maker responded. "You're looking well."

"Thanks," Planck muttered. "So, our final destination is Ignotus?"

Maker frowned. "Ignotus?"

"Sorry," Planck apologized. "That's my name for it — the Vacra homeworld, that is. Ignotus. It's an Old Earth word that means unknown or alien."

"I see," Maker remarked.

There was silence for a moment, and then Maker continued, saying, "Well, we certainly appreciate you agreeing to make the trip, Planck. I know that, given what you've been through, this has to be difficult for you — helping provide a safe escort for one of the people who held you captive."

"Actually, I'm viewing this as closure," Planck replied. "Once we get the sub rosa tech back, I'll be able to close the book on this chapter of my life and move on."

IGNOTUS

Maker gave him a scrutinizing look. "Not to be trite, but that sounds like psychobabble from some third-rate therapist."

Planck laughed. "Yes, I've been seeing someone. Not all of us can blast our way to mental wellness with a handgun."

"Well, a rifle sometimes does the job, too."

Planck chuckled at that, and Maker joined him.

"Anyway," Planck said after regaining his composure, "even if it is psychobabble, it just felt good to talk to someone who wasn't one of my handlers."

Maker simply nodded. The powers that be had kept a close watch on Planck since his rescue from the Vacra. It was really surprising that he was even being allowed to tag along on this mission, as he had a level of knowledge about the sub rosa tech they sought that couldn't be duplicated.

"Well, I'm obviously more of a tough-love guy," Maker declared, "but I'm available if you ever want to discuss anything. Or just talk."

"Thanks, Lieutenant," Planck said. "I may just take you up on that."

IGNOTUS

Chapter 26

As it turned out, Adames really didn't need any help.

"The items coming in are primarily the team's wish list stuff," he explained after Maker and Erlen put in an appearance in the cargo bay. "I told them it's here, so they can pick it up at their leisure. Outside of that, the ship came fully loaded, for all practical purposes, although it won't hurt anything if we're overstocked."

"Sounds good," Maker stated with a nod. "So how do you like our new home?"

"It's nice," Adames admitted. "Maybe *too* nice."

Maker raised an eyebrow. "Meaning?"

"Have you looked at this place, Gant?" the NCO uttered in reply. "A formal dining room, a pool, a rec and game room. Not to mention that it's spacious enough for everyone to have their own separate quarters, complete with king-sized beds sporting thousand-thread-count sheets."

"Let's be serious, Hector," Maker teased, grinning. "Those are eight-hundred-count sheets, max."

They both laughed at that, but then Adames went on.

"It's not that I can't enjoy the finer things in life," the NCO insisted, "but this is completely atypical for Marines. I don't think we want our people getting too used to this."

"I get it," Maker affirmed. "Too much easy living and it becomes the norm. Then when they have to do their jobs and rough it, all they do is complain."

"Exactly."

IGNOTUS

"I'll admit you have a point and it's worth keeping in mind, but let's just see how it plays out. My preference is to give our team the benefit of the doubt, rather than assume they'll be corrupted by soft beds and rich food."

"And if it turns out that I'm right?"

"Then we can always have them start sleeping on a bed of nails or something."

IGNOTUS

Chapter 27

Seeing that everything was under control in the cargo area, Maker spent a few more minutes discussing logistical issues with Adames before departing. As expected, the NCO was completely on top of things, even going so far as to assign quarters to everyone, including the civilians. (All except Browing, that is, who had already staked his claim in that regard.) Maker now understood why Planck had seemingly known where he was going earlier.

Upon leaving the cargo hold, Maker decided that he and Erlen should pick up where they'd previously left off and resume their tour. Thus, they spent the next hour continuing to explore the vessel (except for the cabins that had been assigned and were now occupied). Along the way, they occasionally bumped into other members of their unit, whom Maker would always engage in casual (but brief) conversation. By the time they finished, Maker had a firm idea of where everything on the ship was located, and was able to confirm that it all matched the blueprint of the ship he'd been given.

The last place they visited was the stateroom that Adames had designated for Skullcap. Like all the others, it was far nicer than it needed to be for its intended purpose, and Maker found himself bristling at the thought of the Vacra leader receiving such preferential treatment. Deciding to leave before his anger got too much to bear, Maker and Erlen quickly headed for the exit and back to their own cabin.

Once in their quarters, Maker attempted to get some work done by going to the office and working on a duty roster. Truth be told, however, it was just another

IGNOTUS

task that Adames had already taken care of; all that was really left for Maker to do was review and formally sign off on the job assignments and shifts. However, he had only just begun looking at the document when a chime indicated that someone was at his door.

Already at his monitor, it only took a few seconds for Maker to bring up an image of the area outside his door, where he saw Edison Wayne waiting. Suddenly eager to speak with the young Marine, Maker hurried to the door and ushered him inside.

"Thanks, el-tee," Wayne said as he walked into the cabin. "Is this a bad time?"

"No," Maker answered. "You're actually saving me from dealing with some paperwork. Did you need something?"

"As a matter of fact, I do," Wayne replied with a nod. "Going on the assumption that I'd be the person primarily in charge of engineering, I was giving everything a once-over and detected a problem with the thrusters."

"The thrusters?"

"Yeah, but it's probably easier if I just show you," Wayne stated. "You got time for a quick walk outside?"

"Of course," Maker assured him. "Let's go."

IGNOTUS

Chapter 28

"Okay," Wayne began, "the ship's bugged. Top to bottom, port to starboard, stem to stern."

"How sophisticated? Maker asked.

"There were actually two types of devices: one that I'd consider advanced, and another that was extremely complex, practically avant-garde. However, neither appears to incorporate anything visual — just auditory."

Maker frowned. He and Wayne were currently outside the *Nova*, on the pretext of checking the thrusters. The information being conveyed to him was exactly what he'd been afraid of when — back at the warehouse — he'd given Wayne the task of checking their new ship for listening devices once it arrived. The young Marine was a tech genius, so Maker had been sure he'd be able to locate any bugs, and his confidence had been rewarded.

"Just to be clear," Wayne went on, "I didn't go to every room on the ship. That would have taken too long and aroused suspicion if anyone was paying attention. Instead, I used sampling, going to various areas of the *Nova* and checking them out. That's how I confirmed that the ship was bugged."

"And then I suppose you extrapolated based on the sampling," Maker chimed in, "and concluded there were bugs all over."

"Actually, I took it a step further," Wayne said with a grin. "Without getting into the science too much, all electronics generate an electromagnetic field. After determining that there were listening devices present, I spent a little time getting my hands dirty trying to identify their EMF. Once I knew what it looked like, I jury-rigged

IGNOTUS

a scanner with a broad footprint and conducted a sweep. End result was that I detected bugs everywhere — practically an infestation."

"So they've got people listening to every word we say on the *Nova*," Maker concluded.

"Well, probably not *people*, per se. I suspect everything's being fed to an AI, which is probably programmed to listen for and respond to certain trigger words."

"And how close would that AI have to be to pick up a signal?"

Wayne ruminated for a moment and then said, "I think it would have to be in relatively close proximity — as close as one of the ships at the space station here or in the general vicinity."

Maker mentally chewed on this for a moment, then asked a question that had started buzzing around in his brain.

"You mentioned there were two types of bugs," he said. "What's the purpose of that?"

"At a guess, I'd say it's simple misdirection," Wayne responded. "Basically, I think whoever planted them wanted us to find the less-sophisticated listening devices. They were certainly easier to locate than the others."

"Of course," Maker uttered, nodding. "After finding the first set of bugs, we'd be convinced that confidentiality had been restored, and wouldn't bother with looking for the other devices."

"Makes sense."

"So what's the solution?"

IGNOTUS

"Well, I could round them all up, but then whoever put them there would know that we were on to them."

Maker shook his head. "No. I'd prefer that they keep thinking they've outsmarted us."

"In that case, I should at least collect the lower-grade listening devices. As I said, I think we're *supposed* to find them, so whoever's listening will be suspicious if we leave them in place."

"Okay, say we do that. How do we deal with the others?"

"Well, I can hijack their programming and make them listen on a different frequency range," Wayne noted.

Maker simply gave him a blank look, then stated, "It would be great if you could say that again, but in English this time."

"Sure," Wayne said, chuckling. "Human speech, just like human hearing, occurs within a certain range on the Hertz scale, which is used to measure audio frequency. Basically, humans don't speak *higher* than a certain frequency on one end, or *lower* than a certain frequency on the other."

As he spoke, be put his left and right hands out, palms facing each other, like he was holding an invisible block of wood between them.

"In other words," Wayne continued, "all of our speech occurs within this limited range, and that's the spectrum that the bugs are focused on."

"Ahh," Maker said, finally getting it. "So you're saying you can take control and make them listen to a different frequency band — kind of like forcing them to switch from one radio station to another."

"Pretty much."

IGNOTUS

"What will they hear, then?"

Wayne shrugged. "Don't know, but it won't be human voices. However, that will leave us with the same problem. Whoever put them there will know that we're on to them."

"Hmmm," Maker droned. "Let's say we do as you suggested and get them to monitor a different frequency range. Can we broadcast something into that range for them to pick up?"

"Sure. That's not a problem."

"Then let's do that — maybe loop the same conversation over and over so that this AI you mentioned has something continuous to listen to."

"Sorry, el-tee," Wayne snickered, "but you've been watching too many holo-movies. The AIs we're dealing with are smarter than that. Anything they hear is probably getting compared to prior conversations, and if they hear the exact same thing from the exact same person over and over again, it's going to raise a red flag."

"Maybe that's the answer," Maker said. "A movie."

Wayne suddenly looked perplexed. "Huh?"

"Maybe we just broadcast a string of movies at the right frequency and let them pick up on that."

"It's not a terrible idea, but it won't work."

"Why not?" Maker asked.

"Because, as I mentioned, these bugs are all over the ship. If the AI they're broadcasting to starts hearing the same people having the same conversation simultaneously in different parts of the ship, it's going to realize something's off."

Maker groaned in frustration and wiped his face with his hand.

IGNOTUS

"This is too much," he finally muttered. "Suddenly, I don't care if whoever's listening knows that we're aware of the bugs. Just shut them down and get them off my ship."

"Shut them down?" Wayne echoed.

"Yes," Maker confirmed. "Cut power to them, yank the wiring out, whatever you have to do. Just turn them off and throw them out."

"Hmmm," Wayne droned, scratching his temple. "That actually gives me an idea."

He then laid out to Maker the thought that had just occurred to him.

IGNOTUS

Chapter 29

It was a little rough around the edges and needed a bit of fleshing out, but overall Wayne had the rudiments of a good plan. More to the point, implementing his idea would also provide an opportunity to actualize some thoughts Maker had regarding Skullcap. In fact, he shared those thoughts with Wayne and gave him the job of effectuating them, along with authorizing the younger man to recruit whomever he needed to complete the task.

Satisfied now that he had actually made some forward progress, Maker returned to his quarters and, going straight to the office, began outlining on paper some additional thoughts he had regarding the mission. In fact, he became so engrossed that he didn't realize that a significant amount of time had passed until Erlen padded into the room and growled softly.

"Sorry," Maker apologized, recognizing immediately what the Niotan's issue was. "The time got away from me. Can you wait an hour?"

Erlen's response was something between a purr and a groan.

"Fair enough," Maker said. He then turned on the ship's PA system and began speaking. "Attention all. This is Lieutenant Maker. I'm sure you are all still getting settled in, but I just wanted to take a moment to express my personal thanks to each of you for agreeing to be part of this mission. As you can tell, we've been granted use of a fine new ship for this undertaking, so I was hoping that those of you who are available would join me and Erlen for an inaugural dinner in the formal dining room of our new home in half an hour. That is all."

IGNOTUS

Maker switched the PA off and turned to Erlen. "We eat in thirty minutes. Happy now?"

In response, the Niotan turned and stalked from the room.

IGNOTUS

Chapter 30

Dinner turned out to be a fun time for all. After getting off the PA system, Maker had logged in to the automated galley and told the system to auto-select a meal that could be prepared and ready to serve in half an hour. Thus, by the time everyone began arriving in the dining room thirty minutes later, everything was ready.

There was an automated serving unit that could operate as a waiter of sorts, but it was faster to simply have everyone file through the galley and help themselves. The meal itself consisted of a salad, what appeared to be roast beef, garlic bread, and pie for dessert. After getting their food, everyone retreated to the formal dining room, each taking a seat at an elegant, rectangular table that could actually seat sixteen.

Surprisingly, the cuisine was rather tasty — far from the bland foodstuffs Maker had grown accustomed to. Like the dining room itself (which was populated by fine furniture, beautifully decorated, and accentuated by a chandelier), this was further evidence that the *Nova* was indeed a ship built to impress on all fronts. Even Erlen, who ate his meal in a corner of the room, made a sound that Maker interpreted as a high vote of approval in regard to the fare.

Needless to say, Maker's team was thoroughly taken with their new abode, and the many amenities were the source of much lively conversation during dinner.

"I could get used to this," Wayne announced at one point during dinner, causing Adames to give Maker a pointed *I-told-you-so* stare.

IGNOTUS

Adding to the mood was the fact that Browing had brought two bottles of wine, which were quickly consumed.

Finally, everyone was incredibly excited about getting the items on their wish lists. For instance, Loyola couldn't stop raving about the advanced prototype of a new sniper rifle that she received, and Fierce practically gushed about the cutting-edge medical equipment that had been delivered for the sick bay.

All in all, despite occasional outbursts professing a yen for the high life, the meal — and more so the camaraderie — was thoroughly enjoyable, and it was with a fair amount of regret that it came to an end and everyone decided to turn in.

****

"This is a nice surprise," Chantrey said as she meandered down one of the hallways of the *Nova*.

"What?" asked Maker, strolling along next to her, with Erlen by his side.

"You offering to walk me back to my room after dinner. After not seeing me all day and barely speaking to me while we ate, I was starting to think you'd lost interest."

Maker chuckled. "Well, you'll be happy to know that I actually saw you a couple of times today on the ship's AV system."

"Oh, really?"

"Yes," he replied truthfully. He had indeed glimpsed her several times on the monitor, but had assumed that she — like everyone else — was trying to get settled in and didn't need any unnecessary distractions.

"As to the limited conversation during dinner," he continued, "I think everyone was participating in multiple conversations as we ate, so I'll admit my attention was divided. However, I think you still got the lion's share of it."

Chantrey smiled at this, but didn't immediately comment. A moment later, she asked, "So, is that what dinner will be like every night from now on? The whole crew chowing together?"

Maker shook his head. "Unlikely. After the mission is underway, we'll always need at least one person on duty, but will probably operate two-man teams. That said, tonight was kind of fun, so I may initiate a round robin thing in terms of dinner — let a different person pick the meal five days out of the week."

"And on the other two days?"

"Stand down — let people do their own thing. So if they still want to have dinner together, great. If not, there's no obligation."

"Well, even though I like the rest of your team, it's nice to know we'll still be able to have dinner alone every once in a while."

Erlen let out an inquisitive rumble.

"Semi-alone," Chantrey corrected, smiling. "Anyway, here we are."

Looking around, Maker suddenly realized that they were at the entrance to one of the staterooms. The door slid open; glancing inside, he realized that Chantrey had been assigned one of the more opulent cabins.

IGNOTUS

"Thanks again for walking me to my door," Chantrey said. She then gave him a quick kiss before stepping inside the cabin. "Have a good night."

Maker's eyebrows went up. "So, you're not going to invite me in?"

"I would, but I'm sure you're tired. Plus, you've got to get Erlen back. I'm certain he'd rather spend his first night on the *Nova* in his own cabin."

"First of all, I'm not *that* tired," Maker insisted. "Second, Erlen's presence has never been an impediment to anything in the past. Finally, he knows his way back and the system is keyed to his biometrics, so the door will open for him."

Chantrey seem to consider for a moment, then shook her head sadly. "I'm sorry, but I think we should just call it a night. I'll see you tomorrow."

She gave the two of them a quick wave, then stepped back; a second later, the door closed.

Erlen made an odd sound that was something like a cross between a hiss and a chirp.

"I know," Maker muttered with a nod. "Not how I expected the night to end either."

The two of them turned and began heading back toward their own quarters. However, they hadn't gone more than a step before Maker heard the familiar sound of a door opening behind them. Turning, he saw Chantrey's door standing open, but this time the interior of the cabin was completely dark.

As he watched, a dainty hand slid from the darkness into the light, palm up. The forefinger on the hand suddenly curled quickly three times in a come-hither gesture.

IGNOTUS

Grinning broadly, Maker headed towards the open doorway, casually muttering over his shoulder, "Don't wait up."

IGNOTUS

Chapter 31

The bulk of the next morning was spent running diagnostics on the *Nova*'s various systems: weapons, shields, engines, etc. Taking his place on the bridge, Maker oversaw the various tests and analyses. Technically, he didn't have authority over the three civilians, but he put them to work anyway alongside the members of his team. (His theory was that — whatever happened on this upcoming mission — they were all in it together, so everyone needed to pull their weight.)

It took a little time as the results trickled in, but around noon he got the final word regarding the ship's condition: all systems had checked out.

"All right," Maker said. "Let's take this baby for a spin around the block. Any objections?"

Other than Fierce (who rarely left the medical bay), everyone else was on the bridge. From all indications, no one was opposed to a little joyride.

Maker smiled. "Sergeant Diviana?"

"Yes, sir?" responded Diviana, who was manning the comm.

"Please let the space station know that we'll be going out for a little jaunt, with plans to return shortly," Maker stated.

"Aye," Diviana replied.

While she started speaking into the comm, Maker turned to Wayne, who was in the pilot's seat. "Wayne, fire up the engines."

"Already on it, sir," Wayne stated.

"Lieutenant," Diviana uttered with a sense of urgency. "The space station is denying us permission to leave."

IGNOTUS

Maker raised an eyebrow. "Are they now?"

Diviana nodded. "Yes. They're saying... Wait, I'll put it on the intercom."

She pressed a button on the comm, and a moment later, a man's voice began sounding across the bridge.

"—*ova* is not cleared for departure. Please power down your engines. I repeat, the *Nova* is not cleared for departure. Please power down your engines."

Maker sighed as the message continued to repeat. "Diviana, please let the station know that there's some kind of interference, and their message is coming through garbled and indecipherable."

Looking slightly befuddled, Diviana nodded as she turned off the intercom and began to relay Maker's message. Browing, his face a mask of concern, opened his mouth to speak but was stopped by Maker holding up an open palm in his direction.

"Wayne, get ready to get us out of here," Maker instructed.

"On standby, el-tee," Wayne declared.

Diviana suddenly turned to him. "They're not buying it, Lieutenant. They're refusing to open the bay doors."

"That's funny," Maker observed. "The bay doors are already opening."

Maker tapped a button on a control panel by his bridge seat, and a large monitor on a nearby wall blazed to life. Obviously connected to one of the *Nova*'s external cameras, it showed an image of the bay doors opening, just as Maker had said.

"Wayne, take us out."

IGNOTUS

"Aye, sir," the young Marine replied.

Moments later, they were outside the bay and moving away from the station.

"Sir," Diviana called out. "The space station is ordering us to return to the docking bay. They say they have orders to shoot if we don't."

"Garbled, indecipherable, blah, blah, blah," Maker stated as they continued moving away from the station with increasing speed. He did note, however, the guns of the station swinging in their direction on the monitor.

At this point, there was general consternation plainly evident on the faces of almost everyone present. Browing had a deep frown etched in stone on his face, while Chantrey bit her lip with concern. Even Adames, who trusted Maker implicitly, seemed worried enough to speak up, but kept silent when his commanding officer looked at him and emphatically shook his head.

Maker then turned to Wayne. "Prepare to jump to hyperspace as soon as we're clear."

Wayne nodded. "Will do, Lieutenant. Coordinates are locked."

Moments later, with the guns of the space station unmistakably aimed at the *Nova*, they made the leap to hyperspace.

IGNOTUS

Chapter 32

They were waiting on Maker and his team when the *Nova* came back — Lafayette, Steiner, and Grasso. The three general officers were watching from an observation platform as the ship came in to dock, but hustled down as soon as the bay doors closed. Watching them on the monitor, Maker couldn't read Lafayette's expression, but the other two appeared furious.

Telling his people to sit tight and leaving Adames in command on the bridge, Maker disembarked and was immediately met by an enraged Grasso screaming, "Where the hell have you been?!"

"We just took the *Nova* out for a quick jaunt," Maker replied.

"You weren't authorized for departure of any type!" Grasso countered. "You were ordered to power down by the space station."

"Were we?" Maker asked, eyebrows raised. "I'm afraid we were experiencing some type of interference and the message didn't come through clearly."

"Well, if you didn't understand the message, why did you leave?" Steiner asked.

"Because the bay doors opened," Maker explained. "Thus, we assumed that *they* could understand *us* — even if the reverse wasn't true."

"The bay doors opened because someone hacked the system controlling them," Steiner shot back. "I don't suppose you know anything about that?"

Maker shook his head. "Not at all."

Lafayette seemed to snicker at this, while his two colleagues gave Maker steely looks.

IGNOTUS

"Well, you've been given a ship that's top-of-the-line in all aspects," Grasso said. "Did it ever occur to you that maybe you shouldn't take it out for a joyride?"

"With all due respect, sir," Maker stated, bristling, "it wasn't a joyride. It was a test run."

"A test run?" Steiner repeated.

"Yes, sir," Maker confirmed with a nod. "My team is being asked to leave tomorrow on a mission that's literally taking us into the unknown. I'm not heading into a possible ambush in a ship that hasn't been put through the paces — whose guns haven't been fired and whose shields haven't been tested, among other things."

"Fine," Grasso chimed in. "Assuming that's what happened, it doesn't explain why it took so long. You've been gone over nine hours."

"We had some trouble," Maker confessed. "We went to a star system with an asteroid field in order to test the weapons and shields. Unfortunately, we ran into some kind of electromagnetic interference that knocked everything offline. We didn't suffer any damage, but it took some time to get everything back in working order."

There was silence following Maker's statement, as Grasso and Steiner seemed to stew on what he'd said, while Lafayette continued to look amused.

"If that will be all," Maker finally said, "we still have a lot of preparations to make for tomorrow's departure."

"No, Lieutenant," Grasso said in heated response, "I'm afraid that will *not* be all."

IGNOTUS

Chapter 33

Although they really didn't have anything more to address, Grasso and Steiner spent another ten minutes berating Maker. Without any specific questions to answer, Maker simply stood there and took the tongue-lashing. Eventually, the two general officers seemed to tire of the sport, such as it was, and left. Lafayette, however, stayed behind.

"So," the admiral began after his two colleagues were gone, "I take it you found the bugs."

Maker stayed silent, not exactly sure how to respond.

"Come on, son," Lafayette continued. "We've been doing a good job of being straight with each other thus far. No need to change shoes in the middle of the dance."

"All right," Maker said. "We found your little devices, and I have to say that I'm somewhat disappointed."

The admiral shook his head in frustration. "I told them it was a bad idea, but they wouldn't listen."

"Who?" Maker asked, intrigued.

"My compadres in the Star Chamber, as you put it. I know it may seem like I'm in charge — and, admittedly, my voice *does* carry a little weight — but we're a committee. We do most things by vote."

"And the vote in this instance was to bug the *Nova*."

Lafayette nodded. "Yeah, but you've got to understand: you're dealing with some of the most powerful people in Gaian Space. They're not used to being in the dark about *any*thing, so the notion of not

IGNOTUS

knowing what was happening on this mission — specifically, on the *Nova* — galls them."

"I get that to a certain extent, but it was information that was only going to be available to them for a limited time. I mean, once we make the hyperspace jump to wherever Skullcap guides us, they won't be in proximity to…"

Maker trailed off as a new train of thought unexpectedly popped up in his brain.

"Okay," he finally said. "What aren't you telling me?"

The admiral sighed. "It's not a big deal, but when you leave tomorrow, you won't be going alone. Two battle cruisers are going with you. And before you go there, the specific purpose in assigning them to accompany you was not to pick up the broadcasts from the bugs."

"Of course not," Maker chimed in sarcastically. "Why would I think that?"

Ignoring the lieutenant's comment, Lafayette continued. "They're tagging along primarily in order to transport the sub rosa tech back while you continue escorting the ambassador home. Getting the info from the bugs was just a bonus, although they'll also provide additional protection as long as they're with you."

"So wait," Maker muttered, frowning. "If I'm understanding this correctly, as soon as the tech is retrieved, my squad continues on alone with Skullcap and possibly wanders into a trap, while two battle cruisers immediately return home — safe and sound — with the goods."

IGNOTUS

"Well, it won't be an *immediate* return home," Lafayette clarified. "We'll want Planck to verify that we're getting the real thing first."

Maker's brow furrowed, as he now had an understanding as to why no one had tried to stop Planck from joining the mission. Lafayette and the Star Chamber *wanted* him there.

"I'm sorry if we didn't clarify it before," the admiral stressed, "but that was the deal. The ambassador doesn't want the sub rosa tech anywhere near the Vacra homeworld, so there was always going to be at least one other ship there to take possession of it and bring it back."

"Great," Maker said sardonically. "Anything else I need to know?"

"Not really. However, there is something *I'd* like to know."

"What?"

"You were gone almost nine hours on your little junket. Even if you actually did spend time testing the weapons and shields" — Maker nodded to indicate that they had — "I seriously doubt it took that long to recover from the EM 'interference' you mentioned. So what did you really do the rest of that time?"

Maker smiled. "Just reflect on the joy of being in the Corps, sir."

IGNOTUS

Chapter 34

Maker spent a few more minutes talking to Lafayette, primarily reminding the admiral that he was still owed some things under their agreement. After soliciting a promise that he'd receive everything he was due before the mission formally commenced, Maker went back aboard the *Nova* and sought out Adames on the bridge. The two of them then went to the ship's conference room, where Maker essentially repeated the conversations he'd had with the general officers.

"I turned the exterior cameras on you," Adames said when he'd finished. "There's no audio on those — don't need it in space — but I could see that the discussions were tense."

"It wasn't as bad as it could have been," Maker stressed. "The first two didn't even mention the listening devices, and Lafayette didn't seem that bothered by it. In fact, he seemed amused by the entire situation."

"Are you sure he doesn't know what we were up to while we were gone?"

Maker contemplated the question for a moment, then shook his head. "I doubt it. But even if he did, I get the impression that he wouldn't be too bothered by it."

"I'll tell you what bothers *me*," Adames chimed in. "Having a couple of battle cruisers load up the tech we're risking our lives for and then taking off."

"I know," Maker declared in agreement with his NCO. The sub rosa tech had been, in his opinion, their insurance policy — an unstated guarantee that the Star Chamber expected (no, *needed*) them to come back. Without it, anything that happened to Maker and his team might be considered an acceptable loss.

IGNOTUS

"Anyway," Maker continued, "it's getting late. Let's sleep on it and see if anything new occurs to us tomorrow."

"Sounds good," Adames acknowledged with a nod. "The morning is wiser than the eve, as they say."

"Also, let's do the final briefing in the A.M.," Maker added. "I want to be ready to take off as soon as Skullcap sets foot on this ship."

"No problem," Adames assured him.

IGNOTUS

Chapter 35

Following his conversation with Adames, Maker went to see Chantrey. Needless to say, she was expecting him. After letting him in, she took his hand and led him to a nearby sofa, then sat and pulled him down next to her.

"So, how'd it go?" she asked.

Maker quickly gave her the same overview he'd shared with Adames.

"So you've infuriated two of the three general officers who you've interacted with," Chantrey concluded. "You're losing your touch. Normally all three would be clamoring for your blood."

Maker chuckled. "Guess I'm slowing down in my old age."

"Maybe," Chantrey said with a frown, obviously focused on something else. "And you said that Lafayette wasn't angry about you debugging the ship?"

"No, it was almost like he was expecting it," Maker stated. "Why? What are you thinking?"

"Maybe it was a test."

"A test?" Maker repeated, looking confused. "A test of what?"

"Maybe just to see what you'd do — how radically you'd respond."

He gave her a curious look. "You think what I did was radical?"

"Well, let's consider," she said. "You could have just let Wayne shut the bugs down, but instead you come up with a plan that requires us to essentially violate orders to stand down and hack into the space station bay controls, among other things."

IGNOTUS

"Well, I didn't know what the reaction would be once we deactivated the bugs, and I didn't want someone showing up trying to figure out why they weren't working anymore. As you know by now, we had some things to do on the *Nova* that required a certain amount of privacy."

"I know — you had Wayne put us all to work during our little excursion."

"Well, we only had a limited amount of time to get everything done, so it was all hands on deck."

Chantrey sat back and crossed her arms. "I still can't believe you kept most of us in the dark about what was going on — and especially about the fact that the ship was bugged."

Maker let out an exasperated breath. "Are you kidding? How am I supposed to tell people, confidentially, that the ship is bugged when there are listening devices everywhere? That info couldn't be shared until we were out of range of whoever might have been listening."

"You could have taken us off the ship and told us, the way Wayne did it with you."

"Right," Maker muttered sarcastically. "That wouldn't have looked suspicious: 'Come outside, everyone — I have something to tell you.'" He spoke the last sentence in an excited, conspiratorial voice.

"Okay, okay," Chantrey intoned. "You've made your point. But tell me something: how pervasive were the bugs?"

"Like I said, they were everywhere."

"Okay, let me be precise: I'm asking specifically in terms of our cabins."

IGNOTUS

Maker gave her a skeptical look. "Weren't you around when Wayne rounded them all up?"

Chantrey shook her head. "No, I was busy working on your secret project, so I just gave him a temporary access code."

"Oh," Maker muttered a bit absentmindedly. "Well, my understanding from Wayne is that they were in every area of our living quarters — living rooms, kitchens, bathrooms, etcetera."

Chantrey glanced in the direction of her bedroom and then looked back at Maker expectantly.

"Bedrooms, too," he added.

Chantrey reflected on this for a second and then seemed to mentally shrug, saying, "Well, I hope they got an earful."

Maker looked at her in surprise, and then laughed. "You, lady, have no shame."

Looking at him salaciously, she said, "And this is news to you?"

IGNOTUS

Chapter 36

As promised, Adames had everyone in the *Nova*'s conference room bright and early the next morning. When Maker arrived, with Erlen by his side, everyone was already seated around the table, ready to begin. As he entered, Adames immediately called the room to attention, followed by Maker telling everyone (or rather, the Marines present) to be at ease as he took a position at the end of the table.

"I'll make this quick," Maker began, "mostly because I don't have much more to impart than what you already know. We'll be leaving shortly to escort Skullcap home. As far as I'm concerned, he's an enemy combatant, and for the duration of this mission, we'll be traveling under threat conditions. In other words, everybody needs to stay alert. In addition, there are a couple of other little wrinkles…"

Maker then proceeded to tell them about the battle cruisers that would accompany them for at least part of the mission. However, he hadn't been talking for more than a minute when his p-comp chirped, indicating an emergency message. Glancing at it, Maker was surprised to see a missive from Admiral Lafayette:

Permission to come aboard?

****

As the message had implied, the admiral was indeed outside the *Nova*, where he waited patiently until Maker came to greet him and welcome him aboard. With

IGNOTUS

him was a young Navy captain carrying a briefcase, whom he introduced as his executive officer.

"I have to admit that I didn't expect you this early," Maker confessed as they entered the *Nova*. "In truth, I thought general officers typically slept in."

"That's a rumor that we like to perpetuate," the admiral responded, "so we can catch young officers unawares." He eyed Maker critically for a second as they walked. "Doesn't look like it worked today."

"Sorry to disappoint," Maker quipped. "Will this disqualify me from the mission?"

"Sadly, there's almost nothing that will get you off the hook," Lafayette said jovially. "Anyway, I owe you some stuff, so I'm here to make good on it."

"I was actually in the process of conducting the final briefing when your message popped up. So if you just want to leave it—"

"Nonsense," the admiral said dismissively. "We might as well do this right, and if your people are already assembled, that's perfect."

Maker didn't say anything more but simply led the admiral to the conference room.

As the admiral entered, Adames — who had been keeping an eye on the door — shouted, "Room, ten-hut!"

All of the Marines immediately stood and came to attention.

"As you were," Lafayette said as he took Maker's previous spot at the head of the conference table, then gave everyone a moment to resume their seats before continuing. (Maker unobtrusively stepped to a corner of the room where Erlen lay resting, while Lafayette's executive officer stayed close by the admiral's side.)

IGNOTUS

"For those of you who don't know me, I'm Admiral Lafayette," he began. "Without mincing words, I just wanted to say thanks to everyone in this room for the assignment you've undertaken today. I know that it was a difficult decision, and that each of you volunteered for the mission you're going to embark on, despite your personal misgivings. That kind of action is indicative of the integrity, honor, and bravery of those who serve. And although it isn't often publicly hailed, that kind of act — that kind of *sacrifice* — does not go unnoticed. *Hasn't* gone unnoticed. So today, we honor you for it."

The admiral turned to his exec, who had inconspicuously placed the briefcase on the conference table and opened it while his commanding officer had been speaking. He now handed Lafayette a small, decorated case, which the admiral took.

"Sergeant Diviana," Lafayette said sonorously.

Diviana came smartly to her feet and turned to face the admiral. "Sir, yes, sir."

"Please approach," Lafayette stated.

Diviana marched up to the admiral, who turned to face her as she reached the end of the table and stopped.

"For bravery and distinguished service," Lafayette said, "I present and award to you the Sunburst Medal of Valor."

There were a couple of surprised gasps, and Maker smiled to himself. The Sunburst Medal was one of the highest honors that could be bestowed on a soldier.

Ignoring the excitement his announcement had generated, the admiral opened the case and removed from it a circular, golden medal with a sunburst design on it, attached to a ribbon. Although plainly flabbergasted, Diviana retained enough composure to incline her head,

IGNOTUS

allowing Lafayette to hang the ribbon around her neck. She then stepped back and saluted the admiral, who returned the gesture. Turning, she began marching back to her seat when Lafayette's voice stopped her.

"Where do you think you're going?" he demanded. "We're not done."

IGNOTUS

Chapter 37

Much to her surprise, Diviana received several more medals and commendations. It was, without question, an embarrassment of riches. However, she wasn't the only person so honored. One by one, the admiral called up everyone in the room and presented them with various awards, citing their heroism and gallantry. Even the civilians were not spared, with Chantrey and Planck being honored with non-military awards. (Browing, who was actually an officer in the Reserves, received military awards like the members of Maker's team.)

The last person to be singled out was Adames. After getting a bevy of hardware hung around his neck, he was certain the ceremony — for lack of a better term — was over. Thus, he was caught flat-footed when the admiral told him to remain standing.

"It has been my privilege," Lafayette stated, addressing everyone, "to be here today honoring your prowess on the battlefield. But often we overlook the work that takes place away from the theater of war. Things like training and logistics, that support and enhance our ability to accomplish the mission. People often excel in one area or the other — either on the battlefield or off — so it's a rare treat when you find someone who is adept on all fronts. Someone who takes the initiative in doing what's required without being told. Someone who leads by example. Master Sergeant Adames is such an individual, and so we'd like to reward his skill, knowledge, service, and overall ability by promoting him to *Chief* Master Sergeant, effective immediately."

IGNOTUS

Adames blinked, plainly stunned as a general round of cheers and applause sounded from everyone in the room. He looked at Maker with a *did-you-know-about-this?* expression on his face, but the latter only grinned and clapped along with everyone else. Pressed to say a few words, the NCO — clearly not keen on public speaking — mumbled a quick thanks and then tried to step aside.

"Before I forget," the admiral chimed in, handing Adames a small black jewelry case. He opened it to reveal a metallic set of Chief Master Sergeant insignia.

"Those are actually ceremonial," Lafayette explained. "You'll have a full and official set of your new rank delivered to you before you depart."

"Thank you, sir," Adames said sincerely, as he typically would have had to purchase his own insignia. "That's very kind of you."

"My pleasure," the admiral said with a smile, "and congratulations once again. Now, if you'll excuse me…"

As he trailed off, Lafayette caught Maker's eye and motioned with his head towards the door. As he turned and walked toward the exit, the admiral shouted "Carry on" over his shoulder before anyone could call the room to attention. A moment later, he — along with his exec and Maker —was gone.

That said, the door had barely closed behind the trio of officers before the room exploded with excitement. Everyone began chattering at once, gleefully congratulating one another and admiring their various awards. (All except Cano Snick, that is, who — in keeping with his somber nature — seemed embarrassed by the attention, although he heaped praise on his teammates.)

IGNOTUS

In working the room, so to speak, Chantrey eventually found herself in front of Adames.

"Congrats," she said with a smile. "You deserve it."

"Thanks," he replied, "but I think your comment applies to everybody."

"Including your illustrious leader," Chantrey added. "So what happened to *his* medals? Did he get them in a separate ceremony or something?"

"Uhhh," Adames droned, taking her elbow and guiding her to one side of the room so they could speak somewhat privately. "Maker's not getting any medals."

"Huh?" she muttered in confusion. "Why not? He went on the same missions that the rest of you were recognized for — led them, in fact. Why wouldn't he be entitled to the same thing?"

"Well, I'm assuming *we* got them because Maker nominated us for them."

"So why wouldn't Gant qualify?"

"Because he can't nominate himself. More to the point, typically only a schmuck will declare himself worthy of medals for bravery or something along those lines. What's expected is that your superiors will observe you in action or note what you've done and nominate you accordingly for anything merited."

Chantrey thought about this for a moment, then asked, "So you're saying that no one's nominated him for anything? After all he's done?"

"Maybe you weren't listening the other day, but Gant said it himself: he's radioactive. That spreads in all directions, even up the chain of command. No one's going to nominate him for *any*thing — not a medal, not a

IGNOTUS

promotion, nothing — because he's Madman Maker, and supporting him in any way would taint them."

"But that's not right," Chantrey stated fiercely, with a stern look on her face.

"Why is any of this surprising to you?" Adames asked. "You're a behavioral specialist. You couldn't predict that this would happen?"

"I don't know who makes these decisions, so I can't guess at what they'd do," she said defensively. "Plus, I generally work off psych profiles and other forms of data."

"Well, try not to make a thing out of it," Adames advised. "Gant's made his peace with it."

Chantrey was nonplussed. "What do you mean?"

Adames sighed. "He knew this was what to expect when he came back into the Corps. Professionally, the specter of the *Orpheus Moon* is going to haunt him forever — and now, presumably, the Hundred-and-Twelfth as well."

"And so that's it? No matter what he does or how much he achieves, it will never be enough to banish the ghosts of the past?"

Adames shrugged in exasperation. "You talk like there are a bunch of options here. I agree that the treatment he gets is undeserved, but what exactly do you expect me to do?"

Chantrey gave him a fierce stare. "I think a better question is this: what do you think Maker would do if it was *you* being maligned?"

As she spoke, she reached out and tapped the case holding the NCO's ceremonial rank (which he gripped in his palm), then she turned and walked away.

IGNOTUS

Chapter 38

There was initially silence after Maker — now accompanied by Erlen — left the conference room with Lafayette. The admiral cast a curious glance at the Niotan as they walked, but otherwise didn't acknowledge his presence. (His executive officer, on the other hand, appeared somewhat unnerved by Erlen's presence, but followed his commander's lead and stayed silent.)

"Thanks for distributing the awards," Maker said after a few moments. "It was a nice gesture."

"Think nothing of it," Lafayette replied with a dismissive gesture. "After reviewing the files, I was happy to do it."

"Oh?" Maker droned, raising an eyebrow.

"Admittedly, I could have just rubber-stamped it," the admiral confessed, "but I actually read the recommendations you submitted. Much to my surprise, you didn't overreach in a single instance. Every person you nominated was qualified for and met the criteria for the awards and commendations they ultimately received. Even Adames, in all honesty, hit all the touchstones for promotion to chief."

"Glad to hear you approve," Maker remarked mordantly. "I'm sure your conscience would have given you fits and kept you awake at night otherwise."

Lafayette chuckled. "You never let up, do you?"

Maker merely shrugged in response, noting that they had reached the *Nova*'s exit.

"Anyway," the admiral continued as they left the ship, "just remember that this mission is critical — for a host of reasons. So, for the sake of all that's holy, keep

IGNOTUS

the ambassador safe and keep him alive. Think you can manage that?"

"Sure," Maker responded in a noncommittal fashion.

"Great," the admiral said. "He's all yours."

With that, Lafayette pointed with his chin towards a nearby wall. There, standing between two guards, was Skullcap.

IGNOTUS

Chapter 39

Maker and Skullcap stood across the room from each other, with the former eyeing the latter suspiciously. They were currently aboard the *Nova*, in the quarters that had been designated for Skullcap's use.

After pointing out the insectoid to Maker, the admiral had handed over a data chip containing the hyperspace jump coordinates they needed to use (along with other pertinent info) and then taken his leave. In a similar fashion, the two guards had escorted Skullcap aboard the *Nova* and to the cabin Maker dictated before swiftly departing. (Needless to say, Maker had made the announcement to his crew that their "guest" had come aboard and to make ready for departure.)

As he studied the Vacra leader, Maker tried to make sense of something that had happened earlier — or rather, *hadn't* happened. When Lafayette had drawn Maker's attention to Skullcap, Erlen had been with him. Considering their past run-ins with the insectoid, Maker would ordinarily have expected the Niotan to go on the attack. Instead, Erlen had simply let out a curious rumbling. It was behavior that was out of the ordinary — enough so that it made him even more wary about the mission — and out of concern, he had sent the Niotan back to their quarters once Skullcap was brought aboard.

"This abode will be adequate," the insectoid announced, interrupting Maker's thoughts.

"So glad it meets your approval," Maker quipped acerbically, "especially since it's a take-it-or-leave-it proposition."

"If now is an appropriate juncture, I was hoping we could speak," Skullcap said.

IGNOTUS

"Sure," Maker stated with a nod. "I'll speak, you'll listen. Now, first of all, you're confined to quarters for the duration of this trip, except when your presence is absolutely required elsewhere. To enforce this mandate, the door to this cabin will stay locked and can only be opened from the outside. On those occasions when you leave these quarters, it will be in the company of an armed escort. Any questions?"

"I was not informed that my status would be that of convict."

"On the contrary, you're an honored guest."

"So this is how you treat all envoys?"

"Only the ones who try to kill us."

Skullcap made an odd sound that Maker couldn't interpret, then said, "I am not the enemy you think I am, Maker."

"If not, then it's only because you're worse," Maker shot back. "But if you're feeling shunned and need someone to chat with, talk to Deadeye."

"Dead Eye?" the insectoid intoned, plainly curious.

Maker tapped his p-comp and, with a slight hiss of hydraulics, a panel in the ceiling opened and something like a miniature turret — about the size of a fist — came into view.

"This is Deadeye," Maker declared, pointing up at the device. "He's your new best bud and will be with you wherever you go on this ship in the sense that there's one of these in every room, although not always in the ceiling."

Skullcap tilted his head and glanced up at the mechanism.

IGNOTUS

"Deadeye has scanning technology that's attuned to your biorhythm, so he'll be watching you wherever you go," Maker explained. "More importantly, he has specific instructions regarding how to respond should your behavior become problematic."

"Problematic?" Skullcap repeated.

"Yes. For example, if you try to tamper with the lock on your door, he'll shoot you dead. If you go wandering around the ship without an escort, he'll shoot you dead. If you try to disable Deadeye himself, guess what? He'll shoot you dead."

As he spoke, Maker reflected on the time his people had put into installing this particular safeguard. It was the task he had assigned to Wayne and — after the *Nova*'s unauthorized jaunt the previous day and the debugging of the ship — the younger Marine had utilized the authority granted to him to the fullest. In essence, he had drafted almost everyone on the *Nova* in some capacity or other in order to get the job done in a reasonable span of time.

"So it watches and kills," Skullcap summarized. "Dead Eye."

"You catch on quick," Maker said. "So just obey the house rules, and we won't have any problems."

Without waiting for further comment, Maker left.

IGNOTUS

Chapter 40

"How long before we can leave?" Maker inquired.

"Hopefully in a minute or two," answered Wayne, who was sitting in the pilot's seat again, with the flight and navigation controls at his fingertips.

Maker fought the impulse to drum his fingers impatiently. Sitting in his chair on the bridge of the *Nova*, he turned his attention to the view outside the ship being shown via monitor — namely, two battle cruisers in close proximity.

After leaving Skullcap's cabin (and double-checking that the insectoid was locked in), Maker had gone straight to the bridge. Everyone was already in their appropriate positions, so it had simply been a matter of him giving the word and moments later they were leaving the docking bay. By the time they got clear of the space station, the two cruisers — which had been waiting outside the station on standby — began hailing them. After a brief introduction between Maker and the cruisers' captains, the three vessels had continued moving away until they reached a safe distance for the jump to hyperspace.

Impatience getting the better of him, Maker asked, "What's taking so long?"

"We're traveling in a convoy, so the navigation systems have to sync up," Wayne explained.

"I get that," Maker acknowledged, "but it usually only takes them a few seconds."

"Well, something's throwing them off," Wayne stated. "Maybe it's the data on that chip the admiral gave you, but there's something about this trip they're not liking."

IGNOTUS

"That goes for all of us," Adames chimed in, causing a general round of laughter.

Although he chuckled with the others, Wayne's comment gave Maker something to mentally chew on. Basically, they were about to head well into the unknown, as evidenced by the fact that just getting to their initial destination was going to require multiple hyperspace jumps. The first jump would take them to the Fringe, which was the outermost edge of the Gaian Expanse and human settlement. Every jump thereafter (and there would be at least a dozen more) would take them farther into the Beyond — the region of space that was generally uncharted and unexplored.

"Enough of this," Maker finally muttered, more to himself than anyone else. "Diviana, tell them we're taking off. They've got the coordinates for the first jump point. They can meet us there and then try this syncing thing again."

Diviana, who was manning the comm again, nodded and was about to do as instructed when Wayne spoke up.

"Got it," the young Marine announced. "The navigation systems are synced. We're good to go."

"About time," Maker grumbled. "Diviana, belay that prior order. Confirm that the cruisers are ready and initiate countdown."

Moments later, they made the jump to hyperspace.

IGNOTUS

Chapter 41

They went through the hyperspace jumps without incident. Maker stayed alert but didn't really anticipate any trouble because Lafayette, exhibiting enviable foresight, had sent scout ships to check out the jump points in advance — essentially the moment Skullcap first proffered the coordinates. Their reports were among the info on the data chip the admiral had provided, but the gist of what they'd documented was that the jump points appeared safe.

That said, the trip took the better part of the day — mostly because after every jump, the navigation systems of the three ships needed to sync up again. That part wasn't unusual; ships in a convoy always conferred to make sure there was consensus on where they currently were, and more importantly — after making the jump to hyperspace — where they expected to come out. The issue in this instance was that the computers on the three vessels consistently had trouble reaching an accord with respect to the coordinates. The end result was that they spent far more time at each jump location than originally anticipated.

Maker found it incredibly frustrating, but occupied himself by keeping an eye on Skullcap. From what he could see, the Vacra leader generally stayed standing in one spot in his cabin, rarely moving. He was so still, in fact, that he could almost have passed for a statue.

The only occasions when Skullcap appeared to move normally were mealtimes. The info on the chip had indicated that the "ambassador" preferred to eat four times per day — roughly every six hours. His sustenance

IGNOTUS

consisted of a gooey gray paste that came in unmarked plastic squeeze tubes, each of which (by Maker's estimation) held about sixteen ounces. A crate of the tubes had been delivered, which seemed like far more than what was necessary for the mission.

The protocol for Skullcap's meals was simple: Maker personally delivered the food tubes, carrying them in one hand and holding his sidearm in the other. Somewhat to Maker's disappointment, the Vacra leader gave him no problems at any juncture. In fact, it wasn't until they reached the penultimate jump point that he and the insectoid seriously clashed.

They were nearing the end of the first leg of the mission, with one hyperspace jump left, when Maker decided he needed to have a talk with Skullcap. With that in mind, he went to the insectoid's quarters and — as usual — let himself in unannounced.

Skullcap stood in his usual spot (which was near the far wall opposite the door).

"Maker," he said. "Your visit is unexpected, as it is not the hour for consumption. Am I to assume we have arrived at the final coordinates I provided?"

"Not quite," Maker replied. "We have one more hyperspace jump, but I thought I should ask what to expect when we arrive."

Skullcap's head moved in an odd whirling fashion, as if he were trying to use it to draw a figure-eight in the air.

"I do not understand the question," he declared. "We will arrive in a region of space that is devoid of planetary bodies and celestial phenomena. In essence, there is nothing to 'expect.' As you have had the

IGNOTUS

coordinates for a reasonable amount of time, surely your people have investigated this."

"I'm not talking about meteor showers," Maker retorted, "or a lunar eclipse or anything else you can see. I'm talking about what's likely to *happen*."

"Your query still confuses me."

"Okay, let's go with an example," Maker said. "In the not-too-distant past, you asked to meet with me and a few of my companions under a flag of truce on an uninhabited world. However, you didn't tell us that there was an anomaly on the planet that would drain the power from our ship's engines, so when the ceasefire came to an end, we were sitting ducks."

Maker fought to keep his temper under control. The incident he had just recounted was a perfect example (and needful reminder) of how devious Skullcap truly was, and just thinking about it for too long was enough to make him angry.

Skullcap made an odd breathing sound, then stated, "I recall our prior meeting, and now have a better understanding of your question."

"Great. So, is there anything we're unlikely to anticipate but which we should expect after we make this last hyperspace jump?"

"No," the insectoid assured him. "After the next jump, we will proceed under normal engine power to a nearby star system, where I will initiate the process of returning the articles requested."

"Okay," Maker intoned. "What's involved in this process?"

"In simple terms, I merely have to contact the Vacra currently charged with safeguarding the chattel you desire."

IGNOTUS

"At which point you give us our property and then we take you home. Sounds like a plan to me."

"Indeed. I assume my armor will be brought to me before we arrive?"

"What?" Maker muttered, looking confused.

"My battle armor. You have it, correct?"

"Yes," Maker admitted, and it was true. One of the things that had been brought to his attention was that Skullcap had been in full battle armor when he was initially picked up. The intent was to return the armor when the insectoid reached his homeworld, and Maker stated as much.

"Unacceptable," Skullcap said in an unwavering tone. "I will need it in the near future."

"Frankly speaking, you have a better chance of me giving you a lap dance," Maker quipped. "There's no way I'm letting you get decked out in a full suit of battle armor on my watch."

"I'm afraid it is required if you desire the return of your effects."

Maker gave him a hard look. "Are you saying we don't get our tech back if I refuse?"

"No, that is not what I meant to imply. I only meant to stress that I need my armor, and I am asking this as a" — Skullcap spent a moment trying to determine the proper word — "*favor.*"

Maker snorted in derision. "A favor? That's something that you ask of a friend, not a foe."

Skullcap gave him a blatant stare. "I am not your enemy, Maker."

"Then you must have a twin brother," Maker scoffed, "because there's a guy who looks just like you who's been trying to kill me."

IGNOTUS

With that, he turned and left the cabin, without giving the insectoid a chance to reply.

IGNOTUS

Chapter 42

As Skullcap had assured Maker, nothing untoward happened after the final jump. The *Nova* and its companion ships dropped out of hyperspace in a region that didn't seem to represent a danger on any level. Nevertheless, remembering his past experience, Maker was eager to get moving. The problem was, he didn't know which way to go.

Skullcap had mentioned that they'd be heading to a nearby star system following the last hyperspace jump. However, long-range scans indicated a score of systems that could be their destination — including several with dense interstellar traffic. In short, they were at a juncture that Maker had always known they'd reach, but hadn't really wanted to admit: they needed Skullcap to direct their course forward.

****

Surprisingly, the Vacra leader was very forthcoming in terms of directions when Maker came to discuss the topic with him, providing coordinates for one of the star systems detected by the *Nova*'s scans. However, his apparent helpfulness just served to heighten Maker's suspicions that something dastardly was afoot — especially when Skullcap again pressed the subject of receiving his armor.

"That's not happening," Maker declared, shaking his head. "As I said before, giving you battle armor is insane, tantamount to shooting myself in the head."

IGNOTUS

"And again, I am not your enemy," Skullcap insisted. "Moreover, I have kept faith throughout the course of this agreement."

"Which means absolutely nothing in light of your duplicitous track record."

The Vacra leader made an unusual sound — like a burp and a hiccup, combined with a sigh — and then lowered his head in a forlorn manner, saying, "It is true that my past behavior was disgraceful, and for that I am ashamed."

Maker simply stared at him for a moment, caught off-guard by the fact that the insectoid's statement had sounded sincere. And then he remembered who he was dealing with: a shrewd foe who was also a master tactician. It was probably nothing for him to put on a show of being regretful and contrite.

"Save it for the confessional," Maker grumbled. "I'm not interested in hearing how remorseful you are. You're here to serve a specific purpose, and as far as I know, it doesn't require you to dress up for war."

"Then I have inadequately explained the sequence of events that needs to occur."

Maker was nonplussed. "What are you talking about?"

"If I do not receive my armor, I cannot do what you require of me," Skullcap said plainly. He then began to explain why his armor was imperative.

IGNOTUS

Chapter 43

Maker had initially planned to have a briefing once they got closer to the star system Skullcap had directed them towards. However, after hearing what the Vacra leader had to say, he pushed up his timetable significantly. Fifteen minutes after speaking with the insectoid, he had all his people in the *Nova*'s conference room.

"All right," Maker began. "As with most missions, nothing ever goes a hundred percent right, and this one is no exception. Our esteemed guest, who is supposed to be taking us to the tech they lifted, is now saying he can't hold up his end of the deal without access to his battle armor."

"That's a joke, right?" asked Adames. "Why does he need his armor to lead us to what they stole?"

"It's complicated," Maker stated. "First and foremost, we're obviously in an area of space that we know nothing about. According to Skullcap, our current destination is a commerce planet that is frequented by hundreds of species, most of which — if not all — humans have never encountered. Even the Vacra are only familiar with a limited number of them, and although he's something of a polyglot, our guest says that he needs the translator that's built into his armor to communicate once we get there."

"Wait a minute," Browing interjected. "We have universal translators. Can't he make use of those instead of what's in his armor?"

"The term 'universal translator' is a bit of a misnomer," Wayne explained. "What you're talking about is a device that's the product of what's known as the

IGNOTUS

Universal Translation Project, which itself is a joint effort between hundreds of different species, including humans. Basically, all of those races pooled their collective knowledge to create a tool that can translate any one of their languages into any of the others. Moreover, as new species are encountered, their languages are eventually learned and added as well, even if the species themselves don't officially participate in the project. The end result is an instrument that can translate maybe thousands of languages; however, it's really not a *universal* translator."

"In essence," summarized Snick, dispensing with his characteristic silence, "any languages that haven't been added to the translator's database, so to speak, can't be translated."

"Pretty much," Wayne agreed.

"And you think that's the case with the planet we're headed to?" Chantrey asked, directing her question at Maker.

"Truthfully, I don't know," he answered. "I mean, this is Skullcap we're dealing with — duplicity personified. Who knows if he's telling the truth? He may understand every language spoken in this neck of the woods, but is just looking for an excuse to don his battle suit. However, to be fair, he's been on his best behavior thus far."

"Well, we'll find out soon enough," Diviana remarked. "There's a lot of traffic in the system we're headed to, which means a lot of communications — messages flying back and forth. The bulk of them will probably be shielded, but plenty won't. Our comm equipment can pick those up, and then it's just a matter of seeing if our translators can do anything with them."

IGNOTUS

"That's true," Maker admitted, "but I prefer not having to come up with a plan on the fly if things don't go our way. I'd rather have some options on the table *now* — especially since the translator is only half the reason Skullcap wants his armor."

Surprise registered on everyone's face, and then Loyola asked, "So what's the other reason?"

"Basically, he needs it to track down the tech we want back," Maker replied.

IGNOTUS

Chapter 44

Maker's statement was met with stunned silence, and then Browing said, "You're going to have to explain that."

"Apparently, we've been operating under a false assumption," Maker replied. "Namely, that Skullcap was leading us directly to the missing tech."

"So that's not the case?" asked Chantrey.

"Not quite," Maker stated. "This system we're headed to is called H'rkzn." Maker paused, realizing he'd probably butchered the name (which he'd gotten from Skullcap), then went on. "What we're actually going there for is a Vacra tracking device. Once activated, it will lead us to the sub rosa tech, but Skullcap claims he needs his armor to interface with it."

"Hold up," Adames growled. "So what you're really saying is that Skullcap doesn't actually know where the stuff is that he promised us. Moreover, we have to add another leg to the trip and blindly follow him who-knows-where in order to get it, and hope he's not leading us into a trap."

Maker nodded. "Aside from the fact that Skullcap also wants to wear his armor the entire time, that pretty much sums it up."

Diviana shook her head in disbelief. "No offense, el-tee, but this isn't quite what we signed up for."

"She has a point," Snick added. "This is practically the blind leading the blind."

"You think I'm happy about this?" Maker retorted, speaking to no one in particular. "You don't think the word 'Abort' hasn't been constantly flitting through my brain, accompanied by alarm bells and

IGNOTUS

flashing lights? That's why we're having this discussion — to see if there's any way to continue going forward with this mission without walking into the lion's den."

No one said anything for a few seconds, and then Wayne cleared his throat.

"Ahem," the young Marine began. "I have a thought. It may not prevent us from walking into the lion's den, but it can certainly keep us from putting our head in his mouth."

IGNOTUS

Chapter 45

As with the listening devices, Wayne had come up with a feasible plan that, in this instance, actually needed very little modification. After getting the buy-in of everyone present, Maker dismissed him with orders to begin implementing his idea.

"Okay," Maker said, addressing the rest of those present, "assuming Wayne's idea works, it looks like this mission is going forward. That being the case, we should talk a little about what happens next."

"I would think that's pretty basic," Browing chimed in. "We go in, get this tracking device, and leave."

Maker nodded. "That's it in simple terms, but there are things to consider. But before I begin, I need to make it clear that the info being relayed comes courtesy of Skullcap, so who knows how much of it is reliable."

"Understood," said Chantrey. "Take it with a grain of salt."

"Exactly," Maker stated in agreement. "Now, first and foremost, the cruisers can't accompany us all the way into the star system. The ruling species won't allow it, no more than we'd allow alien battleships into the center of Gaian Space."

There were looks of concerns at this, but no one voiced an opinion or complaint.

"So only the *Nova* goes in," Adames summed up. "Then what?"

"We can get close," Maker noted, "but ultimately we'll have to take the *Nova*'s shuttle down to the planet's surface."

"What's the weather like?" asked Loyola.

IGNOTUS

"Temperate," Maker responded, "but those going down will wear adjustable-temperature bodysuits."

"Atmosphere?" queried Snick.

"Breathable, but not ideal," Maker stated. "Nose filters will probably come in handy."

"Locals?" Adames inquired.

"The species native to this region are called the H'rkzn'ka," Maker replied. "They're friendly, and mostly focus on business and trade. In fact, the entire planetary system is essentially a huge commerce center."

Browing seemed to reflect on this for a moment before asking, "And the planet we're interested in?"

"Home to hundreds of sentient species," Maker said, "most of whom live there in order to be close to the action in terms of business and investing."

"So it's an interstellar commercial hub," Browing concluded. "Much like the historic Wall Street back on Old Earth."

Maker nodded. "In essence, yes. And speaking of Earth things, it's worth noting that humans are virtually unknown here, so we may stick out."

"Good to know," Diviana acknowledged. "Anything else?"

"Yeah," Maker muttered a bit forlornly. "No firearms."

No one immediately spoke, although more than a few glances were exchanged, which indicated that Maker's last comment was less than popular.

"Uh, it seems to me that we tried this no-weapons approach before," Loyola finally said, "and it didn't work out in our favor."

"That was on a planet full of criminals," Maker reminded her, reflecting on the episode in question. "I

IGNOTUS

believe there was concern that we might be bounty hunters, among other things."

"And how is this different?" asked Snick.

"Because this time we'll be on a commercial planet," Maker suggested. "These are business folks. They're used to solving problems with the pen rather than the sword. Plus, there's a lot of wealth there, as you might imagine, and it cuts down on the criminal element to ban firearms. Doesn't mean there aren't any — just that they're illegal."

"Honestly, the more I hear, the less I like this entire thing," Adames chimed in. "Bearing that in mind, please tell me that you're about done with this briefing, because I don't think I can take any more."

Maker nodded. "That's about everything, except who's going down to the planet with me and Skullcap."

"I volunteer," Loyola declared, almost before Maker finished speaking.

"I appreciate that," Maker stated in response, "but I'm afraid I need you to stay on the *Nova*. I think the people going down with us will be Diviana and Fierce."

Maker's statement was met with a horde of frowns and befuddled expressions. Diviana, of course, was an obvious selection given her background in Intel and Special Ops. Fierce, on the other hand, was probably the last person anyone expected to be chosen for something like this.

"Wait a minute," Loyola said. "You reject me as a volunteer but you're conscripting *him*?" She hooked a thumb at Fierce. "Don't get me wrong — I love the guy — but he's a pussycat."

"Thanks, hon," Fierce intoned sarcastically.

IGNOTUS

Ignoring her beau, Loyola went on, saying, "You can't possibly think he's a better asset to have on hand if things go off the rails."

"First of all, despite their nonviolent nature, Augmen are far from useless in combat," Maker noted. "Fierce has proven that on multiple occasions. And as I just stated, we're going to a place where humans are unfamiliar, so no one is likely to know that he's a 'pussycat,' as you put it. Second, he's big and intimidating, and that will go a long way towards making up for the fact that we can't carry weapons. Finally — and most importantly — if someone gets hurt down there, no one's going to know how to treat them because, again, humans are unknown in this part of space. And let me tell you, there's no way I'm getting treated by some alien sawbones who doesn't know which end is up when he looks at me."

There was stony silence as Maker finished speaking, and then everyone burst into laughter.

IGNOTUS

Chapter 46

With the briefing complete, Maker dismissed everyone. As he should have expected, he was approached by a stern-faced Loyola immediately afterwards.

Waiting until everyone else left the conference room, she suddenly turned to Maker and uttered, "Okay, why? Why keep me from going planet-side? Because I'm pregnant?"

"Not exactly," Maker confessed. "There actually are rules about the duties that can be assigned to expectant mothers, but the truth of the matter is that you're a sniper and we're going to a place where firearms are banned."

"Like we haven't smuggled weapons into places before," she admonished. "Or bought them illegally when we had to."

"In case you forgot, our last illicit arms deal was a disaster," Maker stated, reminding Loyola of how they'd been double-crossed by their contact on that prior occasion. "Besides, this is the first time many of these races are going to encounter humans. The last thing we want to do is leave them with a negative impression of our species, such as the inability to obey simple rules."

"All right, I get that," Loyola conceded. "I just don't like the notion of people thinking I need special handling just because I'm having a baby. I mean, I'm not even showing yet."

"Well, nobody else knows, so I assume their attitudes toward you haven't changed. That being the case, if I jump on the bandwagon and continue treating

IGNOTUS

you like a completely expendable grunt, will that make you happy?"

"Very," Loyola assured him, grinning ear to ear.

****

Following his chat with Loyola, Maker went back to his cabin. Erlen practically met him at the door, rising onto his hind legs and playfully pushing Maker's chest with his front paws. At the same time, he let out a curious warbling sound.

"I know, and I'm sorry," Maker apologized.

In essence, Erlen had been cooped up in their quarters all day. Maker had pretty much confined him there, mostly because he didn't know what the Niotan would do with Skullcap on board. Although Erlen hadn't attacked the insectoid earlier, there was no guarantee that his forbearance in that regard would continue.

"All right, we'll go for a walk," Maker said. "However, the same rule applies: do *not* go after Skullcap." The Niotan made a sound of acquiescence, and a moment later they departed.

Since this was Erlen's idea, Maker pretty much let him take the lead and simply meandered along, lost in thought as they walked the *Nova*'s hallways. This mission had left a lot to be desired when he first volunteered; however, in a very short span of time, it had gone from simply bad to repugnant. Even though his team seemed willing to continue, he briefly wondered if he should just pull the plug and go home, despite the repercussions.

No, he ultimately said to himself. *We'll find a way to see this through, regardless of obstacles.*

IGNOTUS

Decision made, Maker suddenly realized that he and Erlen had come to a stop. He looked up to find that they had wandered into the observation lounge — a large, open area with an exterior glass wall that ran from one side of the room to the other. It was effectively a giant window, offering a breathtaking, panoramic view of the stars.

The room itself was designed for comfortably viewing the wonders of space, with numerous chairs and couches throughout, as well as a bar area which — at present — was devoid of alcohol.

When he and Erlen had first come across the lounge during their initial exploration of the ship, Maker had noted the place solely in terms of its functionality — what it was used for. This was his first opportunity to actually experience the room as intended, and he found himself so drawn by the view outside that he didn't even realize that there was someone else present.

"Fancy meeting you here," said a familiar voice.

Maker immediately turned in the direction of the sound, and saw Chantrey sitting on a nearby couch. (In fact, Erlen had joined her and had his head resting in her lap.)

"Oh, sorry," Maker muttered, then began walking towards her. "Didn't see you."

"So, you found my little hideaway," she said as Maker flopped down next to her, opposite Erlen.

"I kind of overlooked this place at first," Maker admitted, "but it's nice."

"I adore it. It's very peaceful and serene, so I like to come here and think."

"Agreed. I'm sure that once we have a little leisure time, more of my squad will find their way here."

IGNOTUS

"A few of them already have, but you guys have stayed pretty busy on this trip."

"True," Maker agreed with a nod, suddenly realizing just how true her statement was. For instance, at that very moment, Wayne was busy attacking the issue of Skullcap's armor, a couple of folks were on bridge duty, and those he'd tasked to go planet-side were probably gearing up for the shuttle ride.

In short, they — like himself — hadn't had much time to enjoy the splendors of the lounge. And with that thought, something new occurred to him.

Turning to Chantrey, he asked, "So, why are you here?"

"Huh?" she muttered in bewilderment. "Like I said, it's tranquil — a good place to think."

Maker shook his head. "No, I mean why are you on this mission? I understand my role and that of my team. I also get why Browing's here. But you…you're an anomaly."

She gave him a coquettish look. "Maybe I'm just here to keep you relaxed."

"Come on — be serious," he implored. "You're not qualified to take on any of the military duties of this mission. You've got no standing with the diplomatic component. You obviously don't need to be here to report on me, since Browing can do that. Moreover, despite anything you were told, any report you submit on me is going to be deemed unreliable because of our relationship. So again, bearing all that in mind, why are you here?"

Chantrey merely stared at him for a moment, then let out a deep sigh. "I can tell you — or rather, take a guess, since no one explicitly told *me* — but you aren't going to like it."

"That's a given."

"Fine," she remarked soberly. "I'm here to keep you under control."

Maker frowned. "What does that mean? Do you have some kind of authority that I'm unaware of?"

"No, not *that* kind of control. Simply put, my presence here is supposed to prevent you from doing anything radical."

"Your presence?" Maker intoned, baffled. And then he understood. "Of course. Because we're in a relationship, I'm unlikely to do anything that will put you — and by extension, the mission — in jeopardy."

"That's the gist of it," Chantrey confirmed. "And I know what you're thinking — that our relationship is once again warping everything, but—"

"No," Maker interjected, adamantly shaking his head. "That's not what I'm thinking in the slightest. I'm actually wondering how they knew you'd go along with it."

Chantrey looked at him in confusion. "What do you mean?"

"Only that your puppet masters are using you as a tool, which doesn't seem to be something you'd normally allow. Somehow, though, they knew you wouldn't object."

"No," Chantrey suddenly hissed fiercely. "No way. I know what you're suggesting, and it's not true. It just isn't."

"But I think you already know that it *is*," Maker insisted. "They've got someone watching *you* now, predicting *your* behavior. Sadly, you've gone from being lead scientist to being a rat in the maze."

IGNOTUS

Chapter 47

Chantrey left almost immediately after Maker's "rat maze" comment, stating a desire to look through some paperwork. Settling for a kiss before she left, Maker imagined she'd spend the next few hours (if not longer) reviewing files in order to determine how likely his assessment was that she was now under the microscope as well.

After her departure, he and Erlen had the lounge to themselves, and Maker spent a little time simply staring out at the stars. He had to agree with Chantrey: it actually was rather relaxing to just sit there with his thoughts. The view was indeed magnificent — the type of thing that everyone should get a chance to enjoy at least once in their life.

They stayed there for maybe half an hour, at which point Maker started feeling a little drowsy. Thinking there was probably enough time for a quick catnap, he and Erlen headed back to their room. Once there, he went straight to the bedroom and stretched out on the bed. He was asleep in less than a minute.

****

Maker found himself roused by an odd buzzing noise. It took him a moment to place it, and then realized what it was: the *Nova*'s bridge crew trying to reach him on his p-comp. He immediately came wide awake.

Tapping a button on his p-comp, he announced, "This is Maker."

IGNOTUS

"About time," grumbled Adames, who was currently in command of the bridge. "I thought I was going to have to send out a search party."

"Not this time," Maker assured him. "What's happening?"

"We're getting pretty close to that star system. There's a lot of traffic up ahead, but it's a sure bet someone's going to notice pretty soon that there's a new kid in the neighborhood."

"All right, keep us out of hailing distance for now, and pass the word to the cruisers as well."

"Roger that," Adames stated, then disconnected.

Wasting no time, Maker promptly reached out to Wayne, who answered almost immediately.

"How's it coming?" Maker asked.

"Just about done," Wayne responded. "It was actually a lot easier than I thought."

"Good to hear," Maker stated. "Finish up and then meet me outside Skullcap's cabin."

"Will do."

"You know what?" Maker intoned, suddenly struck with an inspired thought. "Belay that order. Meet me in the observation lounge instead."

"Roger that," Wayne replied.

IGNOTUS

Chapter 48

"What are we doing here?" asked Skullcap.

"I just thought you'd enjoy a change of scenery," Maker replied. "If it's a problem, you can go back to your cabin. It makes no difference to me."

The two of them were currently in the observation lounge. It was during his conversation with Wayne that Maker had gotten the idea of letting Skullcap stretch his legs. (After all, even convicts in solitary confinement get time out of their cells for things like exercise.) Moreover, bearing in mind the tranquil atmosphere of the place, he had decided to take their guest to the observation lounge.

Maker had chosen to combine this little excursion with Skullcap's mealtime. Thus, he currently held two of the squeeze tubes in one hand, and — as usual — his sidearm in the other. (He had also been careful to walk to the rear of Skullcap as they went through the *Nova*, in case the insectoid tried anything.)

"Well, what's it going to be?" Maker asked. "You prefer to go back to your quarters?"

"No," Skullcap answered almost immediately. "This is...refreshing. Thank you."

"No problem," Maker muttered noncommittally. "Oh yeah — here you go."

Maker tossed the squeeze tubes to the Vacran, who deftly caught them.

"My thanks again," the insectoid said, to which Maker grumbled an unintelligible response.

Opening up one of the squeeze tubes, Skullcap put it up to his mouth while walking forward toward the

IGNOTUS

glass wall. Maker simply stood back and watched as the Vacran fed in silence and took in the view.

****

Skullcap had just finished the second squeeze tube and tossed it into a nearby waste receptacle when Wayne entered the room. The young Marine was carrying a circular device about the size of his palm, with a number of wires trailing from it and numerous diodes on its surface. The Vacran glanced at Wayne (who had headed straight to Maker), and then made a noise akin to a snort. He then began stalking towards the two men with a determined stride.

"Easy," Maker stressed to Skullcap, holding up his free hand, palm outward, while getting a firm grip on his sidearm with the other.

"What have you done?" Skullcap demanded.

"Wayne here simply excised the translator from your armor," Maker explained. "Now you don't have to slog around in that uncomfortable hunk of metal."

"You destroyed my armor?" the insectoid asked.

"Oh, no," Wayne assured him. "That wasn't necessary."

He stepped forward and gingerly handed the translator to Skullcap, while Maker instinctively slid his forefinger onto the trigger of his weapon.

"I did have to disassemble it to a certain extent," Wayne admitted as he stepped back, "but I can put it all back together, no problem."

Skullcap made a sound that Maker interpreted as skepticism, but didn't verbalize a response as he examined the translator.

IGNOTUS

After perhaps thirty seconds, he looked up and said, "It appears to be undamaged and functional. It will serve. For now."

Maker turned to Wayne. "Good job on that."

"Thanks, el-tee," Wayne said with a smile.

"And our other project?" Maker asked.

"It'll be ready shortly," Wayne promised.

With that, Maker dismissed the young man and turned his full attention back to Skullcap.

"Happy now?" Maker queried.

Skullcap made a gesture that Maker interpreted as a shrug. "As I mentioned, it will serve."

"I'm glad our efforts meet with your approval."

"Am I to assume that you will act in similar fashion — further dismantling my armor — regarding the tracking interface?"

Maker gave him a wink. "As I noted before, you're a quick study."

Skullcap let out a sound that might have been a sigh of frustration.

"Very well," the Vacra intoned. "I assume that by giving me the translator now, we are close to H'rkzn?"

Maker nodded. "We'll be in hailing range shortly. Time to earn your keep."

IGNOTUS

Chapter 49

Maker stayed with Skullcap in the observation lounge for perhaps another quarter-hour, at which point Adames reached out to let him know that they were within hailing distance. Maker called their convoy to a halt and then hustled to the bridge with their guest. Upon arriving, he noted that almost everyone was present; the only absentees were Fierce, Diviana, and Planck. (The first two were probably still making preparations to join Maker planet-side, while everyone agreed that it was probably a good idea for Planck to avoid his former captor for the nonce.) Things happened fairly quickly after that.

Within minutes, they were able to make contact with an appropriate authority in the H'rkzn system — an individual who, in Maker's opinion, looked like a lengthy coil of fiber-optic cable on the bridge monitor. Needless to say, it was a species he had never seen or heard of before, and to his naked ear its language sounded like a series of owl-like hoots. (Frankly speaking, it sounded like the *same* hoot repeated over and over again.)

Skullcap, conversing with the wiry individual in Vacran, didn't seem to have any trouble with the translator. The insectoid also seemed incredibly poised, despite the fact that both Adames and Maker held their respective sidearms loosely in their hands near him. Or maybe he'd simply grown accustomed to it. Regardless, after a few minutes of conversation, the Vacran's conference with the H'rkzn official ended and the monitor went dark.

IGNOTUS

"Well?" asked Maker, getting the insectoid's attention.

"It is essentially as I told you before," Skullcap replied. "Your battle cruisers can go no closer. We can direct this vessel to an in-system docking station and from there take a shuttle — our own or one of theirs — to the fifth planet, which is where the tracker is located. Finally, he stated that the ban against firearms is still in effect. That said, you are not precluded from bringing other forms of personal protection."

"How kind of him," Maker remarked sarcastically, then turned to Adames. "Can you escort the ambassador back to his quarters? I need to take care of a few things."

Adames nodded and, seconds later, he and Skullcap were off the bridge.

Almost bursting with excitement, Wayne looked expectantly at Maker.

"Well?" the young man asked eagerly.

"Worked like a charm," Maker said, taking a small hearing device out of his ear. "I could understand everything they said."

"Awesome!" Wayne announced with a grin. "Although in truth, it really wasn't that hard to do. Basically, I just cloned Skullcap's translator, which is geared to convert hundreds of languages — including our own, but most of which we've never encountered — into Vacran. I then tweaked some of the settings and software so that it renders the final interpretation not as Vacran, but as Terran."

"Well, you did great," Maker acknowledged, causing the young man to blush slightly. "And I'm happy to report that Skullcap essentially relayed everything that was discussed truthfully."

IGNOTUS

In light of past experience, that part had actually been something of a surprise. However, it was always possible that the Vacran had used code words or phrases that merely sounded innocuous, so Maker reminded himself to remain on guard.

"Anyway," Maker continued, "great job again on this, Wayne. Now I just need you to make one for everybody, starting with Fierce and Diviana."

"I'm way ahead of you, el-tee," Wayne replied with a grin.

IGNOTUS

Chapter 50

Following the instructions they were given, the *Nova* went forward to the designated docking station, leaving the battle cruisers behind. It wasn't ideal, but Maker took comfort in the fact that this practice was standard in that there were numerous battleships (or rather, alien ships with what appeared to be battleship designs) keeping a healthy distance from the H'rkzn region.

He thought it unusual that those in charge seemingly relied on the honor system in this regard — until they passed a H'rkzn destroyer that was the size of a small moon. The *Nova*'s scanners actually detected several of them nearby, making it plainly obvious why the boundary for visiting gunships was strictly observed. That said, it was understood that almost all ships — even small ones — would have *some* degree of weaponry, so vessels like the *Nova* were allowed to come closer than their fellows.

Once they were docked and ready to depart, Maker found himself facing a decision he had been avoiding up until then: whether to let Erlen go with them. Under normal circumstances, the Niotan accompanied him everywhere, but not solely because Maker was responsible for him; it also partly related to Erlen's nature.

Because the Niotan could reproduce anything he tasted, gaining new experiences — that is, coming into literal contact with the unfamiliar — was an essential part of his growth and development. As they were about to visit a planet and encounter species previously unknown,

IGNOTUS

it was an unprecedented opportunity for Erlen, and Maker didn't want to deny him that.

At the same time, however, Skullcap was going to be with them. More importantly, it had actually been Erlen who had ripped off the insectoid's original arm — the one which had grown back deformed. There was no way Skullcap had forgotten about that. (Also, Maker still didn't completely buy into the story that the Vacra no longer wanted the Niotan.)

In the end, he felt that Erlen's needs outweighed the risks. So, after warning him to stay close at all times and forbidding him to attack Skullcap (which the Niotan didn't seemed inclined to do anyway), Maker decided to take Erlen along.

In addition, Maker picked up a second unexpected passenger in the form of Browing, who hunted him down shortly before they were set to leave.

"This is still officially a diplomatic mission," Browing said. "As the diplomat for our side, I should go with you — especially if we're going to encounter previously unknown races."

Surprising himself, Maker found that he was indifferent to the request.

"Suit yourself," he replied with a shrug.

"Really?" Browing muttered in surprise. "I half expected you to fight me on this."

"No, I just wished you'd told me earlier. I don't know that we'll have time to cobble together a translator for you."

"That's okay," Browing assured him. "It's just important for me to be there. I've been chasing this stuff — the sub rosa tech — for a while now, so the thought of being on the sidelines for any part of its recovery is galling to me."

"I get it," Maker said. "Just get to the shuttle as soon as you can. We're leaving asap."

IGNOTUS

Chapter 51

Diviana served as pilot on the shuttle ride down to the planet, which thankfully occurred without incident. Maker had made it a point to keep Skullcap and Erlen as far apart as possible inside the craft, but the latter barely paid any attention to the former. The reverse, however, was far from true, as Skullcap always seemed to be watching the Niotan. That said, the insectoid remained on his best behavior and did nothing to make a nuisance of himself.

Ultimately, they landed at a large and exceptionally busy spaceport. It was at that juncture, while they were being scanned for firearms, that they ran into their first hiccup.

With Skullcap as part of their group, Maker had insisted that every member of his team bring a weapon. As firearms were verboten, almost everyone chose to bring a blade of some sort. (Fierce, for instance, although adverse to violence and weapons, was able to justify bringing a scalpel as part of a medical kit.) Maker himself chose a vibro-blade.

As expected, everyone passed the weapons scan without issue — until it was Erlen's turn. In essence, although it was pretty clear that he wasn't carrying any weapons on his person, the scanners couldn't penetrate his hide. Thus, there was no way to confirm that he wasn't carrying a ticking bomb inside him, and it was starting to appear as though he wouldn't be allowed to stay on the planet.

Maker and his companions stood patiently to the side while a group of the fiber-cable people calmly

IGNOTUS

discussed what action they should take. Surprisingly, it was Skullcap who came to the rescue.

Stepping over to the wiry group, he declared in his native tongue, "I am the Vacra K'nsl." At this announcement (which Maker interpreted as some type of title), those he had addressed suddenly became incredibly attentive, and the one who appeared most senior inclined his head slightly.

"I personally vouch for the individual you are concerned with," Skullcap continued, "and will accept any and all liability for his actions while on this planet."

That seemed to be good enough for the fiber-optic group. They gave Erlen a pass in terms of the weapons check, and a few minutes later Maker and his team were outside the spaceport, where they suddenly found themselves surrounded by throngs of people (albeit none of them were human).

"Okay," Maker intoned, addressing Skullcap. "Where to?"

"Our destination is not far," the Vacran answered. "We can walk there, if you have no objection."

"None," Maker declared.

"Excellent," the insectoid said. "Please follow me."

He turned and began walking away, with Fierce and Browing on his heels. Maker and Erlen, however, hung back for a moment, along with Diviana.

"You got this?" Maker asked.

"Of course," she replied with a smile. "And my p-comp is synced to yours, so I'll be able to find you when I'm done."

Considering the conversation over, she was about to go when Maker stopped her.

IGNOTUS

"Hold up," he said, seeming to come to a decision. Squatting down, he reached towards Erlen's mouth. The Niotan let out a harsh, guttural cough and spat something into Maker's hand. He stood up and surreptitiously handed the item to Diviana. Although it was covered with an odd fluid, she immediately took and inconspicuously pocketed the object after recognizing what it was: a small firearm.

"Thanks," Diviana said, and then walked away.

As she faded into the crowd, Maker realized that his absence, so to speak, had been noted. Skullcap, Browing, and Fierce — apparently having realized that their party had been chopped in half — had ceased walking and turned around in order to find out what had happened.

Maker quickly moved forward to join them, at which point Skullcap asked, "Where is the female going?"

"Christmas shopping," Maker quipped. "Now let's get moving."

IGNOTUS

Chapter 52

It took them about thirty minutes to reach the place that Skullcap said contained the tracking device. Under normal circumstances, it probably would have taken half the time, but Erlen kept wandering off to "sample" various items; from the clothing individuals were wearing to gewgaws being hawked by street vendors, he tasted everything — either through the papillae in his paws or just licking it outright. (Maker found himself issuing more than one apology to various persons who unexpectedly found a rough tongue or padded paw rubbing against them, although he doubted that anyone understood him.) It also didn't help that the area where they found themselves essentially resembled a giant, open-air bazaar, with representatives from scores of races scurrying about in multitudes. Fortunately, none of their companions complained about the delay incurred by the Niotan's antics.

Eventually they reached their destination, which turned out to be a large building that rose several hundred stories into the air. The exterior wall of the first floor was composed entirely of glass, providing an unobstructed view of the lobby. Inside, Maker saw members of numerous races — all unfamiliar to him — engaged in discourse and seemingly conducting business of one sort or another.

"Come," Skullcap practically demanded, heading toward what appeared to be the building entrance.

Once inside, the insectoid made a beeline for one of several glass tubes in the middle of the lobby. As they drew closer, Maker saw that the bottom of the tube, up to a height of about five feet, was encased in some kind of

IGNOTUS

metallic cylinder that had numerous buttons on it. In addition, the tube — which was about two feet in diameter and went from the floor to the ceiling — appeared to be full of grayish smoke.

As Maker halfway expected, Skullcap stepped forward and pushed one of the buttons on the cylinder. Something akin to the lid of a trash receptacle popped open at the top of the cylinder and Skullcap spat into it. There was silence for a few moments, and Maker was about to ask what they were waiting for when someone spoke.

"We welcome the Vacra K'nsl," said an eerie, disembodied voice that seemed to come from the tube. "How may we serve you?"

"I have property I wish to retrieve," Skullcap stated.

"Certainly," said the voice. As it spoke, Maker noticed various colored lights twinkling within the grayish smoke.

No, not just twinkling, he thought, *but twinkling in conjunction with its speech.*

Maker leaned towards Fierce and whispered, "Have you ever seen or heard of anything like that?"

"No," replied the Augman in a hushed tone, shaking his head. "As weird as it seems, the smog in that tube is somehow alive."

Suddenly, a small, rectangular card extended from a slot on the cylinder that Maker hadn't noticed earlier.

"Here is your pass," said the smoke. "You may proceed to the repository."

"Many thanks," Skullcap replied as he took the card.

IGNOTUS

Suddenly anxious (and wondering what the Vacran was up to), Maker was about to say something when Skullcap spoke again.

"I will also need passes for my companions," he stated, gesturing towards Maker, Browing, and Fierce.

"That is prohibited," the smoke replied. "Only patrons may enter the repository."

"They guard my person," Skullcap explained. "I can go nowhere without them."

"I'm afraid there are no exceptions," explained the smoke. "You must proceed alone or not at all."

Skullcap made some kind of smacking noise that Maker assumed was an indication of disapproval. "If I may not retrieve it myself, then I must insist that you fetch my property."

"Such is not allowed," stated the smoke. "If you were to find it damaged or impaired in some way after delivery, we would be accountable."

"I will absolve you of all potential liability," the insectoid declared.

"That is most kind of you and not unexpected, but we still cannot comply."

Suddenly indignant, Skullcap hissed, "You would deny the Vacra K'nsl? Despite a personal guarantee of absolution?"

There was no immediate reply from the smoke in the tube, which was odd, as the lights inside it were twinkling almost spasmodically. Maker got the impression that it was conversing with someone — presumably a superior.

After what seemed like forever, but was probably no more than thirty seconds, the smoke said, "Your

IGNOTUS

request is most irregular, but we will comply. Please make yourself comfortable and we will deliver your property."

"Many thanks," Skullcap grumbled in a somewhat exasperated tone. Turning to face his three companions, he said, "Apparently we will have to wait for the tracker to be delivered to us."

With that, he stepped away from the tube of sentient smoke.

IGNOTUS

Chapter 53

They ended up taking positions by one of the glass window-walls. Skullcap was at one end of their troop, with Maker next to him. In the middle was Browing and then Fierce, with Erlen on the end next to the Augman. (Typically, Maker would have had the Niotan next to him, but again, he didn't want him in close proximity to Skullcap.)

"So," Maker said to the insectoid, "I thought I heard you use a certain term several times today: the Vacra Counsel?"

"You have a good ear," Skullcap stated, surprising Maker with the compliment. "The Vacra K'nsl," he continued, correcting Maker's pronunciation, "is a title. You would equate it to nobility or gentry."

"So you're a Vacran noble?"

"We do not express it as such, and it is actually a station of appointment rather than birth."

"Ahhh," Maker droned. "You were *selected* for that particular position."

"Yes."

"But it obviously has some meaning to outside species as well."

"In this particular region of space, it means I speak for Vacra."

Maker frowned. "You mean the Vacra as a race? All of them?"

"Yes," Skullcap said flatly.

Maker felt a long series of questions starting to form in his brain, but before he could ask any of them, the ground suddenly shook as a violent tremor passed through it. At the same time, a familiar booming sound reached his ears, which he recognized immediately.

"What the hell?" muttered Browing as their entire group turned almost in unison towards the exterior glass wall.

"Explosion," Maker announced. "Minor — two, maybe three blocks away."

The sound had come from somewhere outside, and he swiftly scanned the area, ignoring the myriad beings around them making sounds he interpreted as gasps of fright and surprise. At the same time, he kept an eye on Skullcap, mindful of the fact that this could be some kind of diversion or trap.

The insectoid, however, seemed as surprised as everyone else. He, like the others in their group, was staring outside, trying to pinpoint the source of the explosion.

After a moment, Maker saw it.

"There," he declared, pointing to area where a dark column of smoke was billowing up between two high-rises.

"I should go see if anyone needs help," Fierce said.

"Negatory," Maker stated in response.

Fierce stared at him for a moment as if he hadn't heard him, then muttered, "Excuse me?"

"Hold your position," Maker ordered. "We're here for a specific purpose, which is to get this tracking device, and then we leave."

Fierce glanced again in the direction of the column of smoke and then back at Maker. "I have to go, Lieutenant. My Hippocratic Oath—"

IGNOTUS

"Applies only to human beings," Maker interjected, cutting him off. "Look around, Doctor. Have you seen a single race or species that you recognize here? Or know how to treat? For all we know, that column of smoke is no different than the one our Vacra friend spoke to a few minutes ago in the tube. If it *is* someone in need of medical attention, you're more likely to harm than help them. I know it goes against your training and your oath, but you need to stand down."

Fierce looked as though he had more to say, but instead simply crossed his arms defiantly. He clearly didn't care for Maker's orders, but at the same time seemed to acknowledge his commanding officer's logic.

"Pardon," said a slightly high voice, sounding unexpectedly close behind them.

Maker spun to his rear (as did everyone else), and found himself staring at what appeared to be a large assortment of multi-colored plastic balls. They varied in size from roughly three to six inches in diameter, and collectively rose to a height of about four feet.

The cluster of balls actually stood closest to Skullcap, and as Maker watched, it extended limbs toward the insectoid that appeared to be little more than triangular-shaped flags made of cloth. Gripped in the ends of those limbs was an object that looked like a metallic pyramid with frosted glass in the shape of a rope coiled around it from top to bottom.

"Your property," said the ball-cluster to Skullcap, presenting the pyramid to the Vacran.

Maker quickly reached out and lifted the pyramid from the ball-being, saying, "I'll take that." No way was he letting Skullcap get his hands on something that, for all he knew, might be a weapon.

IGNOTUS

As Maker tucked the pyramid securely under one arm, the ball-cluster emitted something akin to a squeaking sound, then began to tremble all over in an odd fashion, as if it were experiencing its own personal earthquake.

"All is fine," Skullcap stressed to the ball-being. "My companion has merely offered to carry the item for me."

The balls suddenly ceased their trembling. A moment later, it said, "Thank you for clarifying. Does this conclude your business?"

"It does," the insectoid confirmed. Turning to his human companions, he simply stated, "Come." He then headed towards the exit.

With little choice, Maker and the others quickly followed.

Once outside, they began going back the way they'd come, essentially retracing their steps. They also moved in the same formation as they had previously, with Skullcap walking point, followed by Browing and Fierce, while Erlen and Maker brought up the rear. It was a configuration that Maker felt offered the most protection: if the insectoid tried anything, the Augman's reflexes and strength should be enough to offset any hazards, and Maker himself would deal with any threats from the rear. That said, there were so many people around them (and in such close proximity), that warding off an attack would probably prove difficult.

They had only been walking a few moments, however, when Maker sensed a commotion up ahead of them. Almost immediately, he identified the issue: someone hurriedly making their way through the crowd, forcefully pushing and shoving aside anyone in their path.

IGNOTUS

To his dismay, he suddenly realized a few seconds later that the individual causing the furor was Diviana.

IGNOTUS

Chapter 54

Diviana spied Maker at roughly the same time he saw her and made a beeline for him, striding past the others in their group without so much as a word.

"We gotta go," she announced without preamble once she was in front of him, breathing hard and looking disheveled.

"What is it?" Maker asked.

"I'll tell you on the shuttle," Diviana said, glancing around in a harried manner. "Also, you need to get rid of *this*."

Her last statement was made in a barely-audible whisper. At the same time, without looking down, she stealthily shoved something into Maker's free hand, which he immediately recognized solely by its feel and shape: the gun he'd given her earlier. Without being told, Erlen appeared to inconspicuously lick the hand in question, and when he drew back, the gun had vanished.

"All right, let's keep moving," Maker said.

As might be expected, Skullcap, Browing, and Fierce had all stopped and turned as Diviana went by them. Although he wasn't sure how much they'd heard, Maker was certain that they hadn't seen the gun, which was his main concern. If they *had* seen it, however, no one mentioned it. Instead, they heeded his instructions to get moving, and in seconds they were once again marching towards the spaceport.

Diviana fell into step next to Maker, but as they walked, she kept glancing around, almost as if she had a nervous condition.

"What's with you?" Maker finally muttered under his breath. "Did you go off and get high or something?"

IGNOTUS

"Funny," she noted sarcastically. "No, I just had a little incident."

"Incident?" Maker repeated. "What does that mean?"

"It's kind of complicated," she said, then glanced at the column of black smoke that Maker and the others had noticed earlier.

He followed her gaze, and then understanding dawned on him.

"No," he muttered, shaking his head. "Tell me you didn't cause that explosion."

Diviana winced slightly. "As I said, it's complicated."

Frowning, Maker was about to order her to expound when he realized that their group had come to a halt. Those ahead had stopped so quickly, in fact, that he almost bumped into Browing. He was about to ask what the issue was when someone shouted.

"Return my property!" bellowed a stern voice from somewhere ahead of them.

Maker looked towards where the voice had seemingly originated, but couldn't immediately identify the speaker. Clarity, however, came swiftly as the crowd around them seemed to disperse in record fashion, as if someone had thrown a grenade in their midst.

Within seconds, Maker's group found itself with a wide expanse of circular space around it — a startling contrast to the throngs that had hemmed them in just moments earlier.

"Return my property!" the voice yelled again, and this time Maker saw the speaker: a man-sized creature that seemed to be a cross between a millipede and a grizzly bear, standing perhaps thirty feet ahead of them. It

IGNOTUS

was big and hairy, with a maw full of teeth and a multitude of legs on both sides of its body.

Correction, Maker thought. *There's a multitude of legs on the* left *side of its body.*

On the right side of the grizzly-pede (as Maker thought of it), there was an appreciable gap between two of the limbs on the thing's upper body. More to the point, Maker noted five stumps near the creature's body wall that seemed to be oozing black blood. Obviously, the grizzly-pede had endured some kind of recent trauma.

"Return what is mine!" it bellowed, and at this juncture, Maker noted that it was not alone. There were at least three more of the grizzly-pedes around them — one at the rear and one on each side. They were surrounded.

Furious, Maker leaned forward and growled at Skullcap, saying, "I thought you said this alleged tracker belonged to *you*!"

"It does," the Vacran muttered over his shoulder. "Moreover, the tracker doesn't appear to be what he's interested in."

Confused, Maker glanced at the grizzly-pede and realized that Skullcap was right. It wasn't looking at Maker or the tracker; it was glowering at Diviana.

"Did you steal something from them?" Maker hissed softly at her.

"No!" she shot back in a fervent whisper.

"Then what's he talking about?" Maker asked as the lead grizzly-pede once again demanded its property.

As if reading Maker's mind, Skullcap stepped forward.

"Honorable Xnjda," the insectoid began. "We are newly arrived and have but one thing on our persons that we did not arrive with: a possession retrieved from the repository, which — as you surely know — is only released to the true owner. Thus, we are confused. What is this property of yours we are purported to have?"

"That!" the grizzly-pede insisted, pointing directly at Diviana.

IGNOTUS

Chapter 55

There was stunned silence for a moment (aside from Erlen softly growling), and then Maker practically shouted, "What?"

"The female is mine," the grizzly-pede continued. "She was a *fracg'l* in my household before running away two weeks ago."

"*Fracg'l?*" Browing repeated in a hushed tone to Skullcap, seeming to get the pronunciation correct.

"A pet," the Vacran explained.

"Are you kidding?" Maker uttered.

"Unfortunately, no," Skullcap replied, then turned his attention back to the grizzly-pede. "Great Xnjda—"

"Kpntel," it interjected. "You may address me as Kpntel."

"Thank you, great Kpntel," Skullcap said. "With all due respect, I think you must be mistaken. This female and her male counterparts are my traveling companions. They are neither pets nor property."

"Then I would counter that they must not have journeyed with you for long," Kpntel stated, "for she only recently ran off."

"I appreciate your position," Skullcap retorted, "but — while it distresses me to do so — I must ask if you have proof of ownership?"

Kpntel nodded at one of his fellows standing to the side of Maker's group, who stepped forward and pointed some type of device in their direction. Maker's initial fear that it was a weapon vanished as the object suddenly broadcast a broad beam of bright light that immediately crystallized into an image.

Hologram projector, Maker realized.

IGNOTUS

The image it showed was of a young woman — obviously human — dressed in drab clothing and sitting at the feet of Kpntel. (At least, Maker presumed it was Kpntel in the hologram, but truth be told he wasn't sure he could tell one member of the species from another.) The grizzly-pede was stroking the woman's hair, essentially petting her.

Maker felt himself growing angry as he watched the scene. The notion of human beings as pets was something he hadn't really considered before, and the thought of it disgusted him.

"That's not Diviana," Browing whispered to Skullcap. "They look nothing alike."

It was indeed a true statement. They both had dark hair, but that was about the extent to which Diviana and the woman in the hologram were similar. For instance, whereas Diviana was exotically beautiful, the woman being shown was incredibly plain.

"You need to understand," Skullcap explained. "To most other species, all humans look alike."

Maker was rather taken aback by this, but didn't have time to comment as Kpntel started speaking.

"As you can see," the grizzly-pede said, pointing to the hologram, "the female is a *fracg'l* that belongs to me. Moreover, they are rare creatures, so it is unlikely that this one" — he gestured towards Diviana — "is not the one I owned. Moreover, she is half of a breeding pair, whose offspring command enormous prices."

Maker's eyes went wide at Kpntel's last statement; it was all he could do not to have Erlen cough up the gun again so he could shoot the grizzly-pede dead. More to the point, it was looking like things might head in that direction anyway, as some of Kpntel's cohorts were now

IGNOTUS

holding daggers of some sort, and Maker — still holding the tracker in one hand — didn't fancy getting into a knife-fight with someone who could wield ten blades at once.

"I'm afraid you are once again mistaken," Skullcap said to Kpntel. "Before descending to this planet, I was on a ship full of this species, so their rarity is a thing that is debatable."

"A ship of them?" Kpntel muttered almost to himself, then glanced up at the sky.

"Yes," the insectoid stressed. "I travel with them at present as a guest on their vessel."

"Then they have duped you," the grizzly-pede said, "because they do not have the innate intelligence to operate a spacefaring vessel. That said, they are excellent at mimicking the behavior of more advanced species, and can pantomime not only languages, but skills such as piloting."

"Wait a minute," muttered Diviana to no one in particular. "Is he basically just calling us glorified parrots?"

Ignoring her, Skullcap addressed the grizzly-pede, saying, "Your words carry weight, but I would be remiss if I did not—"

"Enough!" roared Kpntel. "I tire of this banter. I will take my property now, and I would advise any who hold their lives dear not to interfere."

As if on cue, the grizzly-pedes around them began closing in, each carrying at least a half-dozen blades. Even worse, there were at least ten of them, as more had arrived to support Kpntel while Skullcap had been conversing with him.

IGNOTUS

Almost on instinct, Maker's group — including the Vacran — reconfigured itself into a small circle, with their backs to each other, at the same time pulling out their own weapons. Knowing that they needed an advantage, Maker was about to put his hand towards Erlen's mouth when suddenly the Niotan, who had stayed near him but outside their circle, let out a deafening roar.

It wasn't the loudest sound Maker had ever heard from Erlen, but it reverberated in a way that made it appear to last longer (and therefore seem more sonorous) than it actually was. More importantly, it seemed to have a chilling effect on just about everyone except Maker, causing Kpntel's cohorts to cease their advance.

While everyone was still frozen, Erlen dashed towards a metallic pole located a few feet away. It was about ten yards in height, perhaps a foot in diameter, and — in Maker's opinion — resembled a streetlight to some extent. The Niotan swiped at the base of the pole with his paw several times in rapid succession, an action that was accompanied by a tinny, high-pitched ping in each instance.

At first, nothing seemed to happen. After a few seconds, however, an ominous metallic groan began to emit from the pole. As Maker watched, the metal post began to lean forward like an oversized flower bending in the breeze. However, with the metallic groaning escalating in volume, it only took a moment for him to recognize that the pole was actually falling. (He also understood what had happened: Erlen, in fury, had sliced through the metal post with his claws.)

In addition, although he'd later wonder if Erlen had done it on purpose, Maker realized that the pole was falling directly towards Kpntel. More to the point, the

IGNOTUS

grizzly-pede still appeared frozen by Erlen's roar and simply stood there, staring, as the metal pole fell in his direction.

However, just before the pole struck Kpntel (and it surely would have bashed his brains out), it stopped. Amazingly, Fierce had stepped in and caught it, and now held the post (which must have been incredibly heavy) above his head like a powerlifter hoisting weights. And then he unexpectedly, but easily, bent the pole in half with no more effort than Maker would use to fold a piece of paper. When finished, Fierce flung the reshaped piece of metal to the ground near Kpntel's feet.

IGNOTUS

Chapter 56

Maker couldn't really read his expression, but it seemed to him that the grizzly-pede was dumbfounded. Kpntel's eyes seemed to dart randomly back and forth between Erlen, Fierce, and the bent metal post. At the same time, his mouth seemed to work but no sound issued forth. His fellows, meanwhile, seemed to be waiting for some kind of direction with respect to what to do next.

"What's happening?" Maker finally whispered to Skullcap. "Is he in shock or something?"

"At a guess," the Vacran replied, "I'd assume that the actions of the Senu Lia and your subordinate have caused Kpntel to reassess the strength of his position."

"So as far as he knows, all of us can bend steel with our bare hands," Browing surmised. "He's worried that he's bitten off more than he can chew."

"In essence, yes," Skullcap confirmed. "Presumably he is reflecting on some manner of resolving the current conflict without losing face."

"Hmmm," Browing droned. "Maybe I can help."

With that, Browing took a few steps toward the grizzly-pede leader, while Maker and the others quickly closed the gap in their circle caused by his departure.

"Great Kpntel," Browing began, "allow me to apologize for the distress we have caused you and offer our sympathies for the loss of your property. Although our companion is not the female you seek, our preference is to resolve this encounter without either violence or incurring your wrath. To that end, I would propose that we offer you recompense for your, uh, losses." He glanced momentarily at the grizzly-pede's missing limbs. "Is there a price you will accept?"

Kpntel seemed to contemplate for a moment, then said, "Considering the rarity of my *fracg'l* — not to mention my injuries — I had not pondered the notion of a price."

"Then we would be pleased if you would do so," Browing stated. "Although we must continue on our journey, our colleague, the Vacra K'nsl" — he gestured towards Skullcap — "will vouch for payment."

"The Vacra K'nsl?" the grizzly-pede repeated, looking at Skullcap. "You are he?"

"I am," Skullcap confirmed. "I hereby confirm my comrade's statements, and will provide you with a point of contact so that we may converse once you have settled on an asking price."

Kpntel seem to consider the proposal for a moment, his eyes shifting between Browing and Skullcap as he contemplated the matter. Maker, quite certain that they were still going to have to fight for their lives, instinctively shifted his weight to the balls of his feet as they waited for the grizzly-pede to make a decision.

Apparently sensing that Kpntel needed an extra incentive to arrive at the right decision, Erlen coughed and then spat a bluish-green compound in the direction of the grizzly-pede. It landed on the pole Fierce had bent, and a moment later the air was filled with an angry hissing as the sputum began to dissolve the metal, emitting an ominous gray vapor in the process.

Kpntel's eyes went wide for a moment as he watched the metal post being eaten away. He then let out something like a sigh and stated, "So be it. I accept your offer."

IGNOTUS

Chapter 57

With their offer accepted by Kpntel, Maker's group hustled back to the spaceport and a short time later was headed back to the *Nova*. The return trip, however, was an exercise in frustration for Maker. He was dying to debrief Diviana (who was again piloting) in order to find out exactly what had happened, but was adverse to doing it with Skullcap present. Aware that he'd have to wait to get Diviana's story, he settled instead for quizzing their insectoid guest.

"So, who was that guy?" Maker asked Skullcap shortly after they left the planet.

"His race is the Xnjda," the Vacran explained, "and judging by his bands, he is a member of their aristocracy."

"Bands?" repeated Browing.

"Metallic rings worn on several of his limbs," Skullcap explained. "With all the excitement, it's possible you may not have noticed them."

"*I* certainly didn't," Maker admitted.

"How much is he likely to demand in payment?" Browing asked.

"My hope is that he will ask for nothing," the insectoid answered. "The Xnjda are a vainglorious people, for whom pride is practically a necessity of life. After ordering an attack on us, Kpntel could not stand down without experiencing shame, but a defeat at the hands of 'pets' would have been almost as bad."

"And he felt his side would lose after seeing what Erlen and Fierce could do," Maker concluded.

"Correct," Skullcap affirmed. "We offered him a resolution that would not cause a loss of prestige." He

IGNOTUS

turned to Browing. "It was incredibly shrewd of you to make that offer."

Browing shrugged. "After what you said about him losing face, it seemed like the best option. After all, making that concession to him meant nothing to us, although I apologize for putting you on the hook for payment."

Skullcap made a vague gesture. "It was the proper strategy. However, I must admit my surprise at hearing you converse with him directly, as his language should have been foreign to your translators."

"We modified them," Maker admitted, "adopting some of the technology from yours."

"I see," the insectoid said flatly. "In essence, you have been able to understand every word spoken during this jaunt."

"More or less," Maker confessed.

"I applaud your ingenuity," Skullcap remarked in an emotionless tone. "But as I was saying, Kpntel is unlikely to seek redress because we allowed him to save face. With most Xnjda, that alone would be enough to assuage any wounded pride, as they would recognize it as the gift that it is."

"And if he wants restitution anyway?" asked Fierce.

"Then I will pay him," Skullcap stated with finality.

IGNOTUS

Chapter 58

The rest of the shuttle flight was made in general silence. Under other circumstances, Maker might have taken the opportunity to catch a quick catnap, but not with Skullcap on board. The Vacran had undoubtedly been on his best behavior throughout the course of the mission, but Maker was not about to be lulled into a false sense of security.

Once they reunited with the *Nova*, Maker immediately gave the order to depart the station and rendezvous with the battle cruisers. Afterwards, accompanied by Erlen, he escorted their guest back to his quarters, where Skullcap once again tried to engage him in conversation. Maker rebuffed him, and then went to see Wayne. He found him in a small storage room that the younger Marine had commandeered as his own personal workspace.

"I brought you a present," Maker said as he and Erlen walked into the workroom. He then handed Wayne the tracking device, which had been in his possession since he'd taken it from the ball-being.

"This is the tracker?" Wayne asked.

Maker nodded. "Affirmative."

Wayne stepped to the side and placed the device on a nearby shelf. Maker, taking an opportunity to look around the place, noticed first and foremost a large worktable in the middle of the room. More specifically, he noticed what was *on* the table: Skullcap's battle armor (although it was completely disassembled at present).

"So, this is it," he muttered, stepping closer.

"Yeah," Wayne stated with a nod. "All of the offensive capabilities were disabled before I got to it —

presumably by some of our people. I've pretty much shut down the defenses as well, so now it's basically just a metal suit."

"How long will it take you to figure out how the interface with the tracker works?"

Wayne shrugged. "No way to tell. I mean, it's alien technology, el-tee. I've first got to figure out which part of this actually *is* the interface, then I'll concentrate on how to make it work."

"So we don't have a timetable for this."

"Well, if you're in a rush, there is a work-around."

He glanced at Maker hopefully, only to see his commanding officer shaking his head.

"No way," Maker stressed. "Absolutely not."

"Fine by me," Wayne stated noncommittally, "but I don't want you breathing down my neck if I don't produce results as fast as you'd like."

Maker merely stared at him for a moment, then said, "Let me think about it for a minute and get back to you. In the meantime, just see if you can figure it out."

Wayne nodded. "You got it, el-tee."

IGNOTUS

Chapter 59

Upon leaving Wayne's workroom, Maker went in search of Diviana. He found her in her quarters, at which point — after she invited him and Erlen inside — he immediately began questioning her about the situation with Kpntel.

"Okay, so how exactly did that debacle come about?" he asked.

"I was out gathering intel, just as we discussed," Diviana began. "In general, I had no issues initially, and after about thirty minutes I was getting ready to wrap up and come find you when that bug-bear grabbed me."

"Kpntel?"

She nodded. "Yeah. He was screaming something about me being his property and that I was coming with him. Naturally, I reacted."

"I take it that explains his missing limbs."

"When I want a man — or a male of any species — pawing me, he'll know it," Diviana declared. "But in the absence of an invitation from me, it's hands off."

"Or in this instance, *arms* off."

"Well, he's literally got like fifty limbs, so I doubt he even missed them. Plus, it didn't seem to slow him down, because the next thing I knew, he and his cohorts were chasing me."

"And the explosion?"

"Not my fault," Diviana insisted, shaking her head. "Well, not *directly* my fault."

"You're going to have to explain that," Maker said.

"When I mentioned that they were chasing me, they were actually riding in some type of vehicle. My

IGNOTUS

chances of outrunning them on foot were nil, so I took the gun you'd given me and shot at what I thought was the engine."

"Wait a minute," Maker blurted out in a concerned voice. "You actually fired the gun?"

"Yes, but I made sure that no one saw me," Diviana assured him.

He looked at her skeptically, but simply said, "Go on."

"I was only trying to slow them down or — if I got lucky — make them give up pursuing me, but apparently their vehicles operate on principles of physics or mechanics that are somewhat different than ours."

"Let me guess," Maker interjected. "The vehicle blew up."

"Not per se," Diviana clarified. "It actually shot out a spout of flame that sent everybody around it scrambling. The flames ultimately engulfed something like an electrical transformer that was nearby, and *that's* what blew up."

Maker nodded, already knowing the rest of the story. "And a few minutes later, you ran up to us, with your new friends in tow."

"Pretty much," Diviana agreed.

"Okay, so let's put aside your extracurricular activities for a moment," Maker said. "Did you make any headway on the task you were actually trying to accomplish?"

"Of course," she declared matter-of-factly. "What kind of intel agent do you take me for?"

"I don't know," Maker replied. "I'm reserving judgment in this instance until you actually give me some intel."

IGNOTUS

Diviana crossed her arms in a huff. "Fine, but you need to bear in mind that I was limited by time, so it's a small sample size."

"Understood. What did you find out?"

"Following your instructions, I inquired — discreetly — about the presence of any Vacra anywhere nearby. Specifically, I asked if they maintained a permanent presence or outpost anywhere on the planet or in this region of space."

"And?" Maker asked anxiously.

"Well, no one could swear to it on a stack of bibles, but according to the info I got, the Vacra don't have anything like that here. They pass through occasionally, do a little business, and then move on. In fact, no one's seen any of them around here in something like a month."

Maker nodded. Her words gave him a little bit of comfort that there wasn't a fleet of Vacra ships waiting to ambush them.

Not just yet, anyway, he thought.

"Anything else?" he asked.

Diviana frowned. "Yeah, actually. It's a little weird, but everybody seemed to speak of the Vacra in these deferential tones."

"You mean like fear?"

She shook her head. "No, it was actually…reverent. Like they respected them. And when I asked, I was told in no uncertain terms that the Vacra were among the most honorable and noble of any race around."

"Ha!" Maker scoffed. "That has to be a joke."

"No," Diviana insisted. "I mean, I know what you're saying — the Vacra have been nothing but deceitful and underhanded as long as we've dealt with them — but that's not their reputation here. It's the exact opposite, and has been for ages."

Maker frowned. Assuming Diviana's information was accurate, it didn't mesh at all with his own understanding of and experience with Skullcap's race.

"Maybe the Vacra are just like a playground bully," he finally said. "They'll pick on someone they think is smaller or weaker — like humans — but are on their best behavior around anybody they think can give them a thrashing."

"I don't know, el-tee," Diviana muttered, shaking her head. "That's not the impression I got. Maybe there's something here we're not seeing."

"What we've seen is what they've shown us," Maker countered. "And the last time I checked, my vision was twenty-twenty."

IGNOTUS

Chapter 60

As he and Erlen left Diviana's cabin, Maker couldn't help feeling frustrated. The information about the Vacra purportedly being honorable was a new wrinkle that he really didn't want to deal with. Frankly speaking, his method of processing that data was simply to disregard it, because it didn't fit the Vacra behavioral paradigm from his perspective.

That said, it did solidify his desire to complete the current mission as soon as possible. And with that in mind, he came to a decision.

****

It only took a few minutes to round up Skullcap and then march him to Wayne's workroom. As expected, the young Marine was busy scrutinizing a portion of the insectoid's battle armor when they entered, with the tracking device sitting on a nearby table.

"All right, we're going to try this," Maker announced without preamble.

"Great," Wayne replied with a nod.

Upon seeing his disassembled battle suit, Skullcap made a short, low humming sound that Maker assumed was indicative of disapproval.

"I see you did not exaggerate when we spoke previously," the insectoid stated. "My armor is in pieces."

"As I said before, it's nothing that can't be fixed," Wayne assured him.

"Let's stay on task," Maker prompted. He looked pointedly at Skullcap. "You said you needed your armor

IGNOTUS

to interface with the tracker. They're both here, so do your thing."

Skullcap reached for a piece of armor designed to go over the tarsus — the end of his upper forelimb that would be roughly equivalent to a forearm on a human. He picked it up and was about to put it on when Maker spoke.

"Just as a reminder," Maker said, "your buddy Deadeye occupies a comfortable niche in every room, including this one. Basically, if you try anything cute, he's going to shoot you dead. And if he somehow misses, Erlen will melt your face off."

Skullcap glanced at the Niotan, who had entered the room with him and Maker, and now sat attentively by the door.

Turning back to Maker, the Vacran said, "I surmised as much, but does that mean your own weapon is merely for show?"

He gestured toward Maker's hand, which — as usual when he was around Skullcap — gripped his service weapon.

Maker almost chuckled. "To be honest, carrying this when I'm around you has become second nature to me, so I practically forgot I had it."

"Indeed," Skullcap muttered. Then, turning his attention back to the task at hand, he slipped the vambrace (as Maker thought of it) over his forelimb.

As the two Marines watched, the Vacran pressed what appeared to be a button on the side of the armor piece. Almost immediately, a number of diodes on the vambrace lit up, causing Maker to instinctively put his forefinger on the trigger of his weapon.

IGNOTUS

"The battle suit has a general power unit," Skullcap explained, "but this segment" — he gestured to indicate the vambrace — "has its own battery because it has special functions."

"Such as operating trackers," Maker interjected.

"Among other things," the insectoid noted. "However, the battery is of a low-grade variety and incapable of presenting a threat."

"Oh, really?" Maker droned. "You must be disappointed."

"I merely highlighted a fact that would diminish any misinterpretation of my actions," Skullcap remarked, "as well as the odds of me getting shot."

Without waiting for Maker to respond, he then reached for the tracking device. The moment he touched it, the frosted tube around the pyramid seemed to come alive with a soft glow.

"Everything appears to be functioning correctly," Skullcap said after a moment.

"Awesome," Wayne noted. "Which way is it saying we should go?"

"It is not specifying a direction at the moment," Skullcap noted. "It is out of range."

IGNOTUS

Chapter 61

There were four of them in the *Nova*'s conference room: Maker, Adames, Browing, and Chantrey — meeting together in an assembly that was strangely reminiscent of the brainstorming session they'd had days earlier in Browing's apartment.

"So let me see if I've got this straight," Adames said. "The tech we're after is currently located on a Vacra ship, and said ship is in hiding on a distant planet."

"Not *too* distant," Maker corrected. "We can get there in a reasonable time without jumping to hyperspace."

"Fine — it's a stroll in the park," Adames remarked. "On top of that, the tracker you retrieved is currently out of range and therefore useless until we reach the star system where the aforementioned planet is located."

"Correct," Maker confirmed with a nod. "After we get close enough, it'll activate, thereby leading us to the Vacra ship. At the same time, it'll give an all-clear signal to the Vacra on the vessel in question, letting them know they can poke their head up out of the sand. At that point, we'll rendezvous with them, get the tech, etcetera."

Adames frowned as Maker spoke, much as Maker himself had done when he had first gotten the information he'd just relayed from Skullcap. Rather than call everyone together to brief them on the change, Maker had instead simply announced it over the ship's intercom, and then passed it along to the captains of the two cruisers in their convoy (along with the coordinates of their new destination). Almost immediately, however, he had gotten contacted on his p-comp by the trio with him now. But rather than powwow with each of them individually, he'd simply chosen to have a joint session with all of them.

"I'm sure this is starting to sound like a broken record," Adames said, interrupting Maker's reverie, "but this mission seems to get more complicated by the second. At every stage, there are additional steps that we never considered because we never knew about them. I know you, Gant. There's no way you're comfortable with this."

"Frankly speaking, I'm not," Maker admitted. "However, what we're doing now is functionally no different than what we'd have done if the tracker had been within range of the target and simply indicated which direction we should go."

"But if this is how it was supposed to happen, why didn't our little insectoid friend simply tell us all that?" Adames virtually demanded. "He made it sound as though once we got the tracker, we were in business."

"I think what might appear as lack of forthrightness may actually have something to do with linguistics and culture," Browing offered.

"What do you mean?" Maker asked.

"The current situation is similar to our prior dealings with them," Browing replied. "Basically, plans they made with us — such as arranging a rendezvous — were generally skimpy on specifics. They seemed to lack the granular detail that we take for granted. It's a lot like if someone asked you to make them a sandwich, but didn't tell you what kind of meat to put on it, or whether they wanted lettuce, tomatoes, pickles, and so on."

IGNOTUS

Maker pondered on Browing's comment for a moment, then asked, "How's it possible for them to overlook stuff like that?"

Browing shrugged. "It's probably something in the Vacran vernacular that simply doesn't translate when they speak Terran, or — most likely — something cultural that doesn't require the level of particularity that we expect."

"In other words," Maker surmised, "Skullcap's a 'big picture' guy."

"For lack of a better term, yes," Browing agreed.

"But as Maker noted, I'm not sure this changes anything," Chantrey offered.

"I'd argue that it does," Adames said. "At the very least, it alters how we should approach every step of this mission, because we don't know if we're getting all the facts."

Chantrey looked as though she had another comment to make, but before she could form the words, Maker spoke.

"Actually, I think you're both right," he stated, glancing first at Adames and then at Chantrey. "From a macro level, we're still behaving as we would have if the tracker had performed as advertised. But Adames is right in that we probably need to focus a little more on trying to read between the lines. And if that means making Skullcap give us more definitive data, so be it."

IGNOTUS

Chapter 62

Their meeting broke up almost immediately after Maker's last comment. Unfortunately, there were really were no takeaways (other than the general agreement to try to get more specific info from their Vacran passenger). As the others were leaving, Maker got Chantrey's attention and clandestinely asked her to hang around.

"Feels like I haven't seen you in a while," he stated after the other two had gone. "You okay?"

"If you're referring to your prior suggestion that I'm a lab rat in my own experiment, I'm fine," she assured him.

"So you think I was wrong?"

"No, I think you were right on the money. They've got someone performing predictive analysis on me."

"Are you mad?"

"Only at myself," she admitted. "I should have seen this coming, but I guess I relied too much on my past performance and reputation."

"Well, take it from me," Maker said. "Those will only get you so far."

"So I've learned," she remarked. "But do me a favor: don't say it."

"Say what — that I told you so?"

Chantrey sighed. "You do know that's the exact opposite of not saying it, right?"

Maker was silent for a moment, then asked, "So, do you regret it now — this thing between us?"

"That depends," she replied candidly, stepping close. "Are you worth it?"

IGNOTUS

"I'm pretty sure that's a question only you can answer."

"In that case, the jury's still out," she said with a wink. "But you'll get a few more opportunities to make your case."

"That reminds me," Maker uttered, snapping his fingers. "I need to talk to you about something. Can I come see you later?"

"I've got time now," she replied.

Maker shook his head. "I can't right now — bridge duty."

"You're in command. You can be late."

"The leader sets the tone," Maker stressed. "If I want my people to be punctual, then I have to be as well."

Chantrey gave him a skeptical look. "Are you sure this isn't just a ploy to see me again later?"

"Maybe a little," Maker admitted with a grin. "But I actually do have something I need to get your insight on."

"That's fine," she said. "Just swing by whenever you're done. I should be up."

"Thanks," Maker muttered, then headed for the bridge.

IGNOTUS

Chapter 63

Bridge duty, in and of itself, turned out to be fairly uneventful — which was pretty much what any smart soldier wants. No emergencies, no crises, no exigencies. Just a couple of hours passing in routine and unremarkable fashion.

Of course, this was what they had been told to expect by Skullcap. Per their insectoid guest, the area of space they were traversing was uninhabited and seldom visited, so there was no need to expect trouble. Not trusting the Vacran, Maker had made it a point to stay vigilant and told the captains of the two cruisers to do the same.

Thankfully, nothing of note happened during Maker's watch, and he used it as an opportunity to strengthen the connections he had to his team. His squad already had a pretty tight bond, but it never hurt to continue reinforcing it. With that in mind, he made it a point to engage with Loyola and Snick (who were on duty with him) throughout their time on the bridge.

Eventually, Adames showed up to relieve him. Maker quickly relinquished command and departed. Upon exiting the bridge, he momentarily pondered whether he should go find Erlen. The Niotan had essentially been on his own since their earlier confab with Skullcap in Wayne's workroom. Once they were done there, the Niotan had given the impression that he preferred to stroll around the ship rather than go back to their cabin.

Typically, Maker didn't like for Erlen to go wandering on his own. That said, he wasn't likely to get lost on the *Nova*. In addition, the Niotan was fully capable

IGNOTUS

of taking care of himself and knew how to stay out of trouble. (More to the point, he would seek out Maker if the latter were needed for anything.)

Satisfied that Erlen was fine on his own, Maker headed to Chantrey's cabin.

****

She was seated at a small breakfast table when Maker let himself in, with papers strewn all about. However, they weren't just on the table; there were also documents on the countertops, on the coffee table in the living room, and even stacked on the floor in a couple of places.

"What's all this?" he asked as he sauntered towards her, casually observing that many of the papers were comprised of handwritten notes.

"Just some analyses I've been doing," she replied, getting up from the table. "Something to let my puppet masters, as you put it, know that I'm not to be trifled with."

Maker frowned, puzzled. "Should I come back later?"

"No, now's as good a time as any," she stated. She then looped her arm into his and guided him over to the loveseat in her living room. Pulling him down next to her as she sat, she asked, "So, Lieutenant, how can I help you?"

"I need your expert opinion on something," he replied. He then conveyed to her the information Diviana had learned about the Vacra while he and the others had been retrieving the tracker.

IGNOTUS

"Basically," he said in summary, "I've got a guy with the reputation of an angel, but in our past dealings with him, he's been the devil."

"So you're trying to figure out which Skullcap is the real one," she concluded.

"Not just Skullcap — the entire Vacran race," he countered. "Up until now they've presented as one thing, but on this trip, Skullcap has come across as something else entirely. And on top of that, they've apparently got this reputation as a noble race. I'm just trying to get a handle on what I'm dealing with."

"I seem to recall us having a similar conversation before. Just as I said then, my area of expertise is *human* behavior. This is outside my wheelhouse. You'd do better talking to an entomologist."

"And as I said back then, you're the closest thing I've got."

"Okay, I'll give it a whirl," Chantrey decided. "So we've got an individual who displays a different demeanor with two different sets of people: with humans he's generally shady, but with other races he's been morally upright. Truthfully, the dichotomy in his behavior is not particularly unusual."

Maker raised an eyebrow. "It's not?"

Chantrey shook her head. "No. Imagine a guy who thinks a certain girl is pretty. He wants her to like him, so he's always on his best behavior around her. However, there's another girl he thinks is ugly, and he spends his time teasing her and calling her names."

"I get it: he treats separate individuals in entirely different ways. So what — humans are the ugly ducklings of spacefaring races?"

IGNOTUS

"I doubt it's anything like that. But even if that were the case — and using our analogy — Skullcap's not treating separate individuals differently. What he's doing now would be construed as treating the *same* person differently."

"In other words, he's now treating the ugly girl as if she's a beauty queen. The question is why."

"Well, if we were talking about human beings, I'd surmise it was because something changed."

"So maybe the ugly girl actually *is* a beauty queen now. She got her teeth straightened, or her skin cleared up, or she lost weight…something to make her more appealing."

Chantrey gave him a piercing stare. "There are so many things wrong with what you just said that I hardly know where to begin. The misogyny? The objectification of women? The—"

"How about we keep in mind that I was expanding on an analogy," Maker interjected. "Can we work from that perspective rather than assume I was voicing my closeted feelings about women?"

"Fine," Chantrey replied a little tersely. "Skullcap's altered demeanor suggests one of two things: either he's changed personally, or he's the same as he's always been, but whatever motivated his prior behavior has shifted in some way."

Maker ruminated on this for a moment. "So you're saying some outside factor caused him to be a treacherous liar in the past, but its influence has faded."

"Something like that."

"Hmmm," Maker droned. "I'm more inclined to believe there's an outside force at work *now*, which is why he's behaved himself for the most part."

IGNOTUS

"Well, there's a simple way to find out," Chantrey said. Noting the blank look that Maker gave her, she added, "Just ask him."

Maker snorted derisively. "You speak as though he'll just tell me the truth."

"Maybe he will."

"Even if he did, he has to know I'd never believe him," Maker stated, then frowned as he remembered something. "That said, he has been trying to engage me in conversation since the moment he came on board."

"Maybe that's the reason why — he's trying to explain what's different now."

"Ha!" Maker bellowed in disdain. "It's more likely he's just trying to get me to develop Lima Syndrome."

Chantrey's eyebrows rose in surprise. Noting this, Maker began to clarify his statement.

"Lima Syndrome," he repeated. "It's the reverse of Stockholm Syndrome, which is when hostages bond with their kidnappers. With Lima Syndrome, the *kidnapper* bonds—"

"I know what Lima Syndrome is," she interrupted. "Stockholm Syndrome, too. I'm just surprised to hear you mention them."

"Now I understand," Maker groused. "*You* know what they mean, but you're shocked that the big, oafish Marine also knows. Well, let me enlighten you: I'm a soldier, and as such there's always a chance that I can be taken prisoner, or take custody of an enemy combatant. That being the case, those are concepts they taught us to be aware of, so forgive me for paying attention in class that day."

"Are you done?" Chantrey asked, crossing her arms and leaning back. Maker opened his mouth to speak, but she went on without giving him a chance to say anything. "Good. Now, just for the record, I want to make it clear that I know what you're doing, and it's not going to work."

"Oh?" he muttered. "What exactly am I doing?"

"You're trying to manufacture an argument and a reason to be indignant in hopes of making me forget what you said before about women."

"I was working within the confines of an analogy we constructed. It wasn't an independent representation of my opinion."

"And then you incorporated your own standards of beauty that objectify women."

"That's not true," Maker insisted. "You're beautiful, and I don't objectify *you*."

Chantrey blinked, caught off guard. "What?"

"I said that you're beautiful, and—"

"Yeah, I heard you," she interjected, then studied him for a moment. "Pretty slick the way you shifted from indignation to flattery — a seamless transition that would probably beguile most women and make them forgive you."

Smiling, Maker slid closer and took her hand. "I guess the only question is, did it work?"

She grinned back at him and said, "I'll let you know in the morning."

IGNOTUS

Chapter 64

In line with what Skullcap had indicated, they ran into no problems as they traversed the unknown region of space. In due course, the *Nova* entered the star system for which the insectoid had given them coordinates. It turned out to be an expansive solar system consisting of a single star and fourteen planetary bodies. At that juncture, Maker — who was on the bridge — had the Vacran brought in, along with the tracking device.

"Well, we're here," he said to Skullcap. "What now?"

The insectoid glanced at the tracker, appearing to study the glass tube surrounding the pyramid, which now glowed with a blue light. He then turned to the bridge monitor, which showed a panoramic view of the solar system before them.

"The seventh planet," Skullcap stated matter-of-factly. "The water world."

Maker nodded, then gave the order to head for the planet in question. Next, he informed the two cruisers of their destination. (Needless to say, all three ships went on high alert.)

As Maker ended communication with the other ships in their convoy, Skullcap turned to him, saying, "It would be best if I could don my armor now."

"Oh really?" Maker quipped acerbically. "And why is that?"

The insectoid seemed to ponder the question for a moment, then answered, "I will not present well otherwise. The Vacra we are meeting will interpret it as a bad sign."

IGNOTUS

"Bad omens have been par for the course on this mission," Maker stated. "You and your people will simply have to deal with it."

Skullcap made an unusual chirping noise, which might have been indicative of disappointment, but otherwise didn't argue the point further.

"So what exactly is supposed to happen now?" Maker asked.

"The signal from the tracking device should have been picked up by the Vacra on the planet we're approaching. They will hail us when we are in range."

"Sounds good," Maker said, "as long as we're not talking about a hail of gunfire."

IGNOTUS

Chapter 65

Nothing particularly noteworthy happened as they approached the seventh planet of the solar system. Nevertheless, as they drew near their destination, Maker found himself growing slightly apprehensive. It simply felt too much like the calm before the storm.

The planet itself was just as Skullcap had described it: a world completely covered by water, with no visible land whatsoever. Per their insectoid guest, there was a Vacra ship here — presumably below the surface. However, some element in the water made it impossible to scan the depths for any type of vessel.

"This is close enough," Maker announced as they reached orbital height above the planet. "We're not going down into the atmosphere."

"There is no need," Skullcap assured him. "My people should be making contact relatively soon."

As if on cue, Diviana — who was manning the comm — declared, "We're being hailed. It's a Vacra frequency, originating from the planet surface."

"The surface?" Maker repeated.

Diviana nodded. "Yes. Presumably they were beneath the waves before, but apparently they've broken cover."

"Can we locate them with the scanners?" he asked.

"Already on it," Diviana replied, then drew in a sharp breath. "Vacra vessel located — far side of the planet. It's a warship."

Maker cast a sideways glance at Skullcap. "Why am I not surprised?"

"They're still hailing us," Diviana remarked.

IGNOTUS

"Put it through," Maker ordered before turning to Skullcap. "All right, you're up. And remember—"

"I know," the insectoid interrupted. "I will remember to stay ugly."

Maker frowned, trying to make sense of the comment — and then laughed as the insectoid's meaning became clear.

"Exactly," Maker said, still chuckling. "Don't try anything cute."

Skullcap looked as though he wanted to offer additional commentary, but before he could do so, the image on the monitor changed, showing a Vacran in battle armor.

"Commander Vuqja!" exclaimed the insectoid on the screen. "We feared you dead."

Skullcap made a hissing sound that seemed to suggest disdain. "Death fled from me when I was a grub. Should she grow bolder now that I'm a warrior?"

The insectoid on the screen made a sound that seemed to be comprised of a cackle inside a sneeze — presumably laughter. It then stated, "Your words ring true."

A moment later, without warning, the monitor went dark.

Suddenly suspicious, Maker turned to Skullcap, angrily demanding, "What the hell are you up to? You didn't say anything about the tech that we're here for. In fact, you really didn't say anything about anything."

"That was a code phrase," Skullcap explained.

"I gathered as much," Maker shot back. "But what I don't know is what it means to your Vacra buddies."

IGNOTUS

"It was an indication that all is well," the insectoid explained. "That I am not being forced or coerced in any way. What else could it mean?"

"Oh, I don't know," Maker muttered sarcastically. "Maybe, 'Attack and take no prisoners,' or something else along those lines."

"I see," Skullcap intoned. "Obviously, I have done poorly in terms of explaining the safeguards we put into effect to secure the chattels you seek. All that we've had to do thus far — including retrieving the tracker, getting in within range of this planet, and exchanging code phrases — were buffers designed to hinder acquisition of your property by unauthorized individuals."

"Hold on," Maker growled. "So all of these interim steps we've had to take along the way here were intentional? They were part of some kind of security protocol?"

"Yes," the Vacran acknowledged. "My apologies if that was not obvious. Also, I occasionally forget that the human approach to matters is often more meticulous in terms of details than the Vacra require."

Maker frowned, thinking that Skullcap's statement seemed to square up with Browing's earlier assessment.

"So what now?" Maker asked.

"The code phrase was an indication for my people to approach and rendezvous with us," the Vacran said. "Once they are within range, I will join them and assume command. I will then authorize your people to board and—"

"Stop," Maker interjected, holding up a hand, palm out. "That's not going to work. There's no way I'm letting you get on a Vacra warship and simply rely on your word that you'll let us board and scoop up our stuff.

IGNOTUS

For all I know, the only reason they're not blasting us to pieces is because you're here, so I'm not in any hurry to let you waltz out the door."

"I'm not sure there are any other options," Skullcap noted.

"Sure there are," Maker countered. "You can just order your people, from the very spot you're standing, that we're coming on board to get our property and will leave the moment we have it all."

"That is not possible," the insectoid stated.

"Really?" Maker muttered, unconvinced. "Seems pretty straightforward to me."

"You don't understand," Skullcap said. "Under our conventions, I cannot give legal orders until I assume command, and I can only assume command in person."

Maker blinked, not quite believing what he was hearing. "So basically, if we don't let you go board your warship, we don't get our property."

"In essence, yes," Skullcap replied.

IGNOTUS

Chapter 66

A short time later, Maker found himself on the *Nova*'s shuttle, headed for the Vacra warship. As Skullcap had predicted, his people had left the planet immediately upon receiving the code phrase, and soon thereafter were at orbital height near the *Nova* and the accompanying cruisers. Afterwards, it had only taken a quick communiqué to apprise those on the Vacra vessel that Skullcap would be en route shortly to assume command.

It went without saying, of course, that Maker was disgusted by the current turn of events. The very thought of allowing Skullcap to board the Vacra warship was abhorrent to him, but it didn't appear that they had many options — not if they wanted the sub rosa tech back. (Moreover, Skullcap had insisted that if he tried to give orders without assuming command, those on the warship would assume something was wrong, and he couldn't fathom a guess as to what their reaction might be.)

Ultimately, Maker had decided that Skullcap would be allowed to go to the Vacra warship, but he wouldn't go alone. Thus, Maker had ended up accompanying him, along with Adames (who was piloting), Snick, and Planck.

In a perfect world, Maker would have left Adames on the *Nova* so that there would be a seasoned soldier there capable of taking command if things went sideways. The NCO, however, had made a strong argument about the need to take the most competent people (i.e., combatants) to the Vacra warship — namely, himself and Snick. (In that regard, Loyola had again volunteered and adamantly argued that she be allowed to come along, but — as before — Maker had refused.)

IGNOTUS

Planck was the lone anomaly among their group. He wasn't a soldier or a fighter by any stretch of the imagination. However, he had knowledge in two key areas: he was intimately familiar with the sub rosa tech they were after, and he knew the Vacra better than anyone. In fact, it was Planck who had confirmed Skullcap's assertion that the latter needed to be present in person in order to take command.

"It jibes with what I've seen," Planck had said. "In addition, some symbol of authority usually gets passed from one person to another, showing that the new individual is now in charge."

Maker had also taken the opportunity to quiz Planck regarding the information Diviana had obtained about the Vacra's reputation. Planck could only confirm that he'd seen other races treat the Vacra respectfully, although he didn't know if that was done out of courtesy, fear, or as a result of some other factor.

Taken altogether, it meant that Maker had to accede to Skullcap's ultimatum about going to the Vacra warship. However, it didn't mean he had to take unnecessary chances. To that end, he and the rest of those on the shuttle were all armed. (Even Planck, who looked as though he didn't know which end to aim, was carrying a firearm, while Maker brought along his vibro-blade for extra protection.) In addition, the battle cruisers, as well as the *Nova*, were in combat mode; if anything went wrong, they were already set to blast holes in the Vacra vessel.

Fortunately, they had no trouble in terms of approaching or landing on the warship, which was massive in size — bigger than the three ships in Maker's convoy combined. The air inside was tolerable, as they

IGNOTUS

had been informed, but Maker and his people wore nose filters just to be safe. As they exited the shuttle, they were met by a contingent of Vacra soldiers. Just eyeballing them, Maker surmised that they numbered about twenty, which meant that he and his people were badly outnumbered. The only good news was that only one of the Vacra — apparently the leader — was wearing battle armor, *sans* helmet. The fellow was, however, carrying something that looked like a battle-axe.

Skullcap, in the vanguard of those who had exited the shuttle, stepped forward. At the same time, the Vacra in the battle suit walked forward as well, until the two were face-to-face. Skullcap opened his mouth to speak, but what issued forth was a fast-flowing stream of chittering which did not, for some reason, get converted into Terran by their translators.

"What the hell?" muttered Adames in a low voice. "My translator's not getting this."

"It's not the translator," Planck said softly. "It's them. They're speaking some non-standard version of the Vacran language that the device can't decipher."

"The upshot of which is that we have no idea what they're saying," Maker concluded, frowning. This was exactly the situation that he hadn't wanted to be in. Suddenly on edge, he placed his hand on his sidearm, ready to draw and fire at the slightest provocation.

As he watched, the armored Vacra finished saying something and then thrust the battle-axe out towards Skullcap, who took it. The other Vacra then took a few steps backward and resumed his prior place at the head of his fellows.

Turning to face Maker and the others, Skullcap announced, "It is done. I now command this vessel."

IGNOTUS

Maker didn't immediately respond. Instead, his eyes went from Skullcap to the axe he held, and then back to the insectoid's face.

Seeming to understand, Skullcap explained, "It is ceremonial — a symbol of the authority I now wield."

"It looks pretty functional to me," Maker countered.

"It can be utilized as a weapon," Skullcap agreed, "but regalia like this are rarely put to such use."

"Well, let's concentrate on keeping it that way," Maker stressed.

"That is my intent," Skullcap replied. "Now come — I will take you to your property."

He then turned and began walking away — apparently heading for a nearby corridor. With little choice, Maker's team fell into step behind him.

IGNOTUS

Chapter 67

Skullcap marched through the ship unerringly and with a purposeful stride, as if he knew exactly where he was going. Truth be told, that was probably the case; the insectoid was clearly familiar with this ship model (and more likely, with this specific vessel).

Keeping an eye on the insectoid (and more precisely, on the axe he carried), Maker made it a point to stay fairly close to — albeit to the rear of — their erstwhile guide. The battle-axe had a long handle, which meant that Skullcap probably wouldn't be able to use it effectively on someone who was too close.

At the same time, Maker had to keep an eye out for any type of ambush. He'd been on precisely one Vacra ship before (and had spent much of his time fighting for his life during that episode), so the layout was unfamiliar to him. There could be a horde of Vacra, armed to the teeth, waiting around the next corner or in the next corridor. The only silver lining in that regard was that the contingent of insectoids who had met their shuttle hadn't deigned to follow them after Skullcap began leading them through the ship. (Like the people on Maker's own ship, apparently they had other duties to perform.)

The thought of his people made Maker perform a quick visual check on those with him. As he'd figured, Adames and Snick were clearly alert, keenly aware that anything might happen. Planck, however, appeared to be a bundle of raw nerves; he was sweating profusely, and his eyes darted around wildly, like a turkey that had just figured out what Thanksgiving was all about.

IGNOTUS

Of course, Maker thought. *He hasn't been around this many Vacra since we rescued him.* It made sense, then, that Planck was more than a little nervous.

"Steady," Maker whispered to him, hoping to keep the man calm.

Planck gave a curt nod, indicating that he'd heard what was said. Satisfied, Maker gave him a reassuring clap on the shoulder. However, the gesture proved premature, as a moment later a shout from Adames made it clear that their situation was still precarious.

"Heads up!" the NCO bellowed.

They had just entered a corridor that formed an L-shaped junction with the passageway they were departing. Maker, who was at that moment in position to see down both legs of the hallway, noted with alarm that a horde of Vacra soldiers was charging at them from both the front and behind.

Ambush! Maker screamed mentally.

IGNOTUS

Chapter 68

The four men automatically went into a back-to-back formation — or rather, the three Marines did. Maker had to grip Planck's shoulder and manhandle him into position, so that ultimately the two of them faced one leg of the L-shaped corridor while Adames and Snick faced the other. Maker had probably been rougher than necessary, but it had only taken a second. Truth be told, however, a second was probably more time than any of them had to spare, because the next moment they were fighting for their lives.

Maker had instinctively drawn his weapon the moment Adames had shouted. Now he fired indiscriminately at the Vacra bearing down on them, all the while mentally cursing himself for being foolish enough to have trusted Skullcap in the slightest.

As the thought of the Vacra leader crossed his mind, Maker looked for him and caught a glimpse of the insectoid up ahead, surrounded by his fellows. Somehow, while Maker had been trying to calm Planck, the insectoid had apparently put some space between them. Moreover, he could hear Skullcap shouting over the din of fighting.

"Stop!" the insectoid screamed. "Drop your weapons!"

Like hell I will, Maker thought, and continued shooting. It was then that his mind registered something that he wouldn't actually realize until later: the Vacra were charging their position, but not shooting at them.

Maker continued firing, absentmindedly noting that the hallway ahead was starting to fill with bodies. Still, the Vacra were collectively getting closer. There were just too many of them.

IGNOTUS

It was then that Maker took note of an odd fact: he was the only person engaging the enemy in this leg of the hallway. Sparing a quick glance at Planck, he saw the man holding his weapon out, but not firing. Instead, he stood there grimacing, his gun hand trembling slightly.

"Shoot, damn you!" Maker ordered.

"I'm trying!" Planck yelled. "It's not working!"

Maker didn't dare glance behind to see how Adames and Snick were faring; he simply assumed they were taking care of business. But on his side, they were going to be overrun soon with only one person engaging the enemy.

"Here!" Maker shouted, shoving his gun towards Planck. At the same time, he drew the vibro-blade with his free hand and switched it on. And then, almost before Planck had taken the firearm from him, Maker dashed forward shouting, "Stay behind me!" over his shoulder.

For the next few moments, it was essentially a slaughter as the vibro-blade — oscillating at a rate too fast for the eye to follow — severed flesh and bone like a surgical laser. The blade's ability to administer wholesale carnage was on full display as Maker hacked and slashed anything that came near him, and its deadliness initially compensated for the fact that the enemy had more limbs and could, therefore, wield more weapons.

That said, the vibro-blade was designed for close-combat encounters, requiring the person wielding it to be in close proximity to his intended target. Ergo, with the Vacra continuing to charge forward without regard to danger (and even with Planck taking the occasional potshot at the enemy), it was only a matter of time before the inevitable happened. Thus it was that, as Maker was stabbing one of the Vacra in the thorax, another of them managed to grab the wrist holding the blade and then twisted, hard.

Maker dropped the weapon, which immediately stopped oscillating once it left his grip and hit the floor like an ordinary knife. At that juncture, however, he wasn't paying much attention to it; he was too busy throwing kicks and punches in an effort to keep the Vacra off him.

Fighting them hand-to-hand, however, was a difficult chore. The insectoids were built differently than humans — jointed in an unfamiliar fashion, making it difficult for Maker to apply his martial training. Nevertheless, he was initially holding his own until he slipped in something — probably blood or gore. His feet flew out from under him and he banged his head hard on the floor.

For a moment, Maker saw stars. At the same time, klaxons started going off in his brain as he sensed more than observed movement next to him. He shook his head to clear his vision, and then his eyes widened in shock as he saw a Vacra kneeling next to him, stabbing down with a knife.

Acting more on instinct than conscious thought, Maker reached out with both hands and caught the wrist of the limb holding the descending blade, halting its momentum. (Thankfully it wasn't the vibro-blade, but the weapon didn't need any special properties to finish him off; any old stabbing implement would do the trick.) The Vacra then leaned over, putting its weight on the knife, which slowly began to drop toward Maker's chest.

Someone shouted nearby but Maker ignored it, putting all his energy and concentration into stopping the descending blade. However, he found himself slightly

IGNOTUS

distracted when a shadow unexpectedly fell over him. Still fighting for his life, he risked an upward glance and felt unbridled fury at what he saw.

Skullcap.

More to the point, the Vacra leader was still holding the battle-axe, which he had pulled back like a lumberjack attempting to fell a tree in one swoop. And then he swung the axe towards Maker.

IGNOTUS

Chapter 69

"I'm not thanking him," Maker declared.

"For what — saving your life?" asked Snick. "Seems a tad ungrateful, Lieutenant."

Maker frowned at Snick's comment, which alluded to the fact that Skullcap's swing with the axe — rather than serving as a killing blow to Maker — had actually taken off the head of his attacker. Skullcap had then helped a stunned Maker to his feet and a moment later, after somehow establishing control and getting his people to stand down (those that were left, that is), had whisked the four humans to safety.

In this instance, "safety" consisted of being hustled into something like a VIP cabin that they could lock from the inside. A quick search of the quarters had revealed that they were alone. More importantly for Maker, they had come across something akin to towels, and — after a bit of trial and error — he had found some spigots from which he could get water. Together, these two discoveries had allowed him to clean up a bit, namely by letting him wash his face and hands, which had been covered with Vacra blood. (His uniform would have to wait until they got back to the *Nova*, but for all intents and purposes, it was ruined.) Now they were simply waiting for Skullcap to return and let them know…something.

"He's right," chimed in Planck, snapping Maker back to the present. "You do seem unappreciative."

Maker gave him an incredulous look. "Am I the only one who remembers that these things are the enemy?"

IGNOTUS

Adames shook his head. "No, but the fact that Skullcap gave you a hand instead of just letting you die does muddy the water a bit."

"I don't know that he saved my life," Maker countered. "For all I know, this entire thing was a setup."

"To what end?" asked Planck.

"To make us grateful," Maker suggested. "To try to establish a bond of some sort. To make us trust him."

"I don't know, Gant," Adames muttered skeptically. "He didn't really have time to plan anything that elaborate."

"How much planning is needed to say, 'Attack these fools in the west corridor'?" Maker scoffed. "And don't forget, right before he took command, he engaged in some kind of back-and-forth with his buddy that the translator couldn't decipher."

"But at the end of the day, he killed one of his own people to save you," Snick noted. "He cut off his head."

"That doesn't necessarily mean anything," Maker said. "I've mentioned an insect from Old Earth before called a roach that can live for days after its head has been cut off, and certain insectoid races are the same. For all I know, they took that guy around the corner and duct-taped his head back on. He could be walking around now with nothing more than a raspy voice to indicate that his head and neck once had a brief disconnection."

"Well, if that's how you feel, why'd you even let Skullcap stick us in here?" asked Adames.

"Because I fell and hit my head and was still dazed at the time," Maker quipped. "If I'd been in my right mind, I would have gutted him."

IGNOTUS

Maker's words actually did convey his feelings, but it was simple bravado to a certain extent. He hadn't even had his knife on him when Skullcap helped him up. (Much to Maker's chagrin, it was actually Skullcap who had handed the vibro-blade back to him once he regained his feet. Apparently the insectoid had retrieved it at some point while Maker was fighting for his life.)

With his mind now replaying the incident in the hallway, Maker turned to Planck. "You still have my gun?"

"Sorry," Planck muttered apologetically as he handed the weapon over.

"Any particular reason why you didn't shoot Skullcap when he was swinging that axe in my direction?" Maker asked.

"At that point, I understood that his shouts about dropping weapons were intended for his people, not us," Planck responded. "Plus, I could see him ordering them — actually, *forcing* them — to stand down. It didn't seem right to shoot him. Moreover, at that juncture, I realized he was the only thing standing between us and possibly an endless wave of attacking Vacra."

Maker's brow crinkled as he considered Planck's statement. The man was right, of course. Even with the Vacra refusing to use firearms, eventually they would have overwhelmed the four humans. However, that thought brought something else to mind.

"By the way," Maker said to Planck, "what happened to your gun? I checked it myself before we left the *Nova*, so it should have been fine."

Planck lowered his eyes sheepishly. "I actually had Sergeant Adames take a look at it while you were getting cleaned up."

IGNOTUS

Maker waited, expecting Planck to explain further, but after a moment it became clear that the man was having difficulty continuing.

"And?" Maker prompted.

Planck opened his mouth, but no words came out. Obviously embarrassed, he glanced at Adames with a pleading expression.

Taking his cue, Adames said, "Apparently he forgot to take the safety off."

Feeling Maker's gaze angling towards him, Planck stared at the floor, and at the same time began to turn red. He wasn't a soldier, but he felt that his nigh-complete ineptitude had almost cost lives, and it would be no more than he deserved if Maker savagely berated and belittled him. That being the case, he was caught off guard by what actually issued forth from Maker's mouth: laughter. A moment later, Adames and Snick joined him, and soon enough Planck himself cracked a smile.

IGNOTUS

Chapter 70

Shortly after the discussion about Planck's gun, a sturdy knock sounded at the door.

"It is I," bellowed Skullcap before anyone could ask, his voice coming through the door slightly muffled.

Warily, Maker cracked the door open, and was pleased to see that the insectoid was alone. He quickly ushered the Vacran in before closing and locking the door behind him.

"My apologies once again for the incident that occurred," Skullcap began. "Please know that it was in no way planned nor expected on my part."

"So what exactly happened?" asked Maker. "Why did your people attack us?"

"Simply put, they thought I was in danger and being coerced," Skullcap answered.

Maker frowned. "What do you mean?"

"The ceremony you witnessed where I assumed command is usually a formal and solemn event," Skullcap explained. "I should have been in my armor, as was the one who relinquished command to me. The fact that I was not was viewed as unorthodox and sent a signal that something was amiss."

"Wait," Maker interjected, his brow furrowed. "Is that what you were trying to tell me when you mentioned that you needed to wear your armor here?"

"Yes," Skullcap replied. "But in addition to my inappropriate attire, it was also noted that one of you had your weapon drawn almost the entire time you were here."

IGNOTUS

Planck sighed. "That would be me, but to be honest, I must have done it subconsciously. I was barely aware of it until the attack happened."

"Regardless," Skullcap intoned, "it was interpreted as an intent to do me harm, because allies would not need to have their firearms in hand. There was also the fact that I told them you were here to collect your property."

Maker scratched his temple for a moment. "Is that what you were saying when you were chatting unintelligibly with the prior commander?"

Skullcap gave something like a nod. "It is an ancient Vacran dialect that is generally only used for ceremonial purposes. After the formal assumption of command, I inadvertently continued communicating in that manner, but I essentially conveyed why you were here. Considering all the safeguards we have in place concerning those items — and bearing all the other facts in mind — it is not surprising that several Vacra on this vessel grew suspicious."

"So all in all, your people thought you were in danger and mounted an impromptu rescue," Adames concluded.

"In essence," Skullcap confirmed. "A number of them were waiting when we rounded that last corner, and they shoved me to the rear of their group before I realized what was happening. After the skirmish began, I had difficulty asserting control of the situation, although I eventually got them to stand down — but not without having to take certain action."

He glanced at Maker as he made the last statement, but provided no further comment.

IGNOTUS

"Bearing everything in mind, it seems we're lucky the Vacra seem to have an aversion to firearms," Snick chimed in. "Otherwise we'd likely be dead."

"It wasn't aversion," Skullcap assured him. "The design of the corridor increased the odds of friendly fire incidents — especially since there were so many of us and so few of you."

"I think I follow," Adames said. "The corridor being in the shape of an L meant there was a danger of ricochets — especially with Vacra coming from both directions — so your people vetoed firearms."

"Precisely," the insectoid confirmed. "But I should have discerned what was happening — what they were likely to do."

"Didn't they realize that a bunch of them were likely to get killed?" queried Adames.

"Yes," Skullcap answered. "But Vacra do not place as much emphasis on individuality and personal safety as humans. It is the group — the hive — that matters."

"And apparently the hive *leaders*," Maker remarked.

"That is correct," the insectoid stated. "On my part, however, I could not allow harm to come to any of *you*. Your presence here was at my behest, so I was responsible for your safety and required to ensure it above all else — even my own life or those of other Vacra."

Maker let out a snort of derision. "You're laying it on kind of thick, aren't you?"

Skullcap stared at him for a moment, and then said, "I'm not sure I understand."

IGNOTUS

"Forget it," Maker muttered, shaking his head. "But if your people didn't care about their own survival, why does a little friendly fire matter?"

"They wanted to avoid the likelihood hitting *me*," the insectoid replied. "More importantly, we are at a juncture in my people's history where it is anathema for one Vacra to take the life of another."

Maker frowned at this statement, as — if Skullcap were to be believed — it was apparently a core tenet that the Vacra leader had violated when he saved Maker's life. In short, it raised all kinds of questions, but Maker decided not to dwell on it at the moment.

"So what happens now?" he asked.

"I had to spend some time making sure the prior incident would not be repeated, which is why I placed you here," Skullcap explained. "However, everyone on this vessel is now cognizant of the fact that you are here as honored guests and any treatment given to you that is less than respectful will be dealt with harshly. With that understanding, I can now escort you to the goods you were promised."

Despite what he'd heard, Maker still wasn't sure he could trust the Vacran. However, they really didn't have much choice at this point. Even if they decided to abandon the mission, he'd still be taking Skullcap's word that they'd reach the shuttle alive.

"All right," he finally said. "Let's go."

IGNOTUS

Chapter 71

Shockingly, Skullcap was as good as his word. Upon leaving the cabin, he led the human quartet to a massive cargo hold packed with a vast array of tech and equipment, most of which Maker couldn't even classify. In fact, the only person even slightly capable of slapping a label on anything they were seeing was Planck, who — as soon as he laid eyes on the articles around them — became as giddy as a child on Christmas Day.

"I remember this!" he screeched, running up to a device that resembled a metal wagon wheel with a grenade for a hub. "And there's the Poseidic Exsiccator that fool Harris was always working on! And that's—"

"We appreciate the stroll down memory lane, Planck," interjected Maker, "but we really have a job to do here."

"Of course, of course," Planck murmured. "I'm sorry for getting distracted. It's just that, seeing all this…"

"I know," Maker said as the scientist trailed off.

"Anyway, I should get started," Planck remarked. "There'll be time to reminisce later."

Skullcap made an odd noise, drawing everyone's attention. "If you have no further need of me, I will give you privacy to inspect your property. When ready, you may contact me with *this*."

As he finished speaking, he handed what appeared to be a palm-sized voice communicator to Maker, then turned and walked away.

****

IGNOTUS

It took Planck about an hour to go through the items in the cargo hold. While he was busy cataloging, the three Marines basically patrolled the area. In all honesty, Maker didn't think another attack was likely, but he had no intention of getting caught with his guard down. Eventually, Planck called the three soldiers together and announced that he'd reached a conclusion.

"I haven't seen everything, of course," he reported to Maker and the others, "but from what I can gather, most — if not all — of the tech taken from us is here. However, I won't be able to do a full accounting until we get back home."

Maker nodded. "Fair enough. Let's tell Skullcap we're satisfied, get back to the *Nova*, and tell the cruiser captains they can start sending transports for this stuff."

"No," muttered Planck.

Maker looked at him in surprise. "Excuse me?"

"I'm sorry," the scientist apologized. "What I meant to say was that I think I need to stay and make sure everything gets safely loaded. Some of the items here can be dangerous if not properly handled."

There was silence for a moment, and then Adames said, "That plan sounds like it needs to be fleshed out a little more. You do realize you're talking about staying here, by yourself, with a ship full of Vacra soldiers, right?"

Planck nodded. "I do, but it will give me time to catalog more of what's here, so I'll have less to do later."

"That does sound like an efficient use of time," Snick chimed in, "but not the wisest course of action considering the recent hospitality we received here."

"Skullcap's addressed that," Planck noted.

"*Allegedly*," clarified Adames. "Moreover…"

IGNOTUS

Maker turned away as the two Marines continued trying to change Planck's mind. He spent a moment staring at the communicator (and hoping it wasn't some type of bomb) and then activated the device.

"Hello?" he muttered, speaking into the device. "Anyone there?"

"Yes," came the immediate response. As Maker had expected, it was Skullcap speaking.

"We're done with our initial assessment," Maker informed him. "We're ready to start moving this stuff out."

"Very well," the insectoid said. "I will join you momentarily." He then broke the connection.

Having concluded his conversation with the Vacran, Maker turned back to his companions, where Planck was still adamantly standing his ground.

"It's fine," Maker blurted out, interrupting a point Adames was trying to make. "Planck, you can stay."

Adames frowned, obviously concerned. "Gant, are you sure—"

"Not really," Maker admitted, cutting off his NCO. "But if he wants to stay, I'm not going to force him back."

Planck had trouble hiding his surprise. "Really?"

"Yeah," Maker assured him. "Just try not to get killed."

"I'll do my best," Planck said with a smile.

He looked as though he wanted to say more, but at that juncture, Skullcap walked in.

"We're ready," Maker announced before the insectoid could say a word. "Planck, however, will remain here to continue taking a tally of what's present."

IGNOTUS

Skullcap gave Planck a momentary glance and then uttered, "That is acceptable. I will make sure all know he is to remain undisturbed."

With that, he turned to leave, and was quickly followed by Adames and Snick.

Maker, taking the opportunity to address Planck one last time confidentially, said, "You've got your p-comp. If you get the slightest indication of trouble — even just a feeling — let me know and we'll double-time it back here."

"I'm in a cargo bay full of illegal weapons and banned tech," Planck replied with a grin. "I think I'll be okay. And if necessary, I've still got my gun."

Maker raised an eyebrow skeptically. "I thought you weren't keen on using guns to solve issues."

"I was talking about *mental* issues," he corrected. "But to be honest, I've reassessed."

"Oh?" muttered Maker in surprise.

Planck nodded. "Yes — when we were trapped in that hallway, I actually found firing your gun to be quite therapeutic."

IGNOTUS

Chapter 72

Other than a long, hot shower after returning to their ship, the next few hours were fairly uneventful from Maker's point of view. There was hectic activity with respect to the cruisers (which had a constant team of transports ferrying items from the Vacra warship), but the *Nova* was pretty much idle.

Despite having little to do, Maker chose to spend his time on the bridge and kept the crew on high alert. (Skullcap, who had willingly come back on the shuttle from the Vacra warship, was once again confined to quarters.) This was undoubtedly the most important part of the mission — retrieving the stolen tech. In truth, it was the underlying reason why he and his team had been assembled in the first place. It was why he'd volunteered to escort Skullcap home. It's why they were currently putzing around in the middle of nowhere.

Thankfully, nothing untoward happened with respect to the loading and unloading of the sub rosa tech. It all seemed to go as smoothly and efficiently as possible, although Planck proved to be a bit of a micromanager. (He even traveled back and forth on the transports a couple of times to make sure that the off-loading was occurring in accordance with his instructions.) In fact, rather than come back immediately to the *Nova* after the final bit of cargo was placed on the last transport, the scientist went with it to one of the cruisers, determined to make one final inspection.

To a certain extent, Maker sympathized with Planck. The sub rosa tech represented his life's work. He had been captured and held prisoner by the Vacra because of those items. Getting them back was another

IGNOTUS

form of redemption for him. Thus, when the man asked for time to do one final walk-through, Maker saw no reason to deny him. That said, he didn't like the idea of a Vacra warship just sitting idly off their bow.

Seeking a solution to the problem, he went to see their guest. Surprisingly, Skullcap appeared to be expecting him.

"I take it the transfer of your property is complete?" the insectoid queried as soon as Maker entered.

Maker nodded. "Yes, we've finally transported everything to our cruisers. Thanks for your cooperation."

"Excellent. So this means you will escort me to the Vacra homeworld now?"

"That's an option," Maker said. "Of course, assuming certain safeguards can be put in place, you can just go back with your own people."

Skullcap made a bizarre chirping sound, which Maker, of course, couldn't interpret. However, he got the distinct impression that the thought of returning home on the warship had never occurred to the insectoid.

"Thank you for the offer," Skullcap remarked a moment later, "but I think your superiors were desirous that you and your companions receive a formal introduction to my people."

"That's fine, but I have no objection to you making the journey on your warship if you would be more comfortable in that environment."

"Again, your sentiment is to be commended, but I will complete this journey as I began it — with *your* retinue."

IGNOTUS

Maker shrugged. "Fine by me. So if you're certain about that, the next step is to give your friends their marching orders."

****

Skullcap stood on the bridge of the *Nova*, talking to the prior commander of the Vacra warship via the monitor. In essence, he stated in clear and unequivocal terms that the other vessel was to return to their homeworld and that he — accompanied by his new "allies" (Maker almost winced at the word) — would follow shortly thereafter. The warship commander appeared hesitant for a moment, but agreed to comply before breaking the connection.

"Last chance," Maker said to the Vacran. "You can still change your mind and catch a ride with your people. The warship commander sure looked like he'd prefer that."

Maker's comment garnered him an odd look from Browing, who was also on the bridge. (In fact, everyone was present except for Planck and Fierce, who was in the medical bay, as usual.) Thankfully, regardless of what he was thinking, Browing kept his thoughts to himself. His expression, however, was one that Maker had become familiar with, and he knew the man would seek him out later.

"Once again, that is gracious of you," Skullcap noted, "but I feel I should remain in your company for now."

Maker merely nodded in agreement. A few minutes later, as he watched on the bridge monitor, the Vacra warship vanished as it jumped to hyperspace.

IGNOTUS

Chapter 73

Maker found himself filled with conflicting emotions as he escorted Skullcap back to his cabin. On the one hand, he was almost exuberant at the fact that part of the mission was essentially over. On the other hand, he couldn't help worrying to a certain extent about what lay ahead. With that in mind, he thought it best to have a short talk with the insectoid. Ergo, when they reached the Vacran's quarters, Maker went in with him.

"Okay," Maker began once they were inside, "I'd like to avoid a replay of what happened on your warship. Therefore, against my better judgment, I'm going to allow you to wear your battle armor when we take you home."

"That would be prudent," Skullcap agreed, "although you have my word that there will be no repetition of the prior incident."

"Thanks, but in all honesty, I'm not sure what your word is worth."

"Given what has happened, that is not an inappropriate comment, but I am confident that time will reveal that I'm being candid."

"I won't hold my breath," Maker said, walking towards the door. "I'll let you know when we've reassembled your battle suit."

He heard the insectoid mutter a "Thank you" as he exited — and found himself immediately confronted by Browing.

"So what exactly are you up to?" Browing seemed to demand.

Maker didn't even try to disguise his confusion. "What do you mean?"

IGNOTUS

"Back on the bridge, you offered to let Skullcap go back home on the Vacra warship. Why?"

"Because I knew he wouldn't do it, although it felt good to get confirmation."

"How could you know that?"

"Because he saved my life."

Browing frowned. "I heard about that, but I'm not sure how it ties into him wanting to stay on the *Nova*."

"Initially, I wasn't thinking about that part — him staying on the *Nova*, that is. What I focused on at first was the question of why he'd save me — any of us, to be honest — especially after he indicated that one Vacra killing another is abominable. As a matter of fact, while Planck was doing his initial inspection of the sub rosa tech, that's *all* I could think about."

"Maybe he was just adopting the hallmarks of a good host, one of which is that you don't let your guests get killed."

"No," Maker insisted, shaking his head. "I mean, he clearly didn't want us dead, but it wasn't until he came back with us on the shuttle that I realized the reason, which Skullcap just corroborated when he said he'd remain here instead of hitching a ride back with his fellow Vacra."

"Okay, I'll bite: what's the reason?"

"He needs us," Maker declared.

IGNOTUS

Chapter 74

From Maker's perspective, Browing looked like he wanted to laugh at that last comment.

"What do you mean, 'He needs us'?" Browing asked.

"Exactly what I said," Maker answered. "He. Needs. Us."

"But why?"

Maker shook his head. "I don't know, but one thing's for sure: he's sticking close until he gets whatever it is he's after."

Browing rubbed his chin in thought for a moment. "Do you think this is another play for Erlen?"

"I thought about that — how this could possibly be a setup — but it just doesn't feel like it. I'm just not getting that vibe. But more telling is the fact that Erlen himself hasn't tried to claw Skullcap's face off."

"Seeing as he wanted to kill *me* when we first met, I'm not sure your Niotan friend is the best judge of character."

"There's an argument that you actually deserved his ire at the time," Maker noted, chuckling at the memory.

"Where is he, by the way?"

Maker shrugged. "Probably the observation lounge; he likes it there. But getting back to the subject at hand, I don't think that Lafayette and his cronies — knowing what they all know now — would willingly hand Erlen over. It would be tantamount to giving the Vacra a nuclear device."

"So if we're not giving Erlen up and Skullcap's no longer asking for him, what's his angle?"

IGNOTUS

Maker shook his head. "As I said, I don't know, but it's got something to do with him going home, since that's all he's asked for."

Browing pondered this for a moment and then said, "Might be a good idea to ask Planck. He may have some idea since he spent years around the Vacra."

"It's on my to-do list for when he comes back."

"*If* he comes back," Browing corrected.

Maker looked at him with a befuddled expression. "What's that supposed to mean?"

"Planck's the only person with firsthand knowledge of all that sub rosa tech," Browing explained. "That makes him a high-level asset that we can't afford to lose. With that understanding, he's expected to go back home on one of the cruisers."

Maker mentally chewed on Browing's comment for a second before admitting, "I'm not surprised by that. It's been clear that they'd rather kill Planck than have him fall into the wrong hands again. That said, he's given me the impression that he was returning to the *Nova* and—"

Maker found himself cut off as the ship's intercom came on and Diviana's voice sounded from the overhead speakers.

"El-tee, you need to get to the bridge," she announced. "We've got a situation here."

IGNOTUS

Chapter 75

Maker went racing to the bridge, followed by Browing. A few seconds later, they were joined by Erlen, and less than a minute later, they arrived at their destination.

"Okay," Maker said as he took his seat, with Erlen next to him. "What's happening?"

"There's a ship out there," Diviana said. "Still a bit far off, but until about a minute ago they were closing at a fast clip — coming straight at us. Now they've stopped."

The bridge monitor came to life then, showing a vessel with a design that was completely foreign to Maker. That said, it didn't take any special skill to recognize turrets and cannons, and the new ship had plenty. Still, it didn't necessarily mean they were facing an aggressor.

"Have they hailed us?" Maker asked.

"Not as of yet," Diviana answered.

"Maybe they're just passing through," suggested Wayne, who was at the flight and navigation controls.

"I'm not interested in finding out," Maker countered. "Is our navigation system still synced with the cruisers?"

Wayne shook his head. "No. They're going in a different direction than us, so there's no need."

"Great," Maker remarked, and then turned to Diviana. "Tell Planck that if he's coming with us, he's got about a minute to get his butt on a shuttle headed this way. Tell the cruiser captains to go to hyperspace the second Planck is clear of them."

Diviana nodded and relayed the messages. A few moments later, she turned back to Maker.

IGNOTUS

"The cruiser captains acknowledge your message," she stated. "Planck, however, says he needs another five minutes."

"Tell that idiot we may not *have* five minutes," Maker grumbled. A moment later he relented, muttering, "Fine, but tell him in five minutes he'd better be on one ship or the other, or he's getting stranded here."

Diviana acknowledged his order with a nod. Maker drummed his fingers for a moment, thinking, while Erlen — staring at the alien vessel on the monitor — let out a low growl.

Turning to Adames, Maker ordered, "Get Skullcap in here."

****

Adames had the insectoid on the bridge within minutes, at which point Maker explained the situation.

"In short," Maker stated, "we've got an alien ship that's making us jittery."

"It's an Xnjda craft," Skullcap stated after merely a glance.

"Xnjda?" Maker repeated. "You mean like the one who claimed to own Diviana?"

"Indeed," the insectoid replied.

"No way that's a coincidence," uttered Adames.

"Right," Maker agreed. "Diviana, tell Planck to shelter in place — he's stuck over there — and pass the word that we're scattering to the four winds asap."

Diviana nodded to show she understood.

"Wayne," Maker began, "get ready to—"

IGNOTUS

"Already on it, el-tee," interrupted the young Marine. "We'll be jumping to hyperspace before you ca—"

Wayne went silent as a sharp intake of breath from Diviana cut him off.

"What is it?" Maker asked, acutely aware that something was wrong.

"Scanners are picking up four ships that just dropped out of hyperspace in close proximity," Diviana replied. "No, six ships. Eight."

Without being told, Diviana manipulated the view on the bridge monitor, dividing it up into quadrants that showed four different exterior views. Each image showed alien vessels similar in design to the Xnjda craft, which collectively formed a circle around their convoy.

They were surrounded.

IGNOTUS

Chapter 76

"Shields up!" Maker bellowed.

"Activating shields," Loyola said in reply.

Maker breathed a small sigh of relief. Counting the ship they had initially spotted, there were nine Xnjda craft. More to the point, the eight that had dropped out of hyperspace — which were all oversized battleships — had cannons pointed at either the *Nova* or one of the two cruisers. Considering the size of their own convoy, Maker didn't like the odds if things got ugly (and it looked like they were already on that path).

At least the shields will give us some level of protection, he thought, operating on the assumption that the cruisers were following suit. Any relief he felt in that regard, however, was short-lived.

"Problem, Lieutenant," Loyola said. "Shields aren't activating."

"What?" he almost yelled in surprise. "Why not?"

"The defense system is experiencing some type of disruption," answered Loyola. "It's keeping the shields from coming online."

Maker could barely believe what he was hearing. "Can you pinpoint the source of the disruption?"

Loyola was silent for a moment as she stared at information flowing on a screen in front of her, and then she nodded. "It's coming from the shuttle bay."

Maker frowned, but before he could comment, Adames spoke up.

"I'll check it out," the NCO declared.

Adames began jogging towards the bridge exit, but stopped as Skullcap began to speak.

IGNOTUS

"If I might be so bold," the Vacran said, "I would advise that you focus on the exterior of the shuttle."

Adames just stared at him for a moment, then muttered, "Uh, thanks." A moment later, the NCO was gone.

Maker stared fixedly at Skullcap. "That was a pretty specific statement. Do you know something?"

"Not in particular," the insectoid replied. "However, when we were planet-side retrieving the tracker, the shuttle was the area with the greatest ability to be compromised."

Maker could have kicked himself. Skullcap was right. He, Maker, had failed to leave someone in position to guard the shuttle, which was a gross and embarrassing oversight on his part.

"We're being hailed," Diviana announced, cutting into Maker's thoughts.

"Which ship?" he asked.

"The first one," Diviana replied, "which is now moving in closer."

Maker looked at Wayne. "How long before we can jump?"

The young Marine gave Maker a confused look. "Honestly, I can't say, el-tee. The nav system is having an issue with coordinates again."

"What do you mean it's having issues?!" Maker demanded. "We're not synced with the other ships anymore!"

"I know," Wayne admitted, "but the system is still acting confused for some reason."

Maker let out a groan of frustration, then said, "Diviana, find out why those cruisers are still hanging around here."

IGNOTUS

Diviana nodded to show she understood. While she began reaching out to the other ships, Maker got a ping from Adames on his p-comp. It was an auditory communiqué, and the device automatically switched to voice mode as Maker answered.

"Our Vacran friend is right," Adames reported, sounding out of breath. (He had obviously run to the shuttle bay.) "There's some kind of device attached to the bottom of the shuttle. I didn't know what would happen if I touched it, so I left it alone."

"Shouldn't the shuttle's sensors have picked that up?" Maker asked rhetorically. "They're supposed to warn of foreign articles attached to the hull."

"I'm guessing it was cloaked in some way," said Adames. "Headed back your way." He then broke the connection.

Maker's brow creased as he reflected on the implications of everything he'd recently heard: they couldn't shield the ship, they couldn't jump to hyperspace... The situation was getting worse by the second. However, before he could devote more thought to the subject, Diviana began speaking.

"I've received word from the cruisers," she stated. "Their shields are down as well."

Mentally, Maker groaned. If the shields on the cruisers were being affected, it meant that one (or perhaps all) of the alien ships was acting as an amplifier or extender, broadening the effects of the device attached to the shuttle.

"In addition," Diviana continued, "both cruisers got hailed by a couple of those battleships. Basically, the alien vessels are going to fire if they detect any of our hyperspace drives coming online."

IGNOTUS

Maker smacked a fist on the arm of his chair in exasperation.

"Also, we're still being hailed by the first ship," Diviana added.

Maker put a hand up to his forehead, using his thumb and middle finger to massage his temples. In a mere matter of minutes, they had somehow managed to go from successfully completing a major part of the mission to having the rug snatched out from under them.

Actually, it's more like having the rug snatched out from under you and then finding out you're standing over a black hole, Maker thought.

"If I may offer a suggestion?" Skullcap chimed in, getting Maker's attention.

"I'm all ears," Maker said.

Skullcap seemed taken aback by the idiom for a moment (although he may also have been distracted by Adames returning to the bridge), but quickly recovered. "Let me speak with them — the Xnjda. Whatever the issue is, I may be able to help foster a resolution."

Maker glanced at Adames, openly soliciting his input. The NCO, plainly out of breath, simply shrugged.

"Okay, do it," Maker said.

A moment later, the bridge monitor shifted to a different image. Unsurprisingly, it showed Kpntel, who was easily recognizable by his missing limbs.

"Geez," Maker whispered to Skullcap. "Shouldn't he be in a hospital?"

"The Xnjda have a natural ability to deaden nerves at the site of an injury," Skullcap explained in a soft tone. "He won't get feeling again at those points until the limbs regrow."

IGNOTUS

Maker merely nodded, understanding now why the grizzly-pede wasn't in shock or screaming in pain back on that planet where they had initially encountered him.

"Honorable K'nsl," the grizzly-pede began, "I am surprised to see you. I had assumed you left with the Vacra warship."

"As I stated during our previous encounter, I travel with my companions," Skullcap stated, gesturing to include those on the bridge. "Although it is a pleasure to see you again, your statement suggests you have been watching us. Bearing that in mind, I take it you have arrived at a sum that will compensate you for your losses and have approached us to collect."

"Not exactly. But before we converse, I need to stress that none of your ships try to jump to hyperspace. We will open fire if we detect any such attempt."

"We're aware of that stricture," Skullcap assured him. "We also know you've disrupted our shields."

"Excellent," Kpntel commented. "Now, as to your prior statement, you may recall me mentioning that I traffic in rare breeds. Ergo, when you mentioned that there was a ship full of these creatures… Well, I suppose I felt the need to take advantage of an opportunity. And now — discovering that there are actually *three* ships full of them — it's as though I found a *Sl'velta* mine."

A shocked look settled on Maker's face (and pretty much everyone else on the bridge). Skullcap, however, continued talking without missing a beat.

"So," the insectoid continued, "it is your intent to seize everyone on these vessels and sell them as pets."

The grizzly-pede made a gurgling sound that Maker interpreted as laughter.

IGNOTUS

"Oh goodness, no," Kpntel said after regaining his composure. "This many specimens would wreck the market. It would be an oversupply that would drive prices into the ground. No, I would select only the fittest for sale in that regard — after all, I have a reputation to maintain."

"And what of the remainder?" Skullcap asked.

Something akin to a sly grin settled on the grizzly-pede's face. "Let's just say that there are certain races — such as those with expansive mining interests — that have a need for free and permanent labor. They don't ask many questions."

"I see," Skullcap muttered.

"It goes without saying, of course, that you yourself would be exempt from these actions," Kpntel stressed. "We have no wish to offend the Vacra and would allow you, personally, to continue on your way."

"That's kind of you," Skullcap noted, although Maker couldn't tell if he was being sarcastic.

"Of course, I'll need your word that you will not speak of this to anyone," Kpntel said.

"Is that all that you will require?" the insectoid asked, at which point Maker fought the urge to shoot him in the head.

"Of course," Kpntel answered. "Everyone knows that the word of the Vacra, once given, is never broken."

Skullcap seemed to ruminate for a few seconds, then said, "We will need time to discuss your…offer."

"Certainly," the grizzly-pede conceded. "You can have until the time my ship is close enough to begin ferrying my property on board. Also, I would advise you not to tamper with the shield disruptor, as the explosives within it are temperamental. And finally, if you want my

IGNOTUS

advice, life — of any sort — is preferable to being blasted to atoms, which is what will happen if we meet resistance."

He then disconnected and the monitor went dark.

IGNOTUS

Chapter 77

There was stunned silence on the bridge as everyone contemplated what they had just heard. To Maker, it seemed absolutely surreal. As a soldier, the notion of dying on the battlefield was something he'd made his peace with, but ending up as some alien's pet? It was more than he could fathom.

"Please know that I have no intention of deserting you," Skullcap remarked, cutting in on his thoughts. "I will share your fate, whatever it may be."

"Thanks," Maker blurted out in an acerbic tone. "That'll be a great comfort to me when I'm slaving away in an asteroid mine with a control collar around my neck."

Before the insectoid could reply, Maker looked at Diviana. "How long will it take the approaching ship to reach us?"

Diviana checked a monitor at the comm station. "Based on the distance established by the long-range scanners and the craft's current speed, we've got about twenty minutes."

Frowning, Maker turned his attention to Loyola, who was still at the weapon controls. "What are the odds that we can fight our way out of this?"

"Unlikely," Loyola replied. "They got the drop on us, coming out of hyperspace with guns at the ready. We could get off a couple shots from each ship in the convoy, but probably not enough to do any real damage. Moreover, without any shields, we'd just be target practice for them."

IGNOTUS

As Maker reflected on this, Diviana said, "I'm getting messages from the cruiser captains. They want to know what they should do."

"Tell them to stand down for now," he replied. "We're not in a position of strength, and we simply don't have the weapons or firepower to…"

He trailed off as a new thought suddenly blossomed in his brain.

"Get Planck on the comm," he ordered Diviana. "Now."

"Yes, sir," Diviana stated in acknowledgment.

Less than two minutes later, an image of Planck was on the bridge monitor. Maker immediately began asking questions in relation to his idea.

"Planck," he began, "what do you have over there that can help us?"

"Huh?" the scientist muttered, confused.

"You're on a ship full of illegal weapons, banned technology, and outlawed devices," Maker explained. "There's got to be something we can use to fight these guys off."

Planck suddenly looked nervous. "Uh…maybe. I'm not sure that… I mean, there might be something. But it's been so long that I'm not sure what would be best."

"We don't need the best," Maker clarified. "We just need something — anything — that will make these clowns back off."

"All right," Planck said with a nod. "I'll look around, see what's here, and try to come up with something. How much time do I have?"

"You've got about five minutes — max," Maker stressed. "And I suggest you do more than try, unless you

IGNOTUS

want to spend the rest of your life as the main attraction in an alien menagerie."

IGNOTUS

Chapter 78

Planck actually used the full five minutes allotted, but ultimately found something that he thought would work. Being pressed for time, however, he didn't provide Maker with much of an explanation.

"I just need whoever is the best shot with a laser rifle suited up and outside asap," Planck stated. "I'll explain what I need then."

That was as much as Planck was willing to give away in terms of what he had planned. However, with respect to his requirements, there was no question as to who the best shot was — with *any* weapon — in their entire convoy: Loyola.

Thus it was that, a few minutes after Planck made his request, Loyola was at one of the *Nova*'s airlocks, dressed in a spacesuit — which was like a light version of battle armor — and carrying a laser rifle. Maker, not wanting her venturing out without backup (and somewhat curious as to what Planck was planning) accompanied her, leaving Adames in charge on the bridge.

"You ready for this?" Maker asked over the comm system in their suits.

"Desperately ready," Loyola replied. "I've been dying to do something more than sit on the bridge."

"Well, you're getting your wish," Maker stated as he began to open the airlock, and then he halted.

"Listen," he said, "I don't mean to get into your personal life, but I have to ask about this child."

Loyola let out a groan of frustration. "Lieutenant, I understand your concern, but I'm still perfectly fit for duty, and will be for some time to come. It's a baby growing inside me — not a malignant tumor."

IGNOTUS

"I know," Maker declared with a nod, "and that's not where I was going. I'm trying to find out what Erlen's involvement was."

"You mean, whether he caused this to happen."

"That's pretty much a given. I'm more concerned with whether he did it without your consent."

"Consent?" she echoed. "Seems like a weird word to apply to this situation. Truthfully, it's a lot like that rifle I got from my wish list. Sure, it's something that I desperately wanted, but thought I'd never get. However, if someone had just given it to me unexpectedly — as a gift, for instance — I wouldn't say that they did it without my consent. It would be more like I didn't think to ask for it because I didn't believe I could get it. Likewise with this baby. So if you're asking if Erlen did something wrong, I'd say absolutely not."

"So, you're happy about this baby."

"Overjoyed," she said, nodding enthusiastically. "Fierce, too — at least, he'd better be."

Maker laughed. "Okay, I just wanted to confirm that Erlen didn't overstep. I mean, he understands what's acceptable, but I just wanted to make sure. Anyway, let's get back to the job at hand."

With that, Maker opened the airlock. A moment later, the door swung open, and Loyola — opting to go first — stepped out in the void of space.

She floated there for a second, drifting away from the ship, and then activated the jetpack on her suit. The rockets gave her the necessary thrust, pushing her back towards the ship. A moment later, her magnetic boots connected solidly with the *Nova*'s hull.

Upon seeing that Loyola had touched down safely, Maker followed suit, with the interior of his

IGNOTUS

faceplate displaying various information in one corner: speed, trajectory, and so on. (Exiting the airlock separately was a safety measure; it would have been a disaster to leave simultaneously and then discover that neither jetpack was working properly.) Seconds later, he was standing on the hull next to Loyola. Looking around, he noted the two battle cruisers in their convoy nearby. Also, he saw just how badly they were outnumbered and outclassed by the Xnjda battleships, each of which dwarfed their own vessels.

"El-tee," Diviana said, her voice coming through the suit's comm. "We're being hailed by that bug-bear again. Sergeant Adames is letting our Vacra friend talk to him, but thought you'd want to listen in."

"Sounds good," Maker said as he and Loyola stood on the hull.

Seconds later, he heard Kpntel saying, "We've detected movement outside two of your ships. I hope you aren't about to do anything foolish."

"No," Maker heard Skullcap reply. "Your disruptor is interfering with life support systems on the ships, so repairs must be made. Your device is incredibly effective."

"It should be," Kpntel intoned, "considering how much I paid to have it attached to your shuttle. And that was after paying to find out which vessel at the space station was yours."

"You raise an interesting point," the insectoid noted. "Judging by both your own craft and the battleships you have employed to surround us, you are obviously an individual of great wealth. Surely in the face of all you own, the creatures on these few ships are no more than a pittance. It would be of little or no

IGNOTUS

significance to you fiscally if they were allowed to go on their way."

"That is true," the grizzly-pede agreed. "However, I accumulated the wealth you mentioned by taking advantage of *every* opportunity — even the small ones."

Maker felt his hand clenching into a fist as Kpntel spoke. The grizzly-pede was quickly rising through the ranks on Maker's personal hit list, although he'd still have trouble challenging for the top spot.

A subtle chime indicated to Maker that someone was trying to reach him on another comm channel. Loyola was also getting the same notification; as a result, they both switched over simultaneously to find an eager Planck waiting to talk to them.

"I'm outside," the scientist said. "Can you see me?"

Maker looked towards the cruiser that Planck was on, magnifying the image on the interior of his faceplate. Scanning the hull of the other ship, he didn't see anything initially.

"I've got eyes on you," Loyola remarked, at the same time pointing to give Maker an indication of where to look.

Staring in the direction indicated, he finally saw Planck, standing on the outside of the cruiser and wearing a spacesuit identical to his and Loyola's.

"Okay, good," Planck uttered.

As Maker watched, the scientist reached down towards something akin to a spherical metal bin next to him. The bottom of it was apparently magnetized, because it stayed attached to the hull while Planck, working diligently, turned what appeared to be a screw-on top. However, rather than take the top completely off

IGNOTUS

when he was done, he lifted it just a crack and reached into the bin. (Obviously, Planck didn't want whatever was inside the metal container to float away in the zero-gravity of space.) A second later, he withdrew his hand and Maker saw that he was holding what appeared to be a rectangular white box that was perhaps eight-by-five inches in size, and perhaps two inches thick.

"Can you see this?" he asked, holding up the box as he screwed the top back onto the bin with his other hand.

"I've got eyes on it," Loyola replied, looking towards Planck through the scope on her rifle. "White box, one corner red."

Upon hearing Loyola's description, Maker looked again and noted that, as had just been stated, one corner of the box was indeed a deep crimson in color. Somehow, he had missed that detail at first.

"Okay, I'm going to throw this box toward one of the alien ships," Planck explained. "I need you to let it get a little bit away from me, and then shoot only the red corner. Not the entire box — just the red corner. Can you do that?"

"Piece of cake," Loyola replied without hesitation.

Maker couldn't help but be surprised by her confidence. In terms of distances in space, they were close to Planck, but in actuality — per Maker's estimate — they were about a mile apart.

Apparently Planck felt the same, because he asked, "Are you certain?"

"Yes," Loyola said flatly. "It won't be a problem."

"I mean, it's a long way," Planck noted, "and we probably won't have time for an alternate plan if—"

IGNOTUS

"Look, Planck," Loyola chided, "we can stand here shooting the bull about my skill set and what I can do, or you can let me prove it. Personally, I prefer the latter — hopefully before the alien mothership gets here and puts us all in leg-irons."

There was silence for a moment, and then Planck muttered, "Point taken."

"Good to hear," replied Loyola. "Ready when you are."

"All right," the scientist said. "Just remember, let it travel a bit before you shoot."

"How far?" she queried.

"Hmmm," Planck droned. "Just wait about ten seconds, and then shoot it at your leisure."

"Understood," Loyola stated.

"Okay, great," said Planck. "Tossing the first one…*now.*"

He threw the box up in an underhanded fashion, and it went spinning into the void. Knowing that Loyola was concentrating, Maker remained still and silent, although mentally he ticked off the seconds.

One-thousand-one, he thought. *One-thousand-two, one-thousand-three…*

Although he started his countdown from the moment Planck released the box, he actually struggled for a second or two to track the target, but then got it in view. Thus, by the time the ten seconds had elapsed, he was watching and noted when Loyola fired.

A ray of amber light struck the box, which went twirling away at a slight angle due to the impact. Because of its gyrations, it took Maker a few seconds to get a complete view of the box, but eventually he saw that the red corner had been sheared away — presumably by Loyola's shot.

He was about to congratulate her when something else drew his attention: emerald-colored light seemed to be dancing around the box as it continued moving away. For a moment, he thought Loyola had drawn some other weapon and was shooting at the target again, but then he realized that the new light was originating from Planck. The scientist was shining something like a laser pointer at the box, twirling it around.

"Okay, that should do it," Planck muttered, almost to himself.

"Do what?" queried Maker.

"Later," Planck promised, and then reached for the top of the metal bin. "Now for the next one…"

IGNOTUS

Chapter 79

It took only a few minutes for Planck to toss boxes in the direction of all nine alien vessels, saving Kpntel's flagship (as Maker thought of it) for last. It was a bit like skeet shooting, although at a slightly slower pace. That said, Loyola nailed the target — the red corner of every box — on each occasion with a single shot.

When they were done, Planck grabbed his bin and headed back inside the cruiser, while Maker and Loyola did the same on the *Nova*. Maker still had no clue what exactly they had accomplished, but he hurriedly got out of his suit and raced back to the bridge, noting that Loyola arrived only a few seconds after him.

Taking his seat, he asked of no one in particular, "Anything noteworthy happen while we were out?"

"Nothing much," Adames replied. "Just our future lord and master Kpntel saying how much we'll love our new lives as pets."

"That's not happening," Maker declared.

"So does that mean Planck's idea was a success?" Snick inquired.

Maker shrugged. "To tell you the truth, I don't even know what we purportedly did. But Planck seemed satisfied, so keep your fingers crossed that whatever he had us doing out there pays big dividends."

As he finished speaking, he saw Diviana gesture to get his attention.

"We're being hailed," she announced.

"Let me guess," Maker muttered. "It's the Xnjda mothership."

IGNOTUS

"Uh, yeah," stated Diviana, smiling at his phrasing. A moment later, Kpntel appeared on the monitor.

"The time has come," the grizzly-pede declared. "Prepare to be boarded. Also, although it probably goes without saying, any resistance will be met with extreme force."

"We understand," Skullcap said. "Are you certain there is no way to dissuade you from this course of action?"

"I'm afraid not," Kpntel answered. "I am…"

The grizzly-pede trailed off as some kind of commotion began near him. Although not visible on the monitor, it seemed to consist of several voices shouting something that was unintelligible to Maker. A moment later, the *Nova* shook wildly as something like a violent tremor seemed to pass through it. Maker recognized what it was from experience: the concussive blast from an explosion in space. And to the extent he needed confirmation, he got it from Diviana a second later.

"Lieutenant," she began, "scanners show that one of the alien battleships is gone — exploded."

Maker barely had time to digest the news before the *Nova* was rocked again and went lurching sideways.

"Correction," Diviana said. "*Two* of the alien battleships have exploded."

On the monitor, Kpntel seemed to be receiving the same report from one of his people as he stared out angrily at those on the *Nova*'s bridge.

"What did you do?" he demanded. "What did you do?!"

Ignoring him, Maker told Wayne, "Get us out of here." As the young Marine gave a nod of

IGNOTUS

acknowledgment, Maker ordered Diviana, "Tell the cruisers we're on the move." He then turned his attention back to the monitor.

Onscreen, Kpntel was no longer asking what was going on in enraged tones. Instead, he looked as though an invisible person was tickling him with a feather — jerking left and right, and looking all around in bewilderment. It was almost like he was being annoyed by a bug that only he could see. But whatever was going on, it seemed to have an immediate and visible effect on the grizzly-pede physically, as his body seemed to diminish in both breadth and stature. In addition, his face started to look hollow and his eyes sunken; the carapace covering him began to take on an ashen appearance.

"Who…what…?" Kpntel mumbled, plainly addled.

A moment later, the grizzly-pede, now looking cadaverous, seemed to wince, and then he screamed — a long, undulating sound of fear, pain, and anguish. But he was far from the only one; all around him, cries and howls could be heard coming from others on his ship.

Suddenly Kpntel convulsed once, and then appeared to freeze in place, almost as if he'd turned to stone. (Frankly speaking, in Maker's opinion, the grizzly-pede's complexion had unexpectedly adopted a sallow and pasty tone that made him look more like a life-sized clay figurine than a living creature.) Following this, to everyone's shock, Kpntel's body began to peel, his skin breaking off in flakes and scabs that fluttered down like autumn leaves falling from trees. Within moments, it became abundantly clear that his entire body was completely desiccated.

IGNOTUS

Tiring of the gruesome spectacle, Maker declared, "That's enough, Diviana."

The screen mercifully went dark, and a few moments later — as another blast hit the *Nova* — Diviana reported, "All alien ships destroyed."

IGNOTUS

Chapter 80

Thankfully, Maker's entire convoy made it through the encounter with Kpntel essentially intact. Each ship had suffered damage to some degree from the exploding battleships, but it was mostly cosmetic. Aside from making sure their ships were still space-worthy, Maker had two immediate concerns.

The first was the shield disruptor — he wanted it off the *Nova* asap. Fortunately, it had ceased functioning after the destruction of Kpntel's ship (indicating that it was somehow remotely operated). At that juncture, Wayne was easily able to detach and study it.

Reporting his findings to Maker, the young Marine said, "I've disconnected the explosives, but it's definitely what was disrupting our shields."

"Good job," Maker told him. "Now toss it out an airlock or something."

"Will do, but it's weird, though," Wayne noted, scratching his temple. "They knew how to cloak it from our shuttle's sensors and it was designed to disrupt our systems, but humans aren't known in this area of space."

"It's not that weird when you consider that Kpntel sold us as pets, among other things," Maker countered. "He obviously encountered humans at some point in the past and had an opportunity to study our ships and technology."

"In other words, he was a pirate as well as a slaver," Wayne surmised.

"I think recent events have pretty much established that," Maker concurred before sending Wayne on his way.

IGNOTUS

The other concern Maker had was finding out what exactly had happened to Kpntel's ships. For that, he had to wait until Planck returned to the *Nova*, which actually happened sooner rather than later. Ergo, the minute the scientist came on board, carrying a satchel slung over one shoulder, Maker hustled him into the conference room, where they were joined by Browing and Dr. Chantrey.

"Okay," Maker began, "please explain exactly what you did to those alien vessels."

"Happy to," Planck said in a bit of a chipper tone. "One of my former colleagues — Harris was his name — spent years working on a project he called the Poseidic Exsiccator, which basically consisted of nanobots designed to suck water out of compounds."

"And that's what you used on those ships?" asked Browing.

"Yes," Planck confirmed with a nod. "Harris originally conceived of them as being able to help irrigate arid regions, such as being able to burrow down to the water table and then transport water from there to the surface."

"Obviously there were military applications as well," Maker noted.

"Oh, yes," Planck agreed. "For instance, if you were under siege, you could deploy the nanobots to essentially confiscate the enemy's supply of water. Since it's a basic requirement for almost every species we know, lack of water would eventually force them to retreat. That was one of several non-lethal applications for the technology."

IGNOTUS

"Non-lethal?" Maker repeated. "Maybe you missed what happened back there, but that was about as far from non-lethal as you can get."

"I've seen the effect they have on living creatures," Planck said. "And I agree — it's horrific."

Maker simply stared at him for a moment. Although he'd heard Planck's last comment, it didn't sound to him like the man thought it was horrific at all. Instead, he had uttered the phrase with the same dispassion one might display when giving the time of day to a stranger on the street. Maker now vividly recalled that Planck had been the lead scientist in charge of a group making all kinds of nasty weapons, and he suddenly questioned whether it was in anyone's best interest to have Planck return to "normal."

"The problem," Planck continued, "is that the nanobots can't seem to differentiate between living and non-living things."

"In other words, they suck the water — and the life — out of everything around them," Chantrey concluded.

Planck nodded. "Pretty much."

"So how exactly did you get them onto those ships?" Browing queried.

"That's where Sergeant Loyola came in," Planck answered. "The nanobots are generally kept dormant in special containers. However, within each container is a generator. When the generator is turned on, the nanobots are activated."

"So how do you turn on the generator?" Chantrey inquired.

IGNOTUS

"It just needs an influx of power, and it's designed to secure it from myriad sources," Planck explained. "A battery, or a live wire, or—"

"Light," Maker interjected. "Including laser light."

"Exactly," Planck concurred with a smile. "The corner of the containers that Sergeant Loyola shot with her laser rifle were the areas that contained the generators."

"But didn't her shots destroy that section of each container?" Maker asked.

"Yes," Planck admitted, "but the generator only needs power flowing through it for a nanosecond — no pun intended — in order to activate the bots. The laser beam did that. Afterwards, the nanobots came flying out of the container and I used a laser pointer to push them to the alien ships."

Browing frowned. "What do you mean, you pushed them to the ships?"

"When they were being designed, we came up with several methods for making the bots move in the direction we wanted them to go," Planck explained. "One of those techniques was light sails — microscopic sails which, as the name implies, can harness light and use it to move a craft. Of course, it moves them at sub-light speed, but still pretty darn fast."

"So you used the pointer to fill the light sails and send all the nanobots to the various ships," Chantrey concluded.

"Well, not *all* of them," Planck admitted.

"What do you mean?" asked Maker.

"They're microscopic, so it's not like I could actually *see* them," the scientist explained. "But I knew

IGNOTUS

that I'd be able to send enough of them to the various ships to get the job done."

"And the rest are what — just floating out there?" Browing asked. "What if they find their way to *our* ships?"

"That's unlikely," Planck insisted, shaking his head. "First of all, they can't survive — for lack of a better term — in the vacuum of space for very long. In fact, they will avoid non-atmospheric conditions whenever possible. In addition, my laser pointer served as a directional beacon of sorts, kind of like the old laser-guided missile systems. Any nanobots that didn't catch the beam in their light sails would have tried to reach the respective alien ships under their own power because that's where the beam pointed."

"And after they got to the ships, they just went to town, right?" Maker asked. "Swarmed all over each of them and sucked the place dry."

Planck shrugged. "It's what they were designed to do. And again, they're microscopic, so it would have been pretty tough to keep them out once they reached their destination."

"What about the ships blowing up?" queried Maker. "Were they designed to do that as well?"

"No," the scientist admitted. "Without specific instructions regarding what to do with the water they absorb, the nanobots will perform electrolysis — split the water into the hydrogen and oxygen atoms that comprise it. Hydrogen, being a highly flammable gas, may have interacted with something on the ships, which resulted in an explosion. However, my best guess is that the bots attacked some structure that required water or moisture to properly function — a cooling system for the engines or something like that. Since it happened on all the ships,

IGNOTUS

it probably relates to something in their configuration or construction."

"So if Kpntel and his cronies hadn't been turned into dry husks," Browing noted, "they would have gotten blown to bits."

"That wasn't the plan," Planck replied, "but apparently that's how it worked out."

"Well, to be honest," said Chantrey, "I'm more concerned about the nanobots doing something like that on one of our ships — or worse, on one of our worlds."

"No, no, no," intoned Planck. "That will never happen."

As he spoke, he reached into the satchel he was carrying and pulled out something that caused Maker's eyes to go wide with shock: it was one of the containers used to house the nanobots they'd been discussing.

"See, the container that the bots are in is completely sealed," Planck continued, holding up the white box (which Maker could now see was made of metal) for all to see. "Furthermo—"

"Are you crazy?!" Maker bellowed. "You brought one of those damn things on board the *Nova*?!"

"Actually, I brought the last three with me," Planck responded, patting the satchel to indicate that the remainder were inside.

Chantrey, looking pale, asked, "Why would you do that?"

"Well, the captain of the cruiser I was on asked me essentially the same things you did," Planck explained. "After I told him about the nanobots, he didn't want them on his ship anymore. Actually, I don't think he wanted *me* on his ship anymore, either."

"I can't imagine why not," Maker deadpanned.

IGNOTUS

"Anyway, I complied with his wishes, so here we are," Planck said. "But you want to know what's funny? He wanted the nanobots off his ship because he thought they were dangerous, but these things" — he shook the container in his hand for emphasis, causing the other three present to wince — "these things are a Christmas present compared to some of the stuff in his cargo hold."

And then he started laughing.

IGNOTUS

Chapter 81

For Maker, the first order of business after the discussion with Planck was to confiscate the remaining nanobot containers. Fortunately, Planck didn't make a fuss about it, so Maker was able to take possession of them without issue. After doing so, his natural inclination was to strap them to a rocket and fire it into the nearest star. Instead, however, he locked them in the safe in his office. (Also — just in case something happened to him later — he brought Adames up to speed regarding the containers and their location.)

Next, he checked in with the two cruiser captains, who were naturally ready to head back to Gaian Space. With no need for their services anymore (and establishing that neither was willing to take custody of the nanobot containers), he confirmed that they could depart. Within fifteen minutes, the two ships were gone.

With the *Nova* now alone in an unfamiliar (and possibly unfriendly) region of space, Maker was more eager than ever to get the last leg of their journey underway. As before, however, the navigation system was having problems. Focused on getting answers, Maker tracked Wayne down to his workroom, where the latter was busy reassembling Skullcap's armor.

"I can't tell you what the issue is," Wayne declared in response to Maker's inquiries. "I've run diagnostics three times and there's nothing wrong."

"There's got to be *something*," Maker insisted. "I mean, a halfway decent navigator could have calculated a jump by hand at this point." It was a slight exaggeration, but not far from the truth.

IGNOTUS

"I get what you're saying," Wayne countered, "and I don't disagree. But if there's some problem, it's not systemic."

"So what, we just have to wait it out?"

"Apparently," Wayne noted. "But on the bright side, it does give me time to finish putting this" — he gestured towards the dismantled armor — "back together."

Maker gave the pieces of the battle armor a once-over. "How's that coming, by the way?"

"It's pretty straightforward," Wayne said. "I could probably do it with my eyes closed."

"Well, hurry up and finish," Maker admonished, "and then get that nav system working."

"Will do," Wayne replied as Maker left.

****

Maker left Wayne's workroom still feeling agitated. He was ready for this mission to be over. The only thing left on their agenda was getting Skullcap home, but the *Nova* itself seemed to be thwarting their plans.

At the thought of taking their insectoid guest home, however, something new occurred to Maker, and he realized he had to have another conversation with Planck. Thus it was that, a few minutes later, he found himself outside the man's door. Pressing the doorbell, he was surprised when it was opened almost immediately.

"Lieutenant," he said. "Please come in. I've been expecting your visit."

"You have?" Maker asked as he stepped inside and the door shut behind him.

IGNOTUS

"Of course," Planck stated, leading the way to the living room. "Bearing in mind that our final destination is Ignotus, I knew you'd come to see me at some juncture."

He took a seat in an easy chair while Maker sat down on the end of a sofa diagonal to him.

"So," Maker droned. "What can we expect when we get there?"

"Vacra," Planck answered with a grin. "Lots of them."

Maker smiled, appreciating the man's attempt at humor. "Anything more specific?"

"Well, you have to remember I was a prisoner, so it's not like I got the grand tour. I can give you a better description of their holding cells than I can of their guest quarters."

"So you've got no idea what kind of reception we should expect."

"Well, I typically didn't get the invite to formal events. Although occasionally…"

He trailed off, staring into the distance. It was clear to Maker that he was recalling some event or other related to their conversation.

"Occasionally what?" Maker prompted.

"Huh?" Planck muttered, coming back to himself. "Oh, uh, they would, uh, occasionally bring someone to watch when they, uh…when they extracted information from me."

Planck looked down. This was clearly a subject that was difficult for him. That said, it was important for Maker to get whatever he could from the man, although he had difficulty keeping his voice even in light of what he'd just heard.

IGNOTUS

"They invited others to watch while they tortured you?" queried Maker. "Like entertainment?"

"No," Planck responded, shaking his head. "I mean, yes, they did bring others in, but — looking back — I don't think it was just for kicks."

"Still, to parade people through while they put you on the rack and such… It's barbaric."

Planck's eyes narrowed. "Now that I think about it, it actually wasn't an extensive list of people they had me perform for, so to speak. There was really just one person — or just one race, I should say, since I honestly couldn't tell the difference between individuals."

"Did you recognize them?"

"No, they were a species humanity hasn't encountered yet," Planck noted, shaking his head. "They looked like something you'd get if an Old Earth aardvark and a table leg had a baby — a snout, wooden epidermis, light fur, a tail."

Maker frowned. It didn't sound like any race he'd ever heard of.

"Anyway," Planck continued, "more than the physical distress, it was the psychological torture that really broke me down."

Maker merely nodded, not saying anything.

"It was like an extreme version of 'good cop, bad cop,'" Planck went on. "There would be periods where they'd treat me almost humanely, and I'd start thinking that the Vacra weren't so bad. A minute later, they'd be waterboarding me. Sometimes I think it would have been better if it had just been torture all the time, you know? At least then I would have known what was coming. But not knowing what to expect whenever they opened the door — wondering if I was going to get food for the first time in days or get hooked up to a car battery — it was agony."

"And Skullcap was there?" Maker asked.

"Typically," Planck said. "It was like he took a personal interest in me."

"And the sub rosa tech?"

Planck nodded. "I had to tell them about it — show them how to operate it. Not all of it, mind you, but enough. Frankly speaking, I think most of it frightened them. They didn't seem to understand how or why humans would construct some of the things we did."

"Like the Poseidic Exsiccator."

"Exactly. To them, we were playing Russian roulette with our very existence."

Maker didn't comment, but Planck's statements jibed with what he'd been told about the Vacra not wanting the sub rosa tech anywhere near their homeworld.

"Well," Maker intoned, coming to his feet, "I should let you get some rest. I'm sure you must be exhausted."

"A little," Planck agreed, rising as well. "However, I was wondering if I might ask a favor."

"Sure," Maker replied, although somewhere in the back of his mind he was wondering if he'd regret it.

Planck seemed to concentrate for a moment, then let out a deep breath. "As you already know, before the Vacra captured me, I oversaw the development of all kinds of technology and devices — most of which could be weaponized or had some kind of military application."

"Like the nanobots we discussed earlier," Maker chimed in.

IGNOTUS

"Yes," Planck muttered almost sheepishly. "I was a different man back then, just pursuing knowledge for its own sake and not worrying about the effects or long-term outcome of what we were doing. And after today, I suddenly realize how easily I could go back to being who I was — how seamlessly I could slip back into that skin."

Maker frowned. "I thought that's what you wanted — to go back to being normal."

"That's just it — there's nothing *normal* about what I did before. Normal people don't sit around thinking of new ways to kill people, or work on refining weapons that could make an entire race extinct. They don't do what I've done or see the things I've seen, and then sleep like a baby at night."

"You can't look at it like that," Maker stressed. "You have to disassociate yourself — not allow what you do to define who you are. It's like being a soldier; you're required to kill, but it doesn't make you a killer."

Maker worried for a second that the distinction might be lost on Planck, but he seemed to grasp it.

"I understand," Planck stated, "but…" He went silent for a moment, then let out a deep sigh and continued. "I saw the way the rest of you looked at me when I told you about the nanobots. Shock, horror, disgust."

"To be honest, I think it was just fear," Maker interjected. "Nobody wanted to end up a dust bunny."

Planck snickered slightly at that, rewarding Maker's attempt to lighten the mood.

"Regardless," Planck said, "I suddenly realized that people had been looking at me like that for years, and I'd never noticed. But, although I ignored them at the time, your expressions today stuck with me for some reason. And now, I don't want people looking at me like that ever again, but if I go back to having the same duties and doing the same work as before, that's exactly what will happen."

"I understand," Maker uttered, commiserating with the man. "But I'm not sure what the solution is."

"Well," remarked Planck, "I was hoping that — since none of your people appear to judge me for my past — I might become a permanent part of your team."

IGNOTUS

Chapter 82

Maker left Planck's cabin without giving the man a definitive answer. Had the request been made before they left — back when he was bargaining with Lafayette — Maker might have acquiesced. At the moment, however, he felt he had likely used up all his chips in terms of demands and special requests. (Plus, Planck's handlers would probably have a lot of heartburn at the thought of him simply walking away.)

Surprisingly, however, it was something else that kept clawing its way to the forefront of Maker's brain: Planck's treatment at the hands of the Vacra. Not that Maker was unaware of what had happened when Planck was in their custody — everyone on the *Nova* knew. It was more the fact that Skullcap seemed to be taking on the role of staunch ally now. It galled Maker severely, and he unexpectedly found himself filled with a desire to confront the insectoid.

As it turned out, however, Skullcap wasn't in his cabin when Maker dropped in. A quick chat with the bridge indicated that the Vacran was in the observation lounge under the watchful eye of Adames. Maker immediately headed in that direction.

When he arrived, he first noted Skullcap standing near the outer window while Adames, near the rear of the lounge, kept the Vacran in view. Much to his surprise, he saw that Erlen was in the lounge as well, and was also at the window near their guest.

Maker quickly approached Adames, who acknowledged his presence with a nod.

"What's going on here?" Maker asked, gesturing towards Erlen and Skullcap.

IGNOTUS

Adames shrugged. "Beats me. Our Vacran friend requested a little time here, and I figured it was suitable compensation in light of the fact that he behaved himself during that situation with Kpntel. Erlen was already here when we arrived. I thought somebody was going to get mauled to death, but they just sort of fell into place where you see them now."

Maker's brow furrowed as he pondered the NCO's words. Throughout this mission, Erlen had seemingly abandoned his typical attack-on-sight approach when it came to the Vacra, which was downright bizarre. The Niotan now appeared to be on civil — if not openly friendly — terms with their guest.

"So what are you thinking?" Maker asked. "That they declared peace or something?"

Adames smiled. "If not peace, then at least a ceasefire."

Maker was on the cusp of responding to that when he heard Erlen let out an angry growl.

"Looks like the ceasefire is over," he said.

He then stepped quickly towards the observation window, intending to step between the Niotan and the Vacran before anything crazy happened. However, when he reached them, he saw that — although Erlen was still growling — the Niotan's irritation wasn't directed at Skullcap. Instead, it seemed to be focused on something he was seeing through the observation window.

Maker glanced out, trying to determine what was annoying Erlen. However, he saw nothing beyond the usual: stars twinkling, a few heavenly bodies, and the darkness of the void.

"What is it?" he asked Erlen, who simply snarled loudly.

IGNOTUS

"What's going on?" Adames inquired.

"I'm not sure," Maker admitted, frowning. "But there's something out there that Erlen doesn't like."

IGNOTUS

Chapter 83

Maker didn't mince words. Racing back to the bridge, he gave an order that they run every test, every scan, every analysis at their disposal to find who or what was near the *Nova*. To no one's great surprise, the answer was discovered by Wayne, whom Maker had pulled from the task of reconstructing Skullcap's armor.

"There's a ship out there," Wayne said, after having tackled Maker's pet project for about an hour. He made the announcement in the conference room, where Maker had gathered everyone on board (sans Skullcap) after Wayne had given him an initial report of his findings.

"A ship?" Browing repeated. "Are you sure?"

Wayne nodded. "Yes. It's employing some kind of stealth or cloaking technology, so it's not visible to the naked eye or our scanners."

"Then how do you know it's there?" queried Snick.

"There are a couple of giveaways," Wayne replied. "First and foremost, all spaceships have a thermal system to control the temperature inside so that travelers can stay comfortable and operational equipment can perform at peak efficiency. As a result of normal operations, the thermal system generates heat that regularly gets vented into space. In this instance, we've picked up minute increases in temperature with no visible source or cause."

"So you assume it's coming from a ship," Chantrey surmised.

"Correct," Wayne stated with a nod. "Next, going with the theory that there was actually a ship out there, I

IGNOTUS

decided to check to see if that's what was interfering with the navigation system."

Browing frowned. "You mean intentionally?"

Wayne shrugged. "Intentionally, inadvertently, willfully…whatever."

"And?" Browing added eagerly.

"There's a latent piloting algorithm that's been embedded in — and slaved to — our navigation system."

"Excuse me?" muttered Loyola.

"The ship out there is linked to us," Maker explained. "Where we go, they go."

"And it looks like the algorithm that cuffs us together was in the nav system before we even left for this mission," Wayne added. "That's why it's been having trouble from day one."

"So if it was in the system before we left Gaian Space, that means the ship out there is probably one of ours," Adames surmised.

"Bearing in mind that the *Nova* was bugged, we should have expected something like this," Maker noted.

"And since we think it's one of ours," Loyola said, "I take it we can't just blast them to bits."

"That's not high on the list of options at the moment," Maker stated.

"I thought you ran diagnostics on the nav system," Diviana interjected, speaking to Wayne. "How could you miss something like that?"

"First of all, as I said, it's a latent program," Wayne declared defensively. "It stays hidden until we're getting ready to jump to hyperspace. Ergo, when I tested the system, it didn't pop up. On top of that, you have to remember that there's nothing inherently wrong with the

IGNOTUS

nav system, so there was no indication we needed to do a deep dive."

"If there's nothing wrong, then why isn't it working?" Snick asked.

"It *is* working, and working correctly," Wayne countered. "The nav system passed all the requisite diagnostic tests with flying colors. Think of it along the lines of testing a calculator by asking it to add two plus two. If it gives you four, it's working correctly. I got a 'four' out of the nav system, so to speak."

"Then why is it having so many issues calculating a jump?" Snick continued.

"Because on the one hand, we're telling the nav system that we're a single ship attempting a hyperspace jump," Wayne explained. "On the other hand, the hidden algorithm is telling it that we're a two-ship convoy and we need to jump together."

"So it's confused," Adames summed up.

Wayne nodded. "In essence. Moreover, when the navigation program checks with the *Nova*'s other systems — say, the scanners — and tries to figure out where this second ship is located relative to us for purposes of the jump, it's told that there *is* no other ship. It's like we're asking it to do a handstand, and also jump up and down on one leg at the same time. Needless to say, it's having trouble solving this conundrum."

"So what do we do now?" queried Chantrey.

"I can isolate the hidden program and decouple the link so that the other ship isn't slaved to us anymore," Wayne answered. "The next time we jump, they'll stay behind."

"So they'll be stranded here?" observed Snick.

IGNOTUS

"No," Maker insisted, shaking his head. "They presumably have their own navigation system, so we're not leaving them high and dry. They're just not coming with *us*. But they'll still be able to backtrack and go home using the prior coordinates."

"So, how soon before we leave?" asked Browing.

"As soon as the bridge crew can take their seats," Maker replied.

IGNOTUS

Chapter 84

They made the jump almost as quickly as Maker had envisioned it — essentially as soon as everyone was at their duty stations. It only took Wayne a few minutes to terminate the link between the *Nova* and the cloaked vessel, following which the navigation system calculated the hyperspace jump in what felt like record time. Moments later, they were gone.

Maker could only imagine the expressions on the faces of the stealth ship's crew after the *Nova* vanished. The thought of them suddenly running around helter-skelter, trying to find out what had happened, was hysterical to him. In fact, he chuckled at the mental image — although apparently a bit louder than he intended, because several people on the bridge gave him odd looks.

No one said anything to him, but he recognized what he saw in their eyes. It was the same look he himself had given various commanding officers during stressful situations — when said commanders had seemingly pushed themselves to the breaking point.

Maker didn't think he was anywhere near that stage, but he certainly understood that he probably didn't cut a striking figure at the moment. He was long overdue for sleep, couldn't remember the last time he'd eaten, and now seemed to be getting giddy over his own private jokes. Frankly, after dealing with crisis after crisis for hours on end, he was running on fumes and it showed.

He spent a moment reflecting on their current situation. The hyperspace jump they'd just completed was only one of several they'd have to make before arriving at Skullcap's homeworld. Thus, he had time to recharge his batteries, if he so desired. That being the case (and

IGNOTUS

recognizing that he'd want to be at his best when they reached Ignotus, as Planck referred to it), Maker announced that he was going off-duty and left the bridge.

He went straight to his cabin, where — after casually noting that Erlen wasn't present — he wolfed down a couple of protein bars. He then went into the bedroom and practically collapsed onto the bed. Within moments, he was asleep.

IGNOTUS

Chapter 85

Maker awoke to the sound of voices coming from his living room. He recognized them immediately — Chantrey and Adames — but couldn't understand what they were saying. As he sat up, he also realized that someone had thrown a blanket over him while he slept. Tossing it to the side, he hurriedly got out of bed and went into the adjoining bathroom to freshen up. A minute later, he walked into the living room looking far more presentable than he had when he'd gone to bed.

"Look who's awake," Chantrey said with a smile. She was sitting on the sofa with Erlen next to her.

Maker glanced around, frowning. "I thought I heard Adames out here."

"You did," Chantrey confirmed. "You missed him by maybe ten seconds, but he just dropped by to see if you were up on your feet yet."

"Why?" Maker asked, sounding concerned as he sat down beside her. "Did something happen?"

"No, but if you're looking for a status report, the next hyperspace jump takes us to our Vacran friend's homeworld."

Maker fought to hide his surprise at being so close to their final destination. "How soon before we leave?"

She shrugged. "That's up to you. Adames and the rest of your team basically refused to make the final jump while you, their commanding officer, was catching forty winks. They knew you'd want to be there, so to speak."

"They're right about that, but they shouldn't have held things up because of me. How long have I been snoozing?"

"About ten hours, give or take."

IGNOTUS

"Ten hours?" he echoed unbelievingly. "Someone should have just woken me up."

"I think they all realized you needed your beauty sleep."

"Then you should have awakened me with a kiss."

"I tried more than kisses, buddy," she uttered coyly, "but you weren't cooperating."

"So you just settled for grabbing a blanket and tucking me in."

"Actually, the blanket was Erlen's doing," Chantrey clarified, gesturing toward the Niotan (who purred softly as if in confirmation of her statement).

"Still, it was nice of you to check in on me."

"Actually, I only dropped in to check on Erlen," she said jokingly.

Maker glanced at the Niotan and said in a playfully stern voice, "Why do you get all the women?"

"Probably because he takes care of himself," Chantrey admonished, looking Maker over closely. "You know, you really should let Adames put you on the schedule."

"Huh?" Maker muttered, frowning.

"Well, he oversees shift duty for everyone else, making sure they all get adequate downtime. Obviously, you need someone making sure you go off-duty on the regular before you start passing out in the hallway."

"For the record, I never came close to passing out in a hallway, corridor, passageway, what have you."

"Yes, but constantly pushing yourself to the limit isn't healthy — mentally or physically."

"So the next time an intergalactic slaver tries to take us captive, I should just call time-out? Or take a rest

IGNOTUS

break when it's discovered that a ship has been tailing us in stealth mode? Or—"

"Okay, I get it," Chantrey intoned. "This mission's been nothing but a pressure cooker from the moment we started, but you're the only one running themselves completely ragged over every little thing that happens."

"Are you saying I'm wrong to be concerned?"

"I'm saying the leader sets the tone," she countered. "If your people see you wearing yourself to a frazzle, they're going to think it's expected of them as well."

Maker wiped his face with his hand, letting out a groan of frustration.

"All right — point taken," he said. "But seeing as how we're practically at the end of this particular mission, I'll apply your sage advice during the next assignment."

"Then my work here is done," Chantrey declared, rising to her feet. "Anyway, you should probably get ready."

"Get ready?" he echoed, rising as well.

"You're part of the diplomatic corps on this trip, which means you'll be formally introduced to the bigwigs of the Vacran race. With that in mind, you should dress and look the part of a representative of mankind, so that means you need to shower, get cleaned up, put on your good suit, and so on."

"Isn't Browing the chief diplomat on this roadshow? Let him do all that."

"He is, but you — as the military attaché — have a role to play as well. It'll send a mixed message if he looks smart and you look like you just escaped being crushed by a trash compactor."

IGNOTUS

"Fine," Maker muttered in acquiescence. "I'll go get ready. But there's just one thing."

"What?" Chantrey asked, openly curious.

Maker gestured towards the bedroom, saying, "The shower in there — it's kind of big. Gets kind of lonely in there, to be honest."

Chantrey laughed out loud. "Nice try, but we've already wasted enough time just waiting on you to wake up. I'm not going to be the cause of any additional delay."

"How about a rain check, then?" he asked. "After this mission's done?"

Chantrey smiled as she headed towards the door. "I'm going to assume that's a rhetorical question."

IGNOTUS

Chapter 86

The hyperspace jump to Skullcap's homeworld was probably the most anxious of Maker's entire military career. Not only were they headed to what he considered to be enemy territory, but said enemies knew they were coming and were expecting them.

That said, he didn't think any of his anxiety showed. After taking a quick shower, he had made a brief announcement from his office comm that they would be taking the last leg of their journey in short order. He had then put on his service dress and headed out. It wasn't the attire he would normally have chosen, but if this did turn out to be an ambush of sorts, he'd get his final send-off wearing the uniform he had always expected to be buried in.

Thankfully, nothing untoward happened during the jump itself, but they came out of hyperspace in a region that was — not unexpectedly — teeming with Vacra vessels. Almost immediately, they were hailed. Skullcap, dressed in his battle armor as he had desired (minus the helmet that was the source of his moniker), spoke on their behalf when they responded.

"Commander," said an insectoid who appeared on the bridge monitor. "We were informed of your imminent arrival and the Synod is expecting you. Do you require an escort?"

Perhaps sensing Maker's unease at the suggestion, Skullcap replied saying, "The offer is generous but unnecessary. We can make our way to the homeworld without taking Vacra from their duties."

"Very well," the Vacra on the screen replied before terminating the connection.

IGNOTUS

Skullcap turned to Maker. "Was that satisfactory?"

"It'll do," Maker said.

"You still suspect treachery," the Vacran surmised.

"It wouldn't be the first time," Maker replied, "and we all know you're well-versed in the use of code words."

"It you have a method for proceeding that will give you more comfort," Skullcap remarked, "please share."

Maker sighed. "Let's just get this done."

"Very well," the insectoid replied. "Your scanners should be detecting a binary star system nearby with eleven planets in orbit. The tenth is our homeworld."

"What's it called?" Maker asked, realizing for the first time that he hadn't posed the question before.

Skullcap made a sound that was like a buzzing wrapped up in a cough.

"I didn't catch that," Maker said, prompting the insectoid to repeat the same sound.

Maker frowned. Obviously, the planet's formal name was something the translators were having difficulty with.

Throwing up his hands in frustration, Maker declared with finality, "You know what? We're going with 'Ignotus.' It's as good a name as any for a planet."

IGNOTUS

Chapter 87

The *Nova*'s journey to Ignotus occurred without incident, but not without apprehension. Maker could sense it in his team — the disquieting concern that stemmed from the fact that they were in the midst of the enemy. (An enemy which, in the very recent past, had seemed determined to wage war on the human race.) That said, he was still of the opinion that Skullcap needed them for something; however, without knowledge of what that something was, there was no telling when said need might come to an end. Bearing that in mind (as well as all the bad things that could happen now that they were here), Maker had trouble imagining how he'd ever agreed to this mission.

Much like one would expect in Gaian Space, the region around Ignotus was thick with starships — even more than Maker had initially surmised. But it stood to reason: he was at the heart of an interstellar empire. A multitude of ships was par for the course. (It was also a stark reminder that — despite having lost an armada at Maker's hands — the Vacra still had plenty of ships and people to man them.)

As is often the case in such situations, time seemed to drag on forever. To Maker, it felt like each ship within range had an inordinate time to line up their guns and get the *Nova* in its sights (if such were their desire). Eventually, however, they found themselves within shuttle range of Ignotus. At that juncture, Maker had to come to a decision regarding two crucial issues.

The first concerned where to leave the *Nova* while he and others went planet-side. Skullcap had made it clear that they could dock at one of several space stations

IGNOTUS

orbiting above Ignotus, but Maker didn't like the idea of their ride home being anchored, so to speak, to an alien facility. At the same time, he was adverse to the notion of the *Nova* simply floating in open space; she'd be a sitting duck. Even with her shields up, the *Nova* would be susceptible to concentrated fire if a number of ships all targeted her simultaneously.

The other issue related to who exactly should be part of the team that would be visiting the planet. Browing, as the official ambassador, was definitely going, but — aside from Maker — there were no other assigned slots. Considering that this could still be a trap (meaning that it might be a one-way trip for those involved), he found himself spending a fair amount of time weighing the pros and cons of who should stay and who should go.

Ultimately, despite a few misgivings, he settled on Loyola and Snick, who were the best shooter and hand-to-hand combatant, respectively, in their unit. If things went south for some reason on Ignotus, having those two on hand would give the ground team the best odds of coming back alive, if not unscathed. As to the *Nova*, Maker felt there was greater flexibility in keeping the ship in open space, although — once he was gone — Adames would use his best judgment, as circumstances demanded.

With those issues settled, Maker let out a mental sigh.

Time to get this show on the road, he thought.

IGNOTUS

Chapter 88

Snick and Loyola had very different reactions to being told they'd join the team going planet-side; the former was stoic (which was not unusual), while the latter was practically giddy. While those two went to prepare for departure, Maker decided to have one final conversation with Skullcap, who had been on the bridge since the *Nova*'s exit from hyperspace.

After marching the insectoid to the conference room, he wasted no time getting to the point.

"Just to be clear," he said, "we're not handing over our weapons when we get to the planet."

"I had not expected you to do so," Skullcap replied. "The Synod will consider it unorthodox, but will allow it."

"That's the second time I've heard that term — Synod. What is that exactly?"

"They are what you would term our ruling body — a council that governs the Vacra."

Maker blinked in surprise. "That's interesting. I would have thought you guys had a queen or something."

Skullcap's head moved in an odd fashion, as if Maker had just said something shocking.

"Actually, we have an empress," he finally stated, "but the issue is…complicated."

"Well, we promise not to get involved in your internal politics," Maker said. "We'll drop you off, let you make formal introductions, and then take our leave."

"I appreciate your desire for brevity," the insectoid remarked, "but events may have to proceed at a slower pace than you project."

Maker crossed his arms. "Oh, really?"

IGNOTUS

"Yes. First, there is a ceremony in relation to my arrival, although I promise it will not be lengthy. Next, you and the other humans will be formally introduced to the Synod. Following this, I had planned to take the Senu Lia, and—"

"Stop," Maker interjected forcefully. "I thought we had an understanding regarding Erlen, but I'm happy to make it clear. You aren't taking him anywhere. In fact, he's not even going planet-side."

"I understand your desire to protect him, but if I may be allowed to finish my thought?"

"By all means," Maker said. "Go ahead."

"I was going to state that I had planned to take the Senu Lia to the Senu G'Rung."

"Which is what, exactly?"

"The place of his ancestors. Or at least, his people."

Maker merely stared at him for a moment, intrigued, before asking, "What are you talking about?"

Skullcap appeared to reflect for a moment, then answered, saying, "You may recall during our previous encounter my mentioning that the Senu Lia were treasured by my people."

Maker nodded, reflecting on how the insectoid had, at the time, called possession of Erlen a mark of divine favor.

"I did not lie. The Senu Lia were the companions of Vacra royalty for generations on end. They were treated with great honor and respect, and lived among us in the Senu G'Rung — an area in one of the royal palaces dedicated as their residence."

"And you want to take Erlen there," Maker summed up.

IGNOTUS

"Yes," Skullcap admitted. "With his unique gifts, there is much of his history he could learn there."

Maker stood there in stunned disbelief for a moment. Erlen had been entrusted to him by the indigenous race of a distant world. Thus, much of the Niotan's past was a mystery to him, and it galled Maker to admit that the Vacra knew more about his alien companion than he did. However, if Skullcap was telling the truth, there was an incredible opportunity here. With his abilities, how much could Erlen learn if he came across anything from another of his species? A hair, a flake of skin, a spoor? Any of it might contain a treasure trove of information about Erlen's origins. He didn't think he could deny the Niotan that chance.

"I'll think about bringing him along," Maker finally said, not wanting to give Skullcap the satisfaction of being right in any way, manner, or form.

IGNOTUS

Chapter 89

In almost no time at all, the group that was leaving for Ignotus was ready to depart. Against his better judgment, Maker was bringing Erlen along, although he planned to keep a close eye on the Niotan. In fact, Erlen was with him at present, waiting outside the shuttle for the last passenger — Browing — to arrive. (Skullcap, Snick, and Loyola were already aboard, with the insectoid basically under guard of the two Marines.)

Fortunately, Browing didn't keep them waiting long. Decked out in what appeared to be a tailor-made suit, he showed up a few moments later carrying an attaché case and accompanied by Dr. Chantrey.

"About time," Maker muttered. "I was on the verge of leaving you."

"In that case, thanks for waiting," Browing replied.

"What's in the bag?" Maker asked, gesturing towards the attaché case.

"Just a few tokens of mankind's esteem," Browing answered. "Gifts for our new friends. What's in yours?"

As he spoke, he motioned towards a small rucksack that Maker was holding by its straps in one hand.

"Food," Maker replied casually. "I don't expect us to be down there for long, but if we're still there at mealtime I want something my stomach can digest as opposed to an alien version of honey that some insectoid just regurgitated."

"Now there's an image to help me sleep at night," Browing muttered. "Thanks."

IGNOTUS

With that, he entered the shuttle while Maker turned his attention to Chantrey.

"So," he droned with a smile, "come to see me off?"

"Only if 'see you off' means sitting next to you on the shuttle," she quipped.

"Huh?" he murmured.

"I'm coming with you," she explained. "Browing says he can use my behavioral expertise in dealing with the Vacra."

Maker groaned in agitation. "Or more likely, he tore a page out of Lafayette's book, and wants you along to keep me from doing anything crazy."

"Possibly," she agreed.

"Well, did you tell him what you told me — that an entomologist would be better?"

"Yes, but like you, he noted that I'm as good as he can get at the moment."

Feeling vexed, Maker shook his head in agitation for a moment, and then said, "Fine. Just try not to get killed."

"Do I have to?" she droned sarcastically. "Getting killed is in this season. All the cool kids are doing it."

Maker simply stared at her for a moment and then declared, "You're not funny," as Chantrey started snickering. "Did you at least bring a weapon?"

"No," Chantrey answered, still smiling. "But I see you brought yours." She then gestured towards his service weapon, currently holstered on his hip.

"Well, just see Loyola," Maker said. "She lugged aboard a sack full of goodies, so she's bound to have an extra gun or two she can spare."

"Got it," Chantrey said. "See you inside."

IGNOTUS

She then went into the shuttle without waiting to see if Maker had additional comments. Following her lead, he went inside and closed the shuttle door.

IGNOTUS

Chapter 90

Other than the cockpit where Snick (who was piloting) sat, there were no windows on the shuttle. Thus, Maker had to content himself with linking his p-comp to the craft's exterior cameras and watch their approach to Ignotus that way. That said, the shuttle ride down to the planet was practically a non-event, with nothing occurring to rouse his suspicions.

Ignotus itself first appeared as a blue-brown bauble floating in the void. From orbital height, Maker could discern what appeared to be two major continents and several large oceans. However, despite the presence of large bodies of water, he got the impression that most of the land masses were arid.

As they entered the planet's atmosphere, features of the surface began to come into greater focus — mountains, canyons, valleys, and so on. In a similar vein, cities began to take shape as well, and within minutes Maker was seeing what he had generally grown accustomed to when visiting the homeworld of a spacefaring species: numerous cities merged into one giant megalopolis, stretching from one edge of the horizon to the other and covered with monumental skyscrapers, the sky above it thick with aircars and hovercraft.

Needless to say, the architecture deviated in various ways from what Maker was familiar with. Most notable was the fact that the buildings seemed to be constructed in conformity with a hexagonal design rather than squares or rectangles.

Following Skullcap's directions, Snick eventually set the shuttle down on a landing pad atop what appeared to be the largest skyscraper in the vicinity. The rooftop itself was the size of a stadium, and Maker couldn't help but notice quite a few Vacra nearby carrying weapons.

Guards, he thought.

For a brief moment, Maker wondered if a trap of some sort was about to be sprung, but then found himself surprised by the fact that the shuttle still seemed to be moving downward. A second later, he realized what was happening: the entire landing pad, shuttle and all, was descending into the building.

Turning off his p-comp, Maker asked, "Okay, what's going on?"

"We have arrived at the royal palace," Skullcap replied.

"So, I guess we get to meet the queen now," Maker remarked. However, the words had barely passed his lips before Skullcap jerk his head about in something like a double-take and simply stared at him.

"I mean empress," Maker clarified. "Didn't mean to offend."

The insectoid simply stood there, staring at him and not saying anything. A moment later, the shuttle's descent came to a halt, seemingly breaking whatever spell the Vacran was under.

"We should go," Skullcap practically ordered. "The Synod awaits."

IGNOTUS

Chapter 91

Like the air on the Vacra warship, the atmosphere on Ignotus was breathable by humans. However, nose filters — which Maker and his fellows quickly utilized before disembarking — would eliminate any unnecessary discomfort.

As they exited the shuttle, they were met by a single Vacra wearing what looked like a purple robe and sporting a necklace with an odd amulet on it.

"Greetings, Commander," the robed Vacra said to Skullcap, who stood at the fore of the group leaving the shuttle.

"Greetings, Klafrn," Skullcap droned in return. He was now wearing his battle armor, including the helmet with the skull on top. Coupled with the skulls decorating his breastplate, he now looked every bit the intimidating enemy Maker had battled on multiple occasions.

"Where are they?" Skullcap continued.

"The Synod await you in the Chamber of Egg-Flame," the new insectoid replied. "And needless to say, I am at your service."

"Excellent," Skullcap remarked. He then turned to Maker and the others. "This is Klafrn" — he gestured at the robed Vacra — "who has been blessed with the gift of tongues. Because some of the ceremony may occur in an unfamiliar dialect, Klafrn will be on hand to elucidate should you need greater detail about anything said."

Without waiting for a reply, Skullcap turned and began marching away. With little choice, Maker and the others followed.

IGNOTUS

****

They spent about ten minutes marching through the palace — traipsing through expansive hallways and corridors, as well as what Maker took to be antechambers, staterooms, and more. While Skullcap strode stoically in the vanguard of their group, staying silent the entire time, Klafrn played the role of effervescent tour guide, enthusiastically pointing out various items of interest, from rich tapestries to objets d'art.

Maker noted in a detached manner the finery around them as they walked and the wealth it represented. His focus, however, was twofold: first, making sure they weren't being led into an ambush, and trying to remember their route in case they had to find (or fight) their way back. (Erlen, on the other hand, seemingly unconcerned about death possibly waiting around the next corner, ran around like a kid in a candy store, tasting everything in sight.)

Eventually Skullcap led them to a broad door which, due to its hexagonal shape, actually put Maker in mind of a bank vault. There were two guards — one on either side of the door — when they approached, but neither moved to stop the group. In fact, the door seemed to swing open of its own accord as they drew near, clearly indicating that they were expected.

Upon stepping through the doorway, Maker saw that they had entered a vast chamber that was hexagonal in shape, with a diameter of about a hundred yards. Magnificent columns stood at each angle of the hexagon, rising up to an intricately decorated domed ceiling that was about three stories in height. Although he couldn't identify the material, the floor and walls seemed to be

IGNOTUS

made of some exotic natural stone that Maker sensed was exorbitantly expensive. And, as in other parts of the palace, he saw what he assumed were high-end works of art placed geometrically around the room.

All in all, the chamber radiated opulence, and Maker assumed that it was probably the site of much pomp and circumstance — a room where solemn and momentous ceremonies took place. Even the ever-garrulous Klafrn had gone silent, a sure sign of the room's reverential status. (He might also have been quieted by the presence of about a dozen guards posted strategically around the room and who — in Maker's eyes — looked as though they might fire at the slightest sound.)

Unsurprisingly, Skullcap barely paused after entering the chamber. He was clearly on a mission, and quickly resumed striding purposefully towards the far side of the room where — Maker now realized — about a dozen Vacra were seated in ornate, high-backed chairs. For a moment, he wondered how they actually sat given how their bodies were constructed, but as his group drew closer he saw that a portion at the back of the chairs appeared to have been cut away, allowing room for their abdomens.

With that thought, it occurred to Maker that they hadn't made any such accommodation for Skullcap. In fact, he suddenly realized that his archenemy might have spent every moment of the last few weeks on his feet. He had no idea if that was abnormal for a Vacra, but it struck him as cruel, to a certain extent. However, he had no more time to dwell on the subject because at that moment, Skullcap came to a sudden halt. Maker was confused for a second, then became cognizant of the fact

IGNOTUS

that they now stood only about twenty feet from the Vacra who were seated. He had been so lost in thought that he hadn't even grasped that they had crossed to the other side of the room.

Movement out of the corner of his eye caught Maker's attention. Turning in that direction, he saw another Vacra nearby walking towards Skullcap. Maker frowned, angry with himself for being so distracted that he hadn't even noticed another possible combatant in the room. This new insectoid wore a single-piece garment made of some type of shimmering material, and from the way it moved (along with the difference in its figure compared to Skullcap's), Maker assumed it was a female — a fact he felt was confirmed after it spoke.

"On behalf of myself and the Synod," the new Vacra said, speaking joyfully and gesturing towards those seated, "welcome home, Commander Vuqja. We had feared you dead."

"Fortunately, Brzaka, my death is not yet foretold," Skullcap replied in a somewhat ardent tone. "As you might guess, I have come to fulfill my obligation."

"And claim your reward, of course," Brzaka added (with what Maker thought was a smile).

"If such is allowed," Skullcap intoned. "But as you can see" — he gestured toward Maker's group — "I have fulfilled my vow. The Senu Lia and the *Virkbaden* are before you."

Alarm bells started going off in Maker's brain. What he was hearing didn't at all sound like the kind of formal introduction Skullcap had previously indicated he would make. It sounded ominous as hell. He gave Loyola and Snick a hand signal that basically said, *Be ready*. The

IGNOTUS

two Marines gave him subtle nods of acknowledgment in response.

"Hey!" Maker hissed at Klafrn. "That word he used — Virkraken — what does it mean?"

"*Virkbaden*," Klafrn corrected, now looking a little nervous. "It translates loosely as 'Great Slayer,' or words to that effect."

"Slayer?" Maker repeated, frowning.

"Yes," Klafrn said. "It is acknowledgment that many Vacra have died at your hands."

Maker wanted to ask for more detail, but thought it was important to listen as Brzaka started speaking again.

"This is not the status under which they were expected," she stated.

"Status was never discussed," Skullcap insisted. "Only their presence. Thus, I fulfilled my part of the bargain."

Brzaka stared at him for a moment, then said, "The Synod will discuss."

At that juncture, Maker expected her to go report to the Vacra who were seated, who would then…what? Huddle up, maybe? What Brzaka actually did, however, was turn her head to the side, and then appeared to stare off into the distance.

"What's going on?" Browing asked Klafrn.

"Brzaka has the gift of mindspeak," the insectoid responded. "She communes mentally with the Synod."

"She reads minds?!" Maker blurted out, slightly startled. The Vacra had used psychics before, but it had completely slipped Maker's mind. If Brzaka could indeed hear his thoughts…

IGNOTUS

"Her talent does not work on other species," Klafrn assured him, causing Maker to let out a sigh of relief. "And her skill is not really reading minds, but allowing others to conference mentally. And since, by tradition, the Synod seldom speak directly to anyone, someone with her gift is highly prized by them."

Still absorbing what he'd just heard, Maker stepped towards Skullcap.

"What exactly are you up to?" Maker demanded.

"It is difficult to explain," Skullcap offered, "but I would ask that you trust me."

"Trust you?" Maker scoffed. "You've done nothing but scheme deviously from day one. You've got some sort of ploy going right *now*, although I can't see what your endgame is. But you know what? I don't need to. We're leaving."

"If you leave now, your companion will never visit the Senu G'Rung," Skullcap stated. "There is much he could learn there, I'm sure you'd agree. So you must ask yourself, are you willing to trust me, for his sake?"

Maker looked at Erlen. The Niotan had complete faith in him — trusted his judgment, trusted his choices. Trusted that Maker would always have his best interests at heart.

Maker sighed, then gave Skullcap a pointed stare. "Okay, we'll stay, but the minute anything looks off, I'm blowing your brains out."

"I would expect no less from you," Skullcap acknowledged.

The insectoid's comment prompted Maker to say more, but before he could speak, Brzaka appeared to come out of her daze.

IGNOTUS

"The Synod have conferenced on this issue," she said. "The general feeling is that you, Commander Vuqja, have fulfilled the terms of your obligation but not the spirit thereof. However, it cannot be said that you have failed or been untrue to your word. Thus, the Synod will reward you as promised."

Brzaka held out a hand, and something like a spear came flying at her from one of the seated Vacra. She caught it without even looking, revealing the object to be a metal staff. It was presumably made of some precious ore or alloy, and engraved from top to bottom with complex and elaborate designs.

"Commander Vuqja," Brzaka said in a stern tone, "you are hereby declared *Zirxen* and granted the status and rights of that title for all the days of your life."

She held the staff out to Skullcap, and he gingerly took it from her, his hand touching hers and seeming to linger there for a moment in the process. The two of them then began conversing in a language or dialect that the translator couldn't handle. It was eerily similar to what had happened on the Vacra warship, and therefore didn't sit well with Maker.

However, rather than ask Klafrn to translate what was being said, he asked, "So what just happened here?"

"Commander Vuqja has been elevated in rank and title," Klafrn replied. "As a *Zirxen*, only the Synod, queens, and empress outrank him. Moreover, he has earned the right to reproduce with a queen, should such a time come."

Maker frowned. Klafrn's responses seemed to generate more questions than answers, but he focused on staying with his original topic.

"So he just got promoted?" queried Maker.

IGNOTUS

"Correct," Klafrn answered. "It was his promised reward for completing the task he undertook for the Synod."

"Which, I assume, consisted of bringing us here."

"You and the Senu Lia," Klafrn clarified. "Commander Vuqja took a sacred vow to complete that assignment."

Maker chewed on that for a second, then asked, "So what would have happened had he failed? If he simply hadn't located us or something like that?"

"He would have been stripped of all titles and honors," Klafrn replied. "Exiled. In essence, he would have become — in your terms — a nobody."

IGNOTUS

Chapter 92

Maker was livid, so furious he could have kicked himself.

"We had him," he muttered angrily for the umpteenth time. "We had him."

He was, of course, referring to Skullcap. At present, he and the rest of his team were in something akin to a luxurious, two-story penthouse suite, where Klafrn had escorted them after Skullcap received his promotion. The Vacran had then left them alone, promising that Skullcap would join them shortly.

Under other circumstances, Maker might have taken a moment to note their ritzy surroundings and the lavish treatment they were receiving in being placed here. (In truth, it was what Erlen seemed to be doing — running to and fro in an almost helter-skelter manner, rapidly dashing in and out of every room.) Instead, he and the others had gathered in what appeared to be the Vacra equivalent of a great room near the foyer, at which point Maker had gone on an almost nonstop tirade.

"So apparently you were right about Ambassador Vuqja needing you," Browing interjected between Maker's mutterings.

"Yeah — we should have walked away the minute that became clear," Maker stated. "Of course, it all makes sense now."

"What do you mean?" asked Loyola.

"This is why Skullcap ejected in a lifepod after that last battle and allowed himself to be picked up," Maker replied. "He had vowed to haul me and Erlen in before the Synod, but with his armada destroyed, he had no way to make good on that promise. If he had come

IGNOTUS

back here without us, they would have stripped him down to the studs and tossed him out on his keister."

"So he came up with a scheme to get you here," Snick surmised. "Trading the sub rosa tech in exchange for you escorting him home."

"And he knew you'd bring Erlen," Chantrey chimed in. "So it was just a matter of somehow getting you to bring him planet-side with you."

Maker let out an agitated groan, thinking how perfectly Skullcap had baited the hook with the promise of information regarding Erlen (or more specifically, other Niotans).

"And after that," Chantrey continued, "he simply had to convince the Synod that he'd done as promised. Next thing you know, he's big man on campus."

"He played us," Maker stated, shaking his head in disbelief. "He played the Synod. He played *every*body."

"You have to give the guy credit," Browing said. "It takes a lot of chutzpah to come up with a plan like that, and it's not everybody who can outfox not just one but two interstellar regimes."

"Sounds like you admire him," Maker said. "Want me to get his autograph for you?"

"I'm just saying that, in an abstract sense, you have to admire what he's done," Browing remarked. "Very few people could dig themselves out of a hole like that. About the only other person I know who could do it is you, Maker."

"No…don't," Maker stressed, shaking his head. "Don't compare me to that scheming, conniving, calculating fiend."

IGNOTUS

"Strong words from a man who artfully converted an entire ship into a nova bomb," Browing noted. "And then set it off."

"Those were special circumstances," Maker countered.

"And the stuff Skullcap's done was what — part of his daily routine?" Browing shot back. "I'm sure he feels he was facing unique circumstances as well."

Maker had more to say on the subject — plenty more — but was cut off as the door to the suite opened and Skullcap stepped in.

IGNOTUS

Chapter 93

"My apologies for leaving you on your own temporarily," Skullcap began, "but there were some perfunctory duties associated with my new position that I had to perform."

"Well, since you mention your new position," Maker groused as he stalked towards the insectoid, "let me state for the record that I don't appreciate being hustled."

"I am sorry that you feel 'hustled,'" the Vacran intoned, "but I was limited in what I could share with you."

"You didn't share *anything*," Maker retorted.

"I attempted to engage you in conversation multiple times," Skullcap argued, "but you had no interest."

"Well, there wasn't a gag on you," Maker noted. "You could have just blurted it out."

"Actually, I could not," the insectoid countered. "I did not have the authority to fully discuss the situation. However, you are particularly astute, and I had hoped that — if I provided enough clues — you would surmise the truth."

"Well, you've got my undivided attention *now*," Maker insisted. "So drop whatever clues you can so I can figure out what new chicanery you've got going."

Skullcap made a slight buzzing noise that might have been the equivalent of a sigh. "Hints and intimations are no longer necessary. As *Zirxen*, I have the innate authority to apprise you of all relevant facts."

IGNOTUS

There was silence for a moment, and then Maker said, "Well, don't keep us in suspense. Say what you have to say so we can leave."

"Or not," interjected Browing, earning him a glare from Maker (which he ignored). "Part of our mission here is to open diplomatic channels, and my role is to see that done before we depart."

"There will be ample time for introductions," Skullcap stated with assurance. "In the meantime, I will provide the explanation Maker desires. But first, where is the Senu Lia?"

"He's around here somewhere," Maker said. "Probably moping because you haven't taken us to this Senu G'Rung like you promised."

"I don't understand," Skullcap stated. "This *is* the Senu G'Rung."

As he finished speaking, he spread his arms wide, seeming to indicate the entire suite.

****

It took a few minutes to run Erlen down; eventually, Maker found him in an antechamber on the second floor, staring at a mural painted on a wall. Much to Maker's surprise, the image showed a Niotan standing stalwartly next to a Vacran, who sat on something like a throne. Simply seeing another of Erlen's species was enough to give the composition something of a surreal quality, and Maker could understand his companion's fascination with it.

"Come on," he said, leading Erlen away. A few minutes later, they were back with the rest of the group in the great room.

IGNOTUS

"Okay," Maker said to Skullcap, "we're all here and ready for the big reveal."

"Excellent," Skullcap said, "but before I get into the salient facts, I first have to impart certain information about the Vacra — specifically, our process of reproduction."

"Now I wish we *did* have an entomologist here," Maker muttered.

Chantrey gave him a harsh look, then turned to Skullcap and said, "Please go on."

"Thank you," the insectoid droned. "As you might guess, the Vacra population rivals the stars in number. However, what most do not know is that — at any particular point in time — the total tally of fecund Vacra females never exceeds twelve."

"Twelve?" Browing repeated. "Twelve what — twelve million? Billion?"

"Twelve," Skullcap stressed. "As in, one more than eleven."

Silence reigned momentarily as everyone tried to wrap their brains around what they were hearing.

"Just to be clear," Chantrey remarked after a few seconds, "you're saying that your entire species hails from only twelve females?"

"I'm saying that every living Vacra is descended from one of twelve females in the prior generation," the insectoid clarified. "Likewise, every Vacra born in the future will have similar ancestry."

"Family reunions must get a little crowded," Maker joked, earning him another glare from Chantrey.

Ignoring him, Skullcap continued. "The twelve fertile females are known as queens. Eventually, however, they grow old and die. The last surviving queen is designated empress and is usually venerated as the mother of our race. When she ceases to produce young, her biological processes alter significantly in order to produce a special enzyme. She then selects twelve new females and introduces the enzyme to their bodies. The enzyme makes them fertile, creating new queens, and the process begins anew."

"So this enzyme is something like the royal jelly produced by honey bees," Maker surmised. "It makes queens."

"Based on my knowledge of the lifeform you mentioned, that is an accurate assessment," Skullcap agreed.

"But spacefaring species typically number in the trillions," Loyola noted. "With only twelve fertile females at any one time, how do you keep the population from dwindling and dying out?"

"Don't make the mistake of confusing them with humans," Maker interjected. "Other races aren't as limited as we are in terms of how many offspring they produce. There were insects on Old Earth that could lay millions of eggs per month."

"Is it safe to assume that your queens reproduce along those lines?" Browing asked the Vacran.

"A million per *day* would be low volume for a queen," Skullcap answered. "Essentially from the moment of her selection, a queen will produce young almost continuously for the rest of her life."

No one said anything immediately, although something close to shock registered on Loyola's face.

"You know, I'm all for motherhood," she said after a few seconds, "but that sounds horrible."

IGNOTUS

"It's another species," Snick reminded her. "It's not for us to judge."

"Oh, yeah," Loyola snapped acerbically. "Leave it to a man to say how great it would be to spend the rest of your life procreating, with every day an orgiastic bacchanal."

"That wasn't what I said," Snick countered defensively. "I merely stated that we shouldn't judge what's obviously a natural process for them by our standards."

"That does bring up an interesting point," Chantrey noted. "How does fatherhood work with your species?"

"Certain males are sometimes granted a right to procreate," Skullcap answered, "usually under special circumstances."

"And that group includes you," Browing surmised. "Now that you're a *Zirxen*."

"Yes," the insectoid admitted. "Generally, however, the queens select the males with whom they procreate."

"So do they mate for life?" Chantrey asked.

"Hardly," Skullcap responded. "We are naturally cognizant of the risks of inbreeding and the need for genetic diversity. Ergo, our queens can mate with as many males as they like or deem worthy."

"Who's having the orgy now?" quipped Snick, causing Loyola to roll her eyes.

"Okay, we appreciate the Vacran biology lesson," Maker said, "but I'm still confused as to how this relates to us."

IGNOTUS

"I will show you," the insectoid stated. As he spoke, he reached for and removed a hexagonal implement attached at his waist.

Almost instinctively, Maker drew his service weapon, aiming it at Skullcap's head.

For a moment, no one moved, and then Maker — sensing that the object the insectoid held wasn't a weapon — murmured, "Sorry — force of habit."

He then lowered his weapon, but kept it at the ready.

Skullcap pointed the device to an empty area of the room and appeared to squeeze it. Within seconds, it became apparent that he was holding a hologram projector as an image about four feet in height appeared.

Looking at it, Maker immediately recognized that the projection was focused on a female Vacra. Although it was difficult to get a sense a scale, he garnered the impression that she was big — far larger than any Vacra he'd seen thus far. Bearing in mind their similarities with certain insect species he was aware of, he assumed this was a queen. Moments later, Skullcap essentially confirmed this assessment.

"This is our empress," the insectoid announced.

"Empress?" Chantrey echoed. "Then that means all the other queens…"

"They are deceased," Skullcap said. "She is the last fertile female of her generation — and our race."

Maker leaned closer, getting a good look at the hologram. The empress appeared to be lying on a barren floor. From what he could see, aside from a metallic choker of some sort, she was unclothed. (That didn't strike Maker as unusual given Skullcap's description of a queen's reproductive capacity, but he hoped the imagery

IGNOTUS

wasn't about to present that in graphic detail.) Also, although there was no volume, the mouth of the empress seemed to be moving almost spasmodically, voicing something unheard.

Apparently noticing the same thing, Browing asked, "Do you know what she's saying?"

"She's not saying anything," Skullcap replied. "She's screaming. She's being tortured."

IGNOTUS

Chapter 94

It took a moment for Skullcap's statement to sink in with everyone, at which point Loyola shouted, "What?"

"The device you see around her neck is a control collar," Skullcap explained, "capable of administering electric shocks, injecting pain-inducing drugs, and numerous other forms of torment."

"But why?" asked Snick.

Rather than answer, the Vacran seemed to squeeze the object he held again. In conjunction with this, the hologram changed slightly. Now, in addition to the empress, Maker saw two other individuals standing close by. Noting a lengthy proboscis on the newcomers, as well as a ligneous appearance, Maker was reminded of the race Planck had mentioned seeing while he was a prisoner of the Vacra.

"These are the P'ngrawen," Skullcap stated, gesturing towards the two individuals with the empress. "They are a vile and vicious race whom the Vacra warred with for centuries. However, a truce was eventually declared, and we've spent the last few generations in peace — until recently, that is."

Chantrey was openly curious. "So what happened?"

"The P'ngrawen operate under a monarchy," the insectoid explained. "It has become tradition that we meet with them on certain occasions to renew the terms of the truce, including those instances when a new ruler takes their throne."

"So, did they have a new monarch come to power recently?" Browing inquired.

IGNOTUS

"It was actually several years ago," Skullcap noted. "The new king's name was Badukst. When he ascended the throne, we agreed to a meeting to discuss the truce. But, as is typical for the P'ngrawen, Badukst would only meet with a Vacra who he felt was his peer."

"Meaning someone who was royalty," Maker concluded. "One of the queens."

"Precisely," the insectoid confirmed. "However, we were at one of those junctures where the only 'royal' remaining was the empress. With any other race, we would have sent a member of the Synod, since it is they — not the queens or empress — who actually oversee Vacra society. We have tried on numerous occasions to explain this to the P'ngrawen, also making it clear that every Vacra is actually the child of a queen and can thus be considered royalty, but they are stubborn and obstinate in that regard."

"So your empress had to go meet with their ruler," Chantrey concluded.

"She did not *have* to," Skullcap corrected, "and many of us did not want her to. She had stopped producing young, but her body was only just starting the process of producing the enzyme necessary to beget new queens. Thus, it was a critical time, but the empress felt the peace process was vitally important. Moreover, she was confident that nothing untoward would happen, as such meetings had always been held under a flag of truce that neither side had ever violated. However, none of us knew just how depraved and degenerate Badukst was, how wretched and wicked his intentions."

"He kidnapped her," Maker said, understanding what had happened without being told.

IGNOTUS

"He did, violating a truce and a trust that had kept the peace between our races for years," Skullcap stated. "And because of how we reproduce — because they had control of our future and very existence — they gained dominion over us."

"What do you mean?" queried Snick.

"I mean that we do as they say," the insectoid uttered. "Without the empress to pass along the reproductive enzyme, our species faces extinction. Thus, we are obligated to do as they command. If they say go hither, we go. If they demand one of our ships, we give it. If they say attack another race without provocation, we attack."

Maker's brow furrowed as Skullcap finished speaking. "Wait a minute. Are you saying that every time you've attacked human beings, it's been at the behest of this other species?"

"As I mentioned, the P'ngrawen are a corrupt and contemptible people," Skullcap said, "while we pride ourselves on being noble and virtuous. Ergo, they take perverse pleasure in seeing us act in a craven and dishonorable manner, such as double-dealing with those we have bargained with and launching an attack when it is not expected. All done based on the promise that our empress will be returned to us."

"So when you attacked our ship," Browing interjected, "the one you took the tech from that was just returned, that was because the P'ngrawen ordered you to?"

"It was the P'ngrawen who found the means to infiltrate the vessel," the Vacran explained, "but yes, we attacked on their orders. Likewise, on their command, we waylaid those who came to investigate."

IGNOTUS

"That would be me," Maker declared flatly. "I'm the one who investigated and got ambushed, along with my team."

"I recall," Skullcap countered. "I lost an arm during the encounter, so the memory is never far from me."

"Boo-hoo," Maker muttered angrily. "My men lost their *lives*."

"And for that I am truly sorry," Skullcap insisted. "But as you now understand, we had no choice. Likewise on the other occasions when we engaged you in battle."

"Okay," Maker droned, "supposing we buy your story about being forced to attack us time after time, it doesn't really explain what you did to Planck."

"Planck?" the insectoid muttered, clearly not getting the reference.

"The human you captured and tortured for years," Maker explained.

Skullcap seemed to ponder for a moment before answering. "Obviously, I have not adequately explained matters, but I shall make another attempt. In essence, the P'ngrawen wanted the technology and weapons from your vessel. However, they also knew that much of it was incredibly dangerous, which is part of the reason we Vacra were sent to retrieve it."

"You were expendable," Snick summed up.

"Correct," Skullcap acknowledged. "That said, the moment we understood what we had taken, we knew that we couldn't let the P'ngrawen take possession of it. Doing so would have exponentially increased their power and dominance, not to mention their capacity for turpitude. Keeping such technology out of their hands was almost on par with getting the empress back."

IGNOTUS

"So what did you do?" inquired Loyola.

"We manufactured an explosion aboard an unmanned Vacra warship," Skullcap replied. "We then informed the P'ngrawen that everything taken had been destroyed."

"And they believed you?" asked Browing.

"Why would they not?" the Vacran retorted. "They know us as a proud and honorable race. Prevarication is not in our nature. Moreover, they understood how dangerous the devices were that we took — it was why they sent *us* rather than retrieve it themselves — so it was a plausible explanation. That said, they were not happy with the reported turn of events."

"So in the end, you just kept the tech for yourselves," Maker chimed in. "Still doesn't explain why you extended your tender mercies to Planck."

Skullcap seemed to bristle at this. "First, we never coveted the items we took. The Vacra consider them hazardous and unstable, so in truth we wanted them nowhere near us. With respect to the man Planck, the P'ngrawen knew that we had him and wanted him to recreate the articles that they believed had been destroyed. However, rather than take him themselves, it amused them to make us extract information from him. They know that the notion of torture is abhorrent to us, so it was a way to torment us as well as your friend."

Maker snorted in derision. "For a race that claims to loathe torture, you sure did take to it rather easily."

"On the contrary, we typically tried to make your colleague comfortable and treated him well," the insectoid countered. "However, the P'ngrawen regularly checked on the progress we were making with him. Needless to say, it would not have gone well if they

IGNOTUS

discovered that we were not truly focused on interrogating him. It needed to appear that we were putting sufficient effort into the matter — especially when they sent a representative to personally gauge how we were advancing with him."

"So you would torture him occasionally to make it appear that you were playing along," Maker said, mentally noting how this actually jibed with what Planck had told him. "Still, it doesn't quite explain why you implanted a bomb in him."

Skullcap seemed to reflect for a moment before responding. "In all honesty, the man Planck broke rather easily. He had little tolerance for physical pain. However, we misled the P'ngrawen in that regard. We told them your friend was resistant to corporal interrogation methods, but susceptible on a psychological level. In short, we told them that knowledge of the bomb inside him — coupled with the notion that death could come unexpectedly at any time — was fraying Planck's resolve. To appease them, we produced some of the more benign devices from the items we had confiscated and told the P'ngrawen that your colleague had recreated them."

"Okay, I can follow that," Maker stated. "But how does all this relate to Erlen?"

"As I've stated in the past," Skullcap replied, "the Senu Lia have long been a part of Vacra history, dating back to a time when the queens and empress actually did rule our society. The Senu Lia were the companions of sovereigns, and treated as royalty in their own right. More importantly, they seemed to confer an inexplicable form of power to those who possessed them, including protection from harm. Because of this, the P'ngrawen long coveted the Senu Lia and — even during times of war — were known to offer enormous bounties for them. In fact, it wasn't until they ceased demanding the Senu Lia as one of the terms for a truce that progress was made on any peace accords."

"Hear that?" Maker intoned, glancing at Erlen. "You're popular."

Continuing as if uninterrupted, Skullcap said, "Unfortunately, the last of our Senu Lia died many years ago, and we had long assumed the species extinct. Thus, it came as a shock when we discovered a living specimen."

"You mean when we walked into your ambush on the ship you'd raided," Maker chastised.

"You speak as though it was the result of chance or happenstance," the Vacran noted. "We do not believe it such. It was fated that my people would discover the Senu Lia still exist. It was destiny that it take its rightful place with us. Moreover, with its return to us, many felt the Vacra's fortunes would turn for the better."

"So you contacted humanity and offered a trade," Browing stated. "The tech you'd taken for Erlen."

"Yes, but not immediately," Skullcap stated. "Space is vast, and we had never before encountered your species. Moreover, the ship from which we'd taken your possessions gave no indication of where your race hailed from. Given the nature of the items we took, we now know that lack of information about your race's origins was by design rather than an omission. Bearing everything in mind, it took time to locate you, and by that juncture the P'ngrawen had also become aware of the Senu Lia's existence."

"Let me guess," Maker chimed in. "They forced you into double-crossing and attacking us."

IGNOTUS

"Yes, but it was what they were expecting," Skullcap remarked. "Remember, the P'ngrawen were under the impression that everything from your ship had been destroyed. Thus, from their perspective, we had nothing to trade for the Senu Lia and were simply misleading you."

"And if they believed you had nothing to trade," Chantrey noted, "then they felt you were planning to double-cross us all along."

"Precisely, and it was the type of situation that gives the P'ngrawen glee," the Vacran said. "In addition, had we actually gotten possession of the Senu Lia, they were willing to accept it in trade for our empress. Needless to say, it was an offer we could not refuse, although we hoped — by some means — to secure the return of the empress *and* keep the Senu Lia."

"In other words, you planned a *triple*-cross," Maker declared. "So, how do we get from your multitudinous lies, deceptions, and two-timing in the past to this virtue and nobility that we're seeing today?"

"After our last skirmish and the loss of our armada, I realized the futility of our actions," Skullcap replied. "The Senu Lia is not a prize to be captured or possessed; it chooses its companions, as well as where it will stay or go. Trying to forcefully take custody of it has been our undoing. It was wrong, and I apologize both on behalf of myself and all Vacra."

Maker blinked in surprise. An apology from Skullcap was not something he had ever expected, and — in all honesty — he found it remarkable.

"Go on," Maker urged.

"There is little more to tell," Skullcap said. "Following our last engagement, my ship was the sole surviving Vacra vessel. Returning to our homeworld, however, would result in me being stripped of all titles and shunned. Ergo, I ejected in a lifepod, knowing that your people would find me. My hope was that you would be willing to treat with us, and I was not disappointed."

"I think we're all familiar with this part of the story," Browing interjected, "but it's not clear to me that you even had authority to initiate diplomatic relations."

"Such power was vested in me," the Vacran insisted. "I had been given a military command and appointed Vacra K'nsl in order to facilitate my efforts in returning the Senu Lia to us. Treating with other races fell within the ambit of my authority. And, as has been indicated, you know everything that has happened since."

"So, if we're to believe you," Snick summed up, "the Vacra were forced into many of the actions they've taken."

"We were fighting for our lives — facing the death of our entire species," Skullcap insisted. "We *still* are. Would any of you do anything less if it was the human race on the verge of extinction?"

As Skullcap finished speaking, Maker frowned. He couldn't speak for anyone else, but — although it rang of truth in certain respects — he still wasn't completely convinced by everything he'd heard.

"Look, it sounds somewhat reasonable on the surface," he admitted, "but what you've said doesn't explain all the things you've done in regards to your encounters with humans. It's just the tip of the iceberg."

"Then ask what you will," Skullcap suggested, "and I will elucidate."

Maker smiled. "Thanks for the offer. I'll take you up on it."

IGNOTUS

Chapter 95

Over the next half hour, Maker (with an occasional assist from one of his colleagues) grilled Skullcap relentlessly about every instance of questionable behavior he could think of regarding the Vacra. From presumed attacks to backdoor deals, he left no stone unturned.

At the end of that time, however, Maker had to admit to being impressed. Skullcap kept his composure throughout, and no matter the question, he always had an answer that came across as a reasoned and rational response. More to the point, with respect to everything Maker tried to accuse the Vacra of — every bad act, every misdeed, every transgression — the insectoid found a way to blame the P'ngrawen. (As Maker put it at one juncture, it was like Skullcap was "born with his finger pointing at them.")

Even in regard to his armor, the Vacran posited a credible explanation, saying that it was essentially an heirloom passed down from father to son.

"The skull on my helm belonged to a savage beast," the insectoid explained, "slain by an ancestor who barely survived the encounter. Those on my breastplate were all found items — not trophies from kills — and belonged to unknown species at the time they were added to the battlesuit."

"So collecting skulls is some kind of weird family tradition," Maker surmised.

Skullcap made a gesture that seemed to indicate acquiescence. "Although not intended to be such, the helmet became a…conversation piece. It distinguished our line. Later generations simply added to this, in their own way."

Like everything else Skullcap offered, it was a plausible explanation. Ultimately, Maker reluctantly began to accept the fact that the insectoid was probably being sincere in terms of everything he'd shared. (He also understood why one Vacra killing another was detestable: there was no new generation to replace any who died.)

"Okay," he finally said to the Vacran. "Assuming we accept your overall explanation — and your apology, since that's being offered as well — are we essentially done here?"

Before Skullcap could answer, Browing cleared his throat.

"Ahem," he interjected. "I don't think that entirely concludes—"

"Forgive me," Maker interjected tersely. "Aside from the ambassadorial grandstanding, are we done?"

"There is another pressing matter," Skullcap noted, "which will give greater perspective to everything I've said thus far."

"What's that?" asked Chantrey.

"There's a convoy of P'ngrawen ships en route here," Skullcap replied. "They are coming to take possession of the Senu Lia."

IGNOTUS

Chapter 96

It took a second for Skullcap's words to fully register — because Maker couldn't quite believe what he'd heard — but the moment they did, he had his gun up and pointed at the insectoid's head.

"You've got about three seconds to admit that was a joke," he growled, "and in very poor taste."

"If I may explain," Skullcap entreated. "When the Synod were informed that I was returning with you and the Senu Lia, the assumption was that you were in my custody. More precisely, they inferred that we now had the means to secure the return of the empress."

"Through a trade," Snick reasoned. "Erlen for the empress."

"Yes," the Vacran agreed. "They contacted the P'ngrawen, who readily agreed to the exchange."

"So what happens now?" Maker asked. "You send in some Vacra commandos to take Erlen and either kill or subdue the rest of us?"

"No — absolutely not," Skullcap insisted, and then became pensive for a moment before continuing. "The abduction of our empress has fractured the Vacra — created a schism in our people that did not previously exist. There are those who feel that nothing, not even the threat of extinction, merits ignoble behavior. To them, a dishonorable life is no life at all. But there are others, myself included, who feel that we must do all in our power to ensure that the Vacra survive — including acting in ways we completely despise. That said, there are certain tenets that are inviolable among our people, one of which is the concept of an honored guest. Such individuals are treated with esteem and respect, and no harm is allowed to come to them."

Maker, concentrating intensely, had trouble believing what he was hearing.

"You're saying we can leave?" he asked, his tone openly suspicious.

Skullcap nodded. "You are honored guests. You may depart at your leisure. None will stop you, hinder you, or molest you."

"Awesome," Maker uttered, lowering his firearm. "We're outta here."

"If that is your wish," Skullcap conceded. "Although I had hoped that you would consider helping us."

Looking pensive, Chantrey asked, "Help you how?"

"Our empress is still a prisoner," the insectoid stated. "With your help, we could get her back."

"I'm not sure what assistance we could offer," Browing stated. "From what you've said, the P'ngrawen are only interested in…"

He trailed off, glancing at Erlen as he did so. In fact, almost every pair of eyes in the room turned in the Niotan's direction.

"No," Maker said emphatically. "No way. I'm not letting him get involved in this."

"If you're concerned for the Senu Lia's welfare, I will personally guarantee his safe return," Skullcap asserted.

"Oh, really?" Maker blurted out sarcastically. "And just how are you going to do that?"

"I have a plan—" Skullcap began.

IGNOTUS

"I bet you do," Maker growled, cutting him off. "I realize now that you *always* have plans — plans *within* plans, in fact. I've never met anyone with your ability to make truthful statements, but at the same time have the capacity to dupe and deceive. You've raised chicanery to an art form. Well, you can take your plan and stuff it. I'm not letting you bait your hook with Erlen."

"With all due respect, it is not your decision to make," Skullcap remarked, then looked pointedly at Erlen.

Maker followed his gaze, and then turned to the insectoid with a dumbfounded expression on his face.

"Are you kidding?" he scoffed. "Okay, I'm going to say something that — of the people in this room — only you and I probably know: Niotans live far longer than humans." Maker then pointed at Erlen, stating, "He's a *baby* — barely out of diapers by our standards. He doesn't get to make these decisions."

"Then you doom the Vacra to extinction," Skullcap said flatly.

The room was silent as the grim and weighty truth of the Vacran's words sank in.

Maker let out a deep sigh. "Look, despite everything in the past, I'm truly sorry this has happened to your people. It's terrible and tragic on a scale I can't really fathom, and in your position I would probably have done the same things you've done. In all sincerity, I'd help you if I could, but I can't put Erlen in that kind of danger. I'm responsible for him. More to the point, this isn't our fight."

"But it is," Skullcap stressed, "because after they finish with the Vacra, the P'ngrawen will come for you next."

IGNOTUS

Concern was suddenly etched on the faces of Maker and his companions.

"What do you mean?" Loyola asked.

"I previously mentioned that the P'ngrawen want the Senu Lia," Skullcap answered. "What I haven't shared is that they previously had Senu Lia of their own."

Maker fought hard to keep his surprise from visibly showing. "When was this?"

"Millenia ago," Skullcap said. "The P'ngrawen used them to create terrible weapons, which were then employed to subjugate — and occasionally eradicate — other species."

Maker was disturbed by what he was hearing, but didn't doubt the truth of Skullcap's words. When Maker had previously converted a ship into a nova bomb, Erlen had been instrumental in constructing the weapon, producing elements and compounds that Maker never would have been able to procure otherwise. Thus, he had no problem believing that Niotans could be used to create a wide range of catastrophic weapons and devices.

"Are you saying the P'ngrawen will try to conquer humanity?" he asked.

"They've suggested in numerous occasions that they will *extirpate* your race," Skullcap noted.

Browing appeared shocked. "But why? We've never done anything to them."

"It's enough that you — any one of you — has bonded with Senu Lia," Skullcap explained. "It suggests that you may have the means to neutralize any weapons they have or might develop."

"So they'd wipe out humanity simply because of that?" asked Snick.

IGNOTUS

"If they thought it would be entertaining," Skullcap answered, "they'd wipe you out simply to avoid boredom. As it is, your connection to the Senu Lia gives them adequate reason to desire mankind's destruction."

"You mean *my* connection," Maker clarified.

"However you frame it," Skullcap stated, "it places mankind very high on the P'ngrawen's list of targets. Make no mistake — they are coming for you."

Maker frowned. Skullcap could be lying, but again, Maker got the sense that he was being sincere. Still, he wasn't eager to engage in a fight solely on Skullcap's say-so.

"We'll deal with that when the time comes," Maker finally announced, "but right now it feels premature. So, while I wish you good luck in dealing with the P'ngrawen and I pray that your empress is safely returned, there's nothing we can do. I'm sorry."

Skullcap momentarily looked as though he had a comment, but remained silent. There was a sense of forlorn despair and despondency about him that was almost palpable. Even Maker felt it, and — despite the animus and hostility he had harbored against the Vacra for so long — he sympathized with their plight. Looking at the rest of the team from the *Nova*, he knew without asking that they all felt the same.

"Come on," he finally said to his colleagues. "We should leave."

He started walking towards the door, and felt rather than saw the others falling into step behind him. However, he hadn't gone far before he heard Erlen voice something between a growl and a honk.

Understanding that the sound was meant to get his attention, Maker did an immediate one-eighty, at which point he saw that the Niotan hadn't moved. A moment later, however, Erlen began striding towards him, unexpectedly rising up on his hind legs when they were about a foot apart. Placing his forepaws on Maker's shoulders, the Niotan looked him in the eye, then momentarily glanced at Skullcap before facing Maker again.

And then, in a voice that was somewhat odd but slightly reminiscent of an adolescent male, Erlen said, "Maker, help."

It was just two words, but uttered in a way that was both a plea and a statement, as well as a command. Maker was only slightly less shocked than everyone else in the room at what he'd heard. It had always been obvious that Erlen understood human speech, and Maker had always suspected that the Niotan could articulate the requisite sounds. However, having it confirmed in this setting — and in light of what was at stake — was almost prophetic.

Letting out a sigh, Maker stared at Skullcap for a moment and then said, "So tell me about this plan."

IGNOTUS

Chapter 97

"It's a good plan," Skullcap announced.

"Yeah," Maker quipped. "If 'good' is synonymous with 'stupid' or 'ill-advised.'"

Skullcap made a noise that Maker interpreted as the equivalent of a harrumph, but otherwise didn't say anything.

They were currently in the cockpit of a Vacra shuttle, heading towards a trio of ships that had dropped out of hyperspace roughly an hour after Maker had agreed to help his long-time nemesis. Skullcap's plan, hastily explained, had required a few tweaks in Maker's opinion. It was still risky and unsound when viewed in even the best light, but — after the three P'ngrawen ships appeared — they simply had no more time.

Maker took a moment to glance into the passenger compartment of the shuttle, where Erlen was lounging as if he hadn't a care in the world.

"Not too late to change your mind," Maker suggested.

Erlen's reply was a wide-mouthed yawn, as if he were bored. Shaking his head in disbelief at the Niotan's nonchalance, Maker turned back around and stared out the cockpit window.

The three ships they were approaching (which had taken up positions near the edge of the solar system) had a design that was outside his experience. Frankly speaking, they all looked like random chunks of metal haphazardly thrown together. But perhaps they conformed to a pattern that wasn't obvious to the human eye.

"Which is our destination?" Maker asked.

IGNOTUS

"The large one in the middle," Skullcap answered. "That is the flagship of their ruler, Badukst."

"He's here personally?"

"Of course. He would not trust another with custody of the Senu Lia. Also, he prefers to personally torture the empress and send us the recordings, and this may be his last opportunity to do so."

"Sounds like a nice guy."

"Indeed," Skullcap said, a hard edge to his voice.

"I'm surprised they're willing to just waltz in here like this, so close to the homeworld of their enemy."

"They have our empress, so there is little for them to fear from us."

Maker nodded in understanding. "I guess that makes sense."

"Just so you're aware, I have requested that the P'ngrawen have the empress in the landing bay so that the exchange may be conducted as expeditiously as possible."

"Seems like a reasonable request."

"We'll see if the P'ngrawen adopt that view," Skullcap said.

****

The rest of the flight was conducted in silence, although Maker was surprised that it was neither awkward nor uncomfortable. When they were a few minutes from entering the landing bay of the flagship, Maker stepped into the passenger compartment of the shuttle and donned a spacesuit that had been hastily retrieved from the *Nova* while they were fleshing out Skullcap's plan. By the time the Vacran set the ship down, Maker was dressed

IGNOTUS

and had grabbed his rucksack, which he'd also brought along.

"Are we ready?" Skullcap asked as he stepped out of the cockpit.

"As ready as we'll ever be," Maker replied as he slung the rucksack on his back and checked his utility belt, which contained a compact emergency kit, a communicator, and a few other essentials.

Taking that as his cue, Skullcap went to the shuttle door, opened it, and then walked out, with Maker and Erlen right behind him.

They found themselves in an expansive landing bay. Unsurprisingly, there was a contingent of perhaps a dozen uniformed P'ngrawen standing nearby, all apparently guards and holding what Maker immediately recognized as firearms — more precisely, rifles of some sort.

In Maker's opinion, Planck's description of them was fairly accurate. They had elongated snouts and skin that resembled polished wood, with a light covering of fur. They also had what appeared to be vestigial tails.

One of the guards (presumably the captain or commander) stepped towards them.

"I was told to expect a Vacra and a pet of some sort," the guard captain said. "Why are there three of you?"

"This is the creature's handler," Skullcap replied, motioning towards Maker. "It will only eat from his hand, so I assumed Badukst would need him."

"*Lord* Badukst," the captain corrected acidly.

"Of course," Skullcap stated in acknowledgment. "I had requested that the empress be brought to the landing bay for a quick exchange. Where is she?"

IGNOTUS

"Who are you to give commands, *ghangunk*?" the captain demanded. Although his translator clearly had issues finding an equivalent for the last word, Maker had no trouble recognizing that it was an insult.

"It is the P'ngrawen who issues orders to *your* species," the guard commander continued, "not the reverse. You will be taken to your *twanblit* female when it pleases us."

Without waiting for a response (or simply assuming that there would be none), the captain spent a moment eyeballing Maker.

"Why the spacesuit?" he asked.

"Your air is foreign to him," Skullcap explained. "He is unable to breathe it without great difficulty."

It was a true statement, as one of the things that had become clear from the outset was that the P'ngrawen atmosphere was not conducive to human respiration. The guard captain, however, looked like he wanted to test that theory. Still watching Maker suspiciously, he waved over one of his fellows, who carried something akin to a three-foot metal wand.

The newcomer waved the wand in front of Skullcap, taking it from the insectoid's head to his foot, while at the same time looking at a small hand-held display. It didn't take a lot of effort to recognize that this was an obvious scan for weapons. A moment later, it was Maker's turn, and he seemingly passed as well.

"What does the bag contain?" the captain asked, pointing at Maker's rucksack.

"Nourishment for the animal," Skullcap replied. "P'ngrawen foodstuffs will be unfamiliar to him, and he may refuse to eat them initially."

IGNOTUS

The captain turned to the individual with the scanner and ordered, "Examine it."

The fellow carrying the wand waved it around the rucksack, paying careful attention to the display. Maker imagined that it was giving a readout that indicated proteins, carbohydrates, vitamins, and other nutrients. This was seemingly confirmed when, a moment later, the P'ngrawen with the wand made some sort of hand gesture, which seemed to indicate that all was well.

Next it was Erlen's turn. As was typically the case, the Niotan could not be scanned internally. This caused a momentary bit of consternation, as evidenced by a hushed conversation between the P'ngrawen with the wand and the guard captain. Afterwards, the latter stepped away for a moment while he pulled out a communicator of some sort and had a brief conference with someone unseen — presumably a superior. A few seconds later, he returned.

He made a brief gesture that resulted in half the guards stepping back, apparently being dismissed. The remainder took up positions around Maker, Skullcap, and Erlen: two in front, one on each side, and two to the rear.

"*Now* we go to your female," the captain announced. "Come."

IGNOTUS

Chapter 98

Following behind the guard captain, Maker's group (and their escort) left the landing bay through a nearby door. At that juncture, they found themselves in a short corridor that terminated at an elevator. Everyone quickly piled in and the elevator started to rise.

At that moment, Erlen began pawing at his nose and making odd noises, as if he were choking on something while simultaneously trying to sneeze. The Niotan's antics were apparently irksome to some degree, prompting a question from the guard commander.

"What's wrong with that creature?" the captain asked.

"I would guess that he's having an adverse reaction to the atmosphere on your ship," Skullcap stated. "He will adjust, but it may take time."

The guard commander let out something like an audible groan but said nothing. A few seconds later, the elevator came to a halt on a deck that was seemingly near the top of the ship. As they were exiting into an adjoining hallway, Erlen immediately dashed to one side and then, in a fit of coughing, regurgitated a small stream of dark green liquid.

"Your beast is foul," the captain noted with a look of disgust.

"You mean your *ruler*'s beast is foul," Skullcap corrected, "as he now belongs to *Lord* Badukst. You should share your sentiments with him."

The guard commander seemed taken aback by the notion. However, rather than comment, he merely resumed walking down the hallway, obviously assuming that everyone else would follow.

IGNOTUS

****

They stalked through the ship in silence. There was an air about the guard captain that made it clear that conversation, whether idle or of import, was not going to be tolerated. Or perhaps the P'ngrawen were naturally a reticent species, for — as Maker noted — although they occasionally passed others in the hallways, they saw few (if any) discussions between individuals.

Frankly speaking, it felt a bit like a death march (and — depending on the outcome — might turn out to be one, to some extent). The only break in their stride occurred when Erlen, on three more occasions, continued to spew up fluids and such, much to the dismay of their escorts.

Ultimately, after a straight march across what felt like the length of the entire ship, the group reached their destination: a wide door with a pair of P'ngrawen guards standing to either side of it. In Maker's estimation, since leaving the landing bay, the entire trek had taken about twenty minutes. Bearing in mind their apparent location now versus where they had started, it struck him that they were about as far as reasonably possible from their shuttle (which was probably the point).

The guard captain moved towards the door before them, which slid open as he approached, allowing him to enter. Knowing what was expected, Maker and his two companions followed, as did the rest of the guards. Once inside, the door closed behind them; then (to no one's great surprise) Erlen once again spat up — this time at the very foot of the door.

IGNOTUS

Showing little worry about the Niotan, Maker took a look around and noted that they were now in an expansive room, roughly fifty by one hundred feet in size. However, it gave the impression of being larger than it actually was because it was almost completely devoid of décor. All that Maker could spy was a rack on one wall that held an array of unusual devices and implements, a cage next to it that was large enough to hold an elephant, and a large, lumpy mass in the middle of the room that might have been a piece of abstract art.

No, not art, Maker thought as Skullcap suddenly ran towards the bulky object on the floor. *The empress.*

IGNOTUS

Chapter 99

Oddly enough, none of the P'ngrawen moved to stop Skullcap, allowing him to reach the empress without hindrance. Once by her side, he gently reached out, touching her head.

The empress, who lay naked on the floor, huddled in a ball, initially flinched at his touch. But as Skullcap softly stroked the back of her head, she slowly looked up. One side of her face was plainly bruised and swollen. However, the light of recognition showed in her eyes, and she slowly rose up. As she did so, Maker noted that his initial impression from the hologram was correct: she was huge — at least twice the size of Skullcap.

Like her face, her body also bore signs of trauma. Discolored in random spots, it showcased scabrous wounds and contusions — evidence of recent affliction — while in other places Maker noticed wicked scars and pockmarks, indicators of old injuries that had healed.

All in all, it appeared that she had suffered greatly, and for an extended period of time. More importantly, Maker suddenly gained insight with respect to much of what he was seeing — in particular, the various tools on the wall rack. (He did note, however, that a good number of her injuries appeared near the metal collar that was around her neck, just as it was in the hologram.)

"Child, what do you here?" the empress asked in a weak voice.

"Mother," Skullcap said, "I have come for you."

"You should not have," she declared. "These monsters will never let me leave."

"They will now," Skullcap insisted. "They wish an exchange."

IGNOTUS

As he finished speaking, Skullcap gestured towards Erlen, who had meandered forward towards the two Vacra.

Upon seeing him, the empress seemed to catch her breath. Slowly, as if she couldn't believe her eyes, she reached towards the Niotan. Gently, she stroked his back for a moment, and Erlen — apparently appreciating the gesture — turned and licked her hand.

Drawing her arm back, the empress turned to Skullcap again. "No, undo this bargain you've made. The Senu Lia is a treasure. It is not meant to be associated with vile savages like — Aaaaahhh!!!!"

The empress suddenly screamed, wailing in agony and convulsing wildly. As a result of her spasms, she inadvertently struck Skullcap, sending him flying across the room; he hit the floor and skidded momentarily before coming to a halt. Seconds later, the empress ceased howling and dropped to the floor in a heap, looking much as she had when they had first entered.

"My apologies," said someone from one side of the room, voice full of mirth. "She has a tendency to convulse like that when the collar shocks her, although I haven't quite figured out yet whether it's more fun to watch her thrash about in the open or in a cage."

Maker looked in the direction of the voice and saw that another P'ngrawen had come into the room. He was dressed in some type of finery — clothing that almost sparkled with a blue-and-gold hue. Around his neck was a chain that was probably made of precious metal and from which dangled a large medallion, and on each forearm he sported matching wristbands. Finally, he walked with an unmistakable air of superiority.

IGNOTUS

The guard captain and the others who had escorted his group from the landing bay all tilted their heads to the side and made some type of weird hand gesture. Observing them, Maker took their actions, in combination, to represent some sign of obeisance. This new arrival, then, was Lord Badukst, and he had presumably come into the room through some doorway not immediately evident.

As Skullcap slowly regained his feet, Erlen — now standing next to Maker — began making the coughing sound again. The guards, now accustomed to this spectacle, saw no need to worry as Maker bent down to check on the Niotan.

"Is that my new pet?" asked Badukst, staring at Erlen.

"It is, Highness," replied the guard captain.

Badukst frowned. "What's wrong with it?"

"Apparently it is not fully acclimated to our environment," the captain continued.

"And this one?" Badukst asked, gesturing towards Maker while sauntering towards the area where the empress lay.

"Its handler," the captain stated. "Apparently he is the only person it will accept food from."

"Interesting," the P'ngrawen ruler muttered. "I suppose I'll have to—"

"Badukst!" Skullcap shouted, stalking back towards the center of the room. "The Vacra have fulfilled their part of the bargain. Now release the empress."

Badukst appeared to contemplate for a moment, then said, "I think not."

"What?" Skullcap uttered.

IGNOTUS

"I said I don't think I'll be letting the empress go," Badukst stated. "I prefer to keep both her and the Senu Lia."

"That was not the agreement!" Skullcap blurted out angrily, stepping around the empress and in the direction of the P'ngrawen ruler.

Badukst laughed. "Obviously, I'm changing the arrangement."

"You cannot do that!" Skullcap yelled, taking yet another step towards Badukst.

The guards, apparently put on edge by Skullcap's tone (and his increasing proximity to their leader), seemed to make the Vacra the focus of their attention and closed in around him a little more. At the same time, Maker — somewhat forgotten — stealthily slid backwards in the direction of the door they had entered until he was no longer encircled by P'ngrawen. (In fact, they were so fixated on Skullcap that he probably could have turned cartwheels and not drawn any attention.)

"You forget your place," Badukst growled. "I have your empress and the Senu Lia. Thus, I can do what I like. I can—"

The P'ngrawen ruler was cut off as a shrill beeping began to sound loudly. He tapped what appeared to be a button on one of his wristbands, and the noise stopped. He then touched another button, which appeared to open a communication channel.

"What's happening?" Badukst demanded.

"Lord," someone replied nervously, with the beeping noise in the background. "Some kind of corrosive has come on board. It's eating through the decks floor by floor in several areas."

"So neutralize it," Badukst ordered.

IGNOTUS

"We've tried," the voice explained, "but nothing works. It's an acidic compound that we've never encountered. More importantly, one of the areas where it's active is directly above engineering, and if it continues on its current path, it's going to eat right through the main engines. When that happens, they'll explode. The ship may be destroyed. All should evacuate."

Badukst's eyes went wide as the implications of what he was hearing hit him. All of a sudden, he spun towards Skullcap, glaring at the insectoid.

"You…" he hissed. "You did this. Stop it now. Stop it or lose your Emp—"

"Now!" Skullcap shouted, leaping towards the guard captain (who was the closest P'ngrawen near him) and the two of them immediately began a tug-of-war for the latter's gun.

At the same time, Maker opened fire, quickly nailing three of the guards with headshots from a small lasergun he'd obtained via Erlen. (Maker smiled thinking about how, during the Niotan's last purported coughing fit, none of the guards had noticed Erlen spit the gun into his hand). And while Maker was taking potshots at the trio of guards, Erlen spat a glob of goo onto the gun hand of another; a moment later, the guard was screaming in pain as the hand (and part of his firearm) dissolved.

The two remaining guards appeared confused, realizing that attacks were coming from multiple directions but unable to decide where to apply their efforts. Their hesitation was their undoing, as it allowed them to be assailed from a completely unexpected direction: the empress.

Belting a screech of rage, she struck one of the remaining guards with a powerful blow that literally knocked much of the bark off him as he went flying across the room, end-over-end. He struck the wall with a solid thump and then fell to the floor, unconscious.

The last guard got off a few wild shots before the empress knocked the rifle out of his hands. She then picked him up and — with a sound that was reminiscent of wood splintering — literally broke him in two. Flinging the remains aside, she then turned her attention to Badukst.

On his part, the P'ngrawen ruler was aiming something in the direction of the empress and manically shaking it at her. At first Maker assumed it was a firearm, but if it was, it had to be the worst gun in existence because it fired absolutely nothing in the direction of the empress as she stalked towards Badukst: no projectiles, no lasers, no nothing. In fact, the empress grabbed the hand in question and, like someone snapping a pencil in half, broke it off at the wrist.

Howling in anguish, Badukst dropped to his knees, holding the stump where his hand had been, amber ichor pouring from the wound. Ignoring him, the empress took the item from the disembodied hand (which she let fall to the floor) and began to tap at it. A moment later, the collar fell from her neck, and Maker suddenly realized that the item Badukst had been holding was a control device of some sort. From all appearances, he had been trying to shock the empress into submission (or kill her), but it had not worked.

Gunfire drew Maker's attention, reminding him that he had almost forgotten about Skullcap. However, he needn't have worried. The Vacran had apparently been successful in wresting the gun away and had then shot the guard captain with his own weapon. He then ran towards the empress while Maker did the same.

"Mother," Skullcap said, "this is Maker — a friend."

"I surmised as much," the empress said, sounding much better than she had when Skullcap had first spoken to her.

"We should go," Maker said, noting that a furious pounding had begun at the door they had entered through.

The P'ngrawen who had been posted outside (and perhaps others) had probably heard the recent gunplay and were quite likely trying to get inside to protect their leader. The door, however, was going to be an obstacle. Erlen had once spat a compound on an officer's shoes that glued them so solidly to the deck of a ship that the floor had to be cut away to remove them. He had done the same thing when they entered *this* room, producing a substance that had cemented the door in place. Those outside would have to cut the door open with a blowtorch to get inside. That said, Maker had no doubt that they had one nearby.

He was still reflecting on the situation with the door when Skullcap reached down and grabbed the P'ngrawen ruler by the scruff of the neck.

"Up," Skullcap commanded, hauling Badukst roughly to his feet. "You're coming with us."

He then practically frogmarched Badukst to the area where the wall rack was located, with Maker, Erlen, and the empress following. Shoving the P'ngrawen against the wall, Skullcap began scanning the articles on the rack, plainly looking for something specific. After a few seconds, he seemed to identify what he was after as

IGNOTUS

he reached out and took a device that looked like two large, conjoined chicken eggs.

Holding one of the "eggs," Skullcap flicked his wrist. Almost immediately, a low-level humming began. He couldn't tell with the naked eye, but the readout on his faceplate told Maker that the other egg, on the end of the device the Vacran held, was now electrified. In addition, the egg unexpectedly opened up, its exterior separating into strap-shaped ligules that spread apart like the petals of a flower, ultimately taking on the appearance of a mutated daisy.

Without hesitation, Skullcap grabbed Badukst's injured limb and shoved the device he held towards it. The petals immediately closed over the stump, followed by an increase in the volume of the humming noise (which Maker associated with an increased electrical discharge). A moment later, Skullcap pulled the device away. The result — aside from eliciting another agonized scream from the injured ruler — was cauterization of the wound.

Skullcap put the egg-device back in its original position. Maker let his gaze linger on it, as well as the other objects on the rack. He didn't recognize any of them, but it didn't take a lot of imagination to understand that they were all instruments intended to cause torment and suffering. If he hadn't known it before, there was no mistaking it now: this room was a torture chamber.

He was brought out of his reverie by Badukst moaning in pain as Skullcap shook him.

"Where is it?" Skullcap asked the P'ngrawen.

"Where's what?" the injured monarch moaned.

"The entrance," Skullcap demanded.

IGNOTUS

"I don't know what you're talking about," Badukst whimpered.

"When you came into the room, you appeared from this direction," Skullcap insisted. "So there's a door here somewhere."

"You're mistaken," Badukst said. "There's no door over here."

Skullcap started speaking again, but Maker tuned him out, his attention suddenly drawn to a whooshing sound coming from behind them. Turning towards the entrance they had come through, he saw a tongue of flame extending through a small hole in the metal door. As he had suspected, those outside had located a torch and were cutting their way in. (Explosives, of course, would have been quicker, but presumably they wanted to minimize the odds of harming their monarch.)

An angry screech from the empress drew his attention back to the situation with Badukst. Having apparently grown impatient, the empress now had a grip on the P'ngrawen's neck and was holding him against the wall, several feet in the air.

"Would you lie to *me*?" she demanded. "I, who have seen you come and go for years while your prisoner? There is indeed a door here. Now open it, or lose your other hand."

Maybe it was pain or shock, but apparently Badukst had forgotten that the empress knew the truth of this particular matter. That — coupled, undoubtedly, with the thought of having his remaining hand snapped off — eliminated his resolve. He gestured wildly, plainly indicating that he would cooperate, and the empress let him drop. Cradling his wounded arm, he quickly stood up and then tapped the wall in a way that Maker couldn't quite perceive or which was too subtle for him to catch. Regardless, a rectangular expanse of wall swung open, revealing a hidden entrance. Moments later, they were all inside.

IGNOTUS

Chapter 100

They found themselves in a dimly lit corridor. Maker's suit immediately compensated for the lack of light, allowing him to see as though the place was filled with torches. Although modest in size, it was tall enough to allow everyone to walk upright except the empress, who had to bend over almost double.

"Do not mind me," she stated before anyone could question her. "Press on."

Without further prompting, Skullcap shoved Badukst forward, curtly ordering, "March."

Grimacing in pain, the injured monarch led the way (although there was, in truth, only one way to go). Behind him was Skullcap, followed by Erlen, Maker, and finally, the empress. Fortunately, their journey through the secret hallway was short; roughly a minute after they began walking, they emerged through another secret door into what struck Maker as a formal sitting room.

The place was well-lit and perhaps three hundred square feet in size. Although the configuration of the furniture was unusual, the interior design struck Maker as extraordinarily posh and ritzy.

Hearing a grunt of effort behind him, Maker turned just as the empress was exiting the hidden hallway. At that very moment, the entire vessel shook wildly for a second. Maker had trouble keeping his feet, and the empress staggered forward into the room, slightly off-balance.

Maker would have loved to have said that he caught the empress as she stumbled in his direction. In truth, however, she was far too massive for him to have done any such thing. Although, to his credit, he did not move, Maker actually did little more than put his hands out and steady her as the empress regained her balance.

"That was probably the engines exploding," Maker said over his shoulder.

"Yes," Skullcap agreed, "although not as massive as I had expected. They must have found a way to contain it."

Maker was about to comment further when, looking at the empress as he prepared to let her stand on her own, he saw something that made his eyes go wide.

"Skull—" he began shouting, then caught himself and yelled, "Vuqja! You need to see this!"

Half-dragging Badukst along, Skullcap hurried towards Maker, then stopped short as he drew near and let out a curious mewling sound. Maker knew then that the insectoid was seeing the same thing he had only just noticed: a quartet of holes spread across the thorax of the empress, each of which was weeping blood. Maker suddenly remembered one of the guards in the torture chamber managing to fire his weapon a few times before the empress killed him; apparently some of his shots had found their mark.

"Mother..." Skullcap muttered. "Are you—"

"I'm not in pain," she declared, cutting him off but sounding winded. "I do not feel any discomfort, although the wounds are obviously having an effect."

Maker cast a stealthy glance in Erlen's direction, understanding that the Niotan had done something — deadened the empress's nerves, given her a boost of adrenaline, or taken some action along those lines.

However, rather than comment on it, he turned to Skullcap, saying, "We have to get her out of here." (Left

IGNOTUS

unsaid, of course, was the empress's need for medical attention.)

Skullcap roughly shoved Badukst in the direction of a door that led out of the room.

"Move," the insectoid snapped.

Whimpering, Badukst began walking as ordered, with Skullcap and the empress behind him. Maker was about to follow when Erlen began snarling at the wall. Maker was confused for a moment, then understood that the Niotan was growling at the area that masked the hidden hallway they had exited from; the doorway had closed and fit so seamlessly into the wall that Maker had almost lost track of exactly where it was. Still, he understood the message being conveyed.

"We got company coming!" he yelled at Skullcap. He then nodded at Erlen, who dragged a paw across the juncture between wall and floor, leaving a viscous, clear fluid in its wake. It was a subtle reminder that the Niotan could use the papillae in his footpads, like a tongue, to secrete compounds. Confident now that anyone pursuing them would have to cut their way through this door as they had previously, Maker and Erlen hurriedly followed the others.

The adjoining room, like the one they had just vacated, bespoke of great wealth. However, it was at least twice as large, and the overall décor impressed Maker as being even more lavish and luxurious, as evidenced by a two-story ceiling, an elegant staircase ascending to the floor above, art niches that housed exotic creations, and a window-wall that offered a sweeping view of the stars. More to the point, Maker immediately understood that they were in some type of executive lodging or

IGNOTUS

presidential suite — presumably Badukst's private quarters.

Skullcap practically dragged the P'ngrawen leader across the floor to the far side of the room. As he did so, Erlen swiped a paw across the bottom of the door they'd just come through, leaving a liquid trail that would presumably seal this door as well. The Niotan then dashed across the floor towards a set of baroque double doors — apparently the main point of entry — plainly intent on securing those against entry as well.

Summoning a resolve from some internal source, Badukst suddenly hissed, through clenched teeth, "You would be wise to let me go and surrender."

"And what will you do if we refuse?" Skullcap shot back. "You don't appear to be in a position to make demands or issue threats."

"Not me," Badukst clarified as Skullcap marched him down a hall. "My people. They will not take kindly to their beloved leader being harmed."

"Oh yes, having seen it firsthand, I know all about this love you speak of," Skullcap stated. "The P'ngrawen who sold me the blueprints to your flagship wept openly at the thought of what I planned to do to you, crying so forcefully that he could barely count his money."

"What?" Badukst muttered, clearly caught off guard.

Skullcap continued as if no one had spoken. "His blubbering didn't cease until I promised to make your death quick and painless. Of course, if he could see you now" — he gestured towards the injured ruler's stump — "he'd probably accuse me of breaking my word and demand additional payment. He loves you too much to sell you cheaply."

IGNOTUS

In Maker's opinion, Badukst looked as though he wanted to garrote Skullcap with his own tongue.

"You lie!" he screamed as the insectoid pulled him to a stop in front of a large metal door.

"Of course," Skullcap retorted sarcastically. "It's just by happenstance that I led us here, and it's simple luck that I can guess what's on the other side of this hatch."

Badukst looked around in bewilderment, seeming to notice for the first time where they were. (Maker assumed that the physical and psychological toll from losing his hand had caused the P'ngrawen to somehow miss the fact that they had traveled a very specific route through the hallway, which — although it wasn't very extensive — did have several junctions and had required them to go through multiple doors.) An expression that Maker interpreted as fretful settled on the maimed monarch's face.

"Open it," Skullcap demanded.

Badukst hesitated for a moment, causing Erlen (who had rejoined the group) to growl menacingly. Not daring to tempt fate, the P'ngrawen placed his remaining hand on a clear plate next to the hatch. The plate glowed briefly, then Maker heard a number of mechanical clicks — the sound of bolts and locks disengaging. As soon as the noises ceased, Skullcap tried the handle and the hatch swung open.

Skullcap and Badukst went in first, followed by the empress, Erlen, and Maker at the rear. After stepping through and closing the hatch, Maker saw that they were in a small landing bay. There was only one vessel present — a modest-sized but sleek-looking craft that looked factory-new. Maker immediately grasped that this was the

IGNOTUS

personal yacht of Badukst, most likely used to effectuate a fast getaway, if and when necessary.

Skullcap hastily strode toward the ship's entrance with the P'ngrawen ruler in tow. The empress began to follow, but then stumbled unexpectedly. Although she managed to stay on her feet, her breath sounded heavy and uneven. She hadn't complained and had kept up without issue, but she was clearly in bad shape (even if, as she'd said before, she wasn't in any pain). Fortunately, they were in the homestretch at this point.

"We're almost there," Maker said reassuringly.

"Pay me... no mind..." she insisted, moving forward.

Skullcap glanced back in their direction, plainly concerned, but stayed focused on the task at hand. He and Badukst had just reached the entrance to the yacht. It took only seconds to open the door and moments later, they were all inside.

Skullcap practically threw Badukst onto what looked like a P'ngrawen version of a sofa in the main cabin. He then headed to the cockpit, which was just a few feet away. Maker joined him, leaving the empress and Erlen on either side of the one-handed overlord. Even if he were uninjured, Badukst was unlikely to have tried anything under the watchful eye of those two. In his current state, it wasn't even a concern.

Once in the cockpit, Skullcap wasted no time; he immediately began pressing buttons and flipping switches on the instrument panel, obviously preparing the ship for flight. As he did so, various screens and monitors on the panel came to life, providing a wealth of information about the ship.

IGNOTUS

Needless to say, the controls were all completely foreign to Maker. If forced to — and assuming he had enough time — he could probably get the craft powered up and eventually even take off. After that, however, it was likely to be a rough ride, as he had no experience with this type of vessel.

Skullcap, on the other hand, seemed completely at ease with respect to the flight controls, and it took him no more than a minute to get the ship powered up. Still, it felt like it was taking forever.

"You might want to step on it," Maker prompted. "There were guards on our tail, and it won't take them long to figure out where we've gone once they get into their ruler's suite." It also occurred to him that he had failed to have Erlen secure the last door they had come through.

"We'll be gone before they reach us," Skullcap assured him. "The ship is ready, so it's merely a matter of opening the bay doors."

As he spoke, he tapped a few items on a nearby screen and then gripped what Maker had assumed was the control wheel. Glancing out the cockpit window, Maker saw that they were slowly rising, and he felt himself starting to relax.

Unfortunately, it was a short-lived experience as the craft suddenly died on them. The entire instrument panel went dark, and they dropped down to the bay floor with a solid, metallic thud that echoed sonorously.

Fortunately, the yacht hadn't risen very far, so the ship's short plunge had been more unnerving than injurious. That said, what happened next took Maker completely by surprise.

IGNOTUS

An odd noise suddenly began to fill the ship, putting Maker in mind of a songbird trying to warble while simultaneously gulping down a worm. Looking into the main cabin (which seemed to be the origin of the sound), he saw Badukst with his mouth open, shuddering almost uncontrollably. At that moment, Maker had a revelation as to exactly what he was hearing.

It was Badukst. The P'ngrawen monarch was laughing at them.

IGNOTUS

Chapter 101

Deciding to ignore Badukst for the moment, Maker turned to Skullcap, who was hastily fiddling with the control panel again.

"What happened?" Maker asked.

"An unexpected contingency," Skullcap replied. "Apparently the flight controls are DNA-locked. They will fully respond only when a particular person is at the controls."

"No need to guess who that is," Maker said, glancing at Badukst.

"You should have surrendered when you had the chance," the injured ruler said, giggling. "After my people overrun this ship — and they *will* — you can all expect to spend an extended amount of time as my *personal* guests. And I promise, you'll lose a lot more than a hand."

Erlen growled fiercely, but it only seemed to embolden Badukst.

"The Vacra are as good as dead," he continued. "I'll broadcast the execution of your empress live." He then turned to Maker, hissing, "And you…I will use the Senu Lia to completely exterminate your species. It will be a footrace to determine who becomes extinct first, humans or the Vac—"

Badukst found his threats cut off as the empress screeched, drawing back an arm in preparation to strike him.

"No!" Skullcap shouted in her direction, causing the empress to stop. "He stays alive for now." He then turned his attention back to the instrument panel.

"What are our options?" Maker asked.

IGNOTUS

"I can reset the system and override the requirement for a DNA signature," the Vacran replied, continuing to manipulate the controls. "But it will take time."

"How long?"

"Approximately ten minutes."

Maker shook his head. "We don't have ten minutes. We may not even have five."

Maker closed his eyes for a second, releasing a pent-up breath, then opened them again.

"All right," he began, "guards are going to be flocking this way in hordes soon. I'll hold them off as long as I can — buy you some time."

"No," Skullcap retorted. "As I explained, I have a duty to do all in my power to see that no harm comes to you. Thus, it should be *me* who faces the enemy."

"You're right — it *should* be you," Maker agreed. "But as luck would have it, between the two of us, you're the one who knows how to fly this boat, so you get to hang around here." (He didn't even mention the fact that, given the empress's deteriorating condition, every second was critical.)

"But—" Skullcap began.

"You know we don't have time to debate this," Maker said. "So let's just assume that you'd willingly take my place, protect me at all costs, blah, blah, blah."

Skullcap seemed to contemplate for a moment, then muttered, "So be it."

"Now, before I go, how soon can you get the bay doors open?" Maker asked.

"Immediately, I should think," Skullcap answered. "They're not tied to the flight controls, so I'd be surprised if the DNA lock applied to them."

IGNOTUS

"Great," Maker said. "As soon as I'm back inside the flagship proper, open them. It's unlikely that any of the guards have had the foresight to bring a spacesuit, so that will get you a few extra minutes."

"Understood," Skullcap said. Maker thought he detected a twinge of sadness in the insectoid's voice, but figured it had to be his imagination.

"Here," Maker said, taking the communicator from his utility belt and holding it out. "It's encrypted, so we'll be able to chat without being overheard."

"Thank you," Skull droned, taking the device. "Your sacrifice will not be in vain."

"Well, I'm not dead yet," Maker reminded him, "so let's put the eulogy off for a while."

"Very well," the insectoid said, then held out a hand in Maker's direction.

Taken somewhat by surprise, Maker just stood there for a moment. It wasn't just that the Vacran was engaging in a profoundly human gesture; it was also the fact of what shaking that hand would mean. In Maker's mind, Skullcap had been his enemy for years. Shaking the insectoid's hand would seemingly symbolize a new era — a change in their relationship Maker would not have thought possible. Thus, it came as almost a shock to him when he reached out and grasped the proffered hand.

"Good luck," Skullcap said.

"You, too," Maker muttered, still uncertain of what he was doing.

A moment later, Maker released his grip. Skullcap went back to the control panel, while Maker stepped through the main cabin, heading for the exit. But before he got there, Erlen stepped in front of him, whimpering.

Maker bent down and rubbed the Niotan's head.

IGNOTUS

"It's okay," he assured his friend. "Everything's going to be fine."

He then stood up and resumed walking to the door. A moment later, he was outside the yacht and headed to the hatch that connected to Badukst's quarters.

IGNOTUS

Chapter 102

"All right, I'm in," Maker said into his comm unit once he was on the other side of the hatch. There was silence for a moment, causing Maker to reflect on the fact that they hadn't bothered to test the communicator before he'd left Badukst's yacht. Seconds later, he felt relief as Skullcap answered.

"Understood," the insectoid stated. "Opening the bay doors."

Almost immediately thereafter, Maker heard something along the lines of a distant rumbling. Satisfied that his instructions were being followed, he decided to test a theory that had been running through his mind by trying to open the door he'd just come through. On Gaian ships, such a hatch wouldn't open if sensors couldn't detect an atmosphere on the other side. In short, it was a safety measure intended to keep individuals from getting sucked out into space should they carelessly throw wide a door that opened into the void (such as a landing bay which had its bay doors open).

Like its Gaian counterparts, the P'ngrawen door appeared programmed not to open under the current circumstances. Then Maker chuckled to himself, remembering that they'd actually needed Badukst to unlock the door from this side just a few minutes earlier; it probably wouldn't have opened even if the bay doors were closed. Confident that this would present yet another barrier to their enemies, Maker turned his mind back to the task at hand.

As he recalled, they had passed through three doors during their trek from the main part of the suite to the landing bay — including the last hatch. That meant

IGNOTUS

there were possibly two doors between him and any pursuing guards. The next one, if memory served, was around a corner, and as he moved forward, gun in hand, he quickly found out he was right. At that juncture, however, his luck ran out: just as he reached the door, it was being opened by two P'ngrawen guards.

The guards appeared to be engaged in conversation and didn't immediately notice that there was someone in the passageway they were about to enter. Taking advantage of their inattentiveness, Maker shot the first one in the face. The guard flew backwards, crashing into his colleague (who was directly behind him), and they both went down. The first P'ngrawen was obviously dead, and while the second struggled to get out from under his deceased companion and get his gun up, Maker came through the doorway and shot him in the head.

For a moment, Maker simply stared at the dead guards, plainly surprised that there were only two of them. He would have thought that there would be dozens coming after him and his companions, and then the truth dawned on him: the P'ngrawens had no idea which direction they'd gone. Badukst had a palatial suite that guards were probably in the process of searching room-by-room, not to mention various hallways, secret passageways, and so on.

Maybe if they're spread thin enough, he thought, *we'll get all the time we need.*

A moment later, that was shown to be wishful thinking as — at the far end of the hallway, in the direction the dead P'ngrawen had come from — another of their fellows stepped from around a corner and into view. Unlike the first two, the newcomer was vigilant and sized up the situation immediately. In one fluid motion,

IGNOTUS

he brought his weapon to bear and began firing as Maker did the same.

The exchange of gunfire was haphazard, however, as both combatants sought cover while continuing to shoot. The newcomer dove back in the direction he'd come from, taking shelter around the corner of the hallway. On his part, Maker scrambled backward towards the door he'd come through, swinging it almost shut once he crossed the threshold, leaving only a small crack to see — and fire his weapon — through.

Well, if they didn't know where we'd gone before, they certainly do now, Maker said to himself.

****

As Maker suspected, it didn't take long for a bevy of guards to assemble at the far end of the hallway — or rather, that's what he assumed. He couldn't actually see them, but he could hear multiple voices whispering. However, what the parties had was a bit of a standoff. With nothing but a narrow hallway separating opposing forces, neither side could really charge the other's position without taking significant losses.

That said, one of the guards did lean around the corner every ten seconds or so and fire a few rounds in Maker's direction. Although none of them came close to hitting him, he initially returned fire just to keep them honest and let them know he was still present, active, and able. However, he stopped shooting back after he realized their actions were probably just a ploy to get him to exhaust his ammo. Even worse, it had worked to a certain extent. Maker only had the one small lasergun, and its charge was dwindling fast. (He could always try taking

IGNOTUS

one of the dead guards' guns, but he'd have to expose himself, which he was in no hurry to do.)

Frankly speaking, he was surprised they didn't just hurl a grenade at him. Then, of course, he realized that they wouldn't risk it — for all they knew, Badukst was with him, and blowing your monarch to bits is usually a bad career move. (There was also the risk of exposing the interior of the ship to the vacuum of space, which Maker was sure they were loath to do.)

All in all, despite being outnumbered, it was looking like he'd be able to hold the guards off long enough for Skullcap to reset the system on Badukst's escape ship.

Just to be certain, he flipped on his comm and asked, "How's it going?"

"Slower than I anticipated," Skullcap admitted. "We may need additional time beyond my earlier assessment."

Maker was incredulous. "How much more time are we talking about?"

"Five minutes."

"So fifteen minutes total," Maker summed up, peeking out the door as he did so.

"Correct."

Maker shook his head, frustrated. Fifteen minutes was a lifetime for someone under hostile fire. Still, he simply said, "I'm on it."

"Also, there is one other thing," Skullcap stated, "although I do not wish to distract you from your current task."

"What is it?" Maker asked.

"The bridge of the P'ngrawen flagship has been in contact with us. They know where we are and have stated

IGNOTUS

that all three of their ships will fire on us if we leave this landing bay. I wanted you to know that I view those as empty threats and will attempt to escape regardless of odds."

"Understood," Maker acknowledged. "And agreed." He then shut his comm off.

As he broke the connection with Skullcap, Maker suddenly became aware of a new sound — a muted buzzing that seemed to come from behind the wall on one side of the hallway.

No, not just one *wall*, he thought after reassessing. Both *walls*. And *the ceiling*.

Presumably, the P'ngrawen were coming through the walls, this time using some kind of cutting implement. And they were coming at him from all directions.

Maker could have kicked himself. In thinking that he and the guards were at a stalemate, he had completely forgotten about the fact that the walls of ships are seldom completely solid. They contain vents, ducts, access shafts, and more. They have to in order for crews to be able to reach areas that might need repair.

Realizing now that the soldiers at the end of the hallway were just a distraction, Maker closed and locked the door. It wouldn't keep anyone permanently out — the door could be locked and unlocked from either side — but it would keep him from being completely surprised if someone approached from that direction. He then spent a moment listening intently.

From what he could tell, the P'ngrawen were trying to breach the hallway in six places: two on each wall (at the near and far ends of the hallway), and two in the ceiling. As if he needed proof of this, something like a buzz saw breached the wall on the right at the far end of

IGNOTUS

the passageway, sending a shower of sparks cascading into the corridor.

Speculating that his spacesuit would protect him, Maker jogged down the hallway for a better look. However, he'd gone no more than a few feet before a shower of hot sparks rained down on him from above, causing him to dance to the side. As with the wall, the P'ngrawen had also breached the ceiling. Less than a minute later, fiery particles were flying into the room from all six access points Maker had identified, forcing him to take refuge against the wall in the middle of the room — the only place the sparks weren't reaching.

Maker immediately understood that the P'ngrawen had the advantage in this situation. Assuming they were smart (and he had no reason to doubt that they were), they'd time things so that they came through all six "entrances" at once after cutting their way through the walls. Some of them might die, but there was no doubt that Maker would get overrun.

Badukst's yacht would be next. The locked hatched would be an obstacle, but far from a barrier in terms of keeping the P'ngrawen guards out of the landing bay. In short order, they would sweep in, taking everyone prisoner well before the ship was ready to take off. Maker had no doubt that Skullcap and the empress would be tortured and executed. And Erlen? He couldn't imagine all the things they'd do to the Niotan to get what they wanted.

No! Maker said to himself. *I'll never let them have Erlen.*

Turning on his comm, he said, "This is Maker. Can you hear me?"

"Yes," Skullcap replied.

IGNOTUS

"The P'ngrawen are going to overrun my position shortly. My rinky-dink lasergun isn't going to be able to stop them."

"Then you should return. We will make our last stand together."

"No," Maker stressed. "I have a backup plan, but I'm the only one who can execute it. It'll give you the time you need to get out of here. Just get your empress home so your people can survive, and take Erlen to Dr. Chantrey. She'll take care of him."

There was silence for a moment, then Skullcap said, "Maker, I—"

"Don't say anything," Maker interjected. "Just show me some of that vaunted Vacra nobility by doing what I ask, okay?"

Maker got the impression that Skullcap wanted to argue, but instead he acquiesced, saying, "Yes, of course."

"Thanks. Is, uh…is Erlen nearby?"

"Yes. He comes close each time you contact us."

"I should have figured," Maker muttered, smiling. "So Erlen, I need you to listen. When you guys get back, I want you to go to Dr. Chantrey. She'll look out for you, and I need you to look out for her, too. Okay?"

Erlen's reply was a sad, melancholic mewling.

"It's okay, buddy," Maker assured him. "You're going to be fine."

Heart heavy, Maker then shut the comm off. Glancing at the walls, he could see that the P'ngrawen were close to getting in. Recognizing that he was almost out of time, Maker shrugged off the rucksack, unzipped it, and then dumped the contents on the floor.

As he had previously stated, there had indeed been food in the bag: protein bars, snacks, dried fruit, and

IGNOTUS

other edibles. But there was one thing that definitely did not fall under the category of consumable: a box that was all white, except for one corner that was painted red.

Switching the comm on, Maker said, "Oh yeah — one more thing."

"Yes?" Skullcap replied.

"When you leave, don't come back for me. It'll be too dangerous."

Then, after turning the comm off one final time, Maker aimed his gun and fired at the red corner of the box.

IGNOTUS

Chapter 103

Maker came to feeling unbelievably parched, his throat painfully dry. If felt as though someone had sucked all the moisture out of his mouth and then poured burning sand down his throat.

"Welcome back," said a familiar voice.

Maker looked up to find Fierce standing over him. He suddenly realized that he was lying prone in a bed.

"Where…?" Maker wheezed, his voice sounding feeble and weak.

"The *Nova*'s sick bay," Fierce answered, which Maker confirmed with a quick glance around. He also noted that he had an IV in one arm. Feeling around, he managed to find the controls for the bed; a moment later, it began to incline, raising him to a seated position.

"How do you feel?" the Augman asked.

"Thirsty," Maker managed to croak, finding the act of speaking painful.

"That's not surprising," Fierce stated. "You were brought in suffering from severe dehydration and all the attendant symptoms: shriveled skin, highly elevated body temperature, organ failure... In all honesty, I'm surprised you survived."

Maker tried to speak, but ended up launching into a coughing fit. Fierce reached towards a nightstand that was next to the bed, grabbing a bottle of water that was sitting there.

"I know, I know," he droned as he twisted off the cap and handed the bottle to Maker. "You were going to make some wisecrack about not being allowed to die without express permission from the Corps, or something along those lines."

IGNOTUS

His coughing now under control, Maker merely pointed a finger at the Augman and gave a nod of acknowledgment, as if saying that Fierce had read his mind. He then took a sip of water. Swallowing was uncomfortable, but at the same time the water felt soothing.

"Anyway," Fierce continued, "I've been trying to reintroduce fluids to your body as quickly as possible. Fortunately, there are few risks associated with rapid rehydration."

"How...long?" Maker inquired before taking another drink from the bottle.

"You've been here about a day," the Augman answered. "What's the last thing you remember?"

Maker frowned. He had a vivid recollection of shooting the red corner of one of Planck's nanobot containers. A few seconds after that, he started feeling incredibly thirsty. At the same time, his heart started pounding wildly; it felt like a bucking bronco was in his chest trying to kick its way out. Finally, he felt himself getting light-headed. The next thing he knew, he was in the *Nova*'s sickbay, so presumably he passed out.

Fierce nodded as Maker, between sips of water, finished conveying all of this to him. "Yeah, all of that's symptomatic of dehydration — especially the fainting at the end."

"Rendered unconscious," Maker corrected before taking another drink from the bottle.

"What?" asked Fierce.

"Women...faint," Maker stressed. "Men...pass out...or get...rendered unconscious."

The Augman laughed. "Fine, then — you were rendered unconscious."

IGNOTUS

Maker smiled, then muttered in an anxious tone, "Erlen?"

"He's fine, if that's what you're asking — been holding a vigil by your bedside since the moment they brought you in."

Maker felt himself relaxing. Erlen being here meant that Skullcap had managed to get the ship powered up. They had gotten away, and Maker smiled at the thought.

"However," Fierce continued, "I caught him licking your face a few minutes ago when I popped in to check on you, so I sent him out for disturbing my patient. That's around the time you started waking up, so I left him sulking outside."

"It's okay," Maker stated, no longer pained by speaking. "Let him in."

"Will do," Fierce promised with a nod. "What about the others?"

Maker raised an eyebrow. "Others?"

"Yeah," the Augman said with a nod. "You've got a ship full of people all waiting to hear about whether your condition has improved. Because of doctor-patient confidentiality, I really can't give specifics to anyone other than Adames because — as the ranking military member while you're out of commission — he has a need to know."

Maker nodded in understanding. "You can let them all know I'm fine."

"Well, as your doctor I think I'll moderate that message and just tell them you're out of the danger zone."

"Fair enough," Maker acquiesced, smiling as he placed the water bottle back on the nightstand.

IGNOTUS

Fierce looked as though he perhaps wanted to say something else, but instead turned and left the room. A moment later, Erlen practically bounded in. Rising up on his hind legs, the Niotan placed his forepaws on the edge of the bed near Maker's head, and then leaned in and nuzzled his neck.

"I know," Maker said, rubbing the back of Erlen's head. "I missed you, too. Next time, though, feel free to wake me up earlier."

Erlen flopped back down to the floor and began making a curious noise that sounded like a combination of a chirp and a neigh. Maker interpreted it as the Niotan stressing that Maker had needed to rest.

"Okay, okay — I get it," Maker blurted out, causing Erlen to go silent. "Evidently I needed my beauty sleep. Again."

It looked as though Erlen were about to make some type of response, but he never got a chance as a knock sounded at the door. A moment later, it opened a crack and Adames poked his head in.

"So the rumors are true," the NCO remarked. "You *did* survive."

"Yep," Maker said with a nod. "Although apparently by the skin of my teeth."

"Feeling up for more visitors?" Adames asked.

"Of course," Maker replied.

Taking Maker at his word, Adames fully opened the door and entered, followed by Browing and Chantrey.

"Wow," Maker muttered. "I didn't realize it was all three of you. To get here this fast, you guys must have been camped out on my doorstep."

"Not exactly," Adames said with a chuckle. "Fierce let me know the second it looked like you were

IGNOTUS

waking up. I grabbed these two" — he tilted his head at Browing and Chantrey — "and we've been right outside sickbay since, just waiting for the okay to come in."

"Well, you'll all be happy to know I'm perfectly fine," Maker stated.

"No, you're not," Chantrey chimed in. "You almost died."

"That's par for the course in the Marines," Maker quipped. "If you don't come close to dying every day, you're not doing your job."

He and Adames snickered at that, while Chantrey simply rolled her eyes.

"Well, we're all glad you're safe," Browing noted. "But you have to admit it's an odd turn of events: Planck activated a device that sucks the water out of everything around it, and sometime later, you almost die of dehydration. Why do I feel there's a connection here?"

There was silence as everyone looked at Maker, who knew there was nothing to do but tell the truth.

"Ahem," he uttered, clearing his throat. "I guess I, uh, took one of Planck's nanobot containers when we went down to Ignotus."

All of Maker's visitors seemed to reflect on this for a moment, then Browing muttered, "I can't say I'm surprised."

"Hey," Maker intoned defensively, "we were heading into what I felt was almost assuredly a trap. If that happened, it would be us against an entire planet of Vacra. I needed a way to level the playing field, so I smuggled it in with the food in my rucksack."

"And when the P'ngrawen turned out to be the real enemy, you just took the nanobots to your meeting with them," Chantrey surmised.

IGNOTUS

"Again, I was looking for a way to balance the scales," Maker stated.

"How'd you even smuggle that aboard their ship?" Adames asked. "Didn't they scan you for weapons and such?"

"I coated the nanobot container with a special compound," Maker declared, casting a quick glance at Erlen. "It caused the container to read as proteins and such when they scanned it."

"And later on you activated the bots," Browing concluded, "which explains why you ended up on a ship full of mummified P'ngrawens."

"Wow," Maker droned. "I guess my spacesuit must have protected me from the worst effects."

"Yeah — the suit," Browing said skeptically. "That must have been it."

Left unsaid was what Maker — and probably everyone else present — already knew: that Erlen had done something to his metabolism that hindered the nanobots. (Presumably, the Niotan had gotten some sense of what the nanobots were when Maker had him "coat" the box that contained them in order to get past any scanners.)

"Wait a minute," Maker blurted out. "Why did you even risk coming to get me? It was dangerous and stupid."

"Talk to your friend," Chantrey replied, nodding at Erlen.

Maker frowned. "What are you saying?"

"Basically, after he got back on board the *Nova*, Erlen parked himself in front of the bridge and wouldn't let anyone enter until we agreed to go back and get you," Adames said. "I mean, he didn't say it in so many words,

IGNOTUS

but it wasn't hard to figure out what he wanted. Plus, Planck said it was probably safe — something about the nanobots shutting down if they go a certain amount of time without finding water."

"It was still foolish," Maker insisted. "So tell me, who won *that* lotto — Loyola? She's been courting death this entire mission."

"Actually, it was Skullcap," Adames answered.

Maker blinked in surprise. "You're kidding, right?"

Adames shook his head. "No. He volunteered to retrieve your body — said he owed you that much. He'll be happy to hear that you're out of the danger zone."

"Huh?" Maker murmured. "Is he still on the *Nova*?"

Adames shook his head. "No, but we're still in the Vacra region of space, and he asks about your condition almost hourly."

Maker snapped his fingers in recollection. "That reminds me — how's the empress?"

"The empress?" Chantrey echoed, sounding a little unsure of herself.

"Yeah, the empress," Maker said with a nod. "She wasn't looking that great the last time I saw her, but they obviously got away."

"So, no one's told you," Chantrey stated.

Maker frowned. "Told me what?"

Browing, Chantrey, and Adames all exchanged concerned glances, while Erlen let out a melancholic purr.

"No," Maker almost bellowed with a shake of his head, not wanting to believe what the others seemed to be implying. "No."

IGNOTUS

"I'm sorry," Chantrey said. "She died while they were escaping the P'ngrawen flagship."

IGNOTUS

Chapter 104

Maker was in the observation lounge, staring out at the stars with Erlen by his side, when Skullcap tracked him down.

After the news about the empress, Maker had felt troubled in a way he couldn't define, disturbed on a deeply profound level. The others, sensing his mood, had hurriedly departed. (Only Chantrey had lingered, promising to check in on him later.) Shortly thereafter, Maker — stressing the need to stretch his legs and get some air, so to speak — had gotten Fierce to approve him leaving sickbay for a short walkabout. Ultimately, he had found his way to the observation lounge, which was where he was when the insectoid entered the room.

"They told me I could find you here," Skullcap said.

"Someone described the view here as serene," Maker replied, "so I thought I'd check it out."

"I found it to be so," the Vacran said, looking out at the stars.

They stayed like that for a few minutes, neither speaking, just staring out at the vastness of space. Seeing the universe like this, how expansive it was — all-embracing, all-encompassing — just served as a reminder to Maker of how small and insignificant he truly was. How minuscule his impact was. How inconsequential any act that he performed. Yet somehow, in the face of all that, it felt like his failures were somehow magnified, expanded in scope for all the cosmos to see.

"It was a good plan," he finally confessed.

IGNOTUS

"If 'good' is synonymous with 'stupid' or 'ill-advised,'" Skullcap shot back, causing them both to chuckle.

"No, it really was," Maker insisted. "Honestly, I'm shocked at how well you predicted P'ngrawen behavior."

"In truth, there was little I needed to predict. They are a perverse and contrary race, so I knew that my request that the empress be in the landing bay for a quick exchange would be met with opposition."

"No kidding. They basically put her at the other end of the ship."

"Which was as expected. It required us to essentially traverse the length of the ship. At that juncture, it was just a matter of having the Senu Lia spew acid in strategic spots as we walked."

Maker smiled as Skullcap spoke, recalling the surreptitious hand signals the Vacran had given them to indicate where he wanted Erlen to work his magic as they walked through the P'ngrawen ship.

"Choosing a spot over the engines was genius," Maker admitted. "It didn't cause as large an explosion as we wanted, but having a dissolvent eating its way through their vessel — in multiple spots — surely kept a lot of P'ngrawen occupied."

"I suppose that means the money I paid for the ship's blueprints was well-spent," Skullcap remarked, "although in many instances it showed the location of secret entrances and such, but not how to enter them."

"You get what you pay for," Maker said with a chuckle. "Remember that next time."

As soon as the words left his mouth, Maker found himself horrified by the comment he'd made. For the

IGNOTUS

Vacra, there would be no "next time." They had lost everything.

"I heard about the empress," he blurted out, trying to make amends. "Please accept my condolences."

"Thank you," the insectoid said in a sincere tone.

Maker pondered for a moment, focusing on something that had occurred to him when Skullcap and the empress were speaking. It probably wasn't proper etiquette, but he decided to ask anyway.

"When you called her 'Mother,'" he noted, "it wasn't just in the sense of her being the matriarch of your race, was it?"

"I am her offspring," Skullcap admitted without hesitation.

Maker nodded in understanding. "I'm sorry. I didn't know."

"There is no need for sorrow," the Vacran said. "You did all that you could, even attempting to give your life for hers."

"But somehow, I'm still here and she's not."

"Don't blame yourself," Skullcap said. "She was dead before we ever left that torture chamber."

Maker gave him a puzzled look. "What do you mean?"

"Before she snapped his arm off, you may recall that Badukst was attempting to subdue the empress with the control collar."

"I remember that," Maker said.

"In essence, he had the collar do almost everything possible to her: emit electric shocks, inject toxins, and so on. Our medics who examined her body think that her heart ruptured and most of her organs shut down almost immediately."

IGNOTUS

"Geez!" Maker uttered. "It's a miracle she didn't die on the spot."

"Indeed, she should have, but the fact that she didn't seem to feel anything allowed her to keep going — at least for a while."

"I'm not sure it means much, but I'm glad to hear she wasn't in pain."

"Thank you for the sentiment," Skullcap said. "Truth be told, however, I think she had been ready to die for a while. She only held on long enough to die free."

Maker frowned. "How's that?"

"Shortly after our last conversation with you, the threats from the flagship ceased," he stated. "That is, we heard what sounded like wails of anguish, and then nothing. I assumed that, whatever had happened, it was your doing. As soon as the vessel was ready, we left, and almost the moment we were clear of the flagship, the empress died. Thus, she died free — not as a captive, and in the company of another Vacra."

"What will happen to you now?" Maker asked. "The Vacra people, that is."

"At the moment, we are once again in open warfare with the P'ngrawen. It was inevitable, given what happened to the empress, so it was only fitting that the current conflict begin with her liberation."

Maker simply nodded at this, understanding what Skullcap was referencing. The engine explosion on Badukst's flagship had been a signal to attack the P'ngrawen vessels escorting him. Vacra warships had been standing by, and had immediately gone on the offensive.

"How did we do in that regard?" inquired Maker.

IGNOTUS

"One of the escorts was blown apart," Skullcap responded. "The other, recognizing that they were severely outmatched, jumped to hyperspace in a severely damaged condition. Needless to say, having those ships preoccupied during our flight greatly increased our odds of escape."

"And Badukst?"

"He will be tried for his crimes, but it is a foregone conclusion that he will be found guilty and sentenced to death. He, of course, is fully aware of what lies in store for him, and is arguing that he can be useful in ending hostilities."

"Will you take him up on that?"

"He has doomed the Vacra to extinction. For that, many feel the need to exterminate the P'ngrawen — an eye for an eye, in your parlance."

"And how do you feel?"

Skullcap made the odd sound that Maker had started interpreting as a Vacra version of a sigh.

"I have done so much trying to save my people," the insectoid said, "committed so many heinous and abominable acts that it boggles the mind. I've done things to make the Vacra as reviled as the P'ngrawen, so that only in a few places — like the region where we retrieved the tracker — does our original reputation remain intact. But I always told myself that it was for a noble purpose, an honorable goal. That a time would come when I could right any wrongs I'd committed. But now, to engage in what is essentially genocide, with no intent other than the complete obliteration of another species? I understand the desire, but the thought disgusts me."

"So what will you do?"

IGNOTUS

"I don't know. There is a countdown now to the end of the Vacra, a deathwatch on our species. Bearing that in mind, in truth, I would prefer to spend the time I have remaining not making war, but enjoying the company of those I care about."

"Brzaka," Maker said flatly.

Skullcap gave him what appeared to be an appraising glance. "Is it so obvious?"

Maker shrugged. "Not blatantly, but it's clear the two of you care for each other."

"Yes," Skullcap conceded. "Much like you and your mate."

Maker's eyebrows went up in surprise. "Excuse me?"

"Chantrey," the insectoid explained. "She is your woman, is she not?"

"That's not quite the terminology I'd use," Maker said, "but how could you possibly know that?"

"Your scent changes when she is present. Likewise hers when you are in close proximity."

Maker's brow creased as he considered what he was hearing. Many animals and insects had the ability to detect pheromones (which is what he assumed Skullcap was referring to by "scent"), and quite a few sentient species as well. However, it was something he rarely thought about, so the Vacran's statement had caught him a little flatfooted.

"In addition," the insectoid continued, "there are occasions when your scents are notably intermingled, suggesting—"

"Okay, that's enough," Maker interjected. "You called it — we're a couple."

IGNOTUS

He was tempted to say more — explain a little about human relationships — but stopped as the sound of someone coming into the room drew his attention. Both he and Skullcap spun towards the entrance as Browing came in, accompanied by Brzaka.

"You have a visitor," Browing said to Maker, gesturing towards the female Vacra. "Someone previously reported seeing you in here, so I decided to escort her."

Maker nodded in acknowledgment, then frowned as Browing's words brought something to mind: Skullcap had found his way to the observation lounge by himself. It was an indication that Deadeye, which was supposed to shoot Skullcap if he walked through the ship unaccompanied, was not active. (Later he would learn that Adames, going on the assumption that the Vacra were no longer enemies, had ordered it shut down.)

"I bring word from the Synod," Brzaka said as she bent down for a moment to pet Erlen, who had wandered over to her side. Getting a light lick on the hand from the Niotan as a sign of affection, she then stood back up and continued, stating, "The Vacra are grateful for your efforts to rescue our empress. Despite the fact that our behavior towards you and you race — whether forced or not — has been nothing short of atrocious, you still sought to help us in our hour of need, even expressing a willingness to sacrifice yourself in order to do so. It showed us that you and your fellow humans are just as brave and noble as the Vacra. Because of your selflessness and magnanimity towards us, a race that has shown you nothing but malevolence and hostility, we name you our heir."

"Your heir?" Maker repeated. "As in, your beneficiary?"

IGNOTUS

"Yes," Brzaka confirmed.

"This is a great gift," Browing intoned sincerely. "The human race is grateful that you'd find us worthy of this level of generosity."

"No — not the human race," Brzaka corrected. "Maker. The Vacra name him *personally* as the heir of all we possess."

Maker was stunned, so shocked that his mouth almost fell open.

"I, uh... I don't, uhm... I don't think..." Browing murmured, plainly as astonished as Maker by the announcement. "I don't think our laws contemplate this kind of assignation — not to an individual."

"This is not about *your* laws," Brzaka insisted. "This is Vacra canon and decree. Maker is the chosen companion and champion of the Senu Lia. As such, we deem him and only him worthy of this honor."

"But there has to be something you can do other than simply accepting extinction," Maker interjected. "Some way to perpetuate your race. Cloning, perhaps. Or maybe artificial—"

"No," Skullcap stated adamantly. "We know that other races embrace such practices and, although we do not judge, we find them abhorrent."

"The *Zirxen* speaks truth," Brzaka said. "We do not pursue such paths. For us...for us..." She suddenly appeared confused and seemed to sway slightly for a second. "For us, such things are...are..."

As she trailed off, her head seemed to tilt marginally to one side. At the same time, her body oscillated back and forth for a moment, like someone teetering on a high wire. And then she appeared to faint.

IGNOTUS

Somehow, Skullcap managed to get there before her body hit the floor, catching her in his arms.

"Let's get her to sickbay," Browing said.

Skullcap didn't immediately respond. Instead, he stood there with Brzaka in his arms, eyeing her from head to toe, his antennae jiggling wildly the entire time.

"I have to get her to the homeworld immediately!" he suddenly screamed, and then went racing from the room, clutching Brzaka like she was the most precious thing in the universe.

IGNOTUS

Chapter 105

"Pregnant?" Chantrey intoned, not bothering to hide her surprise.

"No, not *pregnant*," Maker corrected. "*Fertile*."

They were in Maker's cabin. Chantrey was sitting on the sofa while Maker lay perpendicular to her with his head in her lap. He had been awake for about twelve hours, and Fierce had reluctantly agreed that Maker was well enough to leave sickbay (although the good doctor wouldn't authorize a return to full duty until at least a day had passed).

"But she can have babies now," Chantrey noted.

"More than that," Maker said. "According to Skullcap, she's also producing the enzyme that can create new queens. I guess things will be buzzing in the hive tonight, with the amount of repopulating they have to do."

"He shared all that with you? So you guys are like best buds now — chatting about all your hopes and dreams?"

"Hardly," Maker countered. "He reached out to apologize for running out the way he did with Brzaka and explain why he did it."

"So how did he know what was happening to her?"

"Apparently, the Vacra have very advanced olfactory organs. He could smell the change in Brzaka's metabolism."

"Hmmm," Chantrey droned. "I don't suppose I need to ask what catalyst prompted this metabolic change."

IGNOTUS

As she spoke, she eyed Erlen, who was on the floor a few feet away, playing with a ball.

Maker shrugged. "I suspect Erlen was able to assimilate the reproductive enzyme from the empress before she died, and then passed it on to Brzaka."

Chantrey gave the Niotan a suspicious look. "Do you think you need to have a talk with him about the birds and the bees?"

"Who, Erlen?" Maker asked.

"Yeah. All of a sudden, females in his vicinity are becoming remarkably procreant. That's worrisome."

"Are you seriously complaining about Erlen saving a race from extinction?"

"Well, he did keep you from inheriting the Vacra empire — which prevents me from having the wealthiest sugar daddy in the universe — but I'm not really talking about that. I'm talking about Loyola."

"Oh," Maker muttered. "You know about that."

"Yeah. As you once said, it's not possible to keep secrets on a ship this small."

"That was on another ship, which actually was somewhat smaller than this one," Maker noted. "But I don't think you have anything to worry about. Erlen knows what is and isn't appropriate regarding reproduction."

"Great, because I'm not eager to have some stupid boy toy be the father of my child."

"Excuse me?" Maker said in mock indignation.

"Not you," Chantrey insisted. "I meant my *other* boy toy."

"Oh, really?" Maker uttered, sitting up.

IGNOTUS

"Don't pout — I was just joking," she insisted, putting her arms around his neck and giving him a quick peck. "You're my only boy toy."

She then started giggling merrily, while Maker rolled his eyes. Before he could make a comment, however, a chime sounded, indicating someone was at the door.

"Saved by the bell," Maker commented to Chantrey as he headed to the cabin entrance. When he opened the door, he found Wayne standing there.

"Sorry to disturb you, el-tee," the young Marine said apologetically, "but this just came in from the naval ship."

He handed Maker a metal cube, roughly five inches in height, length, and width. It was completely smooth except for an oval-shaped groove in the center on one side.

Maker stared at the cube for a moment, then frowned as Wayne's words sank in. "What naval ship?"

"Oh, that's right — you don't know," Wayne muttered. "A Space Navy cruiser dropped out of hyperspace about two hours ago. The captain demanded to speak with you immediately, but Adames said you were still convalescing and couldn't be disturbed. He also ordered the crew not to mention it to you — the naval ship, that is."

Maker smiled to himself, thinking that this was the NCO's way of forcing him to take some downtime. Under normal circumstances, this was the kind of situation where he'd normally assume command again — regardless of doctor's orders or anything else. In truth, however, he was grateful to Adames for running

IGNOTUS

interference. He'd never admit it out loud, but he was enjoying the respite.

"Anyway," Wayne continued, "the cruiser captain sent the cube over. It came with a preeminent security designation, so Adames didn't have the authority to keep it from you. Also, he said to let you know that we're on standby."

"Thanks," Maker said, then closed the door as Wayne turned and walked away.

"Who was it?" Chantrey asked as Maker walked back towards the couch.

"Wayne," he replied as he sat down next to her. "Did you know there was a Space Navy ship here?"

"I may have heard something about it," she said coyly.

"So *everyone's* conspiring to keep me in the dark," he said, feigning anger.

"Everyone's conspiring to keep you from working yourself to death. You should be grateful."

"I know, and I am," he said with a chuckle. "But how'd they even know where to find us? I mean, when the *Nova* left Gaian Space, even *we* didn't have the coordinates to Ignotus."

"Well, when Erlen was keeping everyone off the bridge, the Vacra offered to take a message back for us. Through them, we basically reported that the mission was a success, but you had died. Presumably, with some level of trust established between our races, the Vacra were also willing to provide coordinates for getting here."

"That was nice of them," Maker noted. Turning his attention back to the cube, he continued, saying, "Anyway, I can't put this off."

IGNOTUS

"What exactly is that?" Chantrey asked, staring at the object Maker held.

"An ordinance hexahedron. It's a method of sending sensitive or high-priority communications. Often, but not always, they contain new mission orders."

"Oh," Chantrey murmured. "Should I leave?"

Maker shook his head. "No, I'll just take it in the office."

"Are you sure? I can always come back later."

"Positive," he replied, before giving her a kiss. He then rose to his feet and went to his office.

Once there, seated behind his desk and with the door locked, Maker merely stared at the cube for a moment. As he had mentioned to Chantrey, these devices were usually utilized to send top-secret orders and such. That meant that his team — which had just completed a dangerous assignment — could be leaving again almost immediately. At least Adames, recognizing what the message cube meant, already had the other Marines on standby.

Deciding that he had procrastinated long enough, Maker put the cube on the desk and then placed his thumb into the groove on the top. The area seemed to glow for a moment as his thumbprint was read, and then a small square-shaped corner on top of the box rose slightly. A petite diode began flashing on the square, and a second later, it began broadcasting a hologram onto the desktop — an image of a man that appeared to be about a foot in height.

"Admiral Lafayette," Maker intoned. "Why am I not surprised?"

"Well, you're looking rather spry for a dead man," Lafayette noted, ignoring Maker's jibe.

IGNOTUS

"Death is actually pretty invigorating. You should try it some time."

"I'll take your word for it," Lafayette said, chuckling.

"Anyway, to what do I owe the pleasure? I mean, you obviously knew I was still alive since you sent the message cube to me."

"True, but the first report we received *did* say that you had died, and that the *Nova* was having some kind of trouble, which is why they had the Vacra deliver the message to us."

Maker reflected on how the "trouble" had actually been Erlen blocking the bridge, but didn't feel the need to clarify anything.

"We hurriedly got a ship ready to go offer assistance," the admiral continued, "but before we could send her out, we got word from the Vacra that you were actually alive."

"We also accomplished the mission, but I assume you knew that when the two battle cruisers came back stuffed to the gills with the missing tech."

Lafayette made a dismissive gesture. "I never had any concerns about the mission. I knew you'd get that done."

"And I suppose that faith in us is why you glued a cloaked ship to the *Nova*."

If the admiral was surprised by Maker's statement, he didn't show it.

"That was actually for your protection," Lafayette declared. "Believe it or not, I took your worries about the deceitfulness of the Vacra seriously. The stealth ship was there to help you if things went off the rails — like the incident with the Xnjda."

IGNOTUS

Maker frowned, thinking, and a moment later it came to him.

"The explosions on Kpntel's ships," he concluded. "That didn't have anything to do with the nanobots Planck released — it was the cloaked vessel."

Lafayette gave him a knowing smile. "Stealth warheads are surprisingly effective in combat. The other side never sees them coming."

"You know, you could have said something about that before we left, let us know we'd have an invisible conjoined twin along for the ride."

"Now what fun would that have been?" Lafayette uttered with a grin. "Now, moving on to the real reason of why I sent the message cube."

"Let me guess," Maker said. "Some new mission where my crew gets the honor of risking life and limb several times over?"

The admiral shook his head. "Not at all. If you'll check the cube, there should be a hidden compartment on one side opening up right…about…now."

As if on cue, something akin to a miniature drawer opened on the hexahedron. Glancing inside, Maker saw a pair of shining objects, which he reached in and grabbed. His eyes widened when he saw what he was looking at: a set of captain's insignia.

"It was pretty easy to push through the promotion when everyone thought you were dead," Lafayette stated. "Even the sternest detractors of the infamous Maniac Maker weren't willing to block the posthumous promotion of a soldier who died in battle."

"What are you saying?" Maker asked incredulously.

IGNOTUS

"What does it look like?" the admiral shot back rhetorically. "Congratulations, Captain."

Maker shook his head. "No…it can't… I mean, I'm not dead. It won't stick."

"Of course it will," Lafayette assured him. "It'll simply count as a field promotion. And I've got a bunch of testimonials saying that you earned it."

Before Maker could ask what he meant, an image of Adames's head appeared to the right of Lafayette.

"I've served both with and under the command of Gant Maker," Adames's image said, "and I can assure you there's no finer soldier, officer or enlisted, in the military. He…"

As the hologram of his NCO continued speaking, another face appeared — Wayne, this time.

"Lieutenant Maker is a peerless officer and an unparalleled leader. He's personally saved my life on multiple occasions, endangering himself in the process…"

While Wayne continued speaking, an image of Diviana appeared. Like the two before her, she began spouting a laundry list of Maker's attributes and merits.

"Wait a minute," Maker interjected, at which point all the images other than Lafayette disappeared. "Did they all record messages like that?"

"Every member of your team did," the admiral confirmed, "as well as Browing, Chantrey, and Planck. Most surprising, of course, was this one."

Much to Maker's surprise, Skullcap's face appeared.

"I have been on the battlefield with Maker, both as a friend and a foe, and under either circumstance I can report there is no warrior or soldier more worthy of

IGNOTUS

leading others into battle, or more competent to do so. In addition, he is a shining example of compassion, bravery, and valor. He represents the best of what makes you human. Failure to promote him is a disservice to your military and your species."

Ending the insectoid's endorsement, Lafayette commented, "Well, he's obviously not shy about saying what he feels. But the long and short of it is that this is a promotion that is well-deserved. There are also some other accolades that will be coming as well — medals and all that — but I figured you'd want to wear the rank right away."

"And that's why you sent the message cube," Maker surmised.

"Yes," the admiral stated. "Not exactly proper use of the device, but what good is it to be a general officer if you can't have a little fun every now and then?" He winked at Maker as he finished speaking, causing the latter to grin.

"Well, seeing as I had to 'die' just to make captain," Maker said with a smile, "I'm unlikely to ever find out."

"Hmmm," Lafayette droned. "I'm starting to get that feeling in my gut."

"What feeling?" Maker asked.

"The one that I got the last time we had a conversation like this — where you talk like a chess pawn, but make moves like a queen."

"I'm not sure what you mean, sir."

"That's what you always say, but I'm on to you now," the admiral said, causing Maker to laugh. "Anyway, I understand you're still officially under the weather so I'll sign off now, but we'll talk again soon."

IGNOTUS

"I look forward to it," Maker stated.

Lafayette nodded, and then the hologram disappeared.

Maker sat there for a moment, thinking, then turned on the comm. It took him only a minute or so to get Adames on a secure line.

"So guess what I'm looking at right now?" he asked the NCO.

"New orders from that message cube that came for you?" Adames guessed. "So tell me, what's next on the agenda for us?"

"It wasn't orders," Maker said. "It was captain's bars."

"What?"

"I've been promoted."

"What braindead idiot nominated *you* for captain?" Adames blurted out jovially. "Heads are gonna roll over this."

Maker chuckled. "Thanks, but I've seen the testimonials. So was all that *your* idea?"

"Yes and no. I pretty much orchestrated everything — got people to record their statements while you were shuttling to various places with Skullcap — but it really all started with Chantrey."

"Chantrey?"

"Yeah, your girl gave me a tongue-lashing like you wouldn't believe — completely humiliated and embarrassed me with respect to how I've been supporting you."

"Sorry about that, Hector. I'll talk to her."

"No, Gant. She was right. I wouldn't be wearing these extra stripes if you hadn't fought for me. The same goes for everyone on our team. Who knows where any of

IGNOTUS

us would be if it wasn't for you? Recording those testimonials was the least we could do. We sent them back with the Vacra after we thought you were dead — even got Skullcap to record one as well — but in all honesty, I really didn't think anything would come of it. Glad to know I was wrong."

"Yeah, wonders never cease," Maker said. "Well, I'm still officially laid up, so I'll let you get back to the business of running the ship."

"Aye, aye, *Captain*," Adames replied, snickering as he disconnected.

Taking the cube, Maker left the office. He found Chantrey still on the couch where he'd left her.

"So," she began, "anything important — that you can talk about, that is?"

Maker shrugged. "Apparently I've been promoted to captain."

He showed her his new rank, which she oohed and aahed over for a moment.

"So when did these arrive?" she asked.

"They came in the message cube," he explained. "Apparently there's a hidden drawer on this thing."

He was in the process of showing her where the rank had been contained when, unexpectedly, another secret compartment opened on the exact opposite side of the cube.

Maker and Chantrey stared at each other for a moment, both plainly surprised. Maker then turned the box so that he could get a good look at the contents. It took him a moment, but then he recognized what he was looking at and started laughing.

Chuckling almost giddily (and thinking he'd have to explain everything to Chantrey later), he reached into

IGNOTUS

the compartment and pulled out the item it contained (which had obviously been planted by Lafayette):
A black chess queen.

THE END

IGNOTUS

Thank you for purchasing this book! If, after reading, you find that you enjoyed it, please feel free to leave a review on the site from which it was purchased.

Also, if you would like to be notified when I release new books, please subscribe to my mailing list via the following link: http://eepurl.com/C5a45

Finally, for those who may be interested in following me, I have included my website and social media info:

Website: http://www.kevinhardmanauthor.com/

BookBub: https://www.bookbub.com/authors/kevin-hardman?follow=true

Amazon Author Page: https://www.amazon.com/Kevin-Hardman/e/B00CLTY3YM

Facebook: www.facebook.com/kevin.hardman.967

Twitter: https://twitter.com/kevindhardman

Goodreads: https://www.goodreads.com/author/show/7075077.Kevin_Hardman

And if you like my work, please consider supporting me on Patreon: https://www.patreon.com/kevinhardman

Printed in Great Britain
by Amazon